Intersections

Intersections

Jackson Peoples-Rosenblatt

Copyright © 2015 Jackson Peoples-Rosenblatt
All rights reserved.

ISBN: 0692467343
ISBN 13: 9780692467343
Library of Congress Control Number: 2015909597
CreateSpace Independent Publishing Platform
North Charleston, South Carolina

For Larry "L.C." Cline

Yit'gadal v'yit'kadash sh'mei raba...

The Mourner's Kaddish

SEPTEMBER 11, 2001

I

"You're not too big for me to spank," Eamonn laughed. Around them, the firehouse, one of Manhattan's busiest, was chaotic. Shift changes here had the flavor of Grand Central Station at rush hour.

"Sure, Dad," Mick said. His eyes were a little bloodshot.

Well, who wouldn't celebrate under the circumstances? Eamonn remembered his own reaction to the news of Maribel's first pregnancy. He had never forgotten the ensuing hangover.

"Just try me. I could take you down with one hand tied behind my back," Eamonn said, squaring his shoulders and jaw. This gesture had long sent his four sons into hysterics. Now that they were grown men, it had to be performed with as much irony as swagger.

"You'd like that, wouldn't you?" Mick laughed. "All the guys watching as Firefighter Eamonn Lannaghan takes his strapping offspring over his knee to administer paternal discipline."

"Try me."

"You're going to make one hell of a grandpa."

"I certainly plan to," Eamonn nodded, "but you've got some explaining to do, telling Mom before you told me."

"It just slipped out," Mick said.

"Nothing just slips out of you, Mr. Tightlips," Eamonn said. "Mom and I had to use rubber hoses and bamboo shoots on you whenever we wanted to get to the truth. You haven't changed."

1

"All right," Mick nodded. "Mom guessed. You know she's got that knack. How many times has she looked at one of the aunts or cousins or neighbors and diagnosed a pregnancy before even the woman's gynecologist knew about it?"

"True enough."

"Don't worry," Mick said, "we're planning to let everyone in on it this weekend. Including Eli."

"You know I really will spank you if you leave him out," Eamonn said.

Not that he worried about Eli any more. Now that the boys were grown and the whole damn tribe understood the situation, Eli's inclusion in family matters was pretty much a foregone conclusion. Eamonn just liked giving the warning. It made him feel closer to Eli. Maybe it even made up for all those times he'd made Eli take a back seat. At least a little bit.

■ ■ ■

His first grandchild. Eamonn couldn't believe it. Of course with four adult sons it was only a matter of time, even though only one of them was married at this point and that marriage was on the rocks. It seemed like yesterday he and Eli had stood outside the hospital nursery looking through the spotless glass at newborn Mick. They had only known each other a few months at the time. Eamonn's confession, which might have ended their "friendship", turned out to be the right thing to do. The only thing, really. But what did you know at that age? They were as young then as Mick was now. And almost as clueless. But they'd found their way, and now Mick was going to be a father. Previous generations tried to tell you how fast things went, but you never got it until all of a sudden you were a member of a previous generation yourself. You tried your damndest to hand down the wisdom you'd managed to accumulate, but God only knew if it would do any more good this time around.

Lisa's pregnancy meant there were things that needed to be done. First of all, Mick needed to get off his ass and propose. Eamonn's grandchild should have parents who were married when he or she arrived. It might not be fashionable to worry about a thing like that, but as far as Eamonn was concerned it was a non-negotiable. He wouldn't say anything about it, however. Maribel would take care of that. She'd always been tougher with the boys than he had. Playing "bad cop" had come naturally to her after growing up with that platoon of brothers and male cousins. Thank God. Eamonn had known about teaching the boys to play sports. That and supervising their personal hygiene were about the extent of his parenting skills. By all rights every one of them should be in prison now, based on his expertise. And Eli would take Mick shopping for a ring. That was the kind of thing he was good at. Oh, the irony. Never even a best man, much less a groom. But nobody knew more about engagement rings than Eli except his best friend Josh, who had grown up in the jewelry business. Between them, Maribel and Eli would make sure Mick and Lisa tied the knot properly. And that they found a decent apartment to move into. Neither one of them had a place where there was room for two people to raise a baby. Somehow Mick had never gotten around to asking Lisa to move in with him. He was damned lucky she hadn't ditched him. That, too, was a trait of the Lannaghan men—finding women who let them get away with things they shouldn't expect to.

It was funny how the last few years Eamonn's wife and his male lover had teamed up on all kinds of family projects. Sometimes it seemed as if they were the ones who were actually married and Eamonn was the fifth wheel. It wasn't a dynamic Eamonn had anticipated. But though Maribel and Eli were still a little "artificial" in each other's presence and the terms on which they shared Eamonn had never been explicitly discussed much less negotiated, every now and then he got the uncanny feeling that sometime during the last quarter century they'd gotten together behind his back and hashed everything out.

Eamonn hoped Lisa's parents wouldn't object to the marriage. They seemed like nice people. He realized it made him a little racist, wondering how a Japanese-American family might react to Mick as Lisa's husband. But it wasn't just about east meets west. Eamonn was pretty sure they'd had a banker, doctor, or attorney in mind for Lisa rather than a firefighter, even a third generation one. He hoped this was all in his head.

■ ■ ■

"Aren't you supposed to be off shift?"

"Sure, Jonesey," Eamonn said.

"Then why is your sorry ass still here cluttering up my firehouse?"

"Your firehouse is it?"

"If you'll ever leave," Jonesey growled, "it will be."

"Last I heard it belonged to the people of this fair city."

"You'd pee all over it like a big dog if you thought it would keep anybody else's paws off it."

"Just wanted to see that Mickey got here on time this morning," Eamonn said. "Don't want him getting written up any more. Particularly now that he's in the family way."

"Do tell," Jonesey laughed. "Just like his pop, huh? You never could keep it in your pants, either. Maribel's lucky it was Eli you were shacking up with behind her back. Otherwise she'd have had a whole bunch of bastard stepchildren running around under foot."

"Yeah, yeah," Eamonn said. "You with your four ex-wives. You've got room to criticise."

"Get out of here," Jonesey growled. "And don't come back until you're scheduled to."

■ ■ ■

Eamonn felt like celebrating. But who was there to celebrate with? Maribel wasn't off shift at St. Vincent's yet. Eli was probably already on his way to his office down at the World Trade Center. He liked to get there early. Have the place to himself for a while before the twenty-somethings showed up and ruined his concentration. Liam was God knew where. A surgical resident, his schedule was too chaotic to keep up with. And Tory was on day shift this week over at his engine company on the East Side. That left Renzo, Eamonn's youngest. This time of day, Renzo would be at his gym. Eamonn could head over there, coach Renzo through the tail end of his workout. It would mean telling Renzo about the baby and then swearing him to secrecy until the weekend. That was typical for them. Renzo wasn't just the youngest, he was the son

4

most like Eamonn. But at the entrance to the subway, Eamonn realized he was tired. It was just a few stops and then a couple blocks over to Eli's apartment on Hudson. He'd take Beowulf out for a walk and then sack out there.

II

"Here are the transcripts of *oygn australis'* most recent transmissions, Lev."

Lev Blumenfeld wasn't sure why Sagi always spoke to him in English. It wasn't discreet, if that's what Sagi had in mind. Everybody here spoke English. You might as well send up signal rockets as speak English in this place. Blumenfeld knew that Yiddish was politically incorrect these days, but he preferred it to Hebrew. And Sagi was fluent in the "language of the ghetto" thanks to his grandmother, a survivor from Treblinka. Better they should use that. Sagi had appeared in the doorway of Blumenfeld's office without making a sound. Without alerting him in any way. That took some doing, but that's how good Sagi was. Deficient tradecraft wasn't the reason he'd been pulled off operational assignments.

"Thanks," Blumenfeld said, taking the sheets. Sagi's hand was trembling slightly. It was probably the reason he was no longer on ops. That tremor, microscopic as it was, was the field agent's analogue to a nine point two on the Richter Scale. "You look at them?"

"Why wouldn't I?"

"No reason," Blumenfeld said. "You're cleared for it. Anything catch your eye?"

"No," Sagi said. "Everything's by the book."

He said it a little too fast, Blumenfeld thought. And his eyes were too bright. More evidence.

"You're sure of that."

"It's his m.o., isn't it?" Sagi asked. "He's anal retentive about his transmissions. Always timed to the second. Nothing missing, nothing added. Not a keystroke out of place."

"Yes," Blumenfeld nodded. "That's him all right. Yet something bothers you."

"He's nervous," Sagi said. "His subjects disappeared days ago. He thinks he should have followed them. He was told it's out of his hands now. Yet he's still on station. He wonders why he hasn't been extracted."

"I thought you just said there wasn't anything out of place in the messages."

"There isn't," Sagi said. "Not a single character that didn't come right out of the manual. I'm just reading between the lines. *Something's going on. Why am I sitting on my ass?* This is a natural question for an agent on a surveillance operation when there's nothing left to observe."

"In your experience," Blumenfeld said.

Sagi was twenty-eight going on fifty-five. The baby face gave a false impression. He had lots of miles on him. If nothing else, that was why he wasn't in the field these days. It was the nature of things. Field work was a young man's game. Men burned out early. In agents' years, twenty-eight was—well, who knew? It varied from individual to individual. All you could be sure of was that by the time they were Sagi's age they had paid some kind of price.

"That's right," Sagi said. "In my experience."

Sagi wasn't in the field any more but he wasn't yet ready to run agents. Perhaps he never would be. Then they'd have to "transition" him out of the service. He'd receive a civil service post or return to whatever profession they'd originally recruited him from. Worst came to worst, he'd hire himself to rich Americans as a "security consultant". Blumenfeld had seen dozens of former field agents go that route. There was apparently an insatiable demand for them in the States. South Africa was another booming market. But Sagi had enough potential that he'd been kept on to see how he might develop. He was certainly smart enough. The other relevant questions were esoteric, and, unfortunately, unlikely ever to be answered definitively. People upstairs still weren't absolutely certain about Blumenfeld himself, for instance, yet here he was with half a dozen agents currently in the field.

"Eight thousand miles from home, Lev," Sagi said. "Eight thousand, yes? It's probably not even daylight there yet. An agent can't help feeling isolated. Asking himself questions that no one can answer for him. Inactivity makes it worse."

Was it actually that far? Eight thousand miles? Blumenfeld wasn't certain. He was a little fuzzy on non-metric measurements. He'd have thought it was more like seven, but Sagi would know a thing like that.

"Are you sure you're not the one wondering about an extraction instead of our agent?"

"Lev, please," Sagi protested. "You asked a question. I answered it already. Enough with the cat and mouse."

"So you suggest?"

"Extract him," Sagi said. "I'll book him on the next El Al flight out of LAX. He can travel under his cover or I can have the consulate drop a diplomatic passport for him in any of the usual places. He can be in the secure waiting lounge in less than four hours after the signal goes out, following standard extraction protocols."

"And why am I not going to do that?" Blumenfeld asked. "Do you have a hypothesis?"

"I do not."

Blumenfeld knew he was lying but let it pass. There would be time to follow that up later. If Blumenfeld was right, at least.

"Good," Blumenfeld said. "It is not your job to speculate on what I do or not do running my agents."

"Understood."

"When you run agents of your own, you'll say the same to young men itching to second guess you."

"Also understood."

"There's a possibility that the subjects might return to his area," Blumenfeld said. "A slight possibility. Some might describe it as negligible. But it's there. We might need to resume our surveillance. And if I bring him home now, we wouldn't even know they'd returned. So he'll wait a while longer. While the situation clarifies itself."

"What situation?" Sagi asked.

Of course Blumenfeld couldn't tell him that. Even if he knew. He was about to plead ignorance but Sagi wouldn't believe him, which was exactly what Blumenfeld wanted.

"Yes," he said. "What situation? That's exactly the question."

■ ■ ■

Blumenfeld never really felt at home in Tel Aviv. Ironic, since it was his birthplace. He hadn't actually lived there until after university. Even then, it was mostly no more than his address of record. The city had only become his permanent residence a decade ago. All those years in the field on behalf of a country he was mostly attached to for no better reason than that he carried its passport. He'd spent his childhood and adolescence being moved from place to place as his father's career in the diplomatic corps dictated. Of course that wasn't the real story, but it was the one everybody accepted, the one with official documentation behind it, so it was the one he told. The real story had to do with his mother's career, for which his father's had been a front. Even now Blumenfeld wasn't supposed to know about it. His adolescent suspicions, nursed for years, had been confirmed decades later by diligent reading in the case files. Strictly speaking, he wasn't supposed to know that those files existed or that the agent they referred to was his mother, but a man couldn't help being curious about his family history, and once he started reading those accounts of his alternative childhood he couldn't make himself stop. His main discovery was how accurate his suspicions had been in those days. And if his own had, who else's?

Not that it mattered, because nothing could be done about the past. Still it was good to know. She deserved that—to have someone, some survivor of hers, conversant with the truth.

It was a sweltering afternoon. Blumenfeld had hoped that leaving his office and coming for a walk on the waterfront would dispel his funk, but it didn't. The heat wouldn't allow for it. Even the waves of the Mediterranean looked parched and uncomfortable as they washed up on the sand. The surfers and volleyball players seemed enervated, almost ghostlike. They were only going through the motiongs. The beachfront cafes were deserted. They might as well be closed. The taxi drivers dozed behind their steering wheels, dreaming of who knew what. How he wished he was on a beach somewhere else. They said the weather where *oygn australis* kept his lonely vigil was the best anywhere on earth. Blumenfeld hoped it was true. He'd never been there so he didn't know, but he liked to think that *oygn australis* could at least take comfort in fine weather. Absent further developments, by the time another week had passed Blumenfeld would certainly have to pull him out of there. The top floor—which wasn't really located on the top floor; was just the way his superiors were referred to in casual conversation—was showing signs of nervousness. They'd have insisted on the extraction already, but they were preoccupied. He knew this solely because they hadn't yet insisted on his agent's extraction. That kind of circular logic, inadmissible in the real world, was sometimes highly useful in his line of work.

Really, Blumenfeld would have pulled *oygn australis* already, but he had a point to prove. The top floor suspected him of lacking objectivity in the case of this particular individual. They'd had their suspicions from the moment he first spoke of recruiting the young man. And it was true. Blumenfeld did lack objectivity. What of it? That lack of objectivity was inherent in the relationship between any agent and the man running him. When a man's life was in danger every minute of the day, when he was far from home and in hostile territory and every sunrise might be the last he'd ever see, an agent needed to believe, had to be able to take it as a matter of faith, that the man running him was more than a faceless bureaucrat. That man in that office somewhere had to be closer to him than a friend. Closer to him than his own mother, really. The top floor conveniently disregarded the existential aspects of the work. Yet they could only afford to do so because men like Blumenfeld lacked objectivity. Men like Blumenfeld were the ones who kept the agents feeling like someone was looking out for them. Everything hinged on that. So yes, the situation was exactly as his superiors had implied. Blumenfeld lacked objectivity, and for exactly the reasons they supposed, but he didn't want to give them proof of it. Not just for his own sake. The young man had agreed to have his reputation ruined on behalf of their aims. In Blumenfeld's book, that earned him certain considerations. But the top floor would never make such considerations a central concern in their deliberations. If the agent was going to be protected, it was going to be up to Blumenfeld to do it. So *oygn australis* stayed where he was, like a chess piece unthinkingly left on the board after the players had adjourned for coffee and pastries.

As to *oygn australis* and his observations, Blumenfeld was sure he was on to something big. A piece of the puzzle at the very least. The signs were all in place. His superiors' preoccupation. The anxious looks on the faces of the other agent runners when he encountered them in the corridors. Their more careful than usual avoidance of shop talk in the canteen. Something big was in the air. Something very, very big. Yet there was no mobilization in progress. The civilian population hadn't been alerted to anything beyond the ordinary, unending threats. Something big was coming soon but apparently not coming here.

Blumenfeld hoped the people in charge knew what they were doing.

III

It started out as a lark. By the sheerest chance, Cavendish happened to over-hear Jane Smythe-Smythe attempting to convince Roddy Glendower he should accompany her to New York. Cavendish wasn't sure why Roddy was even at the party, other than that it was such a slapdash, spur of the moment affair any-body might walk through the door. Ordinarily Roddy didn't consort with het-erosexuals, but that was neither here nor there. Cavendish didn't understand that brand of segregation but knew it existed. If Roddy had deigned to join the fun despite his usual inclinations, more power to him. He was as welcome as any other guest.

After hearing from her solicitors that the Decree Absolute was immi-nent, Pippa had said "you know darling, this calls for a celebration, rather" and Cavendish didn't know quite how to discourage or deflect her. That had been the story of their marriage from beginning to end, and it looked increasingly as if it might also be the story of their divorce: Pippa calling the shots and Cavendish standing dumbfounded just out of range of her pitching arm, though not of her voice. He wasn't certain how one might avoid those stentorian tones definitively short of emigrating. She was right, however. Once he took a moment to consider it, he saw that. A major blowout seemed a stunningly appropriate way—the only possible way, actually—to mark the final dissolution of their woefully misbe-gotten marriage. On such short notice it couldn't hope to rival their wedding reception, but with Pippa at the helm it would be the spectacle of the weekend, at the very least.

They had packed the boys off to Gloucestershire to stay with his mum for a fortnight in anticipation of publicity occasioned by the divorce, and once the crucial document was safely in hand Pippa got on the phone. Caterers, florists, bartenders, the paparazzi, a DJ—all those and more were at her fingertips. They started arriving at the flat to set up shop about the time she got around to emailing invitations to potential guests. The party might be impromptu in the extreme, but Pippa always entertained on a grand scale, so a major turnout had to be anticipated. Particularly as it was Cavendish's pounds, shillings, and pence she was spending. Of course shillings had been obsolete since his boyhood, but he still thought of them fondly, still referred to them when quoting prices and values. This required quite a bit of multiplication and division in his head even as he made conversation, constituting a salutary mental exercise if nothing else. He cultivated this eccentricity as one would a delicate, exotic plant. Truly, he still mourned the shilling's passing. *Ah, the noble shilling: gone but never to be forgotten. Not as long as Cavendish draws breath.* By all rights he should have been born a generation, if not a century, earlier. He might well have been his own grandfather, for instance. Spiritually he almost certainly was.

Overhearing Jane boozily making her pitch to Roddy, a process which entailed much fluttering of eyelids—indeed, the full employment of her notorious repertoire of body language, Cavendish sauntered up and said "look here, old thing, why don't I tag along?" in the hope that Roddy might find the offer sufficiently enticing to agree to the adventure. Roddy worshipped at the same gym as Cavendish and had lately developed quite a fine set of accoutrements under the tutelage of some Eastern European individual whose name Cavendish unaccountably couldn't seem to remember and who was financing his trip to the next Mr. Olympia (as a contestant, be it noted) by taking on paying clients. Most of them remained as weedy as ever, but it increasingly looked as if Roddy had what it took. There were bulges where there hadn't been bulges previously. Quite unmistakable and impressive bulges. Roddy had become rather toothsome, now that Cavendish was paying attention.

Though at that juncture Roddy was apparently as addled as Jane, his eyes lit up at Cavendish's suggestion. Unfortunately, it then turned out that a) Jane proposed to embark on the adventure more or less immediately and Roddy couldn't, his second-to-last ex-boyfriend having a gallery opening scheduled for Sunday afternoon which Roddy reckoned could be boycotted much more obviously from the wine bar across the road than from the other side of the Atlantic, and b) Jane's father's Gulfstream was already pretty fully booked for the journey. There would only be seats for two additional passengers even assuming that Cavendish packed light.

Having had all this clarified for him, there was every reason under the sun for Cavendish to turn right around and abandon Jane, Roddy, and the whole scheme, but somehow before he knew it he was clambering up the airstairs into the cramped cabin, which was already teeming with Reginald Smythe-Smythe and his business ramifications (they styled themselves "corporate raiders", which Cavendish judged was as good a euphemism for criminal as any) on their way to New York to make acquisitions. Cavendish's unexpected appearance in their midst occasioned all sorts of commentary, some humorous, some hinting at scandal, due to his long-time association with the eldest son of Reginald's chief rival in such activities, Lord FitzMerlin.

Good old Rupert. How Cavendish missed him, now that he'd been reminded of it. Sorely indeed. That's where he had gone wrong. Pippa instead of Rupert. Live and learn, he supposed.

■ ■ ■

It turned out that Jane's primary motivation for visiting the Big Apple was the presence there of Rupert's brother, Peregrine. Peregrine regularly featured on lists of the U.K.'s most eligible bachelors yet remained unattached in even the most casual manner, and Jane had decided it was her turn to take a crack at him. Knowing them both, Cavendish couldn't believe that was a good idea but wouldn't have dreamed of trying to dissuade her. She was as fierce in her own way as Pippa. And besides, the arguments were all against him. At least the obvious ones. Peregrine was stunningly attractive, for one thing. Almost as attractive as his brother, or at least had been the last time Cavendish saw either of them. And Peregrine would be inheriting the title and the estates, though not for several decades yet going by the astonishing longevity exhibited by that long line of FitzMerlin incumbents. There was the matter of money as well, because the FitzMerlins weren't the typical down-at-the heel variety of aristos you generally encountered these days but rather emphatically their opposite. They made money like most people made toast—frequently and apparently without putting much thought or effort into it. So Jane's interest, not to mention her fervor, made apparent sense. Indeed, her quest had a kind of inevitability to it. But to Cavendish's thinking Peregrine was a pig in every possible way. Even Pippa had recognized it, and that was saying a great deal. Then there was the fact that no FitzMerlin in living memory (meaning by that expression *since the eleventh century*) had actually married an Englishwoman. Rupert and Peregrine's mum was Latvian by way of Paris, for instance. So Cavendish thought of Jane's intentions as quixotic at best. But it did mean a free lift to New York. Given the magnitude of Pippa's divorce settlement, he was going to have to give some thought to economies.

Accompanying Jane to New York would be something to do. Something to take Cavendish away from the British Isles, which he was finding a wearisome locale of late. Something to divert him from his divorce, which, though it had represented a consummation devoutly wished for still managed to leave a bitter taste in his mouth. Shouldn't Pippa have been at least the tiniest bit regretful? Not that Cavendish was himself, but still. Her glee seemed shockingly bad form.

■ ■ ■

It all went swimmingly until they actually arrived on the far side of the Atlantic. Cavendish was able to secure lodgings easily enough, and New York was as ravishing as ever. But it was harder to shake Jane than he had anticipated. Impossible, more or less. And then once Jane finally tracked down Peregrine, Cavendish found himself unable to leave the pair to their own devices because at that point Peregrine took over where Jane had just reached the point of leaving off, insisting Cavendish stay around as a kind of chaperone. This was astute on Peregrine's part but rather difficult to square with his own itinerary. Discouragingly, Jane reminded Cavendish of Pippa more with each passing hour. They were distant cousins, and had been sent down from Rodean in the aftermath of some scandal they had jointly masterminded. Or so Cavendish understood the matter.

Crucially, Cavendish had forgotten how truly identical Peregrine and Rupert were, even with two years between them. One look at the young bounder striding into the lounge of their hotel was enough to convince Cavendish that his journey had been a Very Bad Idea Indeed.

■ ■ ■

And of course, as had so often been the case in Cavendish's wanderings, one bad idea led inevitably to another. Typically an even worse one, in accordance with the dicta of that chap Murphy. Until catching sight of Peregrine, Cavendish's nostalgia about Rupert, though gradually increasing, had been just about manageable. One toss of that impeccably coifed head, however, made matters unbearable. Rupert's hair was just like that if not always quite so ruthlessly groomed, he being much more the athlete and less calculating as well. Jane recognized Cavendish's dilemma immediately, if not its essential nature. "Gosh, yes," she said. "You two were ever such good chums, weren't you? And I'll bet you've scarcely seen each other since your wedding to Pippa." This assumption, uttered without a whiff of innuendo, wasn't entirely accurate but close enough. She hit on the idea of a surprise visit to Rupert as a way of putting three thousand miles between Peregrine and his chosen protector, the better to serve her own aims. Unfortunately, however, there were no direct flights scheduled for the next morning which still had available seats in first class. Cavendish didn't object to traveling coach on socioeconomic grounds, but his six foot three inch, two hundred fifty pound frame protested mightily at the mere suggestion. So here Cavendish was in a departure lounge at Newark about to get onto a plane that would take him to San Francisco, whence he would board another, much smaller, plane for the flight on to San

Diego. By now Rupert had surely received his email. Rupert would either be waiting to greet Cavendish at the airport on his arrival or he wouldn't.

Actually, Rupert was certain to be there. He was too much the gentleman not to show up. But his presence might or might not signify what Cavendish rather hoped it would. Encountering Peregrine had brought him just that much clarity. Bloody long time Cavendish had taken making up his mind. Bloody lot of water under the bridge. Yet things might be salvageable. There would be time during the journey to ponder his tactics.

He knew he'd be able to judge the lay of the land more or less immediately from Rupert's expression when they finally caught sight of one another. Rupert had never been any good at poker. Any card game, really. His expressions betrayed him every time. He was, Cavendish recalled, incapable of guile.

Oh, Rupert.

If worst came to worst, one could turn on one's heel, trudge off in search of a ticket counter, and book one's retreat.

Oh, Rupert.

Roops. . .

"Ladies and gentlemen," the uniformed goddess at the podium drawled into the hand set. These Yanks with their preposterous accents. She might as well have been speaking Urdu. "We're now ready to begin boarding United Flight 93 with nonstop service to San Francisco. First class passengers are welcome to board the aircraft at this time. Anyone requiring additional assistance may approach the podium."

Cavendish checked his Breitling. It looked like being an on-time departure. He hoisted the kitschy carry-on bag he'd purchased at that shop in Times Square and prepared to follow his fellow first-class passengers down the jetway.

AUGUST, 1973

Josh Luxemberg looked around the small living room and took a deep breath. Alone at last. Nanny Freitag and Mom had just left after spending most of the afternoon organizing his kitchen. Considering that said kitchen was six feet square, their efforts seemed more than a little excessive. But he hadn't interfered. Hadn't uttered a word of skepticism. Hadn't made a single suggestion. Mom had written that check for six months rent, after all. More than he'd asked for and way more than he'd been expecting. He knew exactly how his gratitude would best be expressed—let them have their fun. And it was Nanny who chose the two bedroom walkup in a vintage building with a prime Greenwich Village location. Josh had long since resigned himself to a studio on the lower East Side. Probably with a tribe of rats already in residence and squadrons of cockroaches tapdancing on the countertops. So a few hours listening to his female relatives huff and puff and—most of all—kvetch in his new kitchen was a small enough price to pay. Besides, now that they'd worked their magic it was clean enough to eat off the floor in there. Every kitchen gadget known to western civilization was present, accounted for, in perfect working order, and in its proper place. Not that he actually planned on cooking. He wouldn't have known how to begin. He was his mother's son in that regard.

A two bedroom apartment. He couldn't get over it. True, the second bedroom was about the size of a broom closet, but it had to be admitted that relatively few Broadway hopefuls lived on such a scale. Nanny had been intent on that second bedroom "in case of friends from out of town". To her, out of town meant Brooklyn. Or, heaven forbid, Queens. She had come to America steerage class on a steamship out of Hamburg, but nowadays she hated crossing any body of water, no matter how inconsequential, by any means—bridge, ferry, tunnel or even airplane—so she rarely left Manhattan and regarded New Jersey as uncharted wilderness, most likely inhabited by savages.

■ ■ ■

Dad had shelved Josh's record albums just any old way. That was his contribution to the move. He left long before lunch and went back uptown to work. Being around his mother-in-law in such a confined space made him nervous. Especially when she was handling cutlery. Josh was re-alphabetizing the records when the buzzer went off.

"Jeannine," the voice came through the crackly speaker, "it's me, Eli. I locked myself out. Again. Buzz me in, won't you?"

Nanny was fascinated by that speaker apparatus. Josh probably had it to thank for her insistence on this apartment instead of the one in the next block. Most buildings she was familiar with had buzzers only. Being able to speak to visitors and deliverymen waiting on the sidewalk apparently struck her as the height of sophistication. As a Manhattan native, Josh wasn't about to be taken in by that voice. Rapists and axe murders perennially utilized such strategies to gain access to their victims. Not to mention, the occasional Mormon missionary had been known to show up at the occasional front door bent on brainwashing. He turned his attention back to the N's. The buzzer sounded again.

"Jeannine." The voice now had an edge of desperation to it. "Jeannine, are you there? It's Eli. Your upstairs neighbor. Eli from Three B. You know I keep a spare key under the rubber plant next to the mailboxes."

Josh got up, walked the four steps to the apparatus on the wall, and pushed the button.

"I'm sorry," he said. "I believe there's some mistake. There's no Jeannine here. Are you sure you've got the right building?"

"Oh, shit, that's right. She told me she was moving out. You must be the new tenant. Do you think you could buzz me in?"

"I don't know about that," Josh said. "How can I be certain you're not a criminal element?"

But by this time the question was facetious. He had noticed that half dead rubber plant downstairs. He had considered stashing his own spare key there. And the voice couldn't possibly belong to a baddie. He sounded, if anything, like that rabbinical student Josh had dated last summer. Jason? Jordan? There were too many of them to keep track of. Not all rabbinical students, obviously.

■ ■ ■

"Two B?"

Josh looked up from the stack of mail in his hand. All junk. Nobody he knew had his new address yet.

"Yes?"

"Three B," the young man said, pointing at himself. He was in banker drag, apparently just home from work. "Thanks for helping me out the other afternoon. I owe you one."

Eli Danziger, Josh thought. Apparently Eli hadn't recognized him. Reasonable enough. They'd only met once or twice. And both times with hordes of Eli's relatives around making racket and chaos, as Josh remembered it. It might be fun to pretend he didn't recognize Eli either.

"Think nothing of it," he said.

"Oh, but I do," Eli insisted. "I have to. If my past record is any indication, I'm bound to lock myself out at least once more before your lease is up. Probably twice, unless you signed a very short term contract."

"Well, you'll probably have a chance to return the favor before long," Josh smiled, "so I wouldn't worry about it."

"No," Eli said, "not really worry. I wouldn't call it that exactly. But you should at least let me buy you dinner."

"That's not necessary."

"Not necessary perhaps," Eli agreed, "but, well, neighborly. Greenwich *Village*, right? So please?"

"I'm busy tonight."

"Oh, I am too," Eli said. "The rest of the week, really. How about Sunday?"

"Are you the kind of guy who's not going to give me any peace until I say yes?"

"I don't know," Eli said. "Probably."

■ ■ ■

The line outside the room where auditions were being held stretched clear down the corridor to the elevator, but Jill had gotten there early and saved Josh a place. Jill wasn't there to try out. She was there to be his good luck charm. A true Broadway angel, she refused to let him face his first New York audition alone. She'd been cast several months ago in a cheesy but wildly successful Off-Broadway revue whose run kept being extended because everyone wanted to see it despite, or perhaps because of, truly noxious reviews. The producers had hit on the idea of making those reviews part of the show's marketing, going so far as to print lobby posters featuring quotes from the most unflattering of them. More recently Jill had landed a recurring part in a network soap that broadcast from Rockefeller Center. She logged lots of miles on the subway. Ah, the glamorous life of the theatre.

"Darling," she cooed, as he bent to kiss her cheek. She had the face of an ingénue, the delivery of a soubrette, and the heart of a blackjack dealer. As far as Josh was concerned, this was all it took to assure her success.

"Angel," he crooned. "Muse."

"This is your lucky day," she said. "I'm getting vibrations."

"And what extreme good fortune that you weren't called uptown for today's episode," Josh said.

She wrinkled up her face.

"So you could be here with me, I mean," he said. "To see me through this ordeal. Of course it must have been an oversight on someone's part. The individual responsible will probably lose his job when the producers realize what happened."

"Yes, Joshua. I know exactly what you meant. You'll be thrilled to hear that the native drumbeats bring news of major developments in Midtown. My role is to be shaken up. I've been informed, unofficially of course, that I'll soon be playing my own evil twin. In addition to my virtuous, vapid, boring old self. The character's self, that is."

"How delicious would that be?" Josh marveled. "Separated at birth? Or the criminal psychopath newly released from prison?"

"The writers are leaning in the direction of prison," Jill said.

"Prison's probably best in the long run," Josh said. "Great back story."

"Flashback sequences," Jill nodded, "redolent of violence and sexual menace."

"Darling, how I envy you."

"It's one of the most venerable of soap opera clichés, of course," she said. "Nearly as bad as the amnesia gambit. One's almost embarrassed to contemplate it."

"Yet somehow it never gets old."

"At least not in the hands of the right actress. Not just anyone, you realize, can navigate the nuances believably."

"Or manage not to forget who she is in which scene," Josh agreed.

"The wigs alone," Jill mused.

■ ■ ■

"How do you think it went?" Jill asked.

They had waited nearly an hour for Josh to be called in and his stomach was beginning to growl by the time he got out of the audition.

"I sang the hell out of that number," Josh said. "I mean, I really sold it. Not to mention I'm in particularly good voice today."

"And your hair has rarely been so perfect."

"Yes, there's certainly that," Josh admitted, "but who knows what they think they're looking for?"

"I'm sure they'll cast you."

"If they don't it's not the end of the world."

"That's the spirit," Jill said. "Never say die."

"Not that so much," Josh said. "I've got two more shows to audition for next week. Off-Broadway, but work nevertheless."

"Still, I always say that the less you let yourself care about it, the more likely you are to get the part," Jill said. "Come on. Let's have lunch. Then I want you to show me your new apartment."

■ ■ ■

"Darling," Jill sighed, doing a pirouette in the living room, "it's divine."

"You like it?"

"Like it? I covet it. I'm ready to scratch your eyes out with jealousy. These floors. Genuine hardwood. And you actually have a closet."

"Easy, girl."

"What about the neighbors? Have you met them? Are they nice?"

"Funny you should ask," Josh said.

"I sense a story."

"The guy upstairs locked himself out the other afternoon. I buzzed him in. He's taking me to dinner on Sunday."

"Is he cute?"

"Very cute," Josh said. "If you like the type."

"What type is that?"

"That clean cut, suit and tie thing," Josh said, making a face. "Introduce him to your aunties and they'll swoon. Put him in a pair of pajamas from the Sears-Roebuck catalogue and he could do toothpaste commercials."

"You hate that type," Jill said. "I've never understood why. I think those guys are divine. They look completely innocuous, but they have hidden depths. I swear to God, the depths. You should introduce me."

"Hold your horses," Josh said. "Wouldn't work out."

"He's gay?"

"Pretty sure," Josh said.

"How can you say 'pretty sure'? Aren't you the boy with the best gaydar on the East Coast?"

"Oh, I'm sure he's gay," Josh said. "I'm just not sure he knows it yet."

"Then perhaps you should clear it up for him. In spite of your aesthetic misgivings."

"Ordinarily I'd consider it," Josh said. "As an act of charity, you know?"

"That's one name for it. So why don't you?"

"I'm kind of related to him."

"You're joking."

"He's my sister-in-law's first cousin."

"That's not close enough to count," Jill said, "if he's cute enough. And I have a feeling he is."

"I know he recognized me when we ran into each other at the mailboxes. But I pretended not to know who he was. He was too shy to bring it up."

■ ■ ■

Greenwich Village really was a village. The quaint buildings. The narrow streets, some of them paved with cobblestones. The picturesque escape from the tyranny of the grid that governed Midtown and points north. It was perfect for jogging, though Josh had to be careful on the uneven sidewalks. It was perfect for bicycling, but you had to watch the traffic carefully because for the most part it was not watching you. The taxi drivers were downright homicidal. Most of all, it was perfect for looking at boys. There were lots of them. Hordes, really. At every point of the compass. Cute. Pretty. Classically handsome. Breathtaking. Or indescribable. Sexy ethnic boxer/wrestler/gymnasts or icy Nordic types with cheekbones sharp as machetes. Rugged. Downright tough. Or monumental. Young guys like Josh or severe looking daddies. Way more flavors than Baskin-Robbins ever dreamed of serving. They lined the streets. They preened at the intersections. They blasted by on motorcycles. They whizzed past on skates. They displayed themselves from upstairs windows. They lounged on doorsteps.

You looked at them and sometimes they looked back.

■ ■ ■

"So what's your Cousin Talbot up to lately?" Josh asked, falling into step beside Eli. It was Sunday night and Josh was being taken to dinner. He assumed he was the entertainment. "You're Talbot Kleinbaum's cousin, right?"

"Cousin Talbot?" Eli began, then stopped in his tracks and peered at Josh. "You know, I was sure you didn't remember me."

"Of course I remembered you," Josh said. "Why wouldn't I? It hasn't been that long since we last saw each other."

"Three years ago," Eli said. "It was your brother Ike's wedding."

They started walking again.

"Your Cousin Cherie Landau was the blushing bride," Josh said. "You've seen the baby? Genikayte?"

"Only pictures," Eli said. "Cute kid. She's lucky she takes after the Luxemberg side of the family."

"I don't know about that," Josh said. "You're certainly cute enough. And Talbot's an Adonis. Hands down."

"Talbot's kind of a black sheep," Eli muttered.

"So tell me about him."

Josh had a particular reason to ask about Talbot. Or two, to be honest about it.

"Talbot," Eli shook his head.

"Real ladies' man, I expect," Josh said.

There. If that wasn't insinuating enough—no, it had to be insinuating enough. Eli couldn't be that dense.

"Talbot's problem," Eli said, "is that he seems to think he lives in a soap opera. All those women. All that drama. All those broken hearts. It's like he doesn't realize those poor girls are real."

Or maybe Talbot's problem is they're too real, Josh thought. What he'd just found out was that either Talbot's secret was still a secret or Eli wasn't willing to admit to knowing it. It made Eli more intriguing. Of course Talbot was the truly intriguing one.

■ ■ ■

"This was really fun," Eli said, poised for his ascent of the next flight of stairs.

"It was," Josh agreed, half in and half out of his front door.

"We should do it again."

"On me next time," Josh said. "We'll be celebrating my new role."

"Yes," Eli said. "Good luck on that. Make sure you let me know as soon as you hear something."

■ ■ ■

Greenwich Village was like a real village. You bought bread and pastries from a bakery, dropped your shirts off at the laundry, bought fruit from a stand on the sidewalk, ate lunch from a cart. Of course it was like that all over Manhattan. But somehow in the Village it seemed more so.

And the boys. Any time of the day or night, the boys.

■ ■ ■

"I got a callback."

"Bravo, darling," Jill said.

"What's that noise?" Josh asked, holding the telephone away from his ear.

"They're jackhammering downstairs," Jill said. "Something about the sidewalk. They got me out of bed at an ungodly hour."

"Sounds like they're jackhammering in your kitchen."

"I don't believe so," Jill said. "Perhaps I should go check."

"Why don't you congratulate me on my callback instead?"

"Of course, Joshua. Congratulations. There, that's done. You know, I'm not a bit surprised. It was bound to happen. Your shoulders looked particularly broad last Wednesday."

"Did they?"

"I remember distinctly. I'm sure someone in the audition hall noticed. But what I really want to hear about is your dinner with the upstairs neighbor. You're not still pretending that you don't know who he is, I hope."

"No, we cleared that up," Josh said.

"Good. Because those things just get more awkward the longer you let them go on."

"He seemed surprised that I remembered him."

"Why? Isn't he memorable?"

"He could be," Josh said, "with a little effort. His clothing is just so nonde-script. Though I believe it's mostly a question of attitude."

"Ah. So is he or isn't he?"

"Still not sure," Josh said. "I tried to get it out of him. I mentioned his cousin Talbot. To his family, Talbot is this major Lothario. But in reality he's more of a Casanovette."

"I'm afraid I don't follow you."

"Well, I thought that if Eli's gay himself he and Talbot would surely have compared notes. But apparently not."

"That settles it," Jill said. "Now you have to introduce me."

■ ■ ■

"Any news?" Eli asked.

They were checking their mail. Either their schedules were eerily similar or Eli was lurking, hoping to run into Josh down there at the boxes. Josh was a lurk-er of long standing himself and knew all the tricks. He could have given classes.

"I just heard this afternoon," Josh grinned. "It's only the chorus, but I'm officially cast in my first Broadway production."

"That's fantastic," Eli yelped. "Only the chorus, my ass. That's how all the big stars started out. We have to celebrate."

"Monday night," Josh nodded. "Dinner. It's Jill's only night off. She's in a show too. Sunday evenings there's a standing command performance for her grandmother."

"Jill?"

"I'll make a reservation," Josh said, ignoring Eli's curiosity the better to stoke its fires. "I'll let you know the time and place."

■ ■ ■

When they got to the restaurant, Eli had already been seated. Either he had dressed up, which made Josh feel sloppy, or he'd just left work, which made Josh feel socially superior yet at the same time lazy and unproductive. He guessed that was what was meant by the term "bohemian".

"He's a dreamboat," Jill murmured.

"You really think so? You're not being ironic?"

"Irony is your middle name, Joshua, not mine."

"In that case, down, girl."

As they reached the table, Eli stood to greet them.

"You didn't mention he had such nice manners," Jill muttered.

"Josh," Eli smiled.

"Eli," Josh laughed. "I'd like you to meet Jill Wagstaffe. Jill—Eli Danziger."

"Pleased to meet you," Eli gulped.

"Eli, darling," Jill oozed, "the pleasure is all mine."

They all sat.

"Jill is an actress," Josh said. "I think I may have mentioned it."

"Oh, I know exactly who you are, Jill," Eli smiled. "You're on my Nanna Neumann's favorite soap opera."

"Please, darling," Jill interrupted him, "don't speak the title aloud. It's bad luck. It's like saying *Macbeth* inside a theatre. All sorts of misfortunes ensue."

"She's making that up," Josh snorted.

"I am not," Jill insisted. "Dear Joshua is simply unfamiliar with the arcane traditions of soap opera folk."

"Well, all I know," Eli said, "is Nanna's going to be thrilled when I tell her who my new downstairs neighbor's girlfriend is."

"Girlfriend?" Jill giggled. "Who said anything about a girlfriend? I'm afraid dear Josh wouldn't know what to do with such an animal."

"I don't believe I understand," Eli said.

"Oh, I think you do, darling," Jill smiled.

"She's right," Josh laughed. "Queer as a three dollar bill, me."

■ ■ ■

"I know all about Ike of course," Eli said, refilling Jill's wine glass. "He's married to my cousin Cherie. They just had their first baby. But isn't there another Luxemberg brother?"

"My twin, Jake," Josh said. "He ran away to join the circus."

"He's making that up," Jill chortled. "Jake lives on a kibbutz. He goes by Yakov these days."

"My Cousin Fern lives on a kibbutz," Eli said. "Outside Haifa. Maybe it's the same one."

"Probably not," Josh said. "There are lots of kibbutzes over there."

"Anyway, Jake isn't who I was thinking about," Eli said. "Isn't there another brother?"

"Darling," Jill said, "you don't mean Cooper. The black sheep of the Luxembergs. We don't talk about him."

"Really."

"I just got back from delivering him to California a couple of weeks ago," Josh said. "He's starting college out there. He'll probably be expelled by the end of the first week of classes, but at least he's no longer on the East Coast."

■ ■ ■

"So what's the verdict?" Josh asked. He was walking Jill back to her place in deepest, darkest Chelsea.

"Well," Jill said, avoiding a small puddle on the sidewalk from a brief shower during dinner. "I don't know for certain that he's gay."

"He was supposed to come clean when you outed me," Josh laughed.

"Right," Jill said. "That went over like a lead balloon. But I'm sure of one thing. He has a crush on you."

"Oh, no," Josh protested. "He can't. He just can't."

"Nevertheless," Jill said.

If it was true, how was Josh going to get Eli to set him up with Talbot?

II

Josh had been hoping to meet some cute guys among his castmates in case Operation Talbot Kleinbaum fizzled out. There were a few, but they were mostly too femme for his taste. He liked his men rather more stalwart. That was the problem with Eli, really. He was nice enough certainly, just not man enough. There was one guy in the cast, though, Kevin Dietrich, who was butch as hell and went around pawing the turf and smoldering like a campfire after lights out. Trouble was, his girlfriend was also in the cast. They could hardly keep their hands off each other. They practically fucked in the hallway during breaks. If Kevin hadn't been so hot, Josh wouldn't have forgiven him. He wasn't sure he approved of heterosexuality. Behind closed doors was one thing. But they insisted on flaunting their lifestyle. . .

■ ■ ■

Some of Josh's castmates were jaded. He could see it in their eyes. In the way they sauntered into rehearsal just seconds before somebody decided to write them up for being tardy. In the way they worked just hard enough but no harder than they had to in each scene. They were on the way out of the business whether they realized it or not. After this show or maybe the next one, they'd give up. A year from now they'd be out in New Jersey selling carpets.

Josh promised himself he'd never be like that.

■ ■ ■

One of the nellier of the boys in the chorus, C.J., showed up at rehearsal one Monday with a black eye. Lots of razzing about bee stings and unexpected impacts with doorknobs ensued. C.J. took it all like a veteran of the wars. Josh cornered him during break.

"I approached Atilla the Hunk over there with a certain proposition," C.J. said.

"You mean Kevin? He did this to you?"

"I never bought his hetero act, did you?"

"I guess I did, actually."

"Josh, come on," C.J. laughed. "What are you? In third grade? Anyway, now we know the truth. A genuine straight guy would just tell you to get lost. Only a closet case would punch your lights out for offering him a blow job."

■ ■ ■

When Josh got to the restaurant, Eli had already been seated. Which made three times now. That was the type of guy Eli was—get there early, secure the table. No use risking loss of the reservation. He even knew what Josh liked to drink and ordered it. These were sterling qualities, no question. He'd make the perfect boyfriend if it wasn't for the missing sex appeal. He had taken his jacket off and hung it over the back of his chair. He had rolled his sleeves up. His hair was the tiniest bit mussed—it was breezy that day. He was the perfect young Manhattan businessman out for a brisk, efficient lunch. The only thing missing from the picture was a giggling dental hygienist or off-duty stewardess sitting across from him and playing with her hair. Josh kept trying to get Eli to buy some neckties with more zoom to them, but so far with no result. He sensed that Eli's reluctance in that regard was somehow related to the sex appeal deficit.

"Eli."

"Joshua," Eli smiled. "Sit."

Josh sat.

"How's things? Rehearsals going well?"

"O.K." Josh said.

"Just O.K?"

"It's early yet. Before I forget, Jill says to tell you hi and would you please give me your grandparents' mailing address so she can send Nanna Neumann a signed publicity photo from the soap."

"Really?" Eli marveled. "She said that?"

"What she really said," Josh told him, "was that she wants to have your babies. She has formed the opinion that you must be extremely fertile. She suspects you of a propensity to erupt in volcano after volcano of sexual passion and hopes to share at least one such moment with you. *And* would you please give me your grandparents' address, etc."

"She wants to have my baby," Eli murmured, shaking his head with what looked like bewilderment.

"What's good here?" Josh asked, scanning the menu.

"Everything's good here," Eli said. "Just order whatever you think you'd like."

"Not even a hint?" Josh pressed.

"It's like this," Eli said. "I've got this friend. Actually, I'm pretty sure we've all got a friend like this. You mention you're going to Chez Rasputin for dinner next week and he says 'Chez Rasputin? That's my favorite pan-Slavic restaurant. When you go you must try the Duck a la Czarina'. Now you're not that crazy about duck, but he's really insistent. . ."

"This friend wouldn't happen to be Talbot Kleinbaum, would it?"

"Talbot has many bad habits," Eli said, "but not this exact one. I'm actually thinking of one of Talbot's cousins. He just got out of the Peace Corps and he's working on his Ph.D. at Harvard, so he's not in town very often but when he is he's really bossy. Anyway, you order the Duck a la Czarina and when it arrives it's greasy as hell. Honestly, it's an oil slick on a plate. And the sauce has this medicinal edge to it. You can hardly choke it down. At those prices. The evening is pretty much spoiled, and all because Andrew Rubinstein was so insistent. That, my friend, is why I never tell my friends what to order in restaurants."

■ ■ ■

Josh wasn't making it up. Jill had said all those things about Eli. And more. That wasn't why he had repeated them at lunch, however. His motivation for the scene, his subtext so to speak, was the still unanswered question was Eli or was he not batting for Josh's team? And it remained unresolved. What did Josh have to do? Offer Eli a blow job just to see his reaction? C.J. swore by the gambit, but Josh didn't want to risk the consequences. At the very least, some sort of misunderstanding seemed inevitable. The secondary subtext, though of more existential significance to Josh, had to do with his continuing quest to plant his flag at the summit of Talbot KIeinbaum's extremely sexy *corpus delicti* and declare him a possession of Luxemberg.

■ ■ ■

"We're so excited, dear," Mom's voice crackled out of the phone with more than her usual level of intensity. Sometimes Josh wasn't certain she understood that modern day telephone systems featured amplification. "Everybody's coming to your opening."

"Everybody? You mean you found the missing Lindbergh baby and you're bringing him along? Make sure to tell him to bring the Maltese Falcon with him."

"Honestly, Joshua," she sighed. "We spent a small fortune on your education and that damned university sent us back a wiseass. I'm not sure your father would have agreed to it if he'd foreseen that particular result."

Her complaint didn't mesh with the historical record. Josh had gone to university on scholarship. The cost to his parents was minimal. Mom simply chose to remember it differently. Of course he was a wiseass, but he had been since at least kindergarten. And speaking of wiseasses, it was kind of a family specialty. His twin Jake/Yakov was, if anything, even worse. Josh's college education was beside the point.

"It'll be great to have you in the audience," he told her.

■ ■ ■

It was the best feeling in the world. Or maybe the second best. It was hard to beat sex. But when you were actually on the stage taking your bow it was easy to forget, just for a second or two, exactly how great sex was. Of course this was only Josh's first Broadway curtain call. But he sensed that they were all like that. Yes, the first of a long line of them stretching far into the future. Eight shows a week, decade after decade, until the apotheosis marking the close of his illustrious career. By then he'd be a legend many times over. Tony Awards would line his mantel. Cast albums featuring his opulent vocal tones would cram his bookshelves, cheek by jowl with bound volumes of playbills, some of them featuring his photo on the cover.

Tonight was the start. Opening night. His first one in New York. Broadway. A part in the chorus, but still Broadway.

Soon the curtain would close for the night. The work lights would come up onstage. He'd exchange fervent congratulations and sweaty hugs with his castmates. In a few cases the congratulations would be sweaty and the hugs fervent, because he'd been reconsidering C.J.'s failure with Kevin Dietrich and was about to take up the challenge. After that he'd take off his makeup and change quickly into street clothes. He'd go out to meet Mom and Dad and Nanny Freitag. Aunt Rosie and her husband Lou had come as well. Ike and Cherie had taken the train down from Boston. And Jill was there. Jill and funny, uncommitted Eli.

OCTOBER, 1973

"You're awake," the nurse said. "Good. Are you in pain?"

"Not really," Yakov said. The pain was the least of his concerns. The pain had announced to him he was still alive, so it was good news, really. But where was he? How had he gotten there? He couldn't remember anything.

"Stop that," the nurse said. "No heroics. We don't allow any tough guy stuff. Suffering slows down your recovery. It's been scientifically proven. Tell me how bad it is."

"I'll live," Yakov said. His vision was clearing. This was a field hospital, obviously. He hadn't been hurt badly enough to require evacuation to one of the cities. Either that or he had been hurt too badly to be evacuated. Six of one, half a dozen of another. Still alive, though. That was something. He should be happier at the prospect.

"I'll go get you another dose of morphine."

"Morphine?"

"I told you," the nurse said. "We don't believe in heroics here. That craziness stays outside where it belongs."

■ ■ ■

The next time Yakov woke up, a face was staring down at him. He tried to ignore it and go back to sleep.

"Name, soldier?" the man enquired.

Movie star handsome. The kind of man Mom's friends swooned over. American women—sheesh. Maybe Yakov was dreaming.

"Shouldn't that be on my chart?"

"Neurological evaluation," the man grunted. "Humor me."

"Jake—I mean Yakov. Sergeant Yakov Luxemberg."

"American," the man laughed.

"Israeli citizen," Yakov growled, "and soldier."

"Relax, Luxemberg," the man said. "You don't have to impress anyone around here. We know Americans can be tough. I grew up in Montreal myself. Medical school at McGill. So I get it, you see?"

"Get what? Who are you, anyway?"

"Have it your way. I'm Dr. Goldman. And you, Sergeant, were extremely lucky. It wasn't a bad wound, but it nicked an artery. You almost bled out before they got you here. There was a blow to your head, as well. But that seems unusually hard."

"Are you who I've got to thank?"

"Only if you're feeling thankful," Goldman smirked.

"How soon can I go back to my unit?"

"Not soon enough," Dr. Goldman said. "By the time you're sufficiently recovered to go back on active duty, this will all be over with. One way or another."

■ ■ ■

"Nurse," Yakov called. Two days since his arrival he was sleeping less, which meant he got bored. And he wasn't allowed out of bed without assistance, which made it worse. What kind of field hospital was it that babied patients like this?

"Yes, sergeant? More morphine? Coming right up."

"No, nurse," Yakov said. "Not that. I feel fine. Can you tell me what happened to my unit?"

"I don't have that information," she said. "I'll see what I can find out."

"Thank you."

"I can tell you this much," she said. "We didn't have any other patients admitted from your unit."

"That's good."

"Now I'm going to get you some more morphine whether you think you need it or not. To help you rest."

"Or keep me from going back into battle," Yakov muttered to her retreating back.

■ ■ ■

Yakov stared at the ceiling. Which in this case was the underside of the tent. So it wasn't a ceiling, really. He didn't know what to call it. But it was what he had to stare at. From time to time he could hear explosions. Very distant ones. At least he thought they were explosions. He might be imagining it. Or it might be thunder. But whether they were real explosions or not, the fighting was still going on somewhere. His unit was out there battling the Arabs and he was here on his back doing no one any good. This was not what he had come to Israel for. He should be with them, but unless he could get that quack Goldman to authorize his release there was no chance of rejoining them.

He couldn't believe he'd been so stupid. How could he have let something like this take him out of the action?

■ ■ ■

"He's right over here, Mrs. Luxemberg," the nurse said.

Yakov opened his eyes. Who the hell could be here calling herself Mrs. Luxemberg? Not Mom. There was no way she could know he was here.

"Thank you nurse."

He recognized the voice. Anat. What the hell was she thinking? In a few seconds, she was looking down at him.

"Yakov," she said, kissing his forehead.

"What are you doing here?"

"Coming to see my nephew in the hospital," she said, pulling up a chair. "Are you so doped you don't know where you are?"

"I can't believe anyone let you come," Yakov complained. "It can't be safe for you to travel here."

"In case you've forgotten," she laughed, "my husband is a high-ranking Israeli officer. The name Luxemberg cuts through all kinds of red tape, let me tell you. And a little flirting does the rest."

"But the baby."

"The baby will be fine," Anat said. "I'm not due to give birth for a couple of weeks yet. Have you seen the doctor today? What did he have to say?"

"Oh, that rascal Goldman's been here, all right," Yakov growled. "I can't believe anyone licensed him to practice medicine. The man's a quack if I ever saw one."

"Don't be silly," Anat said. "Naftali is one of the finest young surgeons in Tel Aviv. You're extremely lucky he was called up to this particular field hospital."

"Naftali? You know him personally?"

"He's the cousin of a girl I went to school with," Anat said. "I've only met him a few times, but everybody knows of his family."

"Every family has its black sheep," Yakov said.

"Sure, Yakov," she shrugged. "But what did he tell you? About your condition, I mean."

"That I won't be going back to my unit for several weeks. The idiot."

"By then this will be over."

"Exactly," Yakov spat.

■ ■ ■

That rascal Goldman looked in on Yakov again just after his dinner things had been cleared. He had showered and shaved. He smelled good and his hair was ridiculously shiny. He looked like the sexy young doctor on one of Nanny Freitag's afternoon shows. The one who spent all his time hopping in and out of married women's beds. That's what kind of doctor he was—a fake. A fake and a playboy. It was enough to turn your stomach.

"They tell me you're doing fine," Goldman said.

"No thanks to you," Yakov complained.

"Hey," Goldman laughed, "don't blame me. I didn't put you in this bed. Blame that Arab who shot you."

"Just help me find him," Yakov said.

"I hear you had a visitor," Goldman said. "Pregnant lady. Very beautiful, according to your nurse. Like a movie star. Funny, your records don't say anything about a wife."

"My aunt, actually," Yakov said. "My uncle's second wife. You may have heard of him. Colonel Marcus Luxemberg."

"I suppose I should be impressed," Goldman said.

"He'll have your balls for breakfast if I don't get back to my unit within forty-eight hours," Yakov said. It was worth a try.

"Don't hold your breath," Goldman said. "I have an aunt, as well. And she's a member of the Knesset."

■ ■ ■

"It's all right, Sergeant. You were only having a dream."

Yakov opened his eyes. Dr. Goldman was grinning down at him.

"What are you doing here?"

"Your nurse stepped out for a smoke."

"Some doctor you are," Yakov snorted. "Relieving nurses in the middle of the night when you could be saving lives."

"Yes," Goldman laughed. "I'm as bad a doctor as you are a patient."

"Seriously," Yakov said, "is there no way I can convince you to let me go back to my unit?"

"I'm afraid you're going to have to resign yourself to the fact that the nation will probably manage to win this war without any additional contributions from you."

"Bastard."

"Since you obviously don't require further assistance, I'll get back to my book now."

"What is it you're reading?"

Goldman held up the volume so Yakov could see it.

"Proust? In French?"

"I'm from Montreal," Goldman smiled. "Remember?"

■ ■ ■

This wasn't supposed to be happening. Yakov had come to Israel in the first place to get away from it. He had been certain that if he devoted himself to his new homeland, the feelings would go away. And certainly, serving in the armed forces—particularly the Israeli ones—should be enough to make a man of anyone. Even the women he'd gone through basic training with had been hard as nails.

He had known from his first moment on Israeli soil that nothing had changed. Until now he'd been able to ignore it. But for how much longer? Now everything had changed. Nanny Freitag had always said that the Almighty didn't give second chances in order for things to go on as they had in the past. Second chances were only granted for one purpose. They were an opportunity to do things differently. But she couldn't have meant a thing like this.

■ ■ ■

"Good," the nurse said, helping him back into the bed. "Very good, actually. In another day or so the doctor will probably let you walk to the bathroom without help."

"In another day or so," Yakov said, "I'll be back with my unit."

"By the way," the nurse said. "There was a call early this morning. The doctor wouldn't let me wake you. It seems that Mrs. Luxemberg went into labor just about as soon as she arrived back in Tel Aviv. A baby boy. Mother and son both doing well. *Mazel Tov*."

"She's my aunt," Yakov said. "The baby's my cousin."

"Oh," the nurse said. "Well, *Mazel Tov* anyway."

II

"Sergeant Luxemberg, I presume."

The Schlesinger's spacious apartment was crowded with well-wishers. A Brit during wartime was kind of a sensation. Maya Schlesinger, the boy's grandmother, had pulled out all the stops. She was that kind of hostess.

"What the hell are you doing here?" Yakov growled.

"Invited guest," Dr. Goldman grinned. "Friend of the family. You?"

It ought to be illegal for a man to be that handsome, Yakov thought. There was something downright decadent about it. Nurses must line up. Their mothers must. . .

"Family member," Yakov grunted, tearing his eyes away. "Relative of the baby. First cousin, to be exact."

"I hope you're following doctor's orders now that you've been discharged."

"Anat and her mother are like the secret police," Yakov complained. "They don't let me get away with a thing."

"Yes," Dr. Goldman nodded. "I heard you're staying with the Schlesingers. You see that woman talking to Maya Schlesinger? That's my Aunt Naomi."

The woman in question looked like European nobility.

"The Knesset member?"

"The very same. So watch yourself."

"Damn."

"And you're getting along all right on that cane?"

■ ■ ■

Baby Yoel's two brothers, Avi and Zev, were the life of the party. At four years old and two, they certainly knew how to work a room. They charmed everyone in range and had first pick of delicacies from the buffet. It was hard for Yakov to think of them as his first cousins, since they were so obviously members of a different generation. With the baby's half-brothers, Gil and Rafi, he was on firmer ground. Gil was a doctor, an emergency room specialist, and like Naftali Goldman had been called up when the fighting began. His field hospital was still operational, though he said they were seeing very few combat injuries. Still, there was plenty to do. Even when they weren't under fire,

41

soldiers were remarkably accident prone. And there was always some illness or other working its way through the units.

Almost as much as Yoel, Rafi, the oldest of Uncle Marcus' sons, was the center of attention that afternoon. He flew Phantom jet fighters in combat. He had already shot down two MiG's. The women in the room could hardly take their eyes off him, with his dashing looks and stubbly face. He was wearing fatigues so rumpled they looked like they'd been slept in for upward of a week.

■ ■ ■

There had been talk of postponing the event until the end of hostilities, but Yakov's Uncle Marcus vetoed it. It would send the wrong message. Life had to go on no matter how many Arabs were attacking, no matter how many rockets fell on the city. Uncle Marcus had arrived just in time for the ceremony, still dusty from his journey and looking every one of his fifty-one years. He'd been fighting since he was a teenager. First the Nazis as a member of the Dutch resistance, then against the British in the Mandate, and against the Arabs pretty much ever since. There was a real *mensch*. There was someone you could look up to. Try to emulate. There was a man you never wanted to let down.

"My boy," he greeted Yakov. "You're looking well. Under the circumstances."

"And you."

"Old soldiers never die," Uncle Marcus shrugged. "Isn't that what MacArthur said?"

"He was quoting somebody else," Yakov said. He didn't know that for certain, but it seemed likely.

"Undoubtedly. We fighting men don't have much time to sit around thinking up *bon mots*."

"Listen, uncle," Yakov said. "I'd really like to get back to my unit. I'm sure if you made a couple of calls. . ."

"Don't waste your breath, soldier. You don't see it, but I do. You're not up to it. Your duty now is to regain your strength. You did your part. The rest of us will do ours. The tide is turning. We'll soon have our enemies on the run. Stay here and recuperate. You'll see. This isn't the last war Israel will have to fight. You'll get plenty more chances to be a hero. Now, come have a drink with me. We'll drink to my new son, baby Yoel. May he be a fighter as fierce as his Cousin Yakov."

■ ■ ■

"I don't understand why you hate him so," Anat said, pushing the stroller.

Along the beach, you couldn't tell that you were in a country at war. Yakov hobbled along beside his glamorous young aunt, wishing they could talk about anything other than Naftali Goldman. Really, his aunt was obsessed with the man.

Of course, to be quite honest about it, so was Yakov. That was his secret. Or at least part of it. But Naftali Goldman was merely the tip of the iceberg. The secret went far back beyond their first meeting. It was the kind of secret a man was meant to take with him to his grave. It was the kind of secret you didn't even tell your twin brother, and Yakov hadn't. Twins were legendary for keeping each other's secrets, and Josh and he had been typical in that regard. They had "substituted" for each other more times than he could remember. They'd even managed to trick their mother more than once. Their reliance on each other had been total.

But this secret was bigger even than that. And here Yakov was, about to tell it to Anat, who in the grand scheme of things might as well be a stranger. When Josh found out—because once you let a secret like this out into the light of day you had to understand you no longer had any control over it—their relationship would never be the same. Not to mention the rest of the family. But paradoxically, those relationships had never been what everyone thought in the first place. That's what secrets did. Under their power, the "truth" was no more than a convenient myth, and someone as close as your twin brother was actually a stranger and potential enemy.

Still, there was no going back from it. Yakov was alive. He shouldn't be, but he was. And the feelings grew stronger by the day. It was a sign.

"Ah, but you do," he finally managed to choke out. "You know the whole story. You're a fucking mind reader."

"So," she said, turning to look him in the face. "You're finally ready to tell the truth, is it? Well just so you know, I'm not a mind reader at all. You gave it away. I could tell the minute you started complaining about him. You reminded me of me when I first met Marcus. Oy, what a bitch I was. Completely insufferable. I thought Mama was going to throw me out of the house. 'Methinks the lady doth protest too much.' That's what Marcus said to me the third time I lit into him. After that I was totally disarmed. That's what you were doing when I visited you in the hospital. Protesting too much. And that Naftali. He was standing at the nurse's station writing notes as I left. I said to myself 'if that's not Prince Charming, no such person ever existed'. Well for what it's worth, Mr. Tough Guy infantry sergeant, Naftali told his Aunt Naomi it was love at first sight."

"You're joking."

"And the two of you are completely surrounded by *yentas*. Under siege, you'd have to say. So you might as well agree to a cease fire. I know he's ready for it."

■ ■ ■

Yakov's favorite falafel joint in all Tel Aviv. A bunch of open-air tables with the Mediterranean fussing and fidgeting yards away. If Yakov squinted just right it reminded him of Southern California, where his Fugelsang cousins lived. Dr. Naftali Goldman was sitting at a table in the farthest corner. Wearing aviator style sunglasses and with his hair plastered in place in defense against the breeze, he looked like an Italian movie star going incognito.

"Your last chance to bail out, boy," Yakov told himself.

That wasn't scary enough to deflect him. He went to join the doctor.

"Dr. Goldman, I presume."

"Sergeant Luxemberg."

"Reporting for duty."

"Reporting for something," Goldman smirked. "Are you really all right without your cane?"

"Only one way to find out."

"If you say so," Goldman shrugged, "but it looks like grandstanding to me."

Yakov knew he deserved that one.

"I wasn't sure you'd be available to meet me," Yakov said, sitting down across from him.

"They've closed down that field hospital. I'm back to my regular position here in the city."

"That's not what I meant," Yakov said.

"Oh?"

"I've been a real dick."

Behind those sunglasses, the man was inscrutable. Yakov was suddenly terrified. It was worse than fighting the Arabs.

"It hits different people different ways," Goldman finally said. "You were frightened. We doctors can tell stuff like that. And apparently when you get frightened, you growl and try to start fights. When I get frightened, I crack wise."

"It's just that you don't expect to wake up in a field hospital and have a thing like that happen to you," Yakov said.

"I'd say you don't expect to wake up in a field hospital at all."

"Except if you're Israeli you do," Yakov said.

"Right. Back home they don't get that."

"No," Yakov agreed. "Listen, do you think we could start from scratch?"

"I don't believe you really mean that," Goldman said.

"I don't?"

"Why would you want to backtrack? Shouldn't we try to figure out how to move forward instead?"

"It's just that I've been, you know, *such a dick*," Yakov said.

"Not to mention sexy as hell and extremely comical." Goldman was smiling now, so maybe it was O.K. "That's a very potent combination in my book. I think that's what we should be focusing on at this point."

III

Shoshonnah Luxemberg arrived from New York on the first civilian flight to land after the end of hostilities. That was just like Mom, Yakov thought, watching her walk down the steps of the 707 like she owned the whole damn country. Many Israeli women were beautiful, but Shoshonnah wasn't merely beautiful. She was glamorous in the manner of a certain movie star. He halfway expected flashbulbs to go off as she stepped onto the tarmac. Or some small child to approach her presenting a bouquet of roses. He had begged her not to come. But telling her no was like throwing gasoline on an already blazing fire. Anat squeezed his hand. Yoel wriggled in his arms, then went back to sleep.

"She's lovelier than I expected," Anat said.

"That's what people always say," Yakov smiled.

"I don't know why I'm surprised," Anat said. "After all, she is your mother. And you don't look a thing like Marcus."

■ ■ ■

"Oh, my God," Shoshonnah said. "Is this the baby? Let me get a good look at him."

Yakov wrestled with her luggage. There were porters available, but he wouldn't abide the loss of face employing one would entail.

■ ■ ■

Mom held the baby and Anat drove. Avi and Zev were at the movies with their grandmother. Yakov couldn't negotiate the clutch pedal yet with his bad leg, so he rode shotgun. The Peugeot had a particularly recalcitrant clutch pedal. Now that she was here, Mom, who had sounded near hysterical on long distance, was her usual steely nerved self.

"Thank God everything's back to normal around here and everyone is safe," she said.

"There's still fighting going on along the borders," Yakov grunted. "There were a couple of rocket attacks yesterday."

"I thought there was a ceasefire," Shoshonnah said.

"Fucking Arabs," Yakov complained. "They don't know the meaning of the term."

"Are you still in a lot of pain, dear?" Shoshonnah asked.

"I'm fine," Yakov said.

"He won't take his medication," Anat said, pulling out to pass a bus full of soldiers. "Now that you're here, maybe you can make him behave."

■ ■ ■

"I can't believe how much the baby reminds me of Cooper," Shoshonnah said. She had just finished helping Anat bathe him and put him to bed. "It's uncanny. I wish I had some of his baby pictures with me so I could show you, Anat. Cooper's the one of my sons who's a real Luxemberg. He'll look just like Marcus in another thirty years or so. His brothers all take after my family, the Freitags."

"Yes," Anat smiled. "That's what Marcus always says."

"I actually think Yoel looks more like Ike," Yakov said. He didn't mean it. He was just being argumentative.

"Don't play the fool with me," Shoshonnah said. "Yoel doesn't look a thing like Ike, may the Almighty be praised."

■ ■ ■

"So my son," Shoshonnah said. "Now that we're finally alone, what is it that you're not telling me?"

"Mom," Yakov shook his head. He'd been dreading the third degree. The only question was how long it would take her to get around to it.

"Don't even think about it," she said. "I know there's something. You know I can always tell when my boys are holding out on me. Better get it over quickly so we can start enjoying our reunion."

This was how you survived being the mother of four sons. Extremely strong willed ones. You fought fire with fire. You always took the first shot.

"I've met somebody," Yakov said, looking at the floor.

"Really? Here?"

"Yes."

"Not Anat, I hope," she said. "We don't need a complication like that."

"Of course not," Yakov said.

"Because I can tell you're crazy about her."

"Not that kind of crazy," Yakov said. "More like the sister I never had."

"All right," Shoshonnah said. "It could be that, I guess. So it's somebody else. Is it serious?"

"I think so."

"What does that mean, you think so?" she demanded. "It's either serious or it's not. Believe me, I know."

"It's serious," Yakov said.

"Then why do you look like you've just been given a death sentence? That's what I'd like to know. When I met your father, I was walking on air."

"This is hard."

"Not that hard," Shoshonnah snorted. "It's been going on since the Garden of Eden. This is when you tell me about her."

"See, Mom, that's the hard part."

"Now you're just being silly," she said. "Josh was always the silly one. You were always serious."

She'd never let him off the hook before. She wasn't going to start now. Might as well get it over with.

"She's a he, Mom."

"What?"

"His name is Naftali Goldman. He's a doctor. A surgeon. He treated me in the field hospital, but his practice is here in Tel Aviv. And he's just been appointed to a position on the faculty of the university."

"Is this true?"

"Yes," Yakov said.

He watched her face as she made up her mind. It didn't take her long. He wasn't expecting it to, but he had no idea what her decision would be.

"A doctor," Shoshonnah said. "My son is in love with a doctor. Praise the Almighty. Wait until your grandmother hears about this. She will never tell me I've been a bad mother again."

IV

"As soon as I get home, Naftali, I'm going to call your parents in Montreal and tell them I've seen you and you're right as rain. I'm sure they've been as worried as Willi and I were during the fighting."

"Thanks, Mrs. Luxemberg."

"Not Mrs. Luxemberg," Shoshonnah corrected him. "Anything but Mrs. Luxemberg. Call me Shoshonnah, call me Mom, call me 'hey you'. But don't you ever call me Mrs. Luxemberg. Got that, darling?"

"Sure," Naftali grinned.

Every time Yakov saw that grin, he melted.

"We're on the same team now, you and I," Shoshonnah continued. "You have to help me take care of this one. It's not an easy job. He's very hardheaded. It runs in the family, so be warned."

"I promise," Naftali nodded.

"I can tell you've got what it takes," Shoshonnah said.

■ ■ ■

They watched her go up the steps and through the door of the plane.

"Just when you think she's run out of surprises," Yakov said.

"She's one in a million," Naftali said. "That's for certain."

OCTOBER, 1975

"You say you're gay," Josh said, "but as far as I can tell your sexuality is entirely hypothetical."

"What are you talking about?" Eli blushed. He focused on buttering his bagel. When Josh was like this, Eli couldn't stand to look him in the eye. It was like being interrogated by the FBI. No. It was like being interrogated by his grandmother and *tantes*. Far worse than the FBI, in other words. And he wished Josh didn't talk quite so loud in restaurants. He was sure the people at the next table were listening. He had complained about it in the past, but Josh merely said "that's what you get hanging out with someone who works in theatre. Even in our sleep we project."

"You never date anyone," Josh said. "You don't flirt with cute waiters or shop boys. I never catch you staring at handsome police officers. You don't cruise construction workers or truck drivers or bicycle couriers on the street no matter how hot they are. When we walk past fire stations you look the other way. You don't cruise anyone. Hell, you don't even like it when I cruise on the street. You're always complaining."

"You're so blatant."

"That's what cruising is," Josh said. "Blatant. Subtlety doesn't get you anywhere."

"Guys don't appreciate being stared at the way you do."

"Like you know that."

"You could get beaten up."

"It's never happened yet."

"Anyway, Josh, the thing is. . ."

"Spare me the speech about how you have standards," Josh said. "And the one with all the hearts and flowers. I so enjoyed my breakfast and I don't want to vomit it up. You're twenty-five years old. You're cute, whether you realize it or not. You have a great job and a terrific apartment. You even have a personality. At least kind of. It's an offense against the natural order that you're still a virgin."

"Who says I'm still a virgin?" Eli protested.

"Oh, please. Who are you talking to here?"

■ ■ ■

"Where are you taking me?" Eli asked, stumbling on the uneven sidewalk. The block they were on wasn't one Eli would have willingly walked down even in daylight, and as a Manhattan native he didn't spook easily.

"Never mind," Josh said.

It was two days since their most recent discussion of Eli's virginity. Josh hadn't mentioned it since then, but Eli had a feeling.

"I'm not sure this is such a great idea."

"It's for your own good," Josh said, stopping in front of an unmarked door. "Trust me."

"If you say 'this is going to hurt me more than it hurts you' I'm going back home."

"No you don't," Josh said, grabbing his elbow. "Now listen, when we get inside you're going to hand the nice man at the counter five dollars. That's your membership fee. Then you're going to sign his guest book. Don't you dare use your real name."

"What?"

"Inside those walls I'm Spike O'Toole," Josh said. "Think fast."

"Jesus."

"No, that one's taken."

"Josh, what kind of place is this?"

"It's a private club," Josh said, "catering to gentlemen with an interest in athletic pursuits. Wrestling, for instance."

"Wrestling?"

"Yes," Josh nodded. "Wrestling. They're very big on that here. In all possible varieties. Greco-Roman. Turkish. No holds barred. Some guys even go in for tag team action. The nice man at the counter will issue you a towel and a lock."

"Lock?"

"For your locker, silly."

"And the towel?"

"Think of it as a security blanket," Josh suggested.

■ ■ ■

"This is the part where we undress," Josh said, pulling off his t-shirt.

"I don't think. . ."

"Every stitch. It all goes into your locker. Most guys wear the key around their necks. That's why it's on a string."

"Josh."

"Some of the more adventurous types find other ways of wearing their keys. You're free to experiment."

It was like following Alice down the rabbit hole, Eli thought. Except the rabbit hole probably hadn't smelled like this.

"And we'll be splitting up," Josh said. "Around here it's every man for himself."

"But how do I. . . ?"

"You've heard the saying 'when in Rome'?"

■ ■ ■

Most of the guys wore their towels around their waists, Eli noted. Just like in the locker room back in high school. Some draped them around their necks from behind or slung them over one shoulder. A few simply dragged their towels behind them, a la Linus van Pelt with his blanket. Eli adopted the around the waist look. It was the least revealing and made him feel the most secure.

53

Not truly secure, of course. This feeling of vulnerability wouldn't go away until he got back home and bolted his front door. If then. This was a nightmare.

But a nightmare with cute guys in it. Cute naked guys. So far that had trumped his flight impulse.

■ ■ ■

Cute guys notwithstanding, as Eli wandered through the gloomy corridors, all he could think of was wanting to go home. He would have. But he knew that if he didn't spend what Josh considered a reasonable amount of time (whatever that entailed) on the premises he'd just be brought back again and again until he did what was expected of him. It was the gay equivalent of taking the medicine *bubbie* prescribed. Better to get it over with.

■ ■ ■

Of course not everyone there was cute. There was plenty of average and even a surprising number of men Eli wouldn't have thought would want to put themselves on display. In that respect it was a lot like going to the beach. The level of un-self consciousness among the clientele was astonishing. He would have thought gay men would be more particular than that. More careful about presenting themselves in the best possible light or at least concealing their imperfections. Instead there seemed to be a commonly held assumption that your looks, however questionable they might be, didn't preclude your putting yourself on view to the chagrin of all and sundry.

Still, there were enough cute guys scattered around the place to keep Eli interested. And some others who couldn't accurately be described as cute because their looks were far too impressive for a word like that. He wouldn't dream of actually approaching anyone that attractive, but it was certainly fun to look. He'd seen plenty of men pairing off, but he'd also seen plenty being rejected. He couldn't imagine what it would feel like being turned down while other guys were looking on.

■ ■ ■

It was one thing to wander the corridors trying not to stare. What Josh had in mind in bringing him here was something else altogether. Eli could hardly believe it, but he saw it happening all around him. Guys checked each other out. Openly, their agendas all too apparent. And now and then a pair of them—or sometimes more—would disappear into one of the rooms. Just like that. Did they know each other? Had they planned ahead of time to meet there? Or had the impulse struck them as their eyes met? Could you actually do that? Just walk into a room and have sex with a complete stranger?

Apparently you could, though Eli wasn't sure he'd ever be able to go through with it.

■ ■ ■

When the time came, he didn't stop to think about it. That's how spectacular the guy was. Eli had pretty much convinced himself that as interesting as the expedition had been in sociological terms, he'd be perfectly happy to go home and curl up with a good book. Dickens, for instance. Or Thackeray. Something thick, heavy, and soporific, in any case. And suddenly there he was. Eli couldn't have designed a more perfect man if someone had assigned him to, which, he supposed, proved the existence of God. A little above medium height but not actually what you'd call tall, broad, BROAD shouldered, muscled like—well, he looked like Superman with his shirt off. It wasn't just the chest and arms. The other parts were super, too. And he was handsome in that sandy haired, square jawed, archetypally goyish manner that Eli had never been able to resist.

"Right," the guy muttered. "Let's go."

Eli looked around and realized that there was nobody else in the corridor just then.

"Yeah, you," the guy growled.

■ ■ ■

It was everything Eli had ever dreamed of. Actually it was more than that. How could anyone who hadn't experienced it imagine such moments? It was transcendent. Unfamiliar as the sensations were, they felt right in a way nothing in his life ever had. Thank God the guy knew what he was doing. Even with all the visual stimuli forcing him on so ruthlessly, Eli wouldn't have known where to start. The "equipment", which Eli had thought was grotesquely oversized when he first looked at it, turned out to be exactly the right size once it was actually in use. Thank God the guy had picked Eli out of all the men there. Thank God generally. The guy smelled so good. His hairless chest was like satin against Eli's face. His muscles were so big, round, and firm. His hair felt exquisite to Eli's fingertips. His nipples might have been created just for Eli's mouth to worship them.

∎ ∎ ∎

"No, don't get up," the guy grunted, wrapping his towel around his waist. "You look like you could use a nap. Most guys do once I've gotten finished with them."

"I'd like to see you again," Eli stammered.

The guy considered this for a moment.

"I'm here most Thursdays," he said before slipping into the corridor.

II

Before he left for the "club", Eli showered and shaved. It was ridiculous—just like a teenager getting ready for a date. But he needed all the confidence he could muster. The thought of going back there without Josh as his escort terrified him. Still, this was Thursday and that incredible creature had said he'd be there. Or at least that he'd probably be there. Or might be there. If he hadn't been lying about it. Or hadn't forgotten. Or been run over by a bus. But how could someone like that be dishonest? Or forgetful? Or accident prone? It wasn't possible. Except, of course, it was. Eli didn't think he could go on living if he couldn't see that man again. The week had seemed several years long.

■ ■ ■

He trudged around and around the corridors like Hamlet's ghost unable to attract anyone's attention. The place was busy, but there was no sign of Superman. Finally, out of sheer boredom, Eli ended up in a cubicle with a guy who reminded him vaguely of his cousin Talbot's second best friend Carmichael. Carmichael had been on Eli's top ten list since eleventh grade, so that was something. And any sex was probably better than no sex, he reasoned. Then too, having sex with an actual human as opposed to going home and jerking off could be thought of as good practice for the next time he ran into Superman. Because there had to be a next time.

■ ■ ■

The next week it was pretty much the same story, except the guy he ended up with reminded him of Josh. Quite a bit, actually, which was awkward at first but then unexpectedly hot. Until encountering Superman, Eli had been nursing a long term but low grade crush on Josh. So the whole scene was a little ironic. Afterward, Eli chalked it up to experience.

■ ■ ■

When there was no sign of Superman the week after that, Eli told himself he'd better face facts. The guy that week was Italian. Or maybe Puerto Rican.

■ ■ ■

Finally, on the fourth week, there was Superman, more handsome and magnificently built than Eli had recalled. He didn't seem to remember Eli, but once they were safely in a cubicle Eli didn't care. He employed all the tricks he'd learned since their last meeting in the hopes that Superman would be impressed enough to ask him his name.

He didn't.

Afterward they went to the showers together.

At the lockers, they dressed together.

"I'd like to see you again," Eli said as they stepped out onto the sidewalk.

"I'm here most Thursdays," Superman growled.

III

"Eli," Josh sighed.

Eli recognized that sigh as a sign of profound exasperation. Some guys yelled at you. Cousin Talbot had slapped him more than once. Josh got really quiet. And sighed. Once upon a time that sigh would have threatened to break Eli's heart.

"What?"

"Eli, Eli, Eli. Nobody finds a boyfriend at the baths."

"Really? There's some kind of rule to that effect? Who's in charge of enforcing it?"

"Don't be silly," Josh said. "It just doesn't happen like that."

"Except when it does."

"You don't even know his name," Josh insisted.

"Yet," Eli said.

■ ■ ■

Life went on. Thursday followed Thursday.

IV

It was two more months before Eli encountered Superman again. Either the man kept getting better looking and bigger or Eli's memory wasn't as accurate as he'd thought it was. The sex was more amazing than ever.

"I'd really like. . ." Eli said.

"I'm here most Thursdays," the guy said. This time when he said it there was a little grin on his face. "Or you could ask me to lunch. I'm off work next Tuesday."

■ ■ ■

Eli didn't really expect the guy to show up for their lunch date. Much less that he'd be on time. But there he was on the stroke of noon, grinning like he'd just heard the best joke in the world and looking like a million dollars. He was wearing a t-shirt that seemed certain to fall away in shreds if he inhaled too deeply. The t-shirt said "Property of the New York Fire Department."

"Nice shirt," Eli laughed. "Where do you get something like that?"

"It comes with the job."

"You mean. . . ?"

"Eamonn Lannaghan. Engine Company number 28."

"Eli Danziger," Eli said. "Originally of the Upper West Side."

They shook hands. Eli felt like his arm was being jerked out of its socket. It was a surprisingly pleasant sensation.

"Gotta ask you," Eamonn said, "how you know about this place. I thought it was a firefighter secret. But when you mentioned it—well you didn't seem like a member of the brotherhood."

"A friend brought me here," Eli said. A while back Josh had dated a guy who wasn't actually a firefighter but liked to pretend that he was. Eli had chosen the place because there was nothing gay about it. Not a solitary limp wristed waiter. That was saying something for a restaurant in Manhattan.

"A firefighter?"

"Let's just say a guy with a firefighter fetish," Eli said, blushing.

■ ■ ■

They argued over the check. Eli wanted to pay for lunch but Eamonn said they should go dutch.

"But I invited you," Eli protested.

"But it was my idea," Eamonn grinned.

■ ■ ■

"What would you like to do now?" Eli asked as they emerged from the restaurant. "My place isn't far."

"Let's take a walk," Eamonn suggested. "I like talking to you."

■ ■ ■

Eamonn's grandfather had come over from Ireland and gotten a job with the fire department. Three of Eamonn's uncles were firefighters. So was his dad. Two of his aunts had married firefighters, and four of his cousins were firefighters. Two of his older brothers were firefighters and three of his sisters were married to firefighters. There were also a few police officers in the family. No doubt about it: Eamonn's family was a New York Irish cliché.

Except for his mom, who was from Germany. Dad had invaded Omaha Beach on D-Day, fought his way across France and Belgium into Germany, caught sight of that cute blond farm girl driving her cows home from the pasture one evening at sundown, and brought her home to America. There had been lots of friction with Dad's family at first. But the German girl turned out to be an industrious and thrifty housekeeper, and Catholic, and sufficiently fertile. When Eamonn's grandmother criticized her, she didn't talk back. That took the fun out of criticizing her and pretty soon Grandma stopped. Besides, she'd realized by that point that there was hardly anything about her daughter-in-law to be critical about. That's how peace broke out.

Yes, Eamonn did spend most of his spare time at the gym. Yes, he had entered a few bodybuilding competitions around the Greater New York Metropolitan Area. Yes, he'd won a few trophies. Yes, his photograph had even appeared in a couple of the muscle magazines. Yes, there was another contest coming up soon. He'd let Eli know the particulars if he thought he'd like to attend.

Eamonn shared a wealth of biographical detail but didn't address the questions Eli considered most pressing. Such as what was a guy like that doing having sex with men at the baths? And exactly how many men did he have sex with when he went there? And why the hell was he single? Eli couldn't bring himself to ask about any of that.

■ ■ ■

Eventually they did make it to Eli's place.

■ ■ ■

"When can I see you again?" Eli asked as Eamonn was pulling his jeans back on.

"I'll call you," Eamonn said.

"In that case I'd better give you my number," Eli said, pulling a business card out of his wallet and scribbling the number on the back.

"Those business guy pens," Eamonn grinned. "Very fancy, aren't they? That one must have cost you more than we spent on lunch."

"It was a gift," Eli said.

That was Eamonn's cue to ask "from who?" but he didn't.

■ ■ ■

"You what?" Josh gasped.

"We met for lunch," Eli said. "You've heard of it. It's a meal many people are in the habit of eating in the middle of the day."

"I can't believe it," Josh marveled. "I've never known anyone to try and date somebody they tricked with at the baths. Never. And was he a horrible troll in daylight?"

"Anything but," Eli said. "He's absolutely perfect in every way."

He would have said this in any case for the sake of being argumentative. But it was true.

■ ■ ■

Eamonn didn't call. And he wasn't at the club the next two Thursdays. The fires of Eli's obsession blazed out of control. When he got to the club on the third Thursday, Eamonn was waiting out front.

"I checked inside," he said. "You weren't there."

"I gave you my number," Eli said.

"Got it in my wallet," Eamonn said. "Telephones aren't very personal, are they?"

"No," Eli said, heart racing.

"Face to face is better, right?"

"Sure," Eli stammered. "Are we going inside?"

"We should go to your place instead."

"It's just. . ."

"I know the way from here."

■ ■ ■

After that, they didn't ever meet at the baths again. Eli assumed Eamonn still went there to have sex with other guys. But Eli stayed away from the place so he wouldn't see it by accident.

■ ■ ■

Eamonn was a talker. He told Eli about the crazy things he heard people say on the subway, the practical jokes the guys played on each other at the firehouse, the comical mistakes his mother still made speaking English even after all these years. He told Eli about the ridiculous things he overheard in the barbershop and about all the guys he knew at his gym. He narrated the zany antics of his grandparents, uncles, and aunts. He told about the tricks his older brothers and cousins had played on him when they were boys. These sounded like heavy BDSM sessions to Eli but he didn't say so. He wondered what Eamonn's older brothers and cousins looked like.

■ ■ ■

"Have you seen the new guy who's living on the fourth floor?" Josh asked.

"I don't think so," Eli said. He hadn't heard of anyone moving in or out up there.

"I've run into him on the stairs a couple of times the last few weeks," Josh said. "He's astonishing. Shoulders so wide he looks like he must go down the hall sideways just to fit through. Firm chin, square jaw, piercing eyes. Hair like those models in the shampoo ads. You know the part where they run their hands through it? Clark Kent's handsomer brother is who he is."

"Listen," Eli said. "You and Jill and I should get together for dinner. How about Monday?"

■ ■ ■

"Meet some of your friends?" Eamonn asked. "Sure, if you'd like. I'll switch shifts with my cousin Tonio. Or my brother Klaus-Peter, if Tonio's not in the mood to cooperate."

■ ■ ■

"Jill and Josh, this is Eamonn," Eli said. They had met in front of the church in the next block of Hudson from Josh and Eli's building. He thought the open air was a better idea than a confined space.

"Hi," Eamonn said.

"My dear," Jill gaped. "What big shoulders you have."

Eamonn grinned and flexed his left biceps for her and she pantomimed an attack of the vapors.

"Eli, you bastard," Josh fumed, "you never said a thing."

"You're the neighbor on the second floor," Eamonn said. "I've seen you on the stairs a few times."

"Nice to meet you," Josh said in a tone that indicated he wasn't entirely convinced of it but was at least willing to entertain the possibility. "Your buddy Eli's got some explaining to do."

"You knew I'd been seeing somebody," Eli said.

APRIL, 1976

The hospital nursery was quiet. Eli stared through the glass at Eamonn's new son. Michael Kurt Lannaghan. Eamonn's third. When Eamonn sat him down that day a couple of months after they started dating and said "we have to talk", a wife, two small children, and a third on the way wasn't what Eli was expecting to hear about. It was a shock. But it turned out not to be the end of the world. For instance, there wasn't another man in Eamonn's life. That's what Eli had mostly been worrying about. Once they were past that very awkward five minutes, which had ended with Eamonn saying "I love you, Eli", they went on pretty much as before. Sex a couple of times a week and the occasional lunch. It wasn't exactly the kind of arrangement Eli had been dreaming of. But Eamonn was still the man of his dreams. Nothing had changed that. So far it was enough. Eli didn't let himself think beyond that "so far". In his vocabulary, "future" had become a four letter word.

Mickey squirmed in his bassinet and then settled down again. Eli looked at his watch. He had a few more minutes before he had to head back to work. He was tempted to go upstairs to Maribel's room. But what was he supposed to say when he got there? "Hi, my name is Eli. You don't know me, but I'm a friend of your husband?" No. There was no way he wouldn't fuck that up. Better let Eamonn make the introductions when he was good and ready. If that time never came, Eli would just have to deal with it.

■ ■ ■

"The christening is next Sunday," Eli said.

65

"I can't believe you're going along with this," Josh complained.

"Why not?" Jill asked. "I've served as a beard for much worse characters than Eli. I was a beard for Giovanni Bandini, wasn't I? Heir to the notorious crime family. Escorted him to all kinds of functions."

"Sometimes I'm not sure you know the difference between real life and your show," Josh said.

"Of course I do," Jill said. "Real life is so much more dramatic. Soap operas pale by comparison. Can't imagine why anyone watches them. Except shutins and so forth. So fill me in. Who are these people?"

"Well, you know Eamonn of course," Eli said.

"Ah, yes," Jill sighed, "the divine, the magnificent, the near supernatural Eamonn Lannaghan."

"Don't be sarcastic," Josh said.

"I assure you, Josh," Jill said, "when I wax poetical over Eamonn I'm being absolutely sincere."

"His wife's name is Maribel. She's Puerto Rican. Born and raised up here, but the family's very traditional."

"Of course."

"Their son Liam is four, and Victor Antonio is two."

"Do they call him Tony?" Jill asked. "I once dated a Puerto Rican boy named Tony."

"No you didn't," Josh said. "That was another show."

"Was not," Jill insisted. "He had the biggest. . ."

"Spare us," Josh begged.

"Ego on the Lower East Side," Jill grinned.

"They call him Tory," Eli said. "There are too many Vics and Tonys in her family already."

◼ ◼ ◼

Eli was going to the christening as Eamonn's "friend". He understood the need for some kind of designation. Even a euphemistic one. Families required it. Unexplained men on the guest list weren't as troubling as unfamiliar and unexplained women, but it was still a problem. Nevertheless, Eli wasn't sure "friend" didn't create more problems than it solved. He'd been listening carefully all this time as Eamonn talked about his life and its many ramifications and tributaries, and it didn't really sound like he would fit the Lannaghan tribe's preconceived notion of a "friend". Eamonn had friends from Engine Company 28, of course. And people were used to hearing him talk about his friends from the gym. There were lots of those, and Eli was wildly curious about them though he had never given himself permission to ask for details. There were even a few guys Eamonn had known in high school and still saw from time to time. But Eli obviously didn't fit into any of those categories, so what kind of friend was he? In what socially acceptable way could his presence at the christening be accounted for?

He raised this objection the night after Mickey's birth when Eamonn first invited him to the christening. The discussion took place post coitally.

"Don't sweat it," Eamonn said. "Nobody's going to be paying that much attention. Especially not once they start drinking. But if you're really that nervous about it, why don't you invite Jill along?"

■ ■ ■

"I can't understand it," Josh said. "I mean, sure, he's an incredible looking man. And the sex is probably spectacular."

"It is," Eli said.

"But why would you put yourself in a position like that? He's never going to leave Maribel. Not now that he's got three kids. Guys don't do that."

"Guys leave their families all the time," Eli said. "Don't be an idiot."

"He won't," Josh said. "He's not the type to do it. And that's not all. You wouldn't want to have anything to do with him if he was. You couldn't let yourself. No. He'll string you along year after year. Basically until you decide you've had enough. Meanwhile there are all kinds of great guys out there. Single guys."

"Yes," Eli nodded. "At some point in this argument you always point out how many great single guys there are just waiting to be scooped up."

"It's true."

"Yet I notice that you're still single yourself," Eli said. "So what is it? Those guys are great enough for Eli but not great enough for you? Or is there something I'm missing?"

"Now you're just arguing for the sake of it."

"Anyway, how do you know I'm not the one stringing him along?"

"Don't be ridiculous," Josh snorted.

"What's so ridiculous about it?"

"You're you, Eli," Josh said. "You're constitutionally incapable of such a thing."

"Thank you so much for clearing that up," Eli said. "You know, I thought you were supposed to be helping me pick out my suit for the christening."

"Of course I am," Josh said. "You don't think I'd let you wear something you picked out yourself."

"All right. I've got it narrowed down to these two suits."

"The navy one," Josh said. "The charcoal gray is too severe for a christening."

■ ■ ■

Josh's arguments didn't annoy Eli because they were mistaken but because they were accurate. Eli got that. He wasn't stupid. What he was was obsessed. Eamonn was every man smiling from the cover of one of those muscle magazines Eli had hoarded as a boy and kept hidden from his mother. He still had his favorites. Now he had to hide them from Josh. That's how your life changed when you came out of the closet and your best friend lived downstairs. You weren't afraid your mom would find out things any longer. You were free from that fear. Instead, you were afraid your best friend would. In gay, apparently, your best friend disapproved of everything your mother would, although on different grounds. You still had to keep secrets, even if they were no more significant than that opera bored you, for instance. Or that when you were home alone you drank white wine with red meat because you just liked to. Eamonn was every college jock Eli had worshipped from afar, or, in the case of his friend Denise's boyfriend, Kurt, from uncomfortably close up. Eamonn was all those demi-gods flashing their pecs onscreen in those cheesy gladiator movies. Everybody else considered those movies ridiculous, but to Eli watching them was a religious experience. Obsession. Yes.

Which meant that where Josh went wrong was in assuming that Eli was capable of looking at the situation logically and responding to it like a rational human being. He literally couldn't listen to reason, no matter how insistent Josh was. That had been impossible from his first glance at Eamonn in that dimly lit corridor at the baths. That's where his familiar obsession had reasserted its hold over him. Before, it had always been fantasy, arrestingly vivid but completely out of reach. Now it was standing in front of him letting its towel slip onto the floor. And Eamonn had made himself just available enough to keep Eli's obsession fed and watered. Of course the situation sucked. Sex once a week. Sometimes twice, if Eamonn could fit it into his arduous schedule of Engine Company 28, Vito Lupardo's Gym, and the Lannaghan family and its numerous and varied associates. Sex and an occasional lunch date. All these months now and they'd never actually spent a night together. God only knew if they ever would.

Would Eli change it if he could? Sure. Failing that, would he willingly give the current situation up? He couldn't imagine what would make him.

■ ■ ■

"Eli, darling," Jill purred, "what a gorgeous suit."

"You like it? Josh said it was too severe for a christening. He wanted me to wear something else."

"Good for you, then, asserting some independence for once. You're an absolute heartbreaker in that suit."

■ ■ ■

The church was in deepest, darkest Queens. It was a sinister looking place. Eli thought of it as the Bastille's baby sister. Jill seemed unfazed by the atmosphere, but she'd grown up high church Episcopalian.

■ ■ ■

The ceremony itself was crashingly anticlimactic. This did not surprise Eli. He'd had enough goyish friends over the years to know how such things worked. The real significance of the event lay in the size and elaborateness of the party to follow. In that respect Catholics were just like Jews.

■ ■ ■

Eamonn and Maribel both came from large families. They had lots of siblings and even more aunts, uncles, and cousins. The assembled generations crowded the back yard at Maribel's parents' house. They were resolutely middle class, with a heavy emphasis on firefighters and police among the men. In addition there were Coast Guard personnel on Maribel's mother's side and a Marine or two among Eamonn's cousins. There was even a minor league baseball player in the crowd, the fiancé of one of Maribel's cousins, though Eli hadn't heard of him. The womenfolk, those who weren't exclusively housewives, were teachers, secretaries, and nurses. One sold real estate. The gene pools represented were of remarkably high quality. It looked, really, like a location shoot for a christening party scene in a movie. Everyone was pretty to at least some degree, even the representatives of earlier generations. Nobody Eli saw looked remotely Jewish. Or gay. He couldn't have felt more conspicuous if he'd suddenly burst into flame or turned into a unicorn.

■ ■ ■

"Say, Eli," Sean said, "how do you know Eamonn anyway?"

"Yes," Klaus-Peter nodded. "He's never mentioned you."

It was the question Eli had been dreading. Sean and Klaus-Peter were Eamonn's older brothers. Above the neck they looked quite a bit like him. Below the neck they were hefty guys, but not noticeably gymmed.

"Oh, my God," Juanita, Klaus-Peter's wife, shrieked. "I know you. You're Jill Wagner. You're on Maribel's favorite soap."

"Wagstaffe, dear," Jill said. "And please don't go any farther. It's terrible luck to speak the title aloud."

"It is?"

"In front of a cast member it is," Jill nodded. "Among your family and friends it doesn't matter at all. But someone once spoke the title in front of my friend Amanda, and the very next week a mike boom fell on her on the set. Gave her a concussion. The writers had to put her character into a coma while she recovered."

"How awful," Juanita said. "Now before I take you over and introduce you to Maribel, who's absolutely going to faint when she finds out you're here, I have to ask. *Soap Opera Digest* ran an item a week or so ago about an unnamed girl in your cast turning down an offer to pose in *Playboy*. That was you, wasn't it?"

"Sorry, dear," Jill smiled, "but I'm not at liberty to discuss the matter."

"Of course not," Juanita nodded.

Jill wasn't just a beard, Eli thought, watching the two of them head toward where Maribel was sitting. She was a beard in a million. No wonder that Mafia prince had been crazy about her.

"Come on, Eli," Klaus-Peter said, draping an arm across Eli's shoulders, "let's get you something to drink. It'll be hours before the ladies turn your girlfriend loose again."

"I ought to turn her over my knee," Eli growled. "Upstaging the mother at a christening."

"She can't help it," Sean said. "She's a star."

■ ■ ■

"Come here," Eamonn said, steering Eli by the elbow. "I want you to meet Maribel."

The crowd didn't exactly part for them. The obstacle course they ran gave Eli time to collect himself. He was curious and terrified at the same time.

"Maribel, honey," Eamonn said in a tone Eli hadn't heard before, "this is Eli."

"Eli, hi."

She looked like she belonged on the set with Jill. Those huge, soulful eyes. That thick, silky, raven hair. The zoomy figure, even though she'd recently given birth. And that perfect accent. When she spoke, you could hear subway trains in the background.

"Great to meet you," Eli said.

"Eamonn tells me you're quite a guy," she smiled. "Thanks for coming. And bringing Jill with you. What a fantastic surprise. She doesn't know it yet, but she's my new best friend."

■ ■ ■

It was all too beautiful. Regiments of handsome men, their ravishing wives, and their photogenic children. Even the dogs in the scene looked like they came from central casting. These people were living a life Eli had always felt shut off from. Usually he could ignore the pangs, but seeing it playing itself out in front of him with his beloved at its center was excruciating. He'd never be part of it in any real way. And Eamonn so easily, unselfconsciously, inhabited it. That couldn't be a good sign.

"Ready to go?" Jill asked, sidling up.

"Are you tired?"

"No. But it's time to get out of here. You look like Cinderella just before the clock strikes."

■ ■ ■

Eli was astonished the next Tuesday night when Eamonn buzzed in from the street. He'd never shown up unannounced before. Eli's heart raced as he listened to those feet on the stairs. He was waiting with the door open when Eamonn hit the third floor landing.

"This is a surprise," he said, standing aside to let the big guy enter.

"I can't stay," Eamonn said. "I'm on shift."

"Oh?"

Eamonn seemed to take up the whole living room,

"Sean's covering for me," Eamonn nodded.

"What if there's a call?"

"Stomach bug," Eamonn said. "It happens. I didn't mention it to the captain when I came on shift because I thought it would clear up. And then it didn't."

"Right."

"Listen," Eamonn said.

"Why don't we sit down?"

"I told you. I'm not staying. Just wanted to come by and say thanks for Sunday. It was great that you and Jill were there. She really made the party. Maribel still can't believe it. That shot the photographer got of Jill and her with Mickey. She says we have to buy a special frame for it on account of Jill's his fairy godmother now."

"That's sweet," Eli said. "I'll tell her next time I see her."

"And the check you wrote, bud. It was too much."

"Put it in his college fund."

"No, I mean it was way too much," Eamonn said, shuffling his feet.

"Eamonn?"

"What?"

"Are you breaking up with me? Is that why you're here?"

"Breaking up with you? What are you talking about? Of course not."

"It sure sounds like that's what you're working up to."

Eamonn looked at him like a burglar caught in the act.

"Not breaking up," Eamonn insisted. "Nothing like that. Just need to clear the air a little. Right?"

"If you say so."

"Listen, Eli, you're a great guy. Really. I enjoy your company. I've never known anybody like you before. You're smart and funny and kind. The guys I know aren't like that. They're just guys. No smarter than they have to be, funny like tenth graders are funny, and they'd give you the shirt off their backs but they're not very considerate otherwise. You know what I'm talking about. You met them Sunday."

"Yes."

"And the sex is great, Eli. I've got no complaints there."

"That's good."

"I mean, I've had sex with lots of guys. Lots and lots of guys, right? But I've never actually had a—well—relationship with a guy before."

"And you're not. . ."

"Let me finish. See, what you and I have is really special. I know that. I know you know it, too. But, well, this is the part where I really need you to listen, right?"

"I'm listening."

"What I need to say is what we have right now, good as it is, is all we're ever going to have. It's all I can give you. And I don't know if it's enough. I don't know if it would be enough for me if somebody was trying to put me in the situation I'm trying to put you in. But there it is. I love you. I love my wife. I adore my boys. I'm not giving them up for anything or anybody. So I need you to think about that. Think about it real carefully, see? Because the minute you try to make me choose between you and them—the minute, you hear me?—it's over between us."

AUGUST, 1977

Talbot Kleinbaum had ditched his Cuban émigré plutocrat sugar daddy and moved back north from Palm Beach and Key West. He was throwing a housewarming party at his new place in the west forties, and Josh couldn't get away from the theatre fast enough. Maybe this time he had a shot.

■ ■ ■

When he arrived, Eli was already there.

"How was the show?"

"Rough," Josh grunted. "Our leading lady was having an existential crisis."

"Again."

"This time it was bad enough that the understudy had to go on for her. And she was just a little too *under*, if you get my drift."

"Uh, oh," Eli said.

"Anyway, tomorrow is another day. Two more of them, in fact. I can do two shows on Wednesday, but for some reason Saturdays really wear me out."

"The glamorous life of the theatre," Eli nodded.

"So who's Han Solo over there?"

"That would be Andrew," Eli said. "Andrew Rubenstein. I've told you about him before."

"I don't remember."

"Maybe not by name," Eli said. "He's the cousin of one of Talbot's cousins on his father's side."

"The Diamonds?" Josh asked. "Or the Cashmans?"

Josh had made himself thoroughly conversant with Talbot's connections, the better to become one of them eventually. Somehow, however, he'd missed out on Andrew.

"Andrew's mother is a Cashman," Eli said.

"That's his pedigree. How about his vita?"

"Princeton, the Peace Corps, and currently a Ph.D. Program at Harvard," Eli said. "Oh, and the New York, Philadelphia, and Boston Marathons."

"How energetic of him."

■ ■ ■

"I know you don't like me, Josh," Eamonn said, grinning that grin of his. "I don't even blame you for it."

His shoulders seemed wider than the last time Josh had seen him. His hair seemed shinier, too. Every time they met, Eamonn gave the impression that his magnificence perpetually compounded. Like interest.

"You shouldn't," Josh laughed. "You deserve it. And besides, it's nothing personal. I think you're a hell of a great guy, actually. It's just that I'm not crazy about this situation my buddy Eli finds himself in."

"I get it," Eamonn nodded. "You have to think that. You're his best friend and you believe he deserves better."

"That about sums it up," Josh agreed.

"It's not easy for any of us," Eamonn said. "I love Eli. I love my wife. I love my boys."

"How are the boys, by the way?"

"Terrific."

"Glad to hear it. And Maribel?"

"The miscarriage hit her hard. I keep telling her we should stop at three. But she still wants a little girl."

"My mom wouldn't stop at three either," Josh said. "And we got my brother Cooper. That kind of thing never works out the way you hope it will."

"Listen, Josh," Eamonn said, "I never lied to Eli about anything. He knew exactly what he was getting into."

"I know," Josh said. "He and I have been over the whole thing. Just because I understand it doesn't mean I have to like it."

"Nobody said you did."

"Right."

"And the agreement is," Eamonn said, "if he finds somebody he'd rather be with I won't stand in his way."

"He won't," Josh said. "He's not even looking. He says you're the love of his life."

"He says that to me, too," Eamonn said. "So anyway, that's the way it is."

"You know, the two of you are just so fucking reasonable about it," Josh said. "I think that's what really drives me crazy."

■ ■ ■

"News flash, darling," Jill said. "My character is about to turn her back on her life of prostitution and enter nursing school."

"That'll require a major alteration in your wardrobe," Josh said.

"Indeed. The way they're outlining the scripts, it apparently only takes a few weeks to become a surgical nurse."

"I had no idea."

"I've already spoke to Maribel Lannaghan. Her supervisors are going to let me shadow her for a few shifts at St. Vincent's. To research the role. And *Soap Opera Digest* is sending a reporter and photographer along. Isn't that terrific?"

"Fantastic."

"She really is the most gorgeous woman," Jill sighed.

■ ■ ■

"Your usual discussion with Eamonn?" Eli asked.

"Same as always," Josh nodded.

"He really likes you," Eli said.

"And I like him."

"You pretend to like him to make me happy," Eli grinned, "but I see through you."

"Is that how it works?" Josh laughed.

"I know all your tricks," Eli said. "I even know the tricks you don't realize are in your repertoire, so don't try and pull anything over on me."

"Who, me?"

"Speaking of which," Eli said, "Talbot may be back in New York. But he's not exactly available."

"What does that mean?"

"See those two black bodybuilders in the corner?"

"Could anybody actually miss seeing guys that huge? They look like they could hold up the building."

"His new husbands," Eli nodded.

■ ■ ■

"Excuse me."

"Yes?" Josh turned. "Oh, hello."

"Andrew." The man extended his hand.

Josh shook it. Was this why he was here? Not to throw himself at Talbot but to meet this guy? At a party where Talbot wasn't the host, Eamonn Lannaghan wasn't on the guest list, and those two bodybuilders weren't lurking in the corner, this guy would be turning all heads.

"I'm Josh."

"I know who you are," Andrew smiled. "I saw your show last week. With my aunt."

"Oops," Josh said. "It's not a very good show, I'm afraid. But I'm not able to issue refunds."

"You were good in it."

II

"Thanks, Joshua."

78

"Good to see you again, Josh."

"We'll be in touch."

Auditioning never got easier. And this part was the worst, the long walk to the door. If he could just wiggle his nose and disappear like Samantha the witch—or was what she did more of a twitch than a wiggle?—it wouldn't be so bad. But that long, long walk, with the casting people watching his back. Or not watching his back. Which would be even worse, wouldn't it? Looking down at their notes. Staring into space. Looking at the photo of the next hopeful, all thoughts of Joshua Luxemberg banished. What was that quote? "The horror, the horror"?

Out in the corridor, dozens of his fellow thespians waited their turns. They all pretty much had the same dreams he did. Some had less talent than he did, but some had more. Some were better singers, some better dancers, some read their lines more convincingly. It was impossible to quantify, and that made the outcome impossible to predict. Even if he'd been a fly on the wall watching each one of them, he still couldn't have foretold anyone's fate.

Nearly four years now, and he was still waiting for his big break. There was always work. There wasn't a chorus boy in all New York with a better record than he had. "Get me that Josh Luxemberg," the directors said. His agent called him a phenomenon. But seeing himself credited as "swing" over and over again in those playbills—it got a little frustrating.

"*Maybe this time*," he sung softly as he took the steps down to the street.

■ ■ ■

"I know you feel a little disloyal," Jill said, blowing onto her tea, "but you're hardly a rat deserting a sinking ship. And besides, who in his right mind wouldn't want to work with Seamus Steinmetz? I know when he directed me in that thing down in the Village. . ."

"*Eight Lesbians in Search of a Script?*" Josh suggested.

"*Murmurs at Twilight*," Jill corrected him. "And we weren't all lesbians."

"You weren't?" Josh asked. "I must have missed something."

"Some of us were only impersonating lesbians. It was all cleared up in Act II. Or at least partially. Anyway, Seamus was just a dream to work with. He had such empathy with the cast."

"*Empathy with the Sapphists*," Josh said. "It sounds like the title of the next Rolling Stones album."

"Everyone but that odious Destiny Newcastle, that is."

"Oh the irony," Josh laughed, "since she was the one he was fucking at the time."

"Don't change the subject, darling," Jill said. "You've got a very bad habit of doing that just when I'm trying to make an important point."

"Which is?"

"Of course you'll take the part if they offer it. Your current show isn't going to run forever. It never fails, you know. You turn the new part down, and the next thing you know your current show is closing."

"Been there," Josh agreed.

"We all have. So it's settled. Onward and upward."

"Or sideways in this case," Josh said.

"What I really want to talk about is Talbot's party. I hardly got a chance to speak to you there. Did you drag him off and ravish him in the laundry closet?"

"He's already remarried," Josh frowned.

"So soon?"

"Twice."

"That's fast work," Jill said. "Even for Talbot."

"Simultaneously."

"Egad. Still, that's Talbot for you."

"But perhaps it doesn't matter," Josh said. "I think I may have met Mr. Right."

"Oh, Josh," Jill gasped, "me, too."

■ ■ ■

"He invited you where?" Eli gasped.

"You heard me," Josh said. "Temple. It's O.K. He goes to that gay one. They meet somewhere in Chelsea."

"Still," Eli said, shaking his head. "I mean, *temple*. What's supposed to be the point of that? Anyway, you can't go. You work on Friday nights."

"He invited me for Saturday morning service. And lunch afterward. He knows I have an early call for my matinee."

"You're going?"

"Why not?"

"When's the last time you went to temple, anyway?"

"Who knows?" Josh said. "Not counting weddings and Bar Mitzvahs—probably tenth grade. That's when Jake got so heavily into Zionism that I had to do the opposite."

"You won't know how to act at temple."

"Sure I will," Josh laughed. "I'm an actor. 'Think back to a time when you went to temple'. See, it's easy."

"All I can say is it's a hell of a first date."

■ ■ ■

"Thanks for lunch," Josh said. "It was great."

It hadn't been, really. In fact the whole thing had been a bust. But there was just something about Andrew. Josh really wanted to see him again. Maybe it was a sign. Bad first date, terrific marriage.

"I really like this place," Andrew smiled.

"And, uh, temple was. . ."

"You hated it," Andrew said. "I'm not that religious myself. But the traditions are really important to me. Or, to be honest, I'm trying to make the traditions feel important. I don't know if that makes any sense at all."

"No, I just—see, we were Conservative Jews when I was growing up."

"It was too strange for you," Andrew said. "That's O.K."

"I'm sure I could get used to it," Josh said.

"Maybe it would be better if we went to a movie next time," Andrew said.

"That would be nice," Josh nodded. Movies he could do.

■ ■ ■

"Cast, this is your five minute warning."

"*Another opening*," Josh crooned to himself, "*another show*."

They were all out there. Mom, Dad, Nanny Freitag, Aunt Rosie—who wasn't really his aunt, just Mom's best friend ever since first grade—and her husband Lou, Jill and her new girlfriend, Karla, Ike and Cherie, who had come down from Boston. All of them. Except Eli, who had "plans" with Eamonn. They had tickets for next week.

And Andrew. None of them had met Andrew yet. Well, Jill had, of course. But none of the others even knew Andrew existed. It would be interesting explaining his significance without really *explaining his significance*. On the other hand, maybe it was time to come clean. Perhaps Mom and Dad could get over the shock of having two gay sons. They'd certainly taken Yakov's coming out in stride.

Or maybe that had just been the impression they wanted to give. Maybe they'd been O.K. with it because one in four wasn't that bad a percentage. Or maybe Josh thought about things too much.

■ ■ ■

"Cast, this is your two minute warning."

JULY, 1979

"Hold still," Yakov said. "Let me put some more of this on your back. I said, hold still, soldier."

The two older boys, Avi and Zev, took after their mother's family, the Schlesingers. They were slender and graceful and quiet like deer in a forest. They were model children at all times. They never had to be told anything twice. But this one, five and a half year old Yoel, was all Luxemberg. Which meant trouble more or less full time. Yakov finally got him sufficiently greased up and sent him off to join his brothers at the water's edge. How did full time parents stand it?

■ ■ ■

Whenever the boys asked their mother to bring them to the beach—it was all of three blocks from their house, so this was a frequent request—all she could think of was rocket attacks. So she took them to the movies instead. She knew better, but having a roof over their heads seemed safer than out there by the water with nothing but thin air for protection. Consequently they didn't get to the beach very often, though they saw lots of movies. More than their father, Yakov's Uncle Marcus, considered suitable. Marcus had spent twenty years arguing with his first wife and refused to argue with his second. He didn't countermand Anat about the beach or the movies. But lately Marcus had been traveling a lot and taking Anat with him. He was retired from the IDF but hadn't stopped serving his country. His new work as a defense consultant generally took him to European capitals. But wherever the destination, when he and Anat went away the boys stayed with Yakov and Naftali. That's when Yakov and Naftali took them to the beach. Marcus knew about it and didn't object. The boys got to go to the beach fairly often and since everyone concerned, including Anat's parents, had agreed not to tell her about it, everybody was happy.

■ ■ ■

It was another beautiful day. The sun was shining. The Mediterranean was as blue as Yakov had ever seen it. There was enough of a breeze to keep it from getting too hot. The boys played well together. Naftali was enjoying his new book. And there were no rocket attacks. As long as they were all happy, Yakov was happy. He didn't need any further diversion. It was as perfect as things ever got.

■ ■ ■

"Who's hungry?" Naftali called. "It's time for lunch."

The boys headed up the beach.

■ ■ ■

Avi, Zev, and Yoel were their father's second family. His first wife, the mother of their half brothers Rafi and Gil, had died in a rocket attack during the Six Day War in 1967. Rafi and Gil were a generation older than they were, as were Yakov and his brothers, their first cousins on their father's side. Their cousins on their mother's side were their age. Their half brothers had children not too much younger than them who were their nieces and nephews. Avi and Zev had no trouble keeping track of all these complications, but Yoel had no patience for it.

■ ■ ■

They had lunch at the open air café where for all practical purposes Yakov had proposed to Naftali and/or vice versa. Yakov still hadn't forgotten the gleam off Naftali's slicked down hair that day. Chicken kabob for Avi. Shawerma with lamb for Zev. That was easy. They never ordered anything else. Today Yoel insisted on a hamburger. He invariably requested food based on some impulse to be disruptive. If a rumor swept the beach about a shortage of chickpeas, he'd hear it and demand a falafel platter. Naftali quietly circumvented him by ordering a fishburger instead, but a strategic glance from Yakov at just the right moment was still required to head off a confrontation. Naftali was great with the older two boys. Patient. Low key. Humorous. Gentle. Everything Yakov wasn't and just what it took to keep them smiling. Naftali would have made a wonderful father. Everybody agreed that it was a shame he had never become one. Though they expressed this sentiment in the most diplomatic terms possible, Yakov sometimes felt guilty for having kept it from happening.

"That's nonsense," Maya Schlesinger—the boys' grandmother—told him one time when he mentioned it to her. "I've known Naftali since he was a little boy. His aunt is my best friend, after all. He would never have been truly happy if he hadn't met you. And a man who isn't happy as a man can never be happy as a father. It's as simple as that. In a better world, the two of you would be able to adopt or make some other kind of arrangement. But that's for future generations, I suppose. Meanwhile, you should enjoy the time you have with Marcus and Anat's boys. They grow up so fast, I can't tell you."

But Yakov still considered childlessness the tragedy of Naftali's life.

■ ■ ■

The rest of the family saw it somewhat differently. Not that they disagreed with Yakov regarding Naftali's fitness as a parent. But among themselves they agreed that Yakov underestimated his own gifts in that arena. And for proof they had their own observations to go on. Because the reality was that Yoel was a very difficult child. Not even Naftali could handle him, really. He basically ignored anything anyone instructed him to do. He refused to listen either to reason or emotional appeals. Even things he would ordinarily have been inclined to do had he been left to his own devices became matters of serious contention when someone or other told him he should do them. This was true in all cases except that of his cousin Yakov. Cousin Yakov was a captain in the infantry, and when he spoke Yoel obeyed. Unhesitatingly, uncomplainingly, and best of all instantaneously. Just the mention of his name—"your Cousin Yakov wouldn't like that"—was enough to bring him to heel.

Avi and Zev were quiet boys, cerebral, sensitive, eager to please and as happy at home with a book as on the beach or the soccer field or camping in the desert with their male relatives. Yoel was as active and noisy as they were contemplative, a child in more or less perpetual motion. It look all kinds. And may the Almighty be with that boy's mother. After lunch that day, Avi and Zev settled down in the shade with their books. Yakov, knowing it was for the best, took Yoel down to the water. Yoel swam like a fish. He loved the water and playing in it tired him out. Naftali had assured Yakov there was no danger in Yoel going swimming after lunch as long as an adult stayed close.

■ ■ ■

"There's got to be something quiet I could get him interested in," Yakov said that night in bed.

"It's perfectly normal for a boy to be physically active," Nafatli said. "I sometimes worry about the other two, to be frank with you. They're so quiet. It's really not normal."

"What is normal?"

"This really isn't a time for metaphysical speculation," Naftali laughed.

"You see, I'm thinking back on my brother Cooper," Yakov said. "He was just like that. It drove Mom crazy. I know what you're saying, but every young boy also needs to be able to focus quietly on something. It's an important skill for life."

"What happened with Cooper?" Naftali asked. "Did he ever learn to focus on something quiet?"

"He did and he didn't," Yakov said. "Dad set up a weightlifting outfit for us in the basement of our building. The rest of us got tired of it almost immediately, but Cooper practically lived down there. That certainly focused him. And he was out of the house, so it was quiet there even if he wasn't."

"Yoel's a little too young for that," Naftali said.

"You're right," Yakov said.

"So you're saying it's hopeless," Naftali said. "And I'm telling you he's very young and there's no need to worry."

"I'm not finished telling you about Cooper," Yakov said. "Our parents took us to San Francisco one summer. Our Aunt Rivka and her boys lived in Los Angeles and we visited them every year. But one summer Mom and Dad rented a car and drove us up the coast."

"What happened in San Francisco?" Naftali asked.

"Cooper fell in love with architecture," Yakov said. "Don't ask me why. God knows there's plenty of architecture in Manhattan. Perhaps it was because he was seeing it in an unfamiliar context. It was like turning on a light. As sudden as that, and he was never the same. It's why he's making a fortune selling real estate today. He didn't want to design buildings. He didn't have the patience for the study required, but that was beside the point. His passion for architecture was more possessive than that. But he certainly learned to focus. From then on, if you gave him a book about architecture he'd sit looking at the pictures for hours. Mom would practically have to set off bombs to get him to the dinner table."

"You tried architecture with Yoel," Naftali said. "I never understood why."

"It didn't work," Yakov said.

"Maybe there's something else you could get him interested in," Naftali said, "but I still think you worry too much about it. He's not even six years old yet. There's plenty of time."

■ ■ ■

The next day they went back to the beach, and the weather was perfect once again. Sometimes Yakov missed climatic variation. But when Mom wrote about the winters in New York, he didn't.

"I wish Mother and Father would never come back," Yoel told Yakov at lunchtime. "That way we could come to the beach every day."

■ ■ ■

But Anat and Marcus did return, thank God. That remark of Yoel's had given Yakov a terrible night, but there was no air disaster and two days later he and Naftali took the boys to the airport to meet the El Al flight from Paris.

"I wish I could go on a plane sometime," Yoel said as they watched the Boeing come in to land.

"You will," Naftali said. "Traveling is wonderful, and soon you'll be old enough to go anywhere you want."

But Yakov had been listening carefully, and he heard something different in Yoel's voice. When he looked over at his small cousin, there was a strange light in those eyes.

II

Yakov went on maneuvers with his unit. Contemplating the Negev Desert always gave him lots of ideas. He had what he thought was a good one. When he got back, Anat and Marcus were getting ready for a trip to Switzerland. Yakov got ready, too.

■ ■ ■

"All right, young man," he said, toweling Yoel off. "Time for bed."

"It's really not fair that Avi and Zev get to stay up a whole hour later than I do."

"You're absolutely right," Yakov agreed, "and I, your cousin, am doing something about it."

"You're going to let me stay up and watch television with them."

"No," Yakov said. "I'm going to take you in and read you a new book for bedtime."

"I hate books," Yoel said.

"I know that," Yakov said, "and that is why I, your cousin, went and bought a very special book just for you."

"I'd rather stay up with Avi and Zev watching television."

"You'll think differently in about five minutes," Yakov said.

■ ■ ■

"I know you don't know your English alphabet yet," Yakov said. "So you won't be able to read these letters. I will translate the book for you as I read it. It's the pictures in this book that are of the most importance, I believe."

"Great," Yoel said. "You buy me a book that you say is very special but it's not even in Hebrew."

■ ■ ■

"It's his favorite book," Anat said. "I got him a nice book about airplanes in Hebrew, and he loves it. But the one you got him is his favorite. You're a genius to have thought of it. I really can't believe none of us figured it out. With his brother Rafi a fighter pilot, already. How stupid are we?"

"I've sent word to my mother," Yakov said. "She'll be sending more books on the subject. They won't be in Hebrew, either, but it will be something."

"No matter," Anat said. "It will give him an incentive to work harder on his English."

■ ■ ■

Everyone agreed that Yakov was a wizard to have figured out Yoel's undiscovered passion. The boy was noticeably calmer. He even remembered his manners part of the time. But Yakov wasn't satisfied. He had a strong sense of a job yet unfinished.

■ ■ ■

"They're fighting about what movie I should take them to this afternoon," Anat said. For some reason, the telephone made her sound more frantic than usual. "Ordinarily I make them take turns choosing. But then no one is happy."

"I know," Yakov said. "I had three brothers. You have that many boys in a house, it's constant warfare."

"Exactly," Anat said. "Now I hate to ask you to give up an afternoon of your leave. . ."

"Don't be silly," Yakov said. "Naftali's at work anyway."

"If you could be an angel and take Yoel to the movie he wants to see while I take Avi and Zev to the one they want to see, everyone would be happy. Except you, I suppose."

"I have an even better idea," Yakov said. "Drop Yoel here on your way to the theater. I'll bring him home in time for dinner."

■ ■ ■

While Yakov was waiting, he laid out everything he had prepared in the guest room. The kit itself, the paints, the brushes, the glue.

■ ■ ■

"I thought you were going to take me to the movies," Yoel said once his mother and brothers were out the door.

"I hate to disappoint you, my dear cousin," Yakov said, "but I shall be unable to do so because unfortunately there is a project I must take care of here. Which is lucky, really, because you are just the man to help me with it."

"A project?"

"In here," Yakov said, indicating the doorway with a cock of his head.

■ ■ ■

"You see the picture on the box? This type of aircraft is called a Boeing 747. When your father flew to New York last spring that is the kind of airplane he traveled on."

"And we put it together ourselves?"

Finally. There was the light Yakov had seen in those eyes that afternoon at the airport. The books, wonderful as they were, hadn't reignited it.

"Today all we'll be able to do is paint it,"Yakov said. "All the parts must be painted in the correct colors before we can glue them together. And then they must dry completely so we don't smudge them."

"But. . ."

"No, listen. I'll pick you up after school each afternoon this week and we'll keep working on it. By next Sunday the model will be finished."

■ ■ ■

They used the white spray paint on the fuselage, wings, tail planes, and engine nacelles because of course it would be an El Al craft. They used the tiny bottles of paint and the delicate brushes for the smaller parts that needed to be silver, black, or yellow. They left all the parts out on the terrace to dry.

■ ■ ■

"Remember," Yakov said at the end of the afternoon as they went outside to wait for Anat and the older boys, "not a word to them about our project. It's a surprise."

■ ■ ■

"What do we do now that it's finished?"Yoel asked Friday afternoon.

"Nothing just yet,"Yakov said. "*Shabbat shalom.* I'll see you Sunday."

■ ■ ■

"Very good,"Yakov said, asYoel unfolded the step stool. "Right above your bed? Is that what we agreed?"

"Yes."

"Excellent,"Yakov said. He drilled the small hole and snugged the hook tight against the ceiling.

Yoel watched every move.

"Hand me that roll of nylon line. And that pair of clippers."

"Here."

"This is used for fishing," Yakov explained. "It's very strong. And it's nearly invisible. Thus, it's perfect for suspending aircraft models in the air over young men's beds."

He looped the line around the fuselage at two places. He adjusted the line to give the craft a slight nose up attitude, as if it were in a gentle climb. He slipped the line through the ceiling hook. The line stretched slightly as he let the weight hang from it. The model swung gently and turned through forty and then sixty degrees before assuming its preferred position.

"There," he said, climbing down. "What do you think?"

Yoel's eyes gleamed.

"It's the most beautiful thing I've ever seen."

DECEMBER, 1979

Cooper knew Griffin was unhappy about his holiday travel plans. Griffin hadn't complained—not once—but Griffin was no poker player. Whenever Griffin was upset, whether sad or angry, he went silent. It wasn't sulking exactly. What disqualified it from that description was that Griffin didn't seem to be playing to an audience, either real or imagined. If he had been Cooper would have gotten rid of him in a heartbeat. Cooper couldn't stand sulking. It was a form of manipulation of course, and he had no patience with that. If you couldn't come straight out and ask for what you wanted or thought you deserved, you simply weren't an adult. Cooper had been subjected to more of it than any man should have to put up with in a lifetime. It was bad enough from women, but from another man it was intolerable. But what Griffin did was more tuning out than sulking, really. He was assuming a kind of inertness, like a turtle going into its shell. Cooper didn't particularly like it. He'd grown up among people who fought at the top of their lungs and then let go of whatever was bothering them pretty much as soon as they ran out of breath. This was the opposite of that. What it had going for it was that it was easy to ignore. Indeed, being ignored at such times was apparently what Griffin actually wanted. In a matter of hours—or a day or two in more extreme instances—he was back to normal and the original cause of his unhappiness was never mentioned. Cooper was pretty sure this wasn't healthy either for Griffin or for their relationship, but so far it had proven to be extremely convenient. This and the other less desirable aspects of Griffin's behavior could always be dealt with later. If there was a later. Cooper hadn't made his mind up about that yet, though he told himself he was close.

Not that in this instance Griffin didn't have ample cause for dissatisfaction. Cooper understood that and made what he considered appropriate allowances. Sure, he could have decided to stay in San Francisco over Hanukkah and Christmas. He could even have made plans to bring Griffin along with him to New York. That would have taken some negotiation, certainly. He wasn't exactly out to his parents, but he wasn't exactly not out, either. Still, he couldn't just show up on the doorstep with a boyfriend. There was time and opportunity to deal with all that before the trip, but there was nothing Cooper disliked more than having his hand forced. And if he wasn't ready to commit himself with regard to Griffin, he wasn't ready.

Still, he knew he had to make some sort of amends to his boyfriend. And Cooper being Cooper that meant a multipronged offensive. First came the explanation: logical, truthful, unassailable. Nanny Freitag lived with Cooper's parents, and these days her mental state was increasingly erratic. There was no assurance whatever that she'd know who Cooper was when he arrived. About half the time she didn't even know who she was, much less anyone else. And it wouldn't be fair, really, to subject her to the presence of someone totally unfamiliar, someone whose presence couldn't be easily and comfortably explained. Surely Griffin could understand that.

And he had. He'd been unnervingly reasonable about it. Cooper was relieved by his reaction, but at the same time a little uneasy. How honest was it?

Next, he showered Griffin with presents and attention on his birthday, just ten days before his scheduled departure. Dinner at a fancy restaurant, theatre tickets for January and February. March might have been in play, too, but there was that unresolved commitment question. He even considered buying Griffin a used Volkswagen convertible, but discarded the idea as excessive. Not in a material sense. He could certainly afford it. But in the sense that the gesture seemed to imply guilt, Cooper ruled it out. He refused to feel guilty about needing to visit his family by himself. Not to mention, buying Griffin a car seemed to make them a couple. They probably were. Almost certainly. People seemed to have accepted it. At least the people whose opinions mattered to Cooper. But he wasn't ready to make a public gesture confirming it. That made it harder to get back out of, and he still felt he needed an escape clause. He finally settled on jewelry. Griffin didn't own a single piece. He barely had decent clothing. But a ring wouldn't do. A ring of whatever sort carried certain implications. And besides, a ring was a gift of questionable practicality for a classical pianist. Cooper spent several afternoons when he claimed to be showing properties scouring antique shops and eventually found a sterling silver cross on a matching chain—vintage Tiffany, complete with original packaging. Griffin's eyes were wide as he opened the blue box. Cooper was almost home free.

But two weeks was a long time to be away. Griffin would be busy at the record shop during the days leading up to Christmas, and he'd be playing extra gigs at Harry Gordini's piano bar as well, but he'd still be on his own a great deal. The dogs were excellent chaperones in their limited way, but Cooper took steps. He arranged for Griffin to spend Christmas Eve with Ashby—Matt would be flying. Christmas day there'd be the traditional pot luck hosted by Big Steve and Tristan. Cooper's business partners, Ned and Elizabeth, happily agreed to lend a hand for a few lunches and dinners and a symphony concert. And so on. By the time he was done, Cooper had Griffin's calendar so completely booked that he'd barely have time to go to the crapper. It wasn't that he didn't trust Griffin. Who Cooper didn't trust were other guys who might try to use Griffin to get back at him. That was a fairly likely scenario the more he thought about it.

Even then, Cooper wasn't finished. Christmas presents were wrapped and placed under the tree with tags indicating when they should be opened. And finally, the last two nights before his departure, Cooper served up extra helpings of the finest, most exotic courses on his bedroom menu. It would have to be enough.

Still, that last glimpse of Griffin standing at the end of the jetway as Cooper boarded his flight—Griffin was trying not to show his disappointment, but it was as clear as day.

■ ■ ■

Cooper's brother Josh met him at Kennedy. Josh wasn't alone. With him was a tall, blue eyed stranger he introduced as his friend, Martin. Martin was the one with the car. A Volvo, as a matter of fact. Cooper was beginning to think of dark colored Volvos as a gay cliché. That cleared up the mystery. Cooper hadn't had any inkling why Josh had been sent on the errand. As far as Cooper knew Josh didn't even have a valid driver's license. Martin apparently had some kind of job in banking. He and Josh seemed like an unlikely pair of acquaintances, but Cooper didn't question it aloud. They dropped him off at their parents' building but didn't come upstairs. The last time they had been there for dinner, Josh explained, Nanny Freitag thought they were men who'd been sent to take her to the old people's home.

■ ■ ■

"Cooper, darling," Nanny greeted him the next morning when he came into the dining room, "what a surprise running into you here. You never told me you were familiar with this hotel."

Having been warned about her current eccentricities, Cooper was prepared to behave as if she was completely in command of herself.

"It's one of my favorite resorts," he smiled

"I can't imagine why," Nanny said. "The service here is terrible. And the staff are surly. The girl who just took my breakfast order—you'll want to watch her. I think she spits in the food."

"I'm sure they wouldn't keep her on staff if she did such a thing," Cooper said.

"I know what I saw, dear," Nanny said. "But tell me. Where are your wife and children? Sleeping in? I don't see how, with all the racket in this place. I think there must be a boiler factory in the attic."

■ ■ ■

"So who's this Martin character?" Cooper asked.

"Martin Rappaport," Mom said. She was smoking as she tidied the kitchen. Cooper wished she'd stop but didn't want to start the argument just then.

"Rappaport, huh?" Cooper grunted. "He looked awfully goyish. What? His mother Irish Catholic or something?"

"He's as Jewish as you are," Mom said. "And he doesn't look a bit more goyish than your brothers. In any case, I'd hardly call him a character. He's too serious for any sort of mischief."

"He certainly drove like a serious man," Cooper said, recalling the ride in from Kennedy. Martin had steadfastly maintained a speed below the limit, just like somebody's seventy year old uncle. The taxi drivers who ended up stuck behind them must have been apoplectic.

"Your father says a banker who speeds isn't to be trusted."

"I bet he doesn't say anything like that."

"Well, he would if he thought about it."

"But seriously, Mom, who is he?"

"Your brother's friend is who. People have friends, Cooper. I bet you have a few yourself, out there in San Francisco."

"I liked his other friend better," Cooper said.

"Who, sweetie?"

"That guy Andrew."

"Andrew went back into the Peace Corps."

"I heard."

"He's somewhere in Africa, I believe," she said.

"I thought it was Nepal."

"Maybe so."

"Well, I liked him better. At least he had a personality."

"Martin has a personality," Mom said. "He collects stamps. Or coins. Or something—vintage postcards, maybe. Josh told me all about it but obviously I wasn't paying close enough attention."

"Those are examples of neuroses, not evidence of charm," Cooper said.

"I'm sure you're right. But he's Josh's friend."

"And for that matter, there's Josh's upstairs neighbor, Eli. That's what I call a friend."

"Yes, Eli's very nice," Mom smiled. "His mother must be so proud of him."

"Where did Josh and Martin meet, anyway?"

"How should I know?"

"Well, I mean," Cooper said, waving smoke away from his face, "were they in college together or something?"

"I'm sorry, honey, but I have no idea. Martin is just a nice, quiet young man. On the days when your grandmother believes she's a university lecturer in Prague, she insists he's a rabbinical student. I believe your brother finds it soothing to spend his off hours with someone like that. Theatre people are so rackety. But I do know Martin's a theatre buff. They went to London together last spring when Josh was between jobs and saw plays every night. Josh said they had a very nice time."

■ ■ ■

Mom had had Cooper's bedroom painted and bought new furniture. But she hadn't thrown out any of his old stuff. The last time he visited, he went through it all. He shipped the things he wanted to keep out to San Francisco and told her to get rid of the rest. So far, she hadn't. He knew it couldn't be for sentimental reasons. She didn't have a sentimental bone in her body. At least not when it came to things. That was something they'd always had in common. And even if for some reason she was attached to any of it, it was a pretty sorry load of junk. Probably she just hadn't figured out what to do with it all. It was too good to throw away, but at the same time, who'd want any of it?

■ ■ ■

New York never changed. Oh, sure, there were new buildings here and there. New shops. But it was recognizably the same city Cooper had inhabited from birth until high school graduation. It was as if he had a map of Manhattan wired into his brain. Getting lost would have required serious effort. He went out his first morning to experience the Manhattan feeling again. It was cold and crisp and nothing like San Francisco. The buses were noisier and slower than ever, the subway more deafening, the crazies crazier. He would always love San Francisco, but New York would always be home.

■ ■ ■

"Sure," the gym manager said, "I know who you are. You're Eamonn Lannaghan's buddy from San Francisco. He said you'd be coming in. He tells me they really know how to treat firefighters out there."

"They do," Cooper nodded. Eamonn had stayed with Cooper earlier in the year when he visited San Francisco to pose for world renowned physique photographer, Lance Garrison. Cooper's gym buddies pulled out all the stops to make sure that Eamonn was the toast of the city.

"Well, any buddy of Eamonn's is welcome here," the man said. "My name's Ed. You say you're in town for how long?"

"'Til New Years."

"That's lucky," Ed winked, "because the management allows me to extend complementary guest privileges to friends of the gym for exactly two weeks. I'll let the boys know, but if anybody asks you just show them this card."

■ ■ ■

Brooklyn, on the other hand: well, you could have Brooklyn. The street Violetta's salon was on—sheesh. It might as well be Eastern Europe somewhere. But she was Big Steve Fabiani's auntie, and consequently Cooper's auntie surrogate. And she could charm the birds right out of the trees if they hadn't all left for Florida already.

"Cooper, darling," she crooned, charging up to him the minute he got in the door. "My Stefano said you were coming for the holidays. If you'd gotten here an hour later, I'd have been on my way to the airport."

"I was hoping to take you to lunch," Cooper said. "I thought Tristan said you were flying out tomorrow."

"You know, I think I gave him the wrong date. On the phone last night we finally got it cleared up. You'll be back in San Francisco when?"

"On the thirty-first. For Big Steve and Tristan's New Year's Eve Party."

"*Bene.* I'm preparing all the food, you know."

"Everybody in San Francisco knows," Cooper laughed. "They're begging for invitations."

"I'm taking a rain check on that lunch. I'll be staying with them until the fifteenth."

"Great."

"I can't wait to meet that cute new boyfriend of yours that Tristan never stops talking about."

■ ■ ■

When Cooper came in late that afternoon, Nanny was watching the television with the sound turned off.

"You know, Elliot," she said, peering up at him from her rocking chair, "there were Nesses who lived down the street from us in Vienna. Lovely people. Attorneys mostly. I suppose your superiors in the bureau are a little embarrassed that one of their top G-men is Jewish, but I wouldn't let it worry you too much."

"I never worry, ma'am," Cooper assured her.

■ ■ ■

His parents' apartment seemed bare without a Christmas tree. When he was growing up, other Jewish kids had talked their parents into "Hanukkah Bushes," but the Luxembergs always made do without. He'd forgotten what that was like. His friends in San Francisco all had Christmas trees in their places. And he and Griffin had put up a spectacular one. Cooper had a flair for decorating Christmas trees if he did say so himself.

■ ■ ■

"What you should have done was meet us in Boston for Thanksgiving," Mom said, rinsing Nanny's teacup. "We had a lovely visit with your brother and sister-in-law. You wouldn't believe how grown up Genikayte is. Now go get dressed. We're meeting Rosie and Lou downtown for Chinese at seven."

"Nanny coming?" Cooper asked.

"She doesn't do well in restaurants, dear. I'll need you to sit with her while I finish getting ready."

■ ■ ■

"Shoshonnah," Nanny called.

It was almost loud enough to make the windows rattle. Cooper braced himself.

"What, ma?" Mom called.

"Shoshonnah, come in here this minute. You won't believe who just checked into the hotel."

"Who, ma?"

"No, dear, come see."

Mom emerged from the kitchen looking exasperated. How many times a week did this scene or one like it play out?

"Who is it?"

"Don't you recognize him?" Nanny grinned, tousling Cooper's hair.

"I know the face," Mom said, "but I can't put a name to it."

"Silly girl. How could you forget our old friend Bugsy Siegel?" Nanny cackled. "Sorry, Mr. Siegel, I know you prefer to be referred to by your real name. But Ben Siegel sounds like an optician, don't you think?"

■ ■ ■

Josh's friend Jill Wagstaffe had finally moved in with her girlfriend, Karla, who had a place near Stuyvesant Park. Karla was older than Jill by nearly a generation. She taught anthropology at NYU. Their living room looked like backstage at a museum.

"Is Josh really not speaking to Eli?" Cooper asked.

"Josh is really not speaking to Eli," Jill nodded.

"Idiot," Karla said, though it wasn't immediately clear which of the two she was referring to.

"We're not taking sides of course," Jill said, "but between you and me, Josh is really being a dick."

"How long has it been going on?"

"The big blowup was at Thanksgiving," Jill said. "Talbot Kleinbaum hosted a pot luck."

"Egad," Cooper said. "The king of catered affairs?"

"Right," Karla nodded. "He said a pot luck was more in keeping with the spirit of the holiday."

"And they got into it right at the buffet table," Jill said. "Of course the confrontation would never have happened if Eamonn had been there."

"Certainly not," Cooper agreed.

"I thought somebody was going to have to call the police," Jill said.

"It got that bad?" Cooper asked.

"It got that loud," Jill said.

"That doesn't sound like either of them," Cooper said.

"Josh goes in for a lot of verbal aggression in this new role he's workshopping," Jill said. "Karla's theory is he's having trouble stepping out of character."

"Exactly," Karla said, sounding quite emphatic.

"How does that work?" Cooper asked. "I mean with his current show still running?"

"Precisely," Karla said.

■ ■ ■

Martin was waiting right where Josh had said he would be. He was wearing expensive but casual clothes with no pretensions to fashion at all. It wasn't that they were unfashionable. It was more that they seemed to assert that the concept of fashion *per se* didn't exist. They weren't unattractive, just out of place on a thirty year old, which Cooper judged he was.

"Hi," he said.

"Hi," Martin smiled.

"Where's dinner?"

"Place around the corner," Martin said. "You do eat Italian, don't you?"

"I'm sure I'll manage to find something to choke down."

In addition to lacking fashion sense, Martin also seemed to be without a sense of humor.

"The food's good there," Martin said. "And they understand that theatre crowds depend on efficient service. We won't have to worry about being late for curtain."

■ ■ ■

Martin apparently considered himself the ultimate authority on all things New York. During dinner he kept up a monologue focusing on the history and culture of the city as if he were entertaining a newcomer to the Western Hemisphere—or even planet Earth. Whenever Cooper attempted to insert some knowledge of his own, Martin found a way to correct him, if only by way of pointing out some minor detail Cooper had left out of his contribution. If Cooper had taken him seriously at all, he'd have found him insufferable.

Josh's friends had always been a little ridiculous, he remembered. But basically harmless. He hadn't been that crazy about Andrew, but dinner with Martin made him rethink his lack of enthusiasm.

■ ■ ■

Backstage after the performance, everything was pretty subdued. Cooper wasn't sure if it was because the performance had been flat, to put it kindly, or if this was typical of professional actors and actresses. To them it might just be a job. No more glamorous, really, than waiting tables. Which, apparently, was what most of them did between productions.

■ ■ ■

"It's not a very good show," Josh said.

"But you're good in it," Cooper said.

Josh shrugged.

"Didn't you say once that all it takes to make a career is one role?"

"It's true, of course," Martin nodded, "but that role doesn't show up for everyone."

"Obviously," Cooper said.

"Sometimes I think I should throw in the towel," Josh said.

"Surely not," Cooper protested.

"You'll know when it's time," Martin said.

Cooper thought that was interesting. Martin saying "when" as if it was a foregone conclusion. A true friend would have known he was supposed to argue the point.

■ ■ ■

"It's not all confusion, Cooper," Josh said as they walked through Times Square. "Some of it is, of course. But some of it is way too clever for that. You must have noticed. Sometimes she's just playing make believe. Like she's a kid again."

"I don't know," Cooper said.

"Well, I do," Josh said. "And Martin agrees with me. Don't you?"

"Real dementia is like my great-grandmother Nathanssohn," Martin said. "Finger painting on the walls with her own feces."

"Jesus," Cooper said.

"So stop worrying about it so much," Josh said.

■ ■ ■

Cooper parted from them in the subway station. He'd be getting a train uptown and Josh one back to the Village. He had no idea where Martin was headed.

■ ■ ■

One thing had changed about New York after all, Cooper realized, undressing for bed that night. Everywhere you went in the city you saw pairs of young men walking together. Gay wasn't invisible like it had been when he was in high school trying to find his way around.

■ ■ ■

"Funny you should ask," Eli said.

For some reason, Eli had decided that Grand Central Station was the perfect spot for lunch. That suited Cooper just fine.

"Oh? What's funny about it?"

"Nothing, actually," Eli said. "It's just I don't really like Martin. And what do you know? Apparently you don't, either."

"You and Josh fight about it?"

"That's not what the fight was about."

"I know," Cooper said. "The fight was about Eamonn, the same as always. But what about Martin?"

"I never said a thing against Martin in Josh's hearing," Eli said. "It would be hypocritical of me. After all the complaining I've done about Josh criticizing Eamonn, I mean."

"Right," Cooper said, "but you haven't answered my question."

"Yeah, yeah," Eli said. "Who the hell is Martin Rappaport? Here's who Martin Rappaport is. Back when your brother was on the rebound from Cousin Talbot. . ."

"Talbot Kleinbaum? I didn't know they were an item."

"They weren't," Eli said. "That was the problem. Because Josh had a really bad case on him. For years and years. Worst ever, really. Anyway, Josh finally decided he had to move on, and there Martin was. He'd been lurking."

"Excuse me," Cooper said, "but I'm having a hard time thinking of Martin and Talbot in the same—well, time zone. Or on the same planet."

"It's not that unusual for a guy to go for the opposite of someone who disappointed him."

"Really?" Cooper asked. "Sounds like you're giving Josh too much credit for rational behavior."

"Whatever," Eli shrugged. "Thing is, once Josh actually got interested in him, Martin decided to play hard to get."

"Martin?" Cooper said. "Are we talking about the same Martin here? Hard to get? What the fuck is that?"

"I'm just telling you how it was. I can't begin to imagine why Martin thought it made sense."

"Got it."

"So anyway," Eli said, "Martin started playing hard to get and then all of a sudden Andrew showed up and swept Josh off his feet. I may have had something to do with that."

"Really?"

"I invited Andrew to a party I knew Josh would be at."

"Just like high school."

"Anyway, Andrew's arrival on the scene made Martin rethink his strategy. But it was too late. When Andrew went back into the Peace Corps last February, Martin didn't make that mistake again."

"Amazing," Cooper said. "You can't make this kind of shit up. So what don't you like about him?"

"It's nothing I can put my finger on," Eli said, "but I just don't trust him."

■ ■ ■

Only a fussbudget like Josh could have accused Eli Danziger of being difficult and not meant it ironically. From Cooper's perspective, he was the most accommodating of individuals. In fact, if he had one fault it was probably that he was too accommodating for his own good. That flaw certainly had been responsible for the situation Josh disapproved of so strongly that they'd had a shouting match at Talbot's Thanksgiving bash. Cooper could see Josh's point, certainly. Eli deserved better than a part time lover, even if the lover in question was the spectacular Eamonn Lannaghan. But Eli also deserved the benefit of the doubt. They were all adults. They had the right to make their own choices. They didn't need each other's permission, no matter how long they'd been friends.

II

He was just finishing his workout when Eamonn came in.

"Cooper, lookin' good, man."

"Hey. Great to see you."

They went into the traditional meathead hug, completely different from the gay one.

"Likewise. Still putting on lean muscle mass, I see."

"Trying, at least," Cooper said.

"Planning to compete any time soon?"

"Maybe the Californias," Cooper said. "Got a lot on my plate right now. Might put it off another year."

"You about done here?"

"Yes."

"Great. I'm taking you to lunch."

■ ■ ■

"What's good here?" Cooper asked, looking around the diner.

"I've got the cook trained," Eamonn said. "He grills a tuna steak and serves it on a bed of fresh spinach."

"Sounds good."

"Listen," Eamonn said. "Just wanted to thank you for that pep talk you gave Eli the other night. He told me about it."

"Josh is being a dick," Cooper said. "Somebody needed to say it."

"We've all said it," Eamonn said, "but you're, like, a neutral observer."

"The man's my brother," Cooper said. "Nobody knows better than I do how big a dick he can be."

"Fair enough," Eamonn laughed. "You know, it's not like I don't understand where he's coming from. I wish things were different myself. It would be great if Eli and I were raising the boys together."

"You don't have to justify anything to me," Cooper said.

"Josh thinks I should leave Maribel," Eamonn said. "He thinks Eli and I should move in together and try to get joint custody of the boys."

"I don't know how things are here in New York," Cooper said, "but even in San Francisco that kind of thing is very tricky."

"Exactly," Eamonn said. "Not to mention I'm truly in love with both of them, so I'm not sure how divorcing Maribel and moving in with Eli would solve anything. You know, I get the whole political aspect. I really do. Gays have to stick together. Be out and proud. The closet is the enemy. I understand the necessity for that kind of thinking. Someday, maybe a couple of guys like Eli and me could do it to Josh's satisfaction."

■ ■ ■

Of all the men Cooper had ever met, this sleek haired, gray eyed Irish firefighter with size and muscularity at least the equal of his own was the one he should be spending the rest of his life with. Breezy and confident, easy going yet intense, Eamonn exuded the kind of strength, determination, and serene clear-headedness Cooper most valued in himself. It seemed obvious that men as similar in physique, interests, and outlook belonged together, but Eamonnn was apparently just another example illustrating whatever the universe was trying to teach Cooper. Suitability didn't equate to availability. And, Big Steve would have said, it didn't guarantee compatibility, either. That was the worm in the apple. All those similarities Cooper found so compelling and seductive almost inevitability meant that the worst imaginable incompatibility was also in play, the one that had doomed his dreams of a romance with Nick Romanovsky back in his early days in San Francisco. Nick had been old enough and sufficiently experienced to avoid the pitfall that nineteen year old Cooper couldn't have foreseen. Men so compatible in every other respect were, ironically, almost certainly incompatible in bed because their similarities ensured that they wanted the same thing. As a result their satisfaction was mutually exclusive. There was no possible basis for anything beyond friendship.

So that, in addition to everything else Cooper and Eamonn shared, they suffered the same predicament. For all practical purposes, Eli was Griffin's spiritual and emotional doppelganger. They might have been ordered from the same catalogue. Eamonn had found a way to make his peace with loving a man who, on the surface at least, appeared unlikely to be his ideal. Yet Eamonn, for all the complications of his life, was the picture of contentment. It wasn't something Cooper felt free to initiate a discussion about. What he could learn from Eamonn was probably best learned through observation.

■ ■ ■

"So this new guy," Eamonn said. "Tell me about him."

"Griffin's a lot like Eli, really," Cooper said. "I mean, sure, he's not Jewish. And he's as far as you can get from a New Yorker. He grew up on a farm in Kentucky. If he walked in here this minute you'd never say, 'oh, that guy reminds me of Eli'. The similarities are internal. He's extremely patient for one thing."

"That's Eli, all right."

"And he's got this—I don't know exactly what to call it. People see him, they think 'oh, there's a nice, quiet guy. He's probably very easy to get along with.' And he is, but at the same time there's this determination behind it. This refusal, I guess you'd call it, to give up on anything he thinks is really important."

"And you depend on that, don't you?" Eamonn asked.

"I don't know," Cooper said. "I could learn to, I guess."

■ ■ ■

"I'm not even going to ask you what the sex is like," Eamonn laughed. "I know how those quiet ones are in bed. All the stuff they're holding inside the rest of the time comes out like a volcano. It's really wild. You go to bed with a big hulking muscle guy like yourself and you think you're in for something spectacular, but then it fizzles. It isn't the Fourth of July. It isn't even Halloween. It's just another boring night. That's exactly what had happened to me the night I met Eli. Not half an hour earlier, you know? I was just about to head home and jerk off—that's what bad sex the other guy had been. I barely managed to get off. Lucky I hung around. Looking at Eli you'd never think he was a tiger in the sack."

■ ■ ■

Eamonn had put his finger on it, Cooper thought, heading to the subway station. Sex with Griffin. It was the longest Cooper had ever gone having sex with just one person. He hadn't even known if he was capable of it at first. He still wasn't sure. Initially, he'd thought of it as a kind of experiment. Despite Big Steve Fabiani's missionary zeal on the subject, Cooper wasn't convinced that monogamy was even possible for gay men. Some guys, he recognized, seemed to have a predisposition for it. He remembered when his friends Jared and Scott had gotten together. They went to bed on their second date and never looked back. And most recently, Nick Romanovsky, who basically embodied the term sexual omnivore, had become a convert. But even in the face of that, Cooper was ambivalent. Still, though he'd made no rule about it, he was trying it out.

So far it had been fine. Griffin wasn't the best sex he'd ever had, but Griffin was willing and enthusiastic, not to mention a fast learner. And while Griffin wasn't the best sex he'd ever had, he wasn't anything like the worst. Cooper would give him a solid B plus average, with occasional excursions into A minus territory. What that meant long term he wasn't sure of. At the same time, there was a lot about the perpetual hunt for sex that Cooper didn't miss at all. But a lifetime in the land of B plus? Would anybody willingly sign up for that?

■ ■ ■

If Cooper was going to take a break from his experiment, this was the time and place. Back in San Francisco, it would be too easy for it to become a disruption. No matter how careful he was, Griffin was almost certain to find out about it. Cooper dreaded the fallout of that, not because he anticipated any particular guilt over it—God knew he hadn't made any promises to Griffin—but at the same time he recognized that Griffin would inevitably be hurt. They wouldn't necessarily break up over it. But it would put the relationship on a basis that Cooper understood would be less than ideal. If things were going to end, it shouldn't be over some escapade of a sexual nature. It should be about something more fundamental. Compatibility, for instance. The jury was still out on that, too.

■ ■ ■

"Plans tonight?" Mom asked, starting to clear the dinner dishes.

"Nothing in particular," Cooper said.

"Might snow later," Dad said. "Just in time for Christmas Eve tomorrow."

"Be gone by Christmas Day," Mom said. "It always comes too late or too early for a White Christmas."

"Why are there no songs about a White Hanukkah?" Dad asked.

"Because Jews have more sense than that," Cooper laughed.

■ ■ ■

It was one of those typical Greenwich Village bars, which was why Cooper had chosen it. The first two places he'd tried were too chic—guys in cashmere sweaters, guys wearing too much cologne and too much jewelry, guys talking too loud about opera, drag queens at every point of the compass. That was all right if you just wanted a drink and some conversation.

"Hi," the guy said. He was a little like Cooper's gym buddy Jared Bartok and a little like Eamonn Lannaghan.

"Hi," Cooper said. He'd been in the place all of three minutes. New Yorkers worked fast.

"Buy you a drink?"

"Calistoga," Cooper said. "Slice of lime in it."

"Sure."

Cooper looked around the room. Going on six years now he'd spent in places like this, with time off for the current hiatus. Inside walls like these nothing ever seemed to change. It wasn't terrible, but it certainly wasn't the end of the rainbow.

"Name's Patrick," the guy said, handing him his drink.

"I'm Dirk," Cooper said. "Thanks."

"Here's to the eve of Christmas Eve," Patrick said. "You live around here?"

"Just in town for a few days," Cooper said.

"Oh? Where you from?"

"San Diego."

"San Diego," Patrick nodded. "Big navy town."

"That's right."

"But you're not in the navy," Patrick said. "Not with hair that long."

"No," Cooper said. "Former Marine, actually."

"No kidding. You hardly look old enough to be former anything."

"It's the light in here," Cooper laughed.

■ ■ ■

He could have done it, Cooper thought, trudging through a snow flurry toward the subway station. He could have. Patrick was certainly handsome and personable enough. Cooper had had sex with far less attractive men. As far as that went, there had been several other likely candidates in the bar. He knew how to read a room. He could have had any of them. Perhaps more than one. And there had been other bars. Other strangers whose faces would light up when he smiled at them. Other rooms, other jukeboxes, other faces, other pairs of shoulders, other mustaches, other haircuts, other black leather jackets or fisherman's sweaters.

Big Steve and Tristan kept trying to tell him. "Look at Ashby and the Captain," they said. "Look at Jared and Scott."

Hell, even the dogs kept trying to tell him. *A few months of playing house? No, Daddy, more than that. Wake up, already.*

112

You could stay on the hunt forever, if that was your choice. But would you be any better off?

■ ■ ■

Truth to tell, Griffin was not the person he had seemed when Cooper first encountered him. When he imagined it, which was practically never, Cooper's ideal mate was someone self sufficient, fundamentally calm, and absolutely reliable. Spiritually, if not literally, the kind of man his business partner Ned Westerleigh might have hired as a butler, stalwart after the manner of any one of the members of Big Steve's round table, and a wizard in bed. Griffin was none of those things. Not even forseeably. The Labradors' selection had baffled and dismayed Cooper. He understood it from the first, though he'd pretended not to. But once Big Steve announced that Griffin undoubtedly embodied the raw materials, Cooper had to take him a good deal more seriously as a prospective mate.

He had seemed a simple enough guy at first, although so nondescript as to be nearly invisible. Even his growing reputation as a performer at Harry Gordini's legendary Nob Hill piano bar hadn't managed to add much luster to him by the time Cooper took him in hand. At the time it seemed that Griffin needed little more than a decent haircut, some nicer clothes, and a dose of confidence to make him an acceptable companion—at least on a trial basis. There was nothing wrong with his manners, and his vocabulary more than made up for his Kentucy accent, which was atrocious. He was shy, but you could depend on him not to embarrass himself, or you, in public. And he wasn't particularly experienced or skillful in bed, but he was at least accommodating. Not to mention as enthusiastic as anyone could hope for. All that continued to be true as Cooper got to know him better, but it was far from the whole story. And of course, he realized, everything he'd been focused on represented only the most superficial aspects of Griffin's character. When Cooper bought his Jaguar, he'd didn't just kick its tires and take it for a test drive. He looked under the hood, but being no expert that had told him nothing. What he finally did was take it to a mechanic for a full inspection.

As far as he was concerned, that's what the first months of their cohabitation amounted to.

It quickly became apparent that Griffin's psychology was more complicated than Cooper had envisioned. Having grown up with a "performing artist" as a brother, he thought he understood the type. But Griffin and Josh were nothing alike. They were so different from each other, in fact, as to render the concept of "artistic temperament" practically mythical. As Cooper came to understand what made Griffin tick, he realized that the primary springs in the mechanism were his musical abilities, which Cooper admired profoundly without pretending to understand, his enormous insecurity, which was simply baffling, and the almost total sexual deprivation which had apparently been Griffin's perpetual condition in the past. The artistic side of things took care of itself. Griffin was in graduate school, for God's sake. Studying piano performance with none other than Michael Krakowiak. Cooper remembered tricking with Michael once upon a time, probably during his sophomore year at State, but that wasn't important. What mattered was that as a music professor Michael had a national reputation, and under his tutelage Griffin's artistry seemed to be coming along to the satisfaction of everyone concerned. Check that box.

Griffin's insecurity was a challenge. No doubt about it. Whatever its basis, it was so profound that Cooper simply couldn't comprehend it. Praise disturbed Griffin in much the way criticism disturbed other people. He literally seemed frightened of it. And even if that hadn't been the case, praise wasn't a tactic Cooper would have considered employing with any partner. Your pets, certainly. Pavlov and all that. But praise led to dependency, something that was desirable in dogs but not in humans. Praise could turn into manipulation, as could the desire to receive it. There wasn't much to be said in favor of praise. Cooper had seen too many friends and schoolmates ruined by it. The best you could say about it was that it was a constant threat to authenticity in a relationship. What Griffin needed was simply the opportunity to outgrow the worst of his insecurity on his own, however he could manage that, in a supportive environment. And Cooper could certainly give him that. He had the example of Big Steve and the whole gang to go by—that was the kind of thing they did best. Provide Griffin with a kind of emotional safety that was an analogue to the security Cooper gave his dogs. The Labradors again. Could you really treat your live-in the way you treated your pets? Was that the proper care and feeding of a husband? Not that Cooper thought of Griffin as that—yet. But it was Big Steve's preferred term for what he and the rest of the gang all too obviously anticipated Griffin and Cooper would be to each other. And since Big Steve was the one person in the world Cooper could consider taking direction from with regard to his personal life, he agreed to apply that word to Griffin—but so far only in his head.

Dealing with Griffin's sexual hunger was far easier. For one thing, Cooper possessed considerable expertise in that realm. God knows, San Francisco was full of satisfied customers. But it was also because Griffin was just so damned willing. Cooper quickly realized that his lack of experience wasn't due to lack of inclination. And though Griffin never initiated anything, he was surprisingly uninhibited once the action actually got going. In fact, over their months together, Cooper had yet to encounter any resistance from him whatever. No matter what he wanted Griffin to do, Griffin did it. And did it with plenty of enthusiasm. It was the one aspect of life in which he appeared able to step outside his brain and simply let things happen. Griffin might express reluctance about a new sweater or hairstyle (actually, this was a perennial phenomenon) but never about something Cooper demanded in bed. He was almost frighteningly accommodating. Cooper had run up against guys' limits more times than he could remember. It had been one of his primary reasons for avoiding long term arrangements. He never seemed to encounter anyone adventurous enough to take on for the long haul. Not even Kent Norberg, who by the time Cooper met him already had a reputation as one of the nastiest young men in all San Francisco. Kent had been almost as uninhibited as Griffin in bed, but with Kent there had always been some calculation involved. An "I'll let you do that to me, but only if you'll take me to Ned Westerleigh's for tea" or some other such quid pro quo that ultimately kept the sex from being authentic though it had certainly been hot enough. But if you took your time with Griffin, there was apparently nothing he wouldn't do simply for the sake of doing it. Or at least for the sake of pleasing Cooper because pleasing Cooper was apparently a desirable end in itself. Not that Cooper had exhausted either his repertoire or his imagination, but there was no sign so far that Griffin wouldn't accompany him anywhere.

This, Cooper knew, was what the great gay public of San Francisco didn't understand about him and Griffin. They couldn't imagine that a guy as shy and socially awkward as Griffin could possibly be good enough for the amazing and notorious Cooper Luxemberg in bed. And absent that there was no possible reason for the two to still be together. There would have been no point in trying to explain it to them even if Cooper had wanted to. It was none of their business. Over the years he might have conducted himself like a public commodity, but he had never been anything but his own man. In contrast, his real friends apparently didn't question anything about the relationship but his treatment of Griffin. That got old. It would have been intolerable except for his implicit trust in them.

■ ■ ■

It had been a mistake, Cooper thought, sponging the last of the shaving foam off his chest on Christmas Eve morning. He got it now. He shouldn't have come without Griffin. Or at least he shouldn't have come for so long. Nearly two weeks, after all. And without clearing some things up first. He hated the sound in Griffin's voice each night on the phone. Griffin was suffering. He didn't complain, but Cooper knew he was struggling to endure the loneliness.

No, it wasn't the loneliness itself. There were the dogs. There were their friends. It wasn't loneliness *per se*. It was what Griffin suspected the loneliness might signify. If Cooper's absence had truly been necessary, that would have been one thing. But to make Griffin unhappy for no better cause than this?

■ ■ ■

He'd call the airline. It wouldn't be cheap to rebook his flight at such short notice and on a holiday, but you couldn't put a price on what Cooper had decided was at stake.

"Hey, Griffin," he said, rehearsing what he'd say on the phone. "Got a big surprise for you. I'll be in tomorrow afternoon. Pick me up at the airport at. . ."

■ ■ ■

Cooper peeled off two twenties and laid them next to his father's coffee cup.

"What's this?"

It was the mustache, Cooper had finally realized. All this time, and he'd never recognized that his father's face was essentially his face. The same lines and contours. The same nose. The same shape of the eyes. The presence of that mustache had disguised it all. Just like the color and cut of his father's hair had blinded him to its identical texture and growth pattern. Then there were the shoulders. Cooper's years in the gym had been the obscuring factor in that case. This was him thirty years from now.

"I've been spending a lot of time on long distance," Cooper said, pouring himself a cup of coffee and sitting down at the table.

"Crazy bastard," Dad chuckled. "You think we can't afford the phone bill?"

"It's about taking responsibility."

"You've got the rest of your life for that," Dad said. "We're your parents. This will always be your home. Put your money away. There'll be plenty of time to take responsibility later on. Your sons will cost you a bundle, believe me."

There it was. He could leave it alone like he'd been doing for years. Or he could pick up the cue.

"There aren't going to be any sons, Dad."

"Oh?"

"No," Cooper said. "No daughters, either."

"You're sure?" Dad asked. "It's a big thing to be so sure about."

"Yes," Cooper said. "I'm sure."

"I told your mother."

"You did?"

"You think we don't know the signs by now? First Yakov. Then Joshua."

"I'm nothing like them," Cooper said.

"No," Dad nodded. "Except for this one thing, right?"

"I guess."

"So these phone calls," Dad continued. "You must have somebody out in San Francisco."

"Yes."

"Is it serious?"

"Was it serious with Mom? When you'd known her six months?"

"You know the answer to that one," Dad said. "We celebrated our first six months with a wedding. Ike was born nine months to the day after."

"Right."

"I know at this point I'm supposed to ask you all kinds of questions. Yakov's friend is a doctor, you know. Very highly respected. Jewish parents are impressed by such things, I believe."

"Griffin's a graduate student."

"I don't need to know everything about him right this minute," Dad said. "There'll be plenty of time later for me to examine his resume."

"All right."

"Griffin, huh?"

"Griffin," Cooper nodded.

"Not Jewish, I'm guessing."

"Um, no."

"You'll want to go easy telling Mom that part of it."

"Sure."

"You'll bring him with you next time you come," Dad said.

"We'll see," Cooper said.

"Anyway, he'll need a nice present," Dad said, sipping his coffee. "You leaving him alone this time of year. You'll come to the store later and pick out something."

■ ■ ■

"Change of plans, Ed," Cooper told the gym manager. "Flying back to San Francisco tomorrow."

"We'll miss seein' that handsome mug of yours around here, boy," Ed said. "Not to mention the rest of you. Really classed up the place."

"Thanks for everything," Cooper said. "And Merry Christmas."

■ ■ ■

Cooper settled on a bracelet of heavy gauge curb links in white gold. It was outrageously expensive. The Volkswagen convertible he'd considered as a present would have been cheaper. But the bracelet was perfect.

"Your grandfather wore one very much like that," Dad said.

It was all Cooper needed to hear.

"No, son," Dad said. "Put your money away. We gave Ike the engagement ring for Cherie. And we put the down payment on Yakov's house in Tel Aviv. When it's Joshua's turn, may it only happen soon, we'll do something for him, too."

"Dad."

"What's wrong?"

"Um, nothing. Just, well, thanks."

"I'll go in back and get a gift box for this."

■ ■ ■

When Cooper got back to the apartment, he had it to himself. He'd escorted Nanny to the JCC for lunch and mahjong, and Mom was who knew where. For the Luxembergs, Christmas Eve was just another day. He went back to his room and pulled the cassette out of his luggage. Back in the living room, he slipped it into Dad's tape player.

The music swelled into the room. He really had underestimated Griffin. In every possible way. When they first met, he'd thought, "here's a nice, simple kid who plays the piano." The reality was more complex than he could have imagined. He didn't know when or how he'd get to the bottom of it. It was the kind of challenge, he realized, that always brought out the best in him.

■ ■ ■

"What's this you're listening to?"

Cooper hadn't heard her come in. He'd fallen asleep. That's what contemplation always did—put him out like a light.

"It's a tape of a recital a friend of mine gave."

"I had no idea you were interested in classical music," Mom said. "What is that? Liszt?"

"Rachmaninoff."

"Your friend is very talented."

"Yes."

"What's her name?"

"His name is Griffin, Mom."

"Griffin," Mom said.

"Right."

"Just what kind of friend is he?"

"We live together," Cooper said. "Not roommates."

"I see," Mom said. "You know, I told Dad you were like Yakov. Before we even knew about Joshua. Back then, you understand?"

"How could you not have known about Joshua? If there was one of us who. . ."

"It's not something you expect of any of your children, sweetie."

"Right."

"He really does play divinely, doesn't he?"

"He graduated from the conservatory last spring," Cooper said. "He's at the university now, doing graduate work."

"What's his last name, honey?"

"MacDonald."

"That doesn't sound very Jewish."

"He's Scottish Presbyterian from Kentucky."

"You'll want to take it easy telling Dad that part."

MAY, 1980

"FitzMerlin, over here."

The deep rumble of that voice made Rupert tingle all over. It called to mind officers shouting orders at their troops on brisk mornings, jockeys urging on their mounts, coaches exhorting athletes on lush playing fields, a host, really, of masculine and quintessentially British rituals.

"What is it, Cavendish?" Rupert asked.

He knew perfectly well what. It could only be one thing: what it always and invariably was. He asked the question only out of rhetorical imperative. In any such scene, there were conventions which must be observed. It was like high tea at the manor house. Or Kabuki theatre. By sundown of his first day here at Winchester, alma mater of untold generations of Rupert's tribe, the venerable House of FItzMerlin, he had been acknowledged as the most celebrated beauty of his year. Once that was established, he climbed the ladder with astonishing rapidity. Mostly the ascent entailed enduring slobbery kisses from boys a year older than himself or engaging in the occasional wank session with boys a year older than that. Lately he'd ascended even further. And now Cavendish. The summit. At last.

"Because it's there," he muttered to himself. But really, it was far more than that.

Cavendish was comfortably over six feet tall and possessed vast shoulders. His chin was perpetually gritty with black stubble. Rupert couldn't imagine why the masters let him get away with it. They were such sticklers for hygiene they should have required him to shave twice a day if that's what was required to keep him looking less disreputeble. Cavendish's smoky eyes glinted. His raven curls ravished the eye. The younger boys called him "El Greco", but only behind his back and in breathless, reverential whispers. The real El Greco had been a Spaniard, paradoxically enough. Rupert learned this in art class. Cavendish, on the other hand, was as English as steak and kidney pie, the novels of Charles Dickens (save that one aberration), and the sport of cricket, for all his physical exoticism. He was the *ne plus ultra* of lubricious schoolboy fantasy, and he had finally realized he must have Rupert.

Rupert couldn't imagine what had taken him so long. He finally concluded that Cavendish regarded him as dessert. After having dutifully ingested his meat, veg, and starches, Cavendish was ready to indulge in what he'd had his eye on all along.

■ ■ ■

"You know what I like to do best?" Cavendish panted, several geological epochs later.

"One hears you have a particular speciality," Rupert said, pulling down his pants.

"Good lad."

■ ■ ■

Rupert's bum had been widely coveted all that year. Many were the supplicants he had turned away disappointed, including, it had to be noted, more than one of the junior masters. Admittedly, these young men's overtures were sufficiently subtle as to leave them beyond censure should Rupert have taken exception and mentioned it to Matron or the Padre. "*My boy, I'm sure you're just imagining things*" was how the response would have been expressed. And subsequently, Rupert would have found himself on a sort of "watch list" of emotionally unstable types. He couldn't begrudge the masters their caution. Boys might be boys, but a master could end up in a sticky situation indeed. Still, there was little doubt that Rupert had flaunted his prized *asset* with panache and even, it might be said, a certain profligacy, while defending its sanctity with determination and finesse. That defense was due, however, neither to fear of nor distaste for the physical act in question. As the rarest of commodities and a truly breathtaking example of that particular anatomical structure, access to it could only be granted to the most worthy of recipients. Rupert had only one chance to parlay it into the kind of advantages he felt he, and it, deserved. He'd be a fool to squander it foolishly. He had to make the most of the opportunity it presented. He had to save it until the most propitious set of circumstances arrived on the scene.

Benjamin Denis Cosmo St. Claude Cavendish was the only possible man Rupert could conceivably bestow this treasure on. Athlete, scholar, dreamboat, and quiet, behind the scenes hell raiser, Cavendish was like the hero of one of those thick, turgid, morally uplifting yet unconsciously provocative mid-Victorian novels of school life. In other words, he was an archetype. And since Rupert considered himself an archetype as well, if of a somewhat different variety, what passed between them would constitute a kind of collision of archetypes. Or, considered from a Hegelian perspective—because Rupert had just been learning about Hegel—Cavendish was thesis, Rupert was antithesis, and their collision would result in—who knew? Something extremely tasty was his guess. And hopefully lasting.

Rupert considered this collision both necessary and inevitable, which he supposed made him a sort of carnal Marxist, and he spared no effort ensuring that its necessity and inevitability were apparent to Cavendish while at the same time going to great lengths to appear oblivious to the relevant historical forces himself. It wasn't a question of Cavendish's taste. There was no doubt that Rupert's bum ticked that box. That was the most inevitable aspect of the entire matter. But Cavendish, who was almost certain to be appointed head boy for his final year at the school, was discreet about certain activities almost to the point of opacity. And Cavendish, if only one tenth of the rumors were to be believed, had a dauntingly full dance card. Finally, Cavendish was the type of man who would never succumb to the wiles of overt seduction. He had to be the pursuer. His quarry must give the impression of reluctance at the very least, if not outright terror. Otherwise Cavendish lost interest. So

123

Rupert bided his time. "I'll chase Cavendish until he manages by superhuman exertions to catch and subdue me" became his *modus operandi*.

■ ■ ■

"Good lad," Cavendish panted.

"Mmmh," Rupert responded. The intial stages of the encounter had gone better than he dared to hope. Cavendish's physical strength was no surprise, given his impressive physique. The intensity of his attack had been tempered with technique marked by a surprising mastery of nuance, which Rupert judged could only be the result of extensive practice. But the most gratifying aspect of the whole thing was Cavendish's unexpected solicitude. He'd taken surprising pains to ensure that the experience was a highly pleasurable one not just for himself but for Rupert as well. And it had been. For his part, and in deference to both the sensibilities inherent in their socio-cultural context and Cavendish's own psychological makeup, Rupert did everything he could to give the impression that the title of this encounter was "Conquest", though he internally referred to it by the one he preferred—"Merger". Rupert's father, heir apparent to one of Britain's most venerable, if misunderstood, titles, was in addition a businessman of a particularly aggressive type. He invariably called the mergers he engineered between companies he already owned and others he wished to control "acquisitions." Which, Rupert considered, was just another name for plunder. That's how he wanted Cavendish to regard himself. As the supreme plunderer.

II

Now that the initial objective had been achieved, Rupert must consolidate his position. It would be tricky. He had to maintain the role of prey because Cavendish must be allowed to continue to think of himself as predator. But predators by nature were promiscuous in their hunting, and Cavendish somehow had to be prevented from moving on to other, fresher victims, if not in individual instances at least as a habit. Rupert had to find a way to become indispensable.

He had heard it said, by people in a position to know, that a certain species of head boy could rule an entire school merely by judicious exercise of his own willie. Cavendish obviously qualified as an example of the type—at least potentially. What Rupert must do was find a way to rule the head boy by judicious exercise of his own nether regions until such time as he could succeed to the office of head boy himself. And Cavendish could never be allowed to realize that he was being ruled in that way or how his domination had come about.

■ ■ ■

It was hard going at first. Cavendish showed no inclination for a repeat engagement. And there was very little Rupert could do in the way of attempting to convince him otherwise without opening himself to accusations that he was a tart. That would have an opposite effect to what he desired. There were several instructive examples to ponder, and he pondered them at length. In addition, he kept his ear to the ground. Distressing as his observations might prove, he had to keep track of his quarry. Over the first week and a half after their "collision", Cavendish entertained Turner, Williams, Gregory, and Hanson. None of them could hold a candle to Rupert, of course. But they apparently didn't need to. Their availability had been a sufficient precipitating agent. It was all Rupert could do not to march right up to Cavendish and say "now see here." But he didn't.

The next ten days saw Cavendish availing himself of Ronson, Fletcher, and Smythe-Smythe Minor. Still Rupert restrained himself. He couldn't imagine any of those striplings affording satisfaction equal to what he did. Surely Cavendish would realize, sooner or later, that there really was no substitute.

■ ■ ■

"See here, FitzMerlin."

"Yes, Cavendish?"

"I wonder if I might prevail on you to. . ."

"Why certainly, Cavendish," Rupert said, flashing his most winning smile.

"You will? Thanks most awfully, old chap."

JUNE, 1982

Griffin spotted the man again in baggage claim. He'd barely been able to take his eyes off him the whole flight. While Cooper dozed in the seat beside him, Griffin stared. The man was the same physical type as Cooper: just over medium height, with massive shoulders and a ridiculously slim waist. He even had the same black hair, pale skin, and terrifying cheekbones. They could easily have been cousins. Which, Griffin supposed, meant that the man was probably Armenian or Greek rather than Jewish. And not gay—Griffin had been sure of that because Griffin had absolutely no faith in his own gaydar. So there the man was in baggage claim accompanied by a haughty looking blond who could only be a boyfriend. As so often happened, it wasn't Griffin's gaydar that let him down, but his faith in himself.

"We'll drop your luggage at Joshua's apartment and then go uptown and grab dinner. By the time we've walked that off, he'll be ready to leave the theatre," Andrew said. Andrew and Josh had either been together for five years or three years depending on how you accounted for the two years when Andrew had gone back into the Peace Corps. They considered themselves a couple, though Andrew maintained his own residence in New Haven, where he taught at Yale. This made him such a notable figure that Griffin could hardly look him in the eye. He spent weekends in New York, but with matinees Saturdays were Josh's busiest days and thus their weekend was Sunday evening through the departure of Andrew's train early Monday. In other words, their time together was limited, at best. This week, however, Andrew would be in New York full time. The university term had just ended. When he explained it he made it sound as inconsequential as a preschool shutting down for a three day weekend.

Griffin's bags were the first off the plane and Cooper's were the last. That was typical. Cooper's baggage claim karma was the opposite of his parking space karma. It was pretty miraculous when his luggage arrived on the same plane with him.

"You packed heavy," Andrew observed.

Griffin supposed they had by Peace Corps standards.

"We'll be here for a week," Cooper explained. "And then it's directly on to the Caribbean with Mom and Dad."

"You could always do laundry while you're here," Andrew said.

"Where? At Josh's place? Oh, right—no facilities."

"There are laundromats," Andrew suggested. "There's one not a block away from Josh's place."

"Which Josh refuses to go to. He schleps his washing up to Riverside Drive every two weeks," Cooper said. "On the subway, yet."

"You could do that, too," Andrew said.

"Or I could take our stuff over to the East River and beat it against rocks," Cooper suggested. "What do you think, Griffin?"

This wasn't an argument, Griffin recognized. This was just how Jews said hello. By minding each other's business.

■ ■ ■

"This is our favorite Armenian restaurant," Andrew said, leading them down the half flight of stairs from the sidewalk.

They were somewhere a couple blocks off Times Square. Griffin had lost track, and besides, his grasp of Manhattan geography was approximate. He wondered what Armenians ate. This was not idle curiosity. His sensitive digestion and expensive theatre tickets for later in the evening made for a volatile combination.

■ ■ ■

128

Griffin ordered the duck. Duck was one of the few things he was too intimidated by to cook for himself. Besides, Andrew assured him that Josh was crazy about the duck here. Aside from Cooper's business partner, Ned Westerleigh, Josh was hands down the most urbane individual Griffin knew personally, so that was recommendation enough.

"Joshua had never been to Israel," Andrew said. "Can you believe it?"

"Actually, yes," Cooper said.

"Sure," Andrew said. "Of course. But I mean. . ."

"Mom and Dad were pretty much indifferent to the whole thing," Cooper said. "And for that matter, Israel came to us. Uncle Marcus visited regularly. And he brought Aunt Yael and the cousins with him a couple of times."

"Sure," Andrew said, "but it's not the same thing."

"Nothing ever is," Cooper said.

"You'd love the house Naftali and Yakov bought," Andrew said. "In Tel Aviv there are whole neighborhoods of International Style houses. Perfectly preserved. They were built during the twenties. It's one of those."

The duck was as good as Griffin had been promised. And their cute waiter was so flummoxed by Cooper's incandescence that he could hardly talk. It was the perfect New York dining experience. Griffin felt dizzyingly cosmopolitan just to be sitting there.

■ ■ ■

"How was the show?" Cooper asked.

"Grueling," Josh said.

Apparently there had never been a performance in the history of Broadway where anything actually went as intended.

"But you know what they say," Josh said.

"What do they say?" Griffin asked.

"Any performance you can walk away from on your own two feet. . ."

"I thought that was plane crashes," Griffin said.

"It's the same thing," Josh shrugged.

A train pulled into the station, but it wasn't the Number 1, so they kept waiting.

■ ■ ■

When the sofa bed in Josh's guestroom was unfolded, there wasn't space for you to walk around it. If Grifffin needed to go to the bathroom during the night, he'd have to clamber over his husband. As massive as Cooper was, he seemed more so in the confined spaces of Manhattan.

"Welcome to New York, sweetheart," he said, folding his shirt and looking around for someplace to put it down.

"Yes, sweetheart," Griffin said. "Welcome to New York."

■ ■ ■

"Andrew has a family thing he has to go to," Josh explained, "and I've got about a million errands to run before my matinee. So Eli's going to be in charge of you."

Griffin liked Josh's upstairs neighbor, Eli Danziger. He was handsome without being ruthless about it and he had opinions without being ruthless about them, and unlike most of the people Griffin and Cooper hung around with in San Francisco, he didn't look as though he lived at the gym. He was fit the way Griffin was fit and consequently looked normal.

It was the perfect New York Sunday morning, sunny without being too warm, and tranquil enough that Josh's stretch of Hudson Street was virtually traffic free. Even the dogs being walked seemed unusually serene. Of course, Griffin mused, they knew it was the weekend as well as their masters did.

"Those two will be down in a minute," Josh said.

"There's no hurry," Cooper said, more due to his contrarian reflex when dealing with members of his family than as a genuine disavowal of impatience.

Just then, Eli and Andrew erupted through the front door of the building.

"He is not, Andrew," Eli insisted.

"Is, too," Andrew said.

"Cooper," Eli said. "Griffin. Good to see you guys."

He hugged them in succession. Griffin really needed to ask about the cologne he was wearing. Smooth and subtle, it was the antithesis of the take no prisoners scents Cooper favored. It was something Griffin could actually imagine himself wearing. It was a constant source of exasperation for Cooper that Griffin didn't wear any fragrance at all. "*Are you sure you're gay?*" he would ask when Griffin rejected his recommendations.

"Let's go," Josh said.

"I tell you," Eli said, "Cousin Talbot is not a registered Republican. He just said that to provoke you."

"I don't understand," Andrew said. "Why would he do that?"

"Because Talbot is Talbot," Eli said.

"And you're easily provoked," Josh said.

"How far is it to the restaurant?" Cooper asked. "You know about Griffin's blood sugar."

■ ■ ■

After breakfast, their objective was in a park way up on the West Side just a few blocks from where Cooper's parents lived. To one side of the park, rows of apartment houses faced west across it. To the other, the parkway followed the banks of the Hudson River.

"I remember this place," Cooper said.

"The ball field is up that way," Eli said, gesturing vaguely in the direction of the George Washington Bridge.

Griffin braced himself for the spectacle that was Eamonn Lannaghan.

They were just in sight of the baseball diamond when they saw the blur of a child streaking toward them, arms waving frantically and sandy hair flopping in his slipstream. A smaller, black haired boy trailed in his wake, valiantly attempting to keep up.

"Uncle Eli, Uncle Eli," the larger boy called. "Liam just hit a double."

"Did he, Tory?" Eli called back.

"He did," Tory shouted, hurling himself into Eli's arms. "He got two RBI's so far. Two."

By then the younger boy had caught up. He stood looking confused for a moment, then hurled himself into Cooper's arms.

"That's Cooper, Mickey," Eli said. "And the other one's name is Griffin."

"You remember them," Tory assured Mickey. "From Christmas, right? They're cool."

■ ■ ■

Eli's friends mostly didn't approve of Eamonn Lannaghan. Which was a shame, because there was nothing particularly objectionable about the man and a whole lot to like, or at the very least admire. But he was that nemesis, a closet case who married and fathered children in an attempt to pass as straight or, conversely, a straight man who liked a little gay action on the side. Either definition fit, though Eamonn rejected both. He rejected any definition at all. And that couldn't be tolerated. Not in a friend's husband, however quasi. Except that Eli did. Eli had been tolerating it for seven years now. Griffin had heard the situation dissected endlessly, sometimes in Eli's presence but more often not, since first making his acquaintance with this New York branch of Cooper's tribe. He had been as outraged as they obviously expected him to be until he actually met the men involved. Then it got complicated. The more he pondered it, the more it defied conventional analysis.

■ ■ ■

Sitting side by side on the front row of the bleachers, with not a shirt in sight and the legs of their walking shorts rolled up nearly to their crotches the better to expose acres of heroically muscled thigh to the sunshine, Cooper and Eamonn were obviously two of a kind. Had they been standing, they'd have been just enough above medium height for it to be apparent, though no one would have described either of them as actually tall. They had the same improbably broad shoulders, the same densely packed, extravagantly curving and bulging musculature, the same dramatic V-taper down to the same tight waist and washboard belly, and those matching thighs. The differences between them consisted of minor details only, such as which pair of nipples had greater diameter and/or prominence, which navel was an outie, which chest had been shaven most recently, and which man sported the deeper tan. Eamonn was, in other words, Cooper's unmistakable avatar. Or, for that matter, a straying member of the band of demigods of which Cooper was a charter member back in San Francisco.

Above the neck the differences were more obvious. Eamonn was the quintessential square jawed Captain America type, his thick mop of smooth textured sandy hair parted on the right and generally left to its own devices or, as that afternoon, invisible under a New York Yankees cap. Cooper had that sharp-featured European runway model look, and not a strand of his raven hair had ever been seen out of place—at least in public. In Griffin's eyes, pure physical magnificence excused Eamonn of every indictment Eli's "concerned" friends leveled. Looking at Eamonn, Griffin understood Eli's choice perfectly. He'd have made the same choice himself if he'd been required to. He wasn't proud of it. He comprehended the profound transgressiveness of the position, but he knew it wouldn't have dissuaded him. He realized it immediately on meeting Eamonn. He'd heard all the horrifying details of the relationship previously, but meeting the man had negated everything. He turned to Eli and said, just above the threshold of audibility, "I get it completely. If Cooper had been—I mean when I first met him. . . I mean, I just really get it."

That cemented Griffin's friendship with Eli, though it had never been mentioned again.

Griffin knew that somehow Cooper sensed his realization. He thought it was interesting that Cooper never criticized the relationship. When Josh and Andrew and their friends started in on Eamonn, Cooper kept his mouth shut.

■ ■ ■

In the bottom of the final inning, Liam hit a home run with players on first and third that ended the game. Tory and Mickey screamed themselves hoarse as he rounded the bases, but three year old Renzo, namesake of his Grandpa DeBartolomeo, slumbered on in Griffin's lap.

"Don't worry, Uncle Griffin," Mickey said, spontaneously promoting him, "he'll wake up in time for hot dogs and ice cream."

■ ■ ■

Four grown men in charge of Eamonn's four offspring. Liam, age ten, Tory, eight, Mickey, six, and three year old Lorenzo. The odds were strongly against the grownups, Griffin mused. But, as he already knew, the Lannaghan boys were subject to the most stringent of upbringings. High spirited youngsters, they were nevertheless beautifully behaved and well on the way to responsible young manhood. This was apparent when Liam patiently cleaned the mustard off Renzo's face with a moistened napkin *without being told to*, for instance. Or Tory favored Mickey with an impromptu lesson in tying his sneakers. Griffin was dazzled. They weren't merely beautiful.

Of course they were still boys, so hot dogs and ice cream was a rackety repast indeed. In the middle of it Eamonn announced quietly that Maribel had pulled a double shift at the hospital and wasn't expected home until the next afternoon. In response to this, Eli nodded slightly and if Cooper had been one of the Luxemberg-MacDonald Labradors, his chin would have tilted upward as his nose sniffed the air.

■ ■ ■

They trekked back to the park. Cooper lifted Tory onto his shoulders piggy-back, which caused a domino effect. Eli carried Mickey and Griffin carried Renzo. Liam apparently considered himself too grown up for such treatment and sauntered along beside his father. When they reached the Volvo, he supervised passenger loading. Mickey rode shotgun. Eli and Lorenzo got into the back seat. That left the third row for Liam and Tory. Cooper slammed the tailgate shut.

"Great seeing you guys," Eamonn said.

Watching Eamonn and Cooper hug was almost pornographic, Griffin thought. His own hug from Eamonn was sweaty and fragrant.

"See you soon," Mickey called, leaning out the window as the car pulled away.

"Fasten that seatbelt, young man," Cooper cautioned him.

■ ■ ■

As soon as they emerged from the subway station, Cooper's shirt came off again. He never went bare-chested on the streets of San Francisco, but here in New York on a perfect Sunday afternoon, the rules were different. They entered the park and found a bench in the shade.

"How do those two get away with it?" Griffin asked.

"They'll put on a big production of making up the sofa bed in the living room for Uncle Eli," Cooper said. "Wouldn't be surprised if young Liam isn't in charge of the operation. The boys have a very early bedtime, of course, even though school's out. That will leave the coast clear. After Eamonn fucks the living daylights out of Eli they'll hit the showers. Probably together and probably for second helpings. Then Eli will bed down there in the living room, where the first Lannaghan son to get up in the morning will find him. As soon as Eamonn gets up, he'll strip the marital bed and throw the sheets in the washing machine. He'll make it back up with fresh sheets while Eli feeds the boys breakfast. When their grandmother arrives to take care of them for the day, she'll find everything under control. She grew up on a farm in Germany back before and during the war, and she has a very European outlook on male bonding. Nothing suspicious at all about what she sees going on between her youngest son and his best friend. When Maribel gets home later there'll be nothing out of the ordinary for anybody to tell her about. Just 'oh, yeah, mom, after the game Uncle Eli came over and spent the night.' Like he's done dozens of times before."

"How do you know all that?" Griffin asked.

"I don't," Cooper said. "It's just educated guessing. But I'd put money on every detail."

"Amazing."

"Don't get the wrong idea," Cooper said. "Nobody's getting away with anything, really. Maribel knows exactly what's going on. And believe it or not, she appreciates the trouble Eamonn and Eli go to covering their tracks. They're not hiding anything from her. They're helping her hide it from everyone else. That's the one thing she wouldn't forgive. If their families found out."

"Huh?"

"Come on, Griffin. Think about it. He's as spectacular a man as you'll ever meet. He's a fabulous father. You saw that this afternoon. To his buddies at Engine Company Whatever-the-Fuck he's a bona fide hero. His friends all want to be him and their wives all want to fuck him. But his buddies know he'd never think of causing that kind of *tsuris*. They trust him with their lives on the job and around their womenfolk and kids at all times. Maribel trusts him, too. She knows no bleached blond bimbo is ever going to show up on her doorstep carrying a baby and claiming it's his. He's the perfect husband except for this one thing, and she knows she can trust him never to let it ruin what they have. And Praise the Lord, his boyfriend is perfect for the circumstances. As far as she knows, he never makes demands and he knows his place. She'd have to be crazy to blow all that up."

"Lots of women would," Griffin said. "Most of them are emotionally incapable of sharing their husbands that way."

"Not Maribel," Cooper said. "She's willing to pay whatever the market demands for the life she has with her husband and her boys. Eamonn knew when he married her what kind of wife she'd be. Long before he ever met Eli he had the whole thing figured out."

"You've met her," Griffin said. "What's she like?"

"Drop dead gorgeous," Cooper said. "Smart as the dickens. The only reason she didn't go to medical school is in those very traditional Puerto Rican families girls don't do things like that. And she's got a great sense of humor. You'd adore her."

"I can't believe it," Griffin said, shaking his head.

"No," Cooper said. "What bothers you about it is how much sense it makes. How right it seems. You know you're supposed to be horrified like all these jaded New Yorkers, but you're not."

■ ■ ■

On their way to Griffin's in-laws' apartment, they stopped for Chinese takeout, the traditional Luxemberg Sunday supper. Spring rolls. Pot stickers. Barbecue pork ribs. Fried rice. Mongolian beef. General Tso's chicken. Shrimp in lobster sauce. Sweet and sour pork. Pepper steak.

"How many people are we feeding?"

"Mom, Dad, Aunt Rosie, Lou, Nanny, Josh, Andrew, you, and me," Cooper said.

"Better add an order of Cashew Chicken and one of Beef Lo Mein. Mom and Dad will eat leftovers for lunch all week."

■ ■ ■

As they walked up the block in the long shadows of early evening, Griffin thought it must have been like growing up in a magical kingdom.

■ ■ ■

There was more to Griffin's in-laws than met the eye. They owned a successful business and despite being Jews had voted for Reagan, a fact which, when he was reminded of it, made smoke pour out of Cooper's ears. They were, in other words, a kind of sociological stereotype. But at the same time, three out of their four sons were gay and they'd apparently never uttered a word of protest or disapproval. Jake (aka Yakov) had married a surgeon. Josh had married a Yale professor. As a non-Jew, a musician, and now a teacher, Griffin continually expected Shoshonnah and Willi's pent up frustration to be aimed at him. So far there had been no sign of it.

"How do you like your new job?" Shoshonnah asked. Griffin was helping her rinse plates and flatware and load them into the dishwasher. *Chez* Luxemberg, takeout didn't mean paper plates.

"You know, I didn't expect to like it at all at first," Griffin said, "but I really enjoyed it. Of course every day it's a tossup between my students and my colleagues to see who's the craziest."

"And how does that turn out, dear?"

"The adults generally win hands down. The boys are just boys. But some of those teachers are absolute lunatics."

"I'm sure that's true. You must have found it all a big change."

"Sure," Griffin nodded. "You spend a couple of decades communing with your instrument and a bunch of dead composers. Then suddenly you're spending all day every day interacting with live people. Lots of them. It was a real shock. I'm mostly over it now."

■ ■ ■

"Now here's shot of all four of them," Aunt Rosie said. Rosie Stern Wallach was not really Cooper's aunt. She and Shoshonnah met in first grade and had been more or less inseparable ever since. She had been present when Shoshonnah and Willi met and had been the first to know about Shoshonnah's pregnancies. "Cooper must have been three when this was taken. See? You could already tell he was going to be a dreamboat."

"He looks like a baby thug in that picture," Josh snorted. "Like he's hiding a tiny switchblade in his pantsleg."

"He had to get tough in a hurry," Rosie giggled, "with you three and my two older ones torturing him constantly."

"We never tortured him," Josh insisted.

"You were worse than the Spanish Inquisition," Rosie said. "Honestly."

■ ■ ■

"Excited about your Caribbean vacation, gentlemen?" Lou Wallach asked.

"We're just sorry you won't be coming along," Cooper said.

"Lou's not cleared to travel yet," Rosie explained. "On account of the new pacemaker. We'll be down the week after."

"Lucky for you guys," Lou said. "You'll get to put up in the honeymoon suite."

"Honeymoon suite?" Griffin asked.

"Wait 'til you see it," Cooper laughed.

■ ■ ■

Josh and Andrew had gone to Israel back in May. The trip entailed a ten day absence from the show, which hadn't endeared Josh to management.

"You wouldn't believe how much Marcus' youngest boy looks like Cooper," Andrew said.

"It's true," Josh said. "Yoel acts like Cooper, too. Stubborn as a mule."

"I prefer the term 'determined'," Cooper laughed.

"*Farbisn* is what he is," Willi said. "Pig-headed. He's like his grandfather. That was the stubbornest man who ever lived. And his great-grandfather was almost as bad. It's a family trait."

"Yakov's worse than I am," Cooper insisted.

"You wouldn't say that if you saw him now," Josh said. "His husband has him housetrained."

"Oy, that Dr. Goldman," Rosie said.

"Naftali's a sweetheart," Andrew agreed.

"That thick silver hair," Rosie rhapsodized, "and those beautiful manners. Like a United Nations delegate."

■ ■ ■

Nannie Freitag was a charming old woman who seemed confused about who everyone was. She addressed Rosie repeatedly as "your Grace". She referred to Josh as "the Dauphin," and Willi was "the Lord Chamberlain." Coming face to face with Griffin a few minutes after their initial

139

introduction she said "young man, are you a revolutionary? I adore revolutionaries." He told her no but that he'd been raised Presbyterian. She was delighted with that answer. "Why my dear," she said, clapping her hands, "it's practically the same thing."

■ ■ ■

"Is Nanny Freitag all right?" Griffin asked.

"Doesn't she seem all right?" Cooper asked.

"She's having the time of her life," Griffin said. "Except she doesn't seem to know whose life it is."

"Mom says she's faking the gaga thing. We're not supposed to encourage her."

■ ■ ■

"Don't forget," Willi said. "The car will pick you up in front of Josh's building at seven a.m. Saturday."

"And if you're not ready," Shoshonnah said, "you'll be out of luck. He still has to pick us up here and get us all to the airport. It's a very tight schedule. Make sure he gets his packing done the night before, Griffin."

"Aye, aye," Griffin said.

"We can't wait to get there," Cooper said. "We won't be late."

■ ■ ■

"How was the ballgame?" Andrew asked as they waited for the Number 1 train.

"Great," Griffin said. "Liam's a real superstar."

"That bastard's in the wrong line of work," Josh complained. "He ought to quit the fire department and start selling used cars. He'd make a fortune."

■ ■ ■

As soon as they got back to the apartment, Josh and Andrew left for New Haven, where they'd be spending the rest of Sunday night and all day Monday.

"Now's our chance," Cooper said.

"Huh?"

"We can snoop through Josh's stuff."

"You will not," Griffin said.

"Well, I'm at least going to rearrange his socks so it looks like I snooped through his stuff."

"Not even that," Griffin said.

"How are you going to stop me?"

"I have my ways," Griffin laughed, unzipping his jeans.

"Curses, foiled again," Cooper said. "I'm just a sucker for a cute butt."

■ ■ ■

Josh's trip to Israel had forced the postponement of his birthday party. Eli's cousin, Talbot Kleinbaum, had just bought a loft in Soho. He was their host Tuesday evening. The party started early even though the honoree wouldn't arrive until after his evening performance.

"I socked away all the money Oswaldo threw at me," Talbot said, giving them the tour. Oswaldo was his Cubano ex sugar daddy. "That's how I was able to afford that place in the West Forties in the first place. And then after the renovations, I made a killing when I flipped it, so here we are."

"Understood," Cooper said, "but don't Washington and Jefferson require a lot of upkeep?"

Washington and Jefferson were the names of the black bodybuilders Talbot described as his husbands.

"You'd better believe those two are self supporting," Eli said. "And for that matter, our videos are generating quite a bit of revenue."

In the videos, Washington and Jefferson fucked whatever twinkies Talbot was able to round up for them. Sometimes they took turns fucking Talbot himself. In their most recent release, the two men actually fucked Talbot simultaneously, something it hadn't occurred to Griffin was physically possible until he saw it.

Griffin wasn't what you'd call a devotee of porn, but when the porn in question featured people he knew personally, he felt like he at least needed to be conversant with it.

■ ■ ■

The guest list included Josh's long time gal pal Jill Wagstaffe and her new boyfriend, a well preserved fifty something captain of industry type whose ex-wife apparently lived in Florida.

"I thought Jill was a lesbian," Griffin said.

"So did her girlfriend," Eli laughed.

"She's starting law school this fall," Andrew said. "The people at the soap are going to schedule around her classes. But she'll probably have to quit live theatre for the duration."

■ ■ ■

Also present were Andrew's younger brother, Theodore, and his fiancée, Shizuka Nederlander, a half Jewish half Japanese beauty who modeled while working on her Ph.D. in microbiology. On her spike heels, Shizuka was the tallest person in the room even though Andrew and Josh were both six footers.

■ ■ ■

"The boys are crazy about you two," Eli said. "You know what Renzo said?"

"What?" Griffin asked.

"'Uncle Griffin is my best friend'."

■ ■ ■

"What did you guys do today?" Jill asked.

"Tourist stuff," Cooper shrugged.

"The Statue of Liberty, Battery Park, and the observation deck of the World Trade Center," Griffin said, "to be specific."

■ ■ ■

The buffet was heavy on shellfish. Oysters on the half shell. A chafing dish of mussels poached in white wine, garlic and clarified butter. Crab cakes. Shrimp wrapped in bacon and broiled.

"An orthodox rabbi's worst nightmare," Jill said, filling her plate as Griffin tried to make up his mind what to try first. "A roomful of non-observant Jews, many of them homosexual, eating this poison."

■ ■ ■

"You notice who isn't here tonight," Eli said, spooning chopped shrimp in sour cream onto a slice of baguette.

Griffin nodded.

"He wasn't invited. I mean, sure. He's on shift tonight. He couldn't have come anyway. But he would have liked to be invited. They never do unless I practically throw a tantrum."

"That doesn't seem fair," Griffin said.

"Andrew and Josh are always going on about how we have to stand up for our right to be out and proud," Eli said, "but don't Eamonn and I have the right to do it our way?"

■ ■ ■

"So what have you two got planned for tomorrow?" Andrew's brother Theodore asked.

"The Guggenheim," Cooper said.

"It'll probably take most of the day," Griffin said.

"MOMA on Wednesday."

"Another marathon," Griffin said.

"And Thursday?" Theodore asked.

"Probably spend the whole day at the baths," Cooper said.

"I hope you understand that he's joking," Griffin said.

■ ■ ■

"Josh got us theatre tickets for tomorrow, Wednesday, and Thursday nights," Cooper explained to Rance Jefferson, who, it turned out, was about to finish his M.B.A. at Fordham. "So our dance card is pretty full."

"That's cool," Rance said. "It's hard to run out of things to do in New York."

■ ■ ■

"You should really take Griffin out to the island," JoJo Washington insisted. "I have a good friend with a place in the Pines. Fancy? Darling, can we talk? Poor little ol' me could hardly bring myself to move my bowels in the place, that's how fancy it is, and I was only in the downstairs crapper. He'd be happy to put you up for a night. Midweek, you understand? Weekends are way too crowded. Only don't say anything about it to Ms. Talbot. She's a very jealous woman."

■ ■ ■

"I've made a dinner reservation for you for tomorrow night," Andrew said, handing Cooper a business card. "Six-thirty. It's our favorite Italian restaurant. It's just three blocks from the theatre. When you get there, tell them you have an eight o'clock curtain. They'll make sure you're on time. And Griffin should have the *osso bucco*."

■ ■ ■

As instructed, Griffin had the *osso bucco*. It was good, but not as good as at his favorite place in North Beach. The show was good but not great. It was

144

certainly interesting to see Josh on stage. In real life he was a low grade depressive with catatonic tendencies, but on stage he sparkled. He was charismatic. He was ridiculously cute.

"That's how he always was when we were growing up," Cooper said when Griffin mentioned it during intermission. "Nowadays he saves it all for onstage."

"So he's a method chorus boy?"

"Exactly."

■ ■ ■

Just before they left the apartment Wednesday morning, the phone rang. The answering machine engaged, and Andrew's voice came over the line.

"Cooper," he said. "I've made a dinner reservation for the two of you for six-thirty."

He spoke a name and address and then repeated himself.

"It's our favorite Chinese restaurant," he continued. "That address is just around the corner from Rockefeller Center. You can't miss it. And Griffin should have the crispy duck."

"God dammit," Cooper fumed. "What? Does he think we're children? We can't make our own dinner plans?"

■ ■ ■

Griffin had the crispy duck. It was fine, but he'd had better on Stockton Street. Theatre that night was off-off Broadway. He wouldn't have thought a musical based on *Hedda Gabler* could actually work. After the performance he still wasn't sure.

■ ■ ■

"It's right next door to the theatre," Andrew explained, his voice surprisingly nasal over the speaker phone.

Cooper had his fingers in his ears.

"It's our favorite French restaurant. Griffin should order the *boeuf bourgig-non*. It's the best this side of Paris."

Cooper mimed gagging himself and throwing up.

"Six o'clock. I know your curtain is at eight, but tell them seven-thirty."

■ ■ ■

Friday night they were free, and Eli relayed Eamonn's request that the four of them meet for dinner.

"This isn't anybody's favorite restaurant," Eli said, after they'd been seated and were waiting for their drinks to arrive, "and you're allowed to order whatever you want, Griffin. I don't even remember what's on the menu here from one visit to the next."

"How did you know?" Griffin asked.

"He's that way with everybody," Eli laughed.

"Sorry to have to tell you you're not special," Eamonn growled. He'd slicked his hair into place that evening and he was wearing glasses that looked like he'd stolen them off Clark Kent's face. He and Cooper were wearing matching shirts—loose fitting white cotton. They had the same number of buttons unbuttoned.

Griffin wondered if he and Cooper were about to be invited to their first orgy as a couple.

■ ■ ■

Conversation during dinner focused on diet tips, lifting tips, supplementation tips, favorite brands and styles of workout attire, and stories about the worst violations of gym etiquette Cooper and Eamonn had witnessed and how they suppressed them. In other words, it was a lot like brunch in San Francisco.

■ ■ ■

146

"God," Eamonn said, nearly smothering Griffin in a hug almost as fragrant and monumental as the ones Big Steve Fabiani dispensed back home, "I wish we had some friends like you guys around here."

"It was a great evening," Griffin managed to stammer.

Then Eamonn and Eli were off upstairs.

No orgy. Griffin was relieved. But also a little pensive.

■ ■ ■

"Before you ask," Cooper said, "it's called 'Boys' Night Out'. Every guy should get one each week. As long as Eamonn makes his one a.m. curfew, Maribel won't hassle him. The woman is a genius. She could teach a lot of gay couples a thing or two."

"So I'm supposed to give you 'Boys' Night Out' every week?" Griffin asked.

"At our house," Cooper growled, pulling Griffin's shirt over his head, "every night is Boys' Night Out."

■ ■ ■

They were finishing up packing when Josh came in from the theatre.

"I probably won't get up to see you off," he said.

"No problem," Cooper said.

"Thanks for everything," Griffin said. "It was so nice of you to let us stay here."

"You're family," Josh shrugged.

"Love us or leave us," Cooper grunted.

"And speaking of that," Griffin said, "give our love to Andrew."

■ ■ ■

Josh slept through their departure. But Eli came down to the street to wait with them for their car.

"Eamonn says to tell you two that you are now officially his favorite gay couple."

"He's a great guy," Cooper said.

"Josh says I should move to San Francisco," Eli said. "He says you guys have lots of single friends. Guys like Eamonn, you know? Except without encumbrances. I'm supposed to let you two set me up with a 'real husband'."

"We do know some likely gentlemen," Griffin nodded. "We'd be happy to be of service."

"Get them while they're hot," Cooper laughed, staring down Hudson Street. "They're going fast."

"If that's what you really want," Griffin said.

"Exactly," Eli nodded. "That's the catch, isn't it? That man is the love of my life. I adore those boys. I'm sure I'd be crazy about Maribel if she'd ever give me a chance. That's what Josh and Andrew don't understand."

"I get it," Griffin said.

"God, you guys are the best," Eli said. "You know that?"

■ ■ ■

"You know what my ultimate dream is?" Eli asked, hugging Griffin goodbye.

"What?"

"Eamonn and me taking a vacation someday. Just the two of us. I don't even care where we go."

■ ■ ■

After consulting with the driver at length about the arrangement of the luggage, Cooper climbed into the back seat beside Griffin.

"Why are you crying?" he asked.

"They're such great guys," Griffin said. "It's so unfair."

"Stop right there," Cooper said. "There's nothing more to say about it."

MAY, 1984

"Good to see you, old man," Pa said.

"Same here," Rupert smiled.

"Suppose you're wondering why I asked you to meet me here in your Uncle Gervase's chambers."

"Legal matter, what?"

"Manner of speaking," Pa said.

"Well?"

"A trifle embarrassing, actually," Pa said.

"How so?"

"You know that as a man of science I have no patience with superstition of any sort," Pa said.

"Certainly," Rupert said. He recalled more than one nanny having been dismissed for "brainwashing" his younger brothers with nursery rhymes and fairy tales.

"Thing is, old man, it's your mother."

"She hasn't sued you for divorce," Rupert said, suddenly horrified.

"My dear chap. Of course not. Everything's right as rain 'round the old homestead. We hardly see each other enough to get into disagreements. Perfect arrangement, really. No, it's this dratted family curse thing. What with you rising eighteen and your grandfather's age advancing at the same rate."

"Oh, that."

"It's all well and good for you to be dismissive," Pa said. "Your mother is near prostration over it. She's insists that something be done to 'save the lives of my boys' as she so quaintly puts it. And since one hasn't moved quickly enough to assure her that she's been paid attention to, she's taken matters into her own hands."

"Oh, dear," Rupert said. Mum was rather a bull in a china shop when she was moved to act on her own.

"She's proposing a rather radical solution. And she's promised to give me no peace whatever until I've wrapped the business up like a Christmas parcel."

"I see."

"I certainly hope so," Pa said. "Because I have to say I don't at all. Not one bit. But you know your mother. Immovable object as ever was."

More an irresistible force, if you insisted on analyzing the situation in Newtonian terms. Pa was generally the immovable object.

"As you say," Rupert said. "So this radical solution consists of what, exactly?"

"Chap, if there were any other way."

"Out with it, Pa," Rupert smiled, "as the dentist said."

"You sign away your rights as first born. You renounce forever and in perpetuity any and all claims on the title and the estate."

"Sort of an abdication before the fact," Rupert said. This might not turn out so badly now that he thought about it.

"Just so, my boy. Just so."

"In favor of Peregrine, is it?"

"Not exactly," Pa said.

"No?"

"Lots of second sons have fallen victim over the eons as well. Your mother believes it would be safer to take Perry out of the picture too. He is her favourite, after all. Sorry to put it that way, but everyone recognizes it."

"No one more clearly than me," Rupert said.

"Good chap."

"Crispin then," Rupert said.

"Just so," Pa nodded. "Your dear old mum, having statistically analyzed the last nine centuries of family history, has declared that the risk to your brother Crispin is minimal."

"Has she indeed?" Rupert marveled. "Statistically?"

"What she called it," Dad nodded.

"Amazing," Rupert said. "I wasn't aware she was familiar with the concept."

"It's a good thing, actually," Pa said, "because beyond Crispin you're fresh out of siblings and we have to move on to your Uncle Wilfrid's spawn, unspeakable as they are."

"Then I certainly hope mum's calculations are correct," Rupert said. "Though I have to admit to being dubious of her methodology."

"So what do you think?"

"The sooner it's done the better," Rupert said. "I presume that the relevant documents have been drawn up and are currently awaiting my signature."

"You always were quick on the uptake, my boy," Pa said. "Now I don't want you to be worried about a thing. Most of the money is outside the estate, you realize. It's my money that I laboured honestly and tirelessly for and paid ridiculous taxes on and invested carefully and it has no relationship whatever to the title or the land. Except in so far as I've spent a bloody fortune of it keeping the house from falling in on us and the entire deer park from eroding into the river. So I'll be settling some capital on you in compensation."

"A sort of financial analgesic," Rupert nodded.

"Seven figures," Pa said. "Post tax."

"Blimey."

"Well put, son. Well put."

"And Mum doesn't foresee any gruesome consequences of this attempt to circumvent fate?"

"None whatever."

That was discouraging news. But her approval of the plan shouldn't be seen as disqualifying it totally. Behind every silver lining, Rupert knew, lurked a cloud. You had only to find it. For the *schadenfreude*, if nothing else.

■ ■ ■

Pa had earned his Ph.D. in particle physics at Oxford prior to embarking on a career in property development, whence originated the lion's share of his reasonably vast assets. He had been widely regarded as a rising star in that arcane firmament whose prophets were men like Einstein, Heisenberg, and Fermi, a once-in-a-generation (or twice, at most) sort of intellect, it had been claimed. Thus, he considered himself both a man of science and a hard-headed businessman of a particularly rapacious and entrepreneurial stripe. Consequently, Rupert understood, these legal gymnastics, tacitly acknowledging as they did the reality of something Pa had never been willing to entertain seriously, must inevitably constitute a considerable embarrassment to him. So Rupert signed the documents Uncle Gervase presented him as quickly as could physically be accomplished, the better to put the distressing scene behind them. They were home in Knightsbridge well before sundown.

■ ■ ■

The curse of the FitzMerlins might be mythical, but there was a rather terrifying body of empirical evidence corroborating its practical manifestations. Since the eleventh century, not a single first born son of the incumbent had managed to succeed to the title and estates. There had been accidental beheadings, accidental impalements, unanticipated dismountings from horse with resulting catastrophic injuries. There had been accidental poisonings, accidental drownings, deaths by shipwreck, earthquake, and fire. And there had been plenty of garden variety illness, as well. No calamity had been too bizarre, too unpredictable, too unlikely, to fail to obstruct the orderly implementation of the rules of primogeniture. Second sons had succeeded time after time to the title and the estates. Sometimes third sons. Grandpere had been a fourth son who succeeded to the title thanks to Mt. Everest, that blasted *Titanic*, and the Great War. Pa had been a fourth son as well. Polar explorations and the Second World War had exacted a heavy price on his generation. So Rupert was not at all certain that settling the title and estates on Crispin amounted to sufficient insurance. On the other hand, Rupert didn't believe in curses. So it probably wouldn't matter in the long run. There seemed to be enough random bad luck in the cosmos to account for just about any misfortune—even such a long and convoluted chain of them as constituted their family history.

Time, Rupert supposed, would demonstrate whether mum's "solution" actually solved anything.

■ ■ ■

The whole thing was a relief, really. Not that Rupert had ever actually feared for his life. He had grown up in peacetime, he had grown up reasonably risk-averse in an age of seat belts, vaccinations, and cycling helmets, and he had grown up in a country which provided state of the art health care gratis to all its citizens. Surely by the late twentieth century whatever horrible chain of coincidences had so beset the family could reasonably be expected to peter out before claiming him. No. His relief, genuine as it was, arose from different sources.

First was his long treasured dream of living in America. Heretical though it might be for an Englishman of his class, since boyhood he had promised himself an existence on those distant shores. The shores of the Pacific, specifically, since when he thought of America he meant California. And performing his duties as a peer of the realm at such a remove, not to mention maintaining the family estate, remote of location, forbidding of terrain, and ramshackle of condition, seemed too daunting a prospect to consider. He'd spend all his time flying back and forth in jets, and where was the fun in that unless one were at the controls oneself? Then, too, Peregrine seemed nearly as unsuited to the task himself, temperamentally speaking. So leaving it all in the hands of the ridiculously conscientious and terminally unimaginative Crispin seemed a perfect escape.

Furthermore, the new state of affairs admirably accommodated Rupert's lack of dynastic aspirations, to put it delicately. As incumbent he would have, in addition to his other duties, the responsibility to perpetuate the long, basically honourable but admittedly eccentric line of the FitzMerlins in the most existential, i.e., biological manner of all. And though nobody loved sex more than Rupert FitzMerlin, the sex he loved was, it had to be faced, unlikely ever to result in the production of heirs and their backups. Short of some totally unexpected evolutionary leap, at least. So let Crispin handle all that, too, if indeed he was capable of it. Let him find a wife and produce a brood of sons and provide Rupert with an out. Crispin, dim as he might be, was widely regarded as the most photogenic of the tribe, though of a less athletic type than Rupert and Peregrine. Failing some matrimonial catastrophe, the heirs would surely be exquisite.

As soon as he reached the privacy of his bedroom, Rupert made a telephone call. Cavendish was out for the evening, the club porter informed him. Rupert left a message suggesting they meet for lunch the next day.

■ ■ ■

Mum's accent was, to put it kindly, ridiculous. It couldn't possibly be genuine. It called to mind an incompetent actress portraying a dispossessed Ruritanian princess masquerading as a lady's maid in a 1930's West End farce that closed immediately subsequent to its first night, or better yet never opened at all. Despite this her accent was, as it happened, as authentic as dirt. More than merely providing a constant source of comedy, it brought into focus one of the most eccentric of the many FitzMerlin quirks. In all those generations back to the very beginning of the family no FitzMerlin anywhere near the line of succession had ever taken an English wife. The wives had all learned to speak English, at least after a fashion, but they could never reasonably have been described, even though married to British aristocrats, as Englishwomen. Except for, perhaps, the first Lady FitzMerlin, the bride of their patriarch, Olaf the Silent, a Norwegian mercenary who had been instrumental in William of Normandy's conquest of the Island of Britain back in the heady days of 1066. Aethelfreda was a Saxon princess who had been married off to the newly ennobled warrior under the most strenuous protests, the daughter of a particularly fierce and rampantly independent family, who bore Olaf a near horde of suitably robust and warlike if not overly intelligent sons. Since that time, virile young FitzMerlins had ranged far and wide across the Continent in search of brides. The desired type was physically strong, highly temperamental (ferocity being the tribe's most revered trait), and fertile as the dickens. Mostly these were acquired in Scandinavia and the regions along the eastern shores of the Baltic. Rupert's mum's family had come originally from Riga but had transplanted themselves a generation or so before her birth to Paris. That explained her bizarre accent, not quite French and not quite Baltic, with its misplaced emphases and unexpected phonological veerings to and fro.

"Darling," she said, offering her cheek to be kissed as he entered the drawing room dressed for dinner, "your father told me how cooperative you're being about the whole thing. I can't tell you how happy you've made me."

At least that's how Rupert's brain, accustomed to the sound of that voice since infancy, translated the utterance.

"You're welcome," he told her. "Pour you another voddy?"

■ ■ ■

The porter ushered Rupert into the smoking room, where he found Cavendish reclining picturesquely in a club chair that looked as if it might well have come back from Dunkerque on one of those bedraggled fishing boats after the fall of France in 1940. Indeed, Cavendish's club, one of London's most exclusive, prided itself on the advanced state of dilapidation of its facilities. Its servants as well, who tottered around the precincts like inmates of a home for pensioners. It was a little dizzying to think of a man just a few years older than himself being a member of such a rarified establishment as this. That was Cavendish all over. Cavendishes as a tribe, come to think of it. They weren't aristos. They were merely rich. Massively so, that was all. Their money had been made just any old way and was finally old enough to have lost any possible taint. They could have bought dukes and marquesses like livestock. In fact they had, in a manner of speaking. Cavendish possessed squadrons of aunts and girl cousins one was expected to address as "Lady" or refer to as "the honourable".

"Old man," Cavendish growled, rising from the chair slowly and sensuously, with a movement reminiscent of a jungle cat rousing itself after a three course meal and a long nap.

"Cavendish," Rupert smiled.

"Pleased you called. Horribly at loose ends these days."

He sounded as jaded as Nero a couple of weeks after the fire.

"Pa called me up to town," Rupert said. "Family thing."

"Ripping," Cavendish said, nearly asleep on his feet. "Shall we go through to the dining room? I'm told today's fish course isn't totally abysmal."

■ ■ ■

"So you'll be off to Oxford soon," Cavendish said, staring pensively at the remains of his pudding. He had just come down from university, having scored firsts in Literature, History, and Philosophy. Given his apparent obliviousness with regard to intellectual pursuits, this result was generally reckoned so unlikely as to constitute a new subgenre of science fiction, but Rupert wasn't surprised. He knew Cavendish as hardly anyone else did. It took a certain kind of genius to keep genius of such a high order so thoroughly obscured.

"Yes," Rupert said, thinking how much nicer it would be to come to London immediately and take a flat next door to the one he'd insist that Cavendish take.

"Must be rabid to get away from school, chum. Can't imagine how you've stuck it."

"It hasn't been that bad," Rupert said.

"Spare me the unsavoury details. You know how jealous I tend to become."

"Very well," Rupert grinned.

"Oxford's not bad at all. I expect I'll be up there lots at weekends."

■ ■ ■

"It's all meant to be a frightfully deep secret," Rupert said.

"So I should think," Cavendish said, stifling a yawn. This mannerism didn't signify inattention, much less boredom, but was calculated to give the impression it did. Cavendish cultivated inscrutability as some suburban housewives cultivated prize rose bushes.

"The concern is," Rupert continued, "that Grandpere would have a stroke were he to hear of it."

"Confound the efforts of one and all by living to be a hundred and eighty, more like."

They had come to Cavendish's rooms after their meal. These uncannily resembled the rooms he had inhabited at Winchester and those he had recently vacated at Oxford. It was as if he packed up the whole kit and caboodle and brought it along on his migrations. Rupert's Pa didn't believe in clubs, considering them a waste of money. When he wanted to get away from Mum for a little while—which was a great deal of the time, as a matter of fact—he went off somewhere and bought a company, typically one concerned with wine importation or low volume, high prestige publishing. He then ran them as if they were social establishments, with their stated enterprises mere atmospherics. Yet they turned tidy profits. Rupert wondered if he oughtn't to have asked for a handful of those firms in lieu of the capital Pa settled on him.

"Pour you another?" Cavendish asked, brandishing the nearly empty claret bottle.

"No, thanks."

"Sufficiently lubricated, then?"

"You'll just have to find out for yourself."

"Bite that tongue, boy," Cavendish bawled after the manner of a Victorian plutocrat. "I'll have none of your sauciness."

They dissolved into giggles as Rupert began at long last to unbutton Cavendish's shirt.

■ ■ ■

"Crikey," Rupert said, glancing at Cavendish's Breitling, which currently reposed on his own left pectoral. "Is that the time?"

"Of course it's the time, you clot," Cavendish grunted. "That's a very expensive timepiece, I'll have you know. Certified by the Swiss government itself. United Nations as well, I shouldn't wonder. Guaranteed accurate within the tiniest, most miniscule fraction of a second every century or two. Lunar landings have been timed with substantially less precise devices."

"Better be off to my train, then," Rupert said, beginning the laborious process of disengaging himself from Cavendish's outlandishly muscled limbs.

"Sod the train. Now that we're social equals, I suppose I'd better run you down to school in the Aston."

"At current petrol prices? Unthinkable."

"The train is all well and good for members of the peerage," Cavendish said. "They're almost duty bound to travel that way. But as a former member of the aristocracy, however recently, you're far too grand now to make use of public transportation. It wouldn't be suitable at all."

"I wouldn't make too much of that 'former member' business," Rupert laughed. "I'm to be styled 'honourable' and retain all the rights and privileges traditionally accorded a younger son."

"Yes, well," Cavendish mused. "There's certainly nothing honourable about that delicious bum of yours. Ought to be on the official schedule of controlled substances."

■ ■ ■

Cavendish drove like a real racing driver rather than a demented wanker pretending to be one. In other words, with such concentration and smoothness that the velocity they achieved was largely obscured by lack of drama. They arrived at the school in what seemed like record time, though Rupert suspected that some emotional analogue to Einstein's relativity was involved this perception.

"Still being careful, young Roops?" Cavendish murmured huskily as Rupert clambered out of the car. "Still taking all reasonable precautions?"

He meant sexual ones, Rupert knew. Bloody, buggery AIDS. But what did "reasonable precautions" even entail? Nobody seemed to have a clue beyond the obvious—abstinence. He disguised his confusion with a joke.

"I'm exactly as careful as you are."

■ ■ ■

It was just minutes before lights out when Rupert heard the knock on his door. It was tentative. Barely audible, in fact. That could only be Morrison.

"Come."

Morrison entered the room. He was soaked to the skin and shivering. Rain had been coming down in buckets since not long after Rupert's return to school that afternoon.

"Telegram for you, sir," Morrison said.

"Thanks awfully," Rupert said, ripping open the soggy envelope and scanning the message.

Just a thought. On your arrival at Oxford, you might like to give serious consideration to taking up the noble sport of rowing. K.

In correspondence, Cavendish preferred to assume the persona of an Elizabethan rakehell who spelled his name "Kaevyndysshe." This was sound advice, of course. But more than that it confirmed an impending assignation at a disused boathouse of their acquaintance not far from the school. Good old Cavendish.

"Any answer, sir?" Morrison asked through chattering teeth.

"Nonsense boy," Rupert growled in his best Cavendish imitation. "The telegraph office in the village is long since closed, you'd never make it back before lights out anyway, and you're nearly ready to sprout gills as it is."

"Yes, sir."

"There's a wad of pound notes on the table over there. You may take two of them as long as you promise not to breathe a word about it."

"You mean the telegram, sir?"

"No, you twit. I mean the princely gratuity you've just been offered. Though come to think of it you'd best take four of those pound notes."

"Thanks awfully, sir."

"Off with you now. And dry yourself thoroughly. Can't have my man coming down with pneumonia."

■ ■ ■

It was barbaric, of course, having the younger boys wait on the older ones hand and foot, Rupert mused, pulling up the duvet. Strictly speaking he wasn't supposed to have a duvet on his bed but one of the school issued blankets, which were soft as cardboard and effective against cold as tissue. Such comforts as his duvet were held to have a deleterious effect on the character of adolescent males. Eventually the authorities would be alerted to its presence in his rooms and he'd pay a heavy price for his contraband. Which would include but not be limited to the duvet's confiscation. Meanwhile, he found it comforting on a rainy night. Not as comforting has having Cavendish's statuesque person to snuggle with would have been. A poor second to that. But smuggling Cavendish into his room, had he even been available, wasn't worth considering.

He certainly hoped poor Morrison hadn't caught a chill. The telegram could have waited until morning. He'd have to find out who had summoned the boy on a harebrained errand like that in such foul weather. He'd taken Morrison on because as the most fragile boy of his year, he was obviously in need of protection. But if someone was interfering with his defense, Rupert was determined to know about it. Safe to say, Morrison would never complain of it. Schoolboy code didn't permit it. But Morrison's own fear of humiliation was the real guarantee of his silence. A show of weakness on the part of someone so obviously weak would be tantamount to suicide.

■ ■ ■

Rupert defined his dealings with Cavendish as "promiscuous exclusivity". What he meant by this expression was that while up at Oxford and latterly coming down to London Cavendish had availed himself of much of the female population of those cities, specializing particularly in fashion models, heiresses, aspiring actresses, and airline hostesses, he had resolutely abstained from contact with persons of his own sex. That honour was reserved for Rupert absolutely. At the same time, Rupert, still at school, had availed himself of all and sundry eligible partners but in all encounters had performed the role of bugger rather than buggee. He'd built a reputation unmatched by anyone since Cavendish himself as a dispenser of extravagantly priapic favours and took a kind of pride in it, leaving his special place inviolate. This unspoken rule of theirs seemed to demonstrate the importance they placed on fidelity as they defined and were prepared to practice it while at the same time affording each of them the freedom of sexual expression young Englishmen of their respective social positions regarded as a birthright. Not to have taken advantage of the opportunities resulting from their looks, physiques, and charisma might easily have opened them to criticism and perhaps even a level of scrutiny that would have made their continued relations difficult if not impossible to maintain. It might have been nice, from Rupert's standpoint, to have a "boyfriend" devoted to him exclusively and in turn to have reserved himself for that individual only, but Cavendish being who he was such an expectation would have been ridiculous.

So it was without the least reservation that the next afternoon Rupert found himself in one of his favorite places of assignation enjoying the fairly delectable bum of Robinson Minor, a youngster who had recently caught his eye on the rugger pitch. Robinson Minor, if the physical development of his older siblings was anything to go by, would soon grow into a sturdy, well muscled pup, and it was this potential, rather than the current incarnation, which was rather weedy, that Rupert focused on as he pumped away.

■ ■ ■

"I say, old man. The minute you get to Oxford, I mean the very minute, you understand. . ."

"I know," Rupert panted. "Rowing."

"That, certainly," Cavendish panted, "but it's just now occurred to me that. . ."

Amazing. Cavendish had been jackhammering away for a good twenty minutes now and showed no sign of being winded.

"I really ought to give you the address of the gym I used up there," Cavendish continued. "Letter of introduction as well. Did wonders for me, I have to say."

"What do you weigh now?" Rupert asked. "Seventeen stone?"

"Add half a dozen pounds to that," Cavendish said. "And yet, even at a weight like that, one's as lean as a whippet. Truly. And just now one finds oneself contemplating Rupert's shoulders from a particularly felicitous angle, not to mention other parts of Rupert's person—have to say you're quite the well set up lad these days, aren't you?—and thinking what wonders the facility might do for you as well."

The wonders in question, Rupert mused, presumably included the ability to conduct a reasonably coherent conversation without interrupting the rhythm of a certain intensely physical activity. Just then Cavendish succumbed to the frenzy of his own exertions. Rupert felt the explosion internally as well as by way of Cavendish's audible expressions and bodily collapse onto him. Only then did he allow his own long delayed response to occur.

■ ■ ■

It was certainly food for thought, Rupert admitted to himself as he trekked toward school. Cavendish had offered him a lift in the Aston, but arriving in such a recognizable vehicle—being seen to arrive in it—for the second time in barely a week threatened to occasion unwanted speculation, thus disturbing the discipline Rupert had so painstakingly imposed on his underlings that term. And the distance from the boathouse wasn't that arduous even in his depleted state. Yes, Cavendish undoubtedly had a point. Regular, intense exercise with barbells and complicated machinery. Rupert felt stronger, fitter, and more visually impressive just thinking about it.

■ ■ ■

"Visitor in your room, sir," Morrison announced as Rupert hit the bottom of the stairs.

"Who?"

"Didn't actually see him, sir, but the porter seemed happy to admit him in your absence."

"Fine, Morrison. Thanks for the heads-up."

Whatever now? Rupert was hardly in the mood for entertaining. A good long wank to solidify his memories of the last hour and forty-five minutes followed by a good long nap was more what he had in mind. He announced his presence by going up the last few stairs as noisily as he could and then yanked open the door to his room.

"Good heavens," he said, seeing his younger brother lounging in his club chair, "Peregrine."

"Scoundrel," Peregrine snarled. "Nitwit."

"Steady on, old man," Rupert said. "One recognizes these as your perennial salutations of choice. But why should they have brought you all the way down from Eton on a Thursday afternoon? One can only wonder."

"You don't have a brain in your head," Peregrine insisted.

"That, too, I have heard from your lips before," Rupert said, "and I can only repeat my question. Why today?"

"You signed that idiotic document of Pa's," Peregrine said. "Of all the stupid, brainless. . ."

"I did indeed," Rupert said. "What of it?"

"What of it?" Peregrine fumed. "We were meant to present a united front in the face of that ridiculous woman's ill conceived. . ."

"She's our mother, old man."

"More's the pity."

"I really don't think you mean that."

"Don't I? Don't I just? Oh, I can't believe you didn't at least talk with me first."

"Sorry, old thing," Rupert said. "I certainly should have. I see that now. But what I don't see is why it should matter to you whether I signed the bloody thing or not."

"Selling your birthright for a mess of pottage," Peregrine protested.

"Hardly a mess of pottage," Rupert said. "Whatever that may be."

"Don't play the twit with me, Rupert."

"*Play* the twit? Peregrine, you accost me in my own room with the accusation that I'm a half wit. . ."

"Nitwit, I believe I said."

"Nitwit, then," Rupert said, "and now you accuse me of *playing* the twit. It's one or the other. You must realize that. Either I'm an idiot or I'm only pretending to be. Even at Eton they expect greater intellectual consistency than you're exhibiting."

"What you are is immaterial," Peregrine said.

"Not to me, it isn't."

"Very well," Peregrine said, looking exhausted. "Selling your birthright for a measly three million quid. Is that sufficiently literal for you?"

"Literal yes," Rupert said, "but unlike you, I'm incapable of using 'measly' and 'three million quid' in the same sentence. Except of course that I seem to have done so just now. It was inadvertent, I assure you."

"If you were determined to go along with this ridiculous scheme, you should at least have held out for more cash," Peregrine said. "You've put me in an impossible position."

"You're forgetting the FitzMerlin family motto," Rupert said.

"What are you talking about? How is the family motto relevant here?"

"'Every man for himself.' Isn't that how it goes?"

"You know very well it doesn't," Peregrine said. "Not even badly translated from the Latin."

"Old man, don't you see what I'm trying to tell you? If you want Pa to raise his offer, just ask him. He's a businessman. He knows about negotiating. But leave me out of it, won't you?"

■ ■ ■

"I'm afraid your mother is devastated," Pa said. "She never expected that you'd prove to be the reasonable one."

"So Peregrine didn't sign," Rupert said.

"I doubled my offer to him," Pa said. "I'd have made it good with you as well, if he'd agreed to it. In fact, I think I shall just to show that pup."

"Six million? Far too much, paterfamilias dear."

They finally settled on five million.

JUNE, 1986

The funerals were back to back, C.J.'s on Saturday and Dietrich's on Sunday. Dietrich was Jewish, though practically nobody knew it until they got there and yarmulkes were being distributed. Since C.J. and Dietrich had known pretty much the same people, the same mourners showed up both days, many wearing recognizably the same outfits. It was the grimmest possible kind of déjà vu, Eli thought. He couldn't imagine what Josh, who had known both men far better, was thinking.

■ ■ ■

C.J. and Josh had dated briefly and inconclusively back in 'seventy-four. At least Eli thought it would have been around then. He must have known the details at the time but couldn't actually recall much about it. Josh had dated so many people his first few years out of college. It was always hard to keep track. Josh hadn't bothered to himself, just went from one affair to the next. To be accurate about it sometimes they went on simultaneously. Finally Andrew came onto the scene and put a stop to everything. Eli had always envied Josh. He made the whole thing look so effortless. Eli always agonized. At least he hadn't had to agonize for long. Unlikely as it seemed at the time, he settled down well before Josh did. In C.J.'s case Josh wasn't especially moved. Eli remembered that much. C.J. had been sweet but ultimately not very memorable. Pretty much everybody agreed on that.

■ ■ ■

Dietrich was another matter altogether. Back when Josh and Eli first encountered him he was still using his first name, Kevin, and professing to be straight. He was so convincing that hardly anybody questioned it and Josh never bothered trying anything with him, though he came very close to it. Eli remembered Josh and C.J. arguing the question of Dietrich's orientation on at least one occasion. That was after their affair fizzled out. C.J. tried with Dietrich, repeatedly it seemed, and never got anywhere. This appeared to prove the point even though C.J. insisted he was right and Dietrich actually was available. On the other hand, Josh, who generally had sex with everyone he wanted and a lot of guys he really didn't on the principle that you didn't look a gift horse in the mouth, scoffed and made skeptical commentary when Dietrich's name came up. Really, Josh had been so arrogant in those days. Not about everything, it had to be admitted. Just about sex. In any case, with regard to Dietrich, Eli was the one who had actual first hand experience. Not that he'd known who Dietrich was until afterward. During those endless weeks after his first encounter with Eamonn, when he haunted that bathhouse Josh preferred—now closed, of course—up on the fringes of Chelsea in hope of meeting "Superman" again and experiencing at least temporary nirvana, Dietrich was somebody Eli tricked with as a consolation prize. More than once. Not that Dietrich would have remembered it the next morning. If Eli hadn't already fallen in love with Eamonn, still anonymous at that point but nevertheless the man of his dreams, Dietrich might have made a greater impact. But Eli had been as obsessed as humanly possible at the time, and Dietrich, though scorchingly handsome, somehow seemed inconsequential.

■ ■ ■

Which made Eli a minority of one, it turned out. Because even at that embryonic stage in his career, Dietrich was already amassing a reputation bordering on legendary. It wasn't long after Eli's all but forgotten encounters with him that he jettisoned both first name and girlfriend of record—that Barbie doll who went on to fame as a villainess extraordinaire on a long running soap, acing out no less than Jill Wagstaffe, who then sulked off to law school. The next thing anyone knew, Dietrich came roaring out of the closet as if someone had set a fire in there. That's how things went in those days. How many guys had been transformed just like that? Tightlipped, stiff, ex-jock princes one day and screaming queens the next? It seemed like a century ago. Now people seemed hell bent on getting back into the closet as fast as they could and locking and bolting the door behind them. As if you could defend yourself from a virus that way.

■ ■ ■

In any case, C.J.'s funeral was one Eli never would have attended except that Josh didn't like to go to funerals alone and Andrew wasn't in town that afternoon, but Dietrich's was one he wouldn't have missed for anything. C.J. had been a nice young man Eli might well have known in school and his passing was a very sad but ultimately private matter, but Dietrich had ended up being a phenomenon. That made his funeral an event. For the best part of a decade he had defined what it meant to be gay and hot. Just walking down the street, Dietrich was significant. And if he happened to take off his shirt halfway down the block, it constituted an event brunches all around Manhattan would be atwitter over the next Sunday. Since Eli had witnessed the shadowy beginnings of Dietrich's cult, it seemed only fitting to be present as the longboat bearing the remains was set ablaze and shoved out into the turbulent waters just off shore.

■ ■ ■

"I've been thinking about getting tested," Eli said as he got ready for bed that night. Alone. Eamonn was at home with his wife and sons.

The mirror didn't answer. Eli tried it again.

■ ■ ■

A week later, the funeral was for Ellis Robertson, a "friend" of Cousin Talbot. And three days after that they scattered the ashes of Armando Alarcon, the surviving boyfriend of one of Talbot's favorite cameramen who had died in 'eighty-four.

167

"Looking well, Eli," Talbot said when they met at the buffet.

That was his new greeting. Talbot never told people they looked hot any more. Healthy was a significant enough accomplishment. God only knew, it was beyond the aspirations of many.

"You, too," Eli answered.

"My reward for never sleeping with anybody who ever took it up the ass," Talbot gloated. "Genuine top men for me. Exclusively. Not your would be tops who go around beating their chests like mythological heroes yet lie back and spread their legs at the drop of a hat."

"That's not very politically correct of you," Eli said.

"Fuck that shit," Talbot said. "Those political types either didn't want anyone having sex or wanted the hot guys to have to fuck their full allotted quota of fatties, femmes, and trolls before they could take their pick of the ones they really wanted. Look where that got us."

"Uh, I don't remember any such rule," Eli said.

"Because it never took effect," Talbot said. "Guys like me wouldn't allow it. Guys like me never took the political types seriously. We did what we had to do to put them in their places. Anyway, you learned pretty much the same lesson I did, didn't you?"

"How so?"

"That firefighter of yours never took it up the ass, did he?"

"Not that I know of," Eli said.

"Saved both of your lives, didn't it?"

■ ■ ■

Eli wasn't sure of that.

"I'm thinking of taking the test," he said.

Once again, his bathroom mirror didn't answer.

II

"Andrew wants me to get tested," Josh said.

"He does?"

It was Sunday night. Andrew was on his way home to New Haven. He and Josh seemed fated never to actually live in the same city. Josh and Eli were in Josh's living room eating Chinese takeout.

"Actually, he's insisting," Josh said.

"Any particular reason?" Eli asked. "I mean, how would knowing whether you were infected or not change anything?"

"Andrew can't seem to explain that," Josh said. "He just thinks it's the right thing to do."

"Which means he's done it himself."

"Two weeks ago," Josh said. "He was negative."

"And what about the threat of quarantine?" Eli asked. "It could be dangerous having the wrong HIV status appear in your medical records. It could be dangerous having any kind of results in your records, actually. Just being tested indicates that you're a member of an at-risk population, doesn't it?"

"He doesn't worry about that," Josh said. "He says it's just alarmist talk on the part of the activists. He says this is America and it could never come to that. The courts will protect us, etc."

"With Walter Mondale in the White House, he's got a point," Eli said.

"Walter Mondale is nowhere near the White House," Josh said. "I doubt if he's even in Washington these days."

"Exactly," Eli said. "If Andrew trusts the Reagan Administration with our civil rights, he's not as smart as I thought."

"I knew you'd say that," Josh said.

"Why do you bring these things up? You know I'm going to take a position roughly opposite to that of your husband, leaving you caught in the middle and the two of us not speaking until one of us apologizes. Which, come to think of it, is generally me. Even if I don't actually mean it."

"I know you think your ability to offer insincere apologies with apparent sincerity is the glue that holds our friendship together," Josh said.

"Isn't it?"

"Well, yes," Josh said, "that and the fact that I find you indispensable. If I fight these things out with you first, I'm better equipped to deal with Andrew."

"What? Domestic strife by proxy?" Eli laughed.

"Something like that," Josh said. "So you'll come with me?"

"Huh?"

"When I go to get tested?"

"I don't know about that," Eli said.

"I can't do it by myself," Josh said, "and I can't possibly take Andrew along with me. I'll lose my fucking mind."

■ ■ ■

"Josh wants me to go with him to get tested," Eli said, snuggling against Eamonn. Because it was Tuesday, Eamonn had shaved his chest that afternoon. His satiny smoothness was irresistible. Not that he wasn't irresistible under any circumstances, but this condition was a particular favorite of Eli's. There was something downright apocalyptic about Eamonn's nipples when he had just shaved his chest.

"Why?"

"Because he's afraid to go on his own," Eli said.

"No, I get that," Eamonn said. "I mean, why does he think you need to be the one to go with him?"

"Well," Eli said, "Andrew is the alternative, of course."

"And they think our relationship is fucked up," Eamonn laughed.

"Right."

"You know you're all right, don't you?" Eamonn asked.

"That's what I'm told," Eli said.

"I had to get tested after I had that transfusion," Eamonn said, "from that blood bank that everybody was so panicked about."

"Yes," Eli nodded. It had been a terrible time. First Eamonn got injured in that warehouse fire in the Bronx and almost bled to death and then there was the scare about tainted blood. Eli had nearly lost his mind. Eamonn had been steady as a rock through the whole thing.

"And the test came back negative," Eamonn said. "Clean as could be. They did it twice more six months apart just to make sure."

Eli remembered all that horrible fumbling with condoms. Some people did that as a life sentence.

"And if I'm clean, you are. Stands to reason."

"I know that," Eli said, "but if it's all the same to you I think I'll go along when Josh does anyway."

"You worry too much," Eamonn said.

"Agreed."

"You should stop."

■ ■ ■

How arrogant of Eamonn to presume that Eli couldn't have gotten himself infected on his own steam. Did he really think that all those nights when he was home with Maribel and the boys or out with his buddies from the gym or whatever, Eli was curled up with a good book? Like he had no opportunities of his own? Like he was incapable of having sex without Eamonn present? Of course that was pretty much the truth, but Eli didn't like Eamonn taking him for granted that way. It was intolerable, that's what. He really shouldn't stand for it.

His fury must have communicated itself telepathically all the way uptown, because the next afternoon, Eamonn was waiting across the street when Eli emerged from the World Trade Center at the end of the day.

"What are you doing here?" Eli muttered, ecstatic to see Eamonn in spite of himself. "You're supposed to be on shift."

"I am on shift," Eamonn said.

"Right. You're far enough from the house to be declared AWOL, seems to me."

"Had to see you," Eamonn grinned. "You're all bothered, and I need to make it right."

"What do you mean, all bothered?"

"You think I take you for granted. You think that's the reason I said you don't need to get tested."

"Don't be silly," Eli protested.

"Eli, I read you like a book."

"Uh huh."

"You know I do," Eamonn said. "Come on, don't be like this."

"Like what?"

"All stuffy and offended. You think I don't know you're the only man on the planet who could give me everything I want? You think you're the only one in our relationship who worships his boyfriend? You think I don't fall down on my knees every day and thank God for what we have?"

"On your knees? Really?"

"All right," Eamonn admitted. "Figuratively. Listen to me. You have no idea how much I love you. I can't imagine what my life would be like without you. The boys adore you. You even won Maribel over."

"When was that?" Eli asked. "I must have missed it."

"You know she could put a stop to all this in a heartbeat if she decided to. Any other guy, she'd have done it already."

"So she doesn't think of me as a threat," Eli said. "That's all."

"And you see that as some kind of failing on your part," Eamonn shook his head, "when it's the exact opposite of that."

"You're always so sure of yourself," Eli said.

"No," Eamonn said, "you're wrong about that. And if it seems like I take you for granted it's only because I can't allow myself to think of the alternative."

III

In the end all three of them went. Either Josh failed to dissuade Andrew from escorting them, or, more likely, hadn't tried. It didn't matter to Eli either way, except that he hated to see Josh so frantic. In a way it was worse than being nervous himself. Andrew couldn't go anywhere in the city, either on foot or by subway, without providing running commentary during the journey, as if his companions were small children or ignorant out-of-towners. Sometimes this was merely annoying, though Eli was usually silently infuriated by it. Today, however, it was just the distraction he needed. The best thing about it was that it meant neither he nor Josh had to try and make small talk. Eli had never been good at small talk, whereas Josh was too good at it. This was better.

■ ■ ■

"There," Andrew said as Josh emerged from the cubicle. "Isn't that better?"

"Better than what?" Josh asked.

Eli had gone in first so that Andrew and Josh could "talk". He was still in a daze. He couldn't remember a thing that had happened except that he didn't like it. Apparently Josh and Andrew hadn't resolved anything in his absence. Eli wasn't even sure what there was to resolve. Andrew seemed to have a gift for manufacturing small conflicts that were like tiny explosions. They produced light and heat but left no lasting effects. They blew over like sudden squalls, leaving days that were sunny and at least appeared pleasant.

"I'm buying lunch," Eli told them.

"What's the occasion?" Andrew asked, unable to refrain from looking a gift horse in the mouth.

"Ancient festival," Eli said. "Saint Presumptua's Day. Patron saint of optimists."

"You're making that up," Josh accused.

"I most certainly am," Eli smiled.

What he was counting on was one of the most constant of all Andrew's constants: a well-mannered refusal to criticize restaurant food someone else was paying for unless his benefactor did so first.

■ ■ ■

"Strangely anticlimactic, didn't you think?" Josh asked.

Andrew had left them to catch his train back to New Haven. Eli could hardly breathe for the relief brought on by that retreating backside, aesthetically pleasing as it was.

"Only you could say a thing like that at a time like this, Josh."

"But it's true," Josh said. "You sign in with an alias, just like we used to at the baths. You go into a cubicle that smells of disinfectant. Also like the baths, by the way."

"The things you remember."

"They take your blood. It's totally mundane. It didn't feel like life and death at all."

"This part maybe," Eli nodded. "It's a week from now that it turns into outtakes from a bad science fiction film."

■ ■ ■

All over the city, men were dying. That week there were two more funerals. Eli had only known Roger Willcox by reputation and didn't go. But he and Kenny Steinberg had been in high school together. Kenny was handsome, athletic, and a bully. Eli had lost count of the times Kenny terrorized him. It was all a big, nightmarish blur. Years later when they both came out, Kenny went right on as before. There was always someone smaller, shyer, less handsome, unequipped to defend himself, and he unleashed everything he had at these unfortunates. Eli considered it a signal failure of the gay community that it let guys like Kenny get away with such behavior merely because they were hot.

He went to the funeral but once there realized his resentment and disapproval couldn't stand up against the tragedy. Kenny hadn't been hot when he died. Or popular, either. His rich boyfriends had all washed their hands of him, the last one literally throwing him out on the street. It was hard to believe that anyone deserved that kind of treatment, no matter what he'd been guilty of in his previous life.

■ ■ ■

When Eli came back to the city after college, which was in the first years of what was known at the time as "gay lib", he noticed a kind of all-for-one-and-one-for-all spirit among his people. It didn't last long. Soon the community split along the all too predictable fault lines. White gays and black gays didn't

174

mix, really. White gays and Latino gays were hardly any friendlier. Rich gays and poor gays only knew each other when some kind of drug related or sexual transaction brought them together. Middle class gays and gays who were coupled were pretty much invisible. And this caste system was ruthlessly enforced by the queens, with loud but ineffectual resistance on the part of the activists, who called unceasingly for unity but only meant it as long as they got to dictate the terms. Their influence was limited by the fact that they were all too easily co-opted by a stunning face, a monumental pair of shoulders, thighs or pecs, or a spectacular head of hair.

Or, of course, money. For all their utopianism, that was the real downfall of the activist class. Eli's cousin Talbot, the archetypal trust fund baby, had made a hobby of wining and dining activists and then once he'd earned their complete allegiance dropping them like potatoes hot from the oven.

During the first years of the epidemic the old spirit seemed to have been reborn, Eli recalled. People who wouldn't have spoken to each other in 1980 stood side by side in the struggle in '82 and '83. But now, five years in, the camps had resumed their previous positions. It was like living in a medieval village with a rigid caste system. It seemed pointless.

■ ■ ■

Eli got up and went to work every morning just like usual. He went to the gym and worked out like he was committed to it. He went to his Monday night discussion group and studiously pretended not to envy the younger, cuter guys there. He met Jill Wagstaffe for lunch on Tuesday like always.

"Darling," she said, wriggling with *schadenfreude*. "Tell me. What was it like? Terrible? Surreal?"

So she hadn't spoken to Josh. She was really more Josh's friend than Eli's. He wondered if this betokened some premonition on her part. Jill was a great one for having premonitions. Occasionally one of them even came true.

"I know," she said. "One isn't supposed to ask. But my friend Editha is up for a part as an AIDS victim. . ."

"You're not supposed to call them that," Eli said.

"Really? Why ever not?"

"The activists don't like it."

"Really? What are we supposed to call them, pray tell?"

"PLWA's."

"What the hell is that supposed to represent?" Jill asked.

"People Living with AIDS," Eli said.

"Ridiculous."

"Nevertheless," Eli shrugged.

"Do you suppose there's an activist in this restaurant right now taking notes on our conversation?"

"Almost inevitably," Eli said. "That busboy, for instance."

He just said it to be provocative, of course. The busboy didn't look any more like an activist than Eli's Nanna Neumann did.

"Really," Jill said.

"No, don't turn around."

"Well, anyway, Editha's dying to know. What was it like?"

"Flossing," Eli said.

"What?"

"You know you're supposed to do it because it's good for you. But it's not altogether pleasant."

■ ■ ■

Eli would have given anything for an hour alone with Eamonn, but it was a school holiday and he'd taken the boys camping somewhere upstate. He'd been right about everything, as usual, and Eli wished he could tell him so. He had been oversensitive as usual, looking for offense where none had been intended. He had whined. He had clung. In other words, he'd been *that guy*, and he hated it. He wouldn't blame Eamonn for never showing up again.

■ ■ ■

176

Thursday night he had dinner with Talbot. Talbot exemplified the highest reaches of the gay food chain and was always good for amazing dish if nothing else.

"They said it would ruin me," Talbot gloated. "They said nobody would watch porn with condoms in it."

They had indeed said that. And worse. In this case, "they" were everyone who was anyone in the community. Talbot was going out on quite a limb, being the first gay pornographer to insist on safe sex precautions being taken on set. You'd have thought he'd bombed Nagasaki for all the criticism and second guessing that ensued. Eli heard the debate raging across countless brunch tables, ricocheting around countless cocktail parties, echoing in the expanses of countless intermissions and gallery openings. As always in what Eamonn referred to as Modern Gay Life, the louder people made and defended their assertions the more certain you could be that they were dead wrong. The more revered the speaker, the more likely he/she was to be talking utter nonsense. It was the aspect of the gay community that most resembled its straight analogue. Talbot himself had said that equality would only be realized when gays had the freedom to be as stupid as breeders. It looked like that day was just around the corner.

"But guess what?" Talbot continued. "Sales have skyrocketed. It turns out that the eroticization of safe sex was exactly what people were waiting for. Everybody thought I was filthy rich before. Just wait until next quarter's receipts become common knowledge."

"That won't be long," Eli observed. Talbot was a genius at self promotion.

"Damn right."

"Tell me," Eli said. "Do you use condoms yourself? In real life, as it were?"

"That would be just about as pointless as eating gourmet takeout with the plastic wrap still on it," Talbot said.

"Then. . .?"

"Listen, little cousin," Talbot said, "when you know your way around as I do, using condoms is pointless because unnecessary. You see a chap at the gym that you like the look of. A few seconds close observation is all that's required to ascertain the nature of his preferences and experience, which inevitably indicates the state of his health. Nothing to it, really."

■ ■ ■

Eli's fear was irrational. He understood that. But what if? What if one of those few guys, a scant handful honestly, had been infected. Sure. All the way back there in 1975, when nobody suspected anything like this could ever happen. They said it had been around that long ago, though perhaps not in Manhattan. But suppose it had. Suppose Eli, with his perennial evil luck, had had sex with one of the miniscule number of men in the city at the time capable of giving him that death sentence. Dietrich, for instance, could have been infected that long ago. Suppose Eli had, despite all the talk of how unlikely it was, been able to precipitate a case of bottom-to-top transmission and had given it to Eamonn. And Eamonn's recent and multiple test results to the contrary had been mistakes. Suppose all that.

Ridiculous, yes. But he couldn't help himself. He worried. He obsessed.

The week dragged unbearably.

IV

"I lied to him is how," Josh said.

"You lied to Andrew?"

"He thinks the appointment is tomorrow," Josh nodded. "I couldn't face this with him there. He's the love of my life, but sometimes he doesn't know when to shut up."

"Or even how," Eli nodded. "Poor you, though. Stuck with me."

"You always sell yourself short, Eli."

"I have plenty of help with that," Eli said.

■ ■ ■

Eli knew the minute Josh emerged from the cubicle that the news wasn't good. He might have been the toast of Broadway (chorus boy edition) not too long ago, but nobody was that good an actor. The shoulders drooped ever so slightly. The feet shuffled just north of the baseline level of human perception. He stared at the floor. Eli rose from his seat. Josh was taller and his shoulders broader, but as Eli hugged him he was, for once, the strong one.

"God, Josh," he said. "I'm so sorry. It's the most terrible thing."

He sobbed once.

"You're o.k. of course," Josh said.

"Yes," Eli nodded.

"I'm not surprised," Josh said, "about you or about me. There wasn't any reason to expect a different outcome."

"That doesn't make it any easier to hear the news," Eli said.

"No," Josh said. "That's for sure. You know what Andrew will say about this."

"Pretty much," Eli nodded.

"He'll remind me that the experts are saying only a certain percentage of those infected will actually get sick."

"Right."

"And that they're developing treatments as quickly as medical science can perform its magic. He'll go down the list of all the early warning signs and remind me that I haven't experienced any of them. He'll promise me that whatever happens we'll get through it together."

"That's right," Eli said. "I know I don't have the best attitude about him sometimes, but he's a really good guy. You can always depend on him. You two will be fine."

"He is a really good guy," Josh said. "And I love him, and he's right about all those things. But you're the one I wanted with me today. Because when I came out of that room you knew the words I needed to hear first."

■ ■ ■

As he came in through the door, Eli could hear Andrew's voice talking to his answering machine.

"I know you're anxious about getting your results tomorrow. But please don't be. Remember that regardless of what happens, Josh and I will be right there facing it with you. You're his oldest friend, and there's no way he'd turn his back on you."

Poor schmuck, Eli thought.

■ ■ ■

"I told you everything would be fine," Eamonn said, sponging him off with a wash cloth.

"That's right," Eli yawned, "you did."

What a fucked up world. No matter how happy you might be, outside your door—or in this case, in the apartment downstairs—someone less fortunate than you was miserable.

Eamonn came back into the bedroom from rinsing the washcloth.

"Scoot over," he said.

"Isn't it time for you to be heading home?"

"Not tonight," Eamonn said, climbing in behind him.

"What about Maribel?"

"Ssh," Eamonn said, kissing him on the top of the head.

Eli exhaled slowly, relaxing into the embrace of those huge arms.

"Tonight I'm staying with you."

JULY, 1988

66 . . . *God save our gracious queen, God save the queen.*"

Like everything else about him, Cavendish's voice was ridiculously over-sized. Raspy and not especially tuneful, it nevertheless managed to be perfectly on pitch. Afraid he'd burst into tears with the emotion of the moment and mindful of his own voice's propensity to crack on the high notes, Rupert refrained from joining him in the anthem, though he mouthed the words for the benefit of the cameras.

It was, he supposed, as close as one got in this irreverent age to an apotheosis. Winning Olympic bronze for England, and winning it in collaboration with the man who'd stolen his heart years before and still kept it under lock and key. It was hard to imagine life holding anything more thrilling than that in store. What could one possibly do for an encore? Graduating from Oxford weeks earlier with triple firsts paled by comparison, though it was, at least arguably, a far more practical accomplishment. Even so, Rupert knew which of the two he reckoned more meaningful. His career at university had largely been passed as a series of interregnums—interregni?—during which Cavendish's person had been unavailable to him due to exigencies of time and space and other circumstances of an exceedingly pragmatic nature, rendering the whole experience of higher education almost totally insignificant from Rupert's perspective. Whereas this Olympic quest had been rather the opposite of that, necessitating as it did extreme and prolonged proximity—though not always of a sexual nature—to said person and predicated in the first instance on said person's explicitly communicated wish. Indeed, the presence of those bronze medals dangling against their chests as the orchestral music

181

soared and the flag rose into the Olympic firmament, was due to nothing more or less than Cavendish's will. And what were those oars he and Rupert had wielded in pursuit of that goal other than analogues of Cavendish's own mighty implement?

So: apotheosis—yes.

■ ■ ■

Two days later the apotheosis renewed itself as they won silver in double sculls. But while apotheosis it might be, the reality of the situation was that Rupert's future remained distressingly undetermined. It was something about which Cavendish had expressed no intention whatever. Indeed, Cavendish refused to be drawn on the subject. And the absence of an expressed intention or even any inclination toward discussion of such seemed to bespeak a lack of engagement Rupert found infuriating, frustrating, and, by implication, heartbreaking. Wasn't this an instance, he felt like demanding, in which living happily ever after was the only appropriate next step?

He had found himself on the point of making this very argument more than once in the days leading up to their events and was deterred from doing so only by the thought that any response could only be premature. But now, surely now, Cavendish himself would speak, and Rupert's own sentiments would sound in that deep growl.

■ ■ ■

Their private celebration that night was sufficiently carnal to satisfy a six pack of sexual compulsives. In the profound serenity of its aftermath, Rupert thought surely the time had come for Cavendish to declare his intentions and chart the next leg of their course. But aside from some deeply satiated sounding grunts, Cavendish made no utterance. Soon they were asleep.

■ ■ ■

The Manhattan based publicist Cavendish had hired months earlier certainly earned her retainer. They were besieged with requests for interviews and photo shoots prior to their arrival at the games. Cavendish decreed an embargo prior to their events, the better to ensure that their concentration remained at its peak. But the morning after their second victory, fagged as he was, Rupert was forced to run the gauntlet. He'd practiced modest looking smiles in the mirror until he could muster an almost sincere one without even thinking about it, but that day's array of "opportunities" and "meet and greets" taxed him sorely. Cavendish sailed through them like a veteran of the celebrity wars, apparently with something at least approaching relish, but Rupert just wanted to be gone and more or less invisible. He understood Cavendish's impulse to capitalize on their success and the attending notoriety but found himself yearning for a deserted tropical island where they'd be able to go perpetually without clothing.

■ ■ ■

Around them, the games continued unabated. They attended several events. Cavendish had arranged for prime seats and even directed Rupert's attire and grooming choices. Nothing, it seemed, was to be left to chance. They were to appear where and as the greatest advantage could be gained. Rupert kept expecting Cavendish to pull him away suddenly from some venue or other, spirit him off in a waiting car, and breathlessly declare his undying love, but such a life altering event failed to occur.

When something finally did happen to totally redirect Rupert's course, it came without either warning or fanfare. Indeed, Rupert recognized it for what it was only retrospectively. Otherwise, he might have played the scene differently. But one always thought that after the fact.

II

"My dear boys," Selina Monagu-Withers purred, approaching their luncheon table. Dripping with furs and jewelry and far too heavily made up for a forenoon, she was as out of place in the athletes' village as a giant squid in the food court at Harrod's. Rupert wondered if she'd bribed someone to gain admission. "They told me you'd left the city."

Selina had married and divorced multiple titles of nobility on both sides of the Channel and emerged each time wealthier yet surprisingly little the worse for wear. Rupert had no idea what her background was, though there were persistent rumours of adolescent indiscretions at Rodean.

"Decoys," Rupert said. "Cavendish here hired at least a dozen sets of them."

"Really?" she asked, "how frightfully clever you are, darling."

That she swallowed such a ridiculous line only served to reinforce Rupert's faith in her stupidity.

"You can't put a price on your solitude," Cavendish growled, with a fervor that suddenly made Rupert wonder if he hadn't accidentally hit on the truth with that offhand quip.

"Quite right, my dears," she said. "Now just look who I happened upon outside the aquatic pavilion."

"I believe it was the velodrome you were in front of, my dear," the tall, distinguished gentleman at her elbow corrected her.

"Indeed," she nodded. "One wonders what the bloody buggery a 'velo-drome' is. One envisions squads of ostriches—or is the plural ostrichi?—skittering around on unicycles."

"I believe it's where the equestrian events are held," Cavendish said, eyeing the gentleman with an expression Rupert found disconcerting. "It's Ned Westerleigh, isn't it?"

"Pleased to see you again, my boy," the gentleman smiled, "and you, too, of course, FitzMerlin."

"Always a pleasure," Rupert said.

"You all know each other?" Selina asked. "Where's the fun in introducing your friends to people they already know?"

"Cavendish is always 'fun', I believe," Westerleigh said, "and as for my young kinsman, here. . ."

"Don't tell me you're related to him, too," Selina complained. "Honestly. I can't take you anywhere without you turning up some second cousin three times removed or whatnot. It's a positive menace."

"The Westerleighs are extremely well connected, I believe," Cavendish said.

"Not to mention comprehensively," Rupert smiled. "Didn't we meet last at Margot Ranulfssen's engagement party?"

"We did indeed," Westerleigh said.

"Which one?" Selina asked. "That girl's been engaged more times than one can count."

"Paris," Westerleigh said. "That Canadian actor."

"Idiot girl," Selina fumed. "She really should have gone through with it and married that one. Worth thirty million and gay as a goose."

"Dear boys," Westerleigh said, "we wouldn't dare presume on any more of your time."

"We wouldn't?" Selina asked.

"Certainly not," Westerleigh said. "Now young Rupert, I understand you've just finished your degree at Oxford."

"Triple firsts," Cavendish nodded.

"Just so," Westerleigh nodded. "Perhaps you'll do me the honour when you return to London. Luncheon at my club. Just ring up when you get to town. Cavendish has the number."

Cavendish has the number. Whatever could that signify? Of course Cavendish had every telephone number worth having, and Ned Westerleigh's surely figured among them. But Rupert found the declaration curious nonetheless.

III

Almost the minute they got to London, Cavendish was off again. This time it was Hong Kong.

"I don't see why you didn't go there directly from Seoul," Rupert said.

"Wanted to spend time with you, didn't I?"

"On a commercial flight," Rupert said, not seeing the point.

"In the first class cabin," Cavendish pointed out.

"Yes, but."

"Not everything is about sex."

"Since when?"

"For that matter, I'd already arranged our triumphant entrance," Cavendish grinned. "Sauntering down the aircraft stairs to the applause of thousands."

This was no exaggeration. There had actually been thousands at Heathrow for their arrival. Rupert still wasn't convinced that Olympic bronze or even silver rated such adulation. Plenty of gold had been won by British athletes at the games. Well, not plenty, perhaps. But some. Yet as far as Rupert knew, none of those other athletes were being similarly feted. Of course when you came right down to it, none of the other medalists was even half as photogenic as Cavendish was.

"I'll drive you to the airport in the morning," Rupert suggested.

"You won't," Cavendish said, starting to unbutton Rupert's shirt.

"Why not?"

"You're to be seen just after sunrise rowing on the Thames down by Richmond. The paparazzi have already been alerted."

"Oh."

"Make sure you're bare-chested," Cavendish said, going after Rupert's left nipple, which was the more sensitive of the two.

"All right."

"And use some of my stuff and slick your hair back."

"Really."

"Attention to detail is crucial in these situations," Cavendish said. "It's supposed to be an accidental sighting, but nothing about your presentation can be left to chance."

"How long will you be gone?" Rupert asked, suppressing a moan.

"Not sure," Cavendish muttered, really intent on the task at hand now. "Might be as long as a fortnight."

III

In the event it was exactly a fortnight. A fortnight without so much as a phone call, which left Rupert feeling particularly bereft. Then, without warning, he opened the front door of the mews house he was renting while he pondered his future, and there Cavendish was.

"You're back."

"And your backside," Cavendish grunted, pushing Rupert back inside and slamming the door behind them, "been dreaming about it. Regularly. Incessantly. Almost lost my mind."

"And you expect to just show up here and make demands," Rupert laughed.

"Problem with that?"

"Suppose not," Rupert said, unzipping.

■ ■ ■

"Ever see that cousin of yours?" Cavendish asked. His head was pillowed on Rupert's chest. Rupert loved stroking those coarse curls.

"Cousin?" Rupert asked.

"Westerleigh chappie."

"Oh, right," Rupert said. "Ned."

"That one."

"Tea at his club," Rupert said. "Last week."

"Try to recruit you for the spooks, did he?"

"What?"

"Did me," Cavendish said. "Once upon a time."

"You never said."

"One's not supposed to," Cavendish grunted. "One's not even supposed to recall the overture having taken place."

"Right."

"So did he?"

"I thought one wasn't supposed to speak of it," Rupert said.

"Only if he did," Cavendish said, "shouldn't be too quick to turn it down. Opportunity to serve. All that."

"Did you turn him down?"

"Didn't make the cut," Cavendish said.

"Oh."

Somehow the idea of Cavendish failing to meet the requirements of the Secret Service, whichever branch Ned was involved with, seemed unbearable.

"Temperamentally unsuited," Cavendish said. "What they told one. God knows what the real reason was."

"Do you regret it?"

"Don't be silly," Cavendish said. "Far too risky, that game. One could be killed. Or maimed. And one's always on the go in that line of work. Moment's notice. Godforsaken places. Sri Lanka. Kuwait. Bananastan. Not like the flicks make it look at all, women dripping off one and speeding around in fancy cars."

"That rather describes you already," Rupert observed.

"Chap," Cavendish yawned.

"So you think I shouldn't go with them?"

"Aha," Cavendish said. "So Westerleigh did try."

"Bastard."

"Any chance of seconds on that entrée?" Cavendish asked, giving Rupert a tweak. That left nipple was raw.

"Since you asked so nicely," Rupert said, readying himself for the onslaught.

■ ■ ■

With Cavendish back in London, everything that had been on hold sprang into motion. Interviews. Photo shoots. Appearances at charity functions. The two of them were the toast of the city. It would never have occurred to Rupert that winning Olympic medals was something that could be exploited, but the opportunities weren't lost on Cavendish. It wasn't as if either of them needed the money. It was, rather, like Hillary gazing thoughtfully at that damned peak.

■ ■ ■

There was even to be a poster put on sale, a shot of the two of them, bare-chested except for their medals, posed side by side. Cavendish left not a single detail of the image uncalculated. He was to smolder in the shot, for instance, whilst Rupert offered a boyish aspect.

"What's with you and this stuff?" Rupert complained as the makeup chappie plastered his hair down with grease.

"Stop trying to identify a sinister agenda in everything," Cavendish grumbled. "The shot is to be a study in contrasts, that's all. You're blond, I'm dark.

You have that satiny tan, and I'm pale skinned. I have this ridiculous mop of curls, like a Renaissance Italian prince. So of course we have to present you as a member of the Hitler Youth."

"If that's not sinister, I don't know what is," Rupert said.

"Just a touch more grease," Cavendish suggested. "It doesn't look quite slick enough. Needs to seem blinding."

■ ■ ■

Rupert had told Ned he needed time to consider the proposition. And as a practical matter his calendar was impossibly clogged at the moment, leaving him hopelessly distracted. A few weeks merely, and he'd be able to give the matter the attention it deserved. It seemed a perfectly reasonable request, and if Ned suspected there was more to it than that he gave no indication. Still, before he ended their interview he begged Rupert's indulgence as he laid out the case a last time. Like Ned himself, Rupert had relatives all over the Eastern Bloc and thus possessed a convenient excuse for wide ranging travel in the region. Also like Ned, Rupert spoke fluent Russian, albeit, it had to be said, in a form heavily inflected with archaisms and obsolete idioms which made it, and him, seem rather quaint. Not to say prehistoric. He was a recognized authority on Soviet literature, having distinguished himself through the publication of a handful of scholarly articles on the subject during his recently concluded undergraduate days. And his accomplishments in sport provided him with access to a domain which was of great importance in contemporary Soviet life, while his reputation as the "peer who gave it all up", made him fascinating to the Soviet overlords, who, despite their constantly proclaimed horror of the aristocracy, were some of the world's biggest snobs. Rupert detested that soubriquet. He'd never been more, really, than a peer twice removed, but the press loved the idea of it and resurrected the phrase for its coverage of the Seoul Games. Indeed, Ned averred, Rupert was of such potential importance to the service that if he hadn't existed someone would have been forced to invent him. Except that doing so would have taken more time and required far more resources than could have been allocated to such a project in these straightened times. Nevertheless, a more appropriate candidate for a position on the staff of the cultural attaché in

Moscow could hardly be conceived of. And here he was, at loose ends. It was nothing less than kismet.

Yes, Rupert saw all that, he assured Ned as he beat his retreat.

Time. He needed time. Surely Cavendish must come to his senses soon. The prospect of Rupert's recruitment and dispatch to parts unknown seemed to guarantee it.

■ ■ ■

What Rupert actually needed was a sign from Cavendish. And he got it, but not in the way he'd hoped. Leaving Ned that afternoon he understood clearly that their interview wasn't to be spoken of. Then Cavendish had. Rupert had been hopeful that Cavendish would return from Hong Kong prepared finally to declare himself, to insist that they set up housekeeping, or at least bachelor's hall, together. Some sort of formalized arrangement between them seemed well overdue. But instead of that, Cavendish alluded to his own abortive "recruitment" by Ned Westerleigh's masters and implied that Rupert ought to give it a go. It was heartbreaking. Were he to do as Cavendish advocated, further delays and disruptions in their affairs were inevitable. Rupert couldn't go along with it.

But that assumed Cavendish was telling the truth about having been turned down for the service. And he'd have to say that, wouldn't he? He couldn't come out and say something like "put in a good word for you with Control"—or whatever they called the man in charge—"they're taking quite an interest in you, my dear". Could he? And wouldn't an espionage career explain Cavendish's comings and goings, his globetrotting, his all too frequent *incommunicado*? How many times in the past year alone had he been unreachable? Yes, it all fit. Cavendish as a sort of James Bond in the raw.

Unless it didn't.

■ ■ ■

In any case, the sign Rupert had been hoping and praying for never materialized and didn't appear likely to. It was a bitter pill. Meanwhile, however, Cavendish was back in London for however long, and was apparently content to make his person available to Rupert on a more or less constant basis. That was something. But Rupert couldn't help but be troubled by the way Cavendish, every day or so, asked if he'd seen or heard anything else of Ned. That had to mean something, didn't it?

■ ■ ■

So finally he made the call and put in his second appearance at Ned's club, which was even more exclusive and disastrously down at the heel than Cavendish's, if such were possible.

"My dear boy," Ned smiled as the porter delivered Rupert to the table in the dining room where the remains of a full English breakfast moldered enticingly. "How lovely to see you. Please tell me you haven't eaten. Osgood here will bring you a plate."

"Thanks awfully," Rupert said. He'd been too nervous earlier to think about eating before he left home, but seeing that debris jump started his appetite.

"Osgood," Ned said, "if you please."

"As you wish, sir," Osgood nodded.

■ ■ ■

"Well, this is very good news indeed," Ned said almost before the words were out of Rupert's mouth. "Now I scarcely need to remind you. . ."

"Understood," Rupert said. "Not a word to anyone."

"My dear," Ned said, "that hardly needs to be mentioned. What I meant to say was that we're not Americans. Obviously. They'd greet you on the front stairs as you left the building a few minutes hence and spirit you off to training camp. But here these things take time. You'll have to be thoroughly vetted. You have been already, of course, but they'll go back over it again. Perhaps twice more. It may be several weeks before the matter can move through channels. So I wouldn't hold my breath if I were you."

"I see."

"I'll just have to ask you to keep me advised of your comings and goings," Ned said, "where you can be located on a more or less day to day basis, so to speak. So as to pass the word along as needed."

■ ■ ■

Meanwhile, Cavendish was uncharacteristically present. He passed his days moving from Rupert's bed to Rupert's kitchen to Rupert's bathroom to the gym where they both worshipped regularly and back again. He was as seldom out of sight as out of mind. And he was rarely clothed to any meaningful extent. This was welcome, certainly, but baffling. Could all this proximity possibly be coincidence? There was, Cavendish explained, a smell in his rooms at the club which necessitated his bunking with Rupert for several weeks while things were sorted out. And next, the flat he'd bought over in Chelsea required extensive renovations before he could even think of moving into it. And the squads of young women whose hospitality he might easily have availed himself of proved, each and every one of them, to possess some minor but disqualifying flaw when push came to shove. And so on. It was as close to a declaration as Rupert was likely to get, he reasoned. And yet it was no declaration at all.

More than once, he resolved to have it out with Cavendish. Just spill out his feelings like so much beer sloshing onto the floor of a pub on a post-Test Match evening and see what came of it. He was rehearsing his painstakingly composed speech one afternoon as he jogged down the Embankment after his workout when he caught sight of Ned Westerleigh striding along in his direction with a furled umbrella over his shoulder. He was about to call a greeting when something indefinable in Ned's posture dissuaded him. The next thing he knew two brawny gentlemen had him by the arms and were "helping" him toward the curb, and an instant after that he was in a taxi sweating onto the upholstery as the vehicle weaved through traffic in a direction away from the river.

Away from his flat, as well, where he'd left Cavendish in a profound post coital slumber. He hoped Ned would find a way to get word to him that he shouldn't be concerned at Rupert's disappearance. Because that's what this all too obviously was. Then again, if his suspicions were correct, Cavendish had probably known that today was the day well before they tumbled into bed together after lunch.

MARCH, 1990

I

"You're only sixteen," Yakov said. "What's the rush?"

"Almost seventeen," Yoel said, "so there's no time to lose. And if I start private flight school now, there's a much better chance I'll get into military flight school later."

"So you can fly fighters like your brother," Yakov said. "I get it."

"It's not really about Rafi," Yoel insisted.

This was probably true. Yakov knew how much Yoel hated being compared with his half brother, who was a full generation older. Yakov's age, in fact.

It was uncanny how much Yoel reminded Yakov of his younger brother, Cooper. The main difference was that Cooper had never bothered to learn a word of Hebrew. Not even for his Bar Mitzvah. He had copied his Torah portion out phonetically on tiny pieces of paper and slipped them into his shirt cuffs for later reference. Rabbi Schoenstein nearly had a stroke when those notes slipped out during the ceremony.

"So what's stopping you?" Yakov asked.

"I'm guessing Dad won't like it," Yoel said.

"When has that ever kept you from doing what you wanted?"

"He's still a very influential man," Yoel said. "In the military, I mean. He has all kinds of ways of stopping me without seeming to interfere."

"Well, you know what I think," Yakov said.

"Not that again," Yoel complained.

"Yes, that again," Yakov said. "You should talk to him about it."

■ ■ ■

"All right," Naftali nodded. "He asked you for advice. You gave it. It was very good advice, too. He'll either take it or he won't. End of story."

"I just wonder if I should talk to Marcus."

"Sweetheart, they have to work it out between them. Marcus might not mind at all."

"Oh, he'll mind," Yakov said. "None of his sons have gone into the armored corps. And you know how Marcus is about his precious tanks. Yoel's his last chance for a true successor."

"Marcus is a bigger man than that," Nafatli said. "And even if he isn't, it's not your business. Let your talk with Yoel be an end of it."

■ ■ ■

Naftali was right, of course. Naftali was almost always right. And Yakov took his advice at least half the time.

■ ■ ■

From what Yakov could tell, every boy who ever lived had made a shrine of his bedroom. At least every boy blessed with a bedroom or other suitable space of his own had done so. Every time he stepped into Yoel's room, he recalled his own room and the rooms of his brothers. They'd been as personal as diaries. If you knew what you were looking at, you could even read them that way. Each one was a kind of archaeological dig in the making.

Yoel's room was a monument to aviation. The model aircraft hanging from the ceiling. The shelves of books on the subject. The posters on the walls. They spoke to this great love of Yoel's life. At the same time this monument also gave mute testimony to the very particular fervency of its curator. Many boys could be devotees but, being boys, a certain chaos reigned overall. The artifacts might all be present, but disorder governed their deployment and worship. In this case, however, the room had the quality of a museum exhibit dedicated not to its apparent subject but to a certain model of boyhood itself.

That was thanks to Naftali. Yakov might have unearthed and awakened Yoel's latent obsession, but it was Naftali who gave it discipline. He had to. Yakov had been away with the army so much of the time. Naftali was the one present day to day, the true *in loco parentis*. His surgeon's sensibility insisted on everything having its place and always being there. The result was a room that for all the objects it contained gave the impression of the cell of a medieval monk. Or, for that matter, the barracks room of a junior officer in the Israeli Defense Force. Spartan. Orderly. Hygienic. That was the room. And for that matter, it was the boy himself. Yakov had helped him discover his passion for humankind's conquest of the skies. Naftali had taught him to love discipline.

For Yakov, Yoel's presence in their home had been a chance to redeem his single boyhood failure. He'd all but ignored the existence of his youngest brother. His two regrets as he'd lain in that field hospital during the Yom Kippur War contemplating his existence to that point were that he'd never been in love and that he'd never really bothered to know Cooper. Ike had been omnipresent as older brothers inevitably are. And Josh and Yakov were identical twins. That spoke for itself. Cooper had been little more than an interloper. And annoying into the bargain. Yakov's most vivid memories of Cooper had to do with their arguments. Cooper rarely won those disputes but he never lost them. Life and time had redeemed both of Yakov's regrets. Life had sent him Naftali almost immediately, and in time, circumstances had sent him Yoel. Yoel was Cooper in a younger avatar—less obnoxious not because Yoel himself was less obnoxious than Cooper had been but because by the time he moved in with them, Yakov himself was old enough to know better how one went about being a brother. For Naftali, Yoel was the son he'd never had. It had been a blessing.

Marcus and Anat, may the Almighty continue to bless them and make them and their children prosper, had, incomprehensibly, given him and Nafatli a free hand in dealing with Yoel. For Anat it was undoubtedly a relief. Yakov still couldn't imagine what had induced Marcus to accept it.

Of course there was one thing that made the arrangement possible. Yakov and Naftali always deferred, or at least pretended to defer, to the boy's real father.

■ ■ ■

"I suppose I should feel guilty about it," Anat said, "but I don't."

"I don't understand," Yakov said. "Why would you?"

"A mother isn't supposed to farm out the raising of her son," she laughed.

"Nonsense," Yakov said. "All parents need help from time to time."

"Yes, but the way you and Naftali pretty much took over. It was the last thing I expected Yoel to say when my mother asked him what he wanted for Hanukkah that year."

"'I want to leave home'," Yakov laughed. "At age six, yet."

"Exactly," Anat nodded, "but what a stroke of genius for him to move in with you and Naftali. We all recognized it."

"Out of the mouths of babes."

"Avi and Zev were so easy. I hardly had to think about what to do with them. They were quiet and clean and obedient and I convinced myself that I was really good at being a mom. And then Yoel came along and he was simply too much to cope with. I couldn't do anything right. God knows how he'd have turned out but for the two of you."

"I think we got the better end of the deal, actually," Yakov said.

"I don't see how you could possibly say that," Anat said.

"No matter what happened," Yakov laughed, "I always knew that we could send him back to you."

"So you admit he was a handful."

"If you'll admit that you've never been able to tell when I'm being facetious," Yakov said. "The thing is, Yoel's given me a second chance at being a big brother. I don't know if that makes any sense, but it's how I feel. Joshua and I were too wrapped up in each other to pay much attention to Cooper."

"You were twins," Anat shrugged. "That's how it works."

"Yes," Yakov said. "Of course. But Yoel helped me realize what I'd missed out on. And he gave me a second chance at it."

"You and Naftali would have made such great fathers," Anat said. "When I think of how unfair. . ."

"Stop right there," Yakov said.

■ ■ ■

"Where's our boy?" Naftali asked.

"Where else?" Yakov asked. "Either the beach or the gym."

"Ah yes," Naftali nodded. "The two babysitters. Where would we be without them?"

"He's hardly a baby."

"I know. Last week I saw him playing volleyball out on the beach. He looked like a twenty year old. An extremely well-built one."

"It's that Luxemberg stock," Yakov said. "Look at his father. The man's never been in a gym except perhaps in pursuit of Arab gunmen, yet his arms are like tree trunks."

"What's for dinner tonight?"

"What else?"

"I know." Naftali rolled his eyes. "Yoel's in training, so that means either chicken or fish."

"It's good for us, too."

"That's not why our diet is the way it is. Some people would say you spoil him."

"Yes. Like the commanders in the Spartan army spoiled their soldiers," Yakov said. "It may look like he's being catered to constantly. But I assure you, that young man does not have an easy time around here."

"Exactly," Naftali smiled. "That's what those people don't get. You're crazy like a fox."

"Hardly," Yakov said. "I just think back to all the things my parents should have done in dealing with my brother Cooper, and I do them."

"Your parents didn't do so bad a job," Naftali said. "Cooper's already a millionaire. And he isn't thirty-five yet."

"He isn't quite a millionaire," Yakov protested.

"Well, he's close."

"Close, yes," Yakov admitted. "The point is this. By pretending that Cooper was just like the rest of us and treating him accordingly, my parents set themselves up for all kinds of *tsuris*. He was a special case, and things would have gone better if they had instituted a different regime for him. I'm not really doing all these things for Yoel."

■ ■ ■

Yakov found Yoel at the gym, where he was being coached in posing by the current Mr. Israel, Lev Blumenfeld. Blumenfeld was certainly the man for the job. He'd managed to place in the top six in his weight class at the World Championships, a notoriously hostile venue for Israeli athletes, so he knew his stuff. Whether the rather unsavory rumors about his extracurricular activities were true or not was a matter of some debate. Whatever indiscretions he was guilty of apparently took place outside the borders of Israel, which even the most skeptical critics agreed was creditable. Yakov wasn't sure Blumenfeld could be considered a good influence on Yoel, but the boy was bound to encounter all kinds, and here in Tel Aviv Blumenfeld could hardly flex his biceps without the gossips taking note, so it was probably safe enough.

Whether or not Yoel would enter that year's Mr. Israel competition in the junior division was still up in the air, but preparations were taking place based on the assumption that he would. Naftali wasn't sure he approved of Yoel's bodybuilding beyond the fact that it taught self-discipline and required an extremely hygienic regimen, but Yakov considered the phenomenon inevitable. As had been the case with regard to Yoel's flying, Yakov was responsible for this interest, too.

He and Naftali had taken Yoel and his older brothers to New York one year during their school holidays. They had never been to the States, and their mother, particularly, was anxious for them to go. Not anxious enough, however, to want to take them there herself. Traveling with the boys exhausted her, she claimed, though Yakov thought it had to do more with her reluctance to be recognized as a woman old enough to have sons that age. In any case, they went and stayed with his parents in the apartment on Riverside Drive where he and his brothers had grown up.

They did all the things tourists do—attractions, museums, Central Park. Avi and Zev had done extensive research beforehand, and as each site was systematically explored they checked it off their lists. Evenings there were symphony concerts, a trip to the ballet, and Broadway shows. On these excursions they were accompanied on several occasions by Yakov's brother, Josh, Josh's partne,r Andrew Rubinstein, and Josh's best friend, Eli Danziger. Each night Avi and Zev were captivated, but Yoel's responses were cooler, almost distant, and Yakov knew some kind of eruption was eminent. Eli must have sensed it too, because sitting in the Roxy Deli after a performance of *Cats*, he said, "I have an idea. My buddy Eamonn is competing in a bodybuilding show on Saturday night. We should all go."

In the event they didn't all go. Avi and Zev opted for yet another night of theater—Beckett in Greenwich Village of all things. Josh, Andrew, and Naftali took them. But Eli and Yakov escorted Yoel to the Brooklyn Academy of Music, the venue for Eamonn's contest, as unlikely as that seemed. The event was a revelation. Yakov had heard of such competitions, of course, but the reality exceeded his expecations. It wasn't nearly as seedy an affair as he'd expected. The audience was surprisingly respectable, the competition itself well regulated, serious, and almost genteel. Backstage afterward, Yoel had his photo taken with the triumphant Eamonn, whose own sons were present along with their uncles and cousins.

At Eli's apartment afterward, he delivered the *coup de grace*.

"Your cousin Cooper is a bodybuilder too, you know," he explained to a dazzled Yoel. "Here's a picture he sent Eamonn a couple of years ago when he won his weight class at the California Championships."

Yakov watched Yoel studying the picture carefully. His resemblance to his exotic, West Coast cousin had been remarked on extensively ever since their arrival in New York. Seeing Cooper in this previously unsuspected manifestation changed Yoel's life just as surely as that fateful visit to Ben Gurion airport had that long ago afternoon. By the time they returned to Tel Aviv, Yoel's obsession with aviation had been joined by its new twin, the iron game. As always, Yakov had been the first in the family to recognize the inevitable. He set up the weightlifting equipment for Yoel in a disused room off their back veranda and got him a trainer who specialized in working with boys not yet in their teens. She was an IDF veteran, a lesbian Sabra who was easily tough enough to keep Yoel in check.

The rest of the family figured that such hard work would get old in a hurry and the obsession would peter out. But Yakov knew that gleam in Yoel's eye for what it was. He even started working out himself, just a little. To keep Yoel company.

■ ■ ■

Lev Blumenfeld was a ridiculously handsome man. And the way he spoke to you seemed to confirm at least some of those rumors about male brothels in Frankfurt and escort services in Manhattan. Every time Yakov encountered him, he felt like one or the other of them should be wearing a condom.

"So what's the verdict?"

"I didn't know court was in session," Blumenfeld grinned.

"About our boy," Yakov growled. He had decided that his only defense, really, was a show of irascibility.

"He's ready," Blumenfeld shrugged. "He'll win the junior division in a walk."

"But will he enter?"

"Who knows?"

"Well, if you don't know his plans. . ."

"He doesn't confide in me," Blumenfeld said. "I'm his technical advisor only. I realize you and Naftali believe I'm some sort of Svengali, but it's as simple as that."

"So you honestly don't know what he's going to do?"

"No inkling," Blumenfeld said. "I'll tell you this much. He's waiting for some kind of sign."

"What does that mean?"

"He hasn't yet found the answer in himself," Blumenfeld said.

"Is that where it is?" Yakov asked.

"You of all people should know the answer to that," Blumenfeld said. "No great achievement takes place without it."

"I suppose that's true."

"But as for Yoel, he seems obsessed with that brother of yours. The one in San Francisco."

"Cooper," Yakov nodded. "They've never met. I didn't realize they were in touch."

"I don't know that they are," Blumenfeld said, "at least directly. There's some man in New York who's a kind of intermediary."

"Eli Danziger," Yakov said. "His lover and Cooper are long distance gym buddies."

"That's the one," Blumenfeld said. "Yoel seems to spend lots of time pondering the question what would Cooper do. Meanwhile, the man in New York keeps sending him photos of Cooper in action."

"God help us."

"I didn't realize it was a bad thing."

"Oh, I don't suppose it is, really," Yakov said. "Cooper's a solid enough citizen. His husband keeps him in check, from what I'm told. And he's certainly a success in business. Yoel could do worse for a muse."

■ ■ ■

"I'll tell you what it is," Marcus said. "He assumes I'll say no to this plan of his because of Rafi. He thinks I hold the air force responsible for Rafi moving to the States. Being a veteran pilot gave him opportunities over there, and he went."

"Isn't that the truth?" Yakov asked.

"It is and it isn't," Marcus said. "It's true that Rafi's experience flying fighters in combat made things easier for him over there. What isn't true is that I blame him for going. He's a man. He was within his rights to make the decision he did. There is no question of blame. Any more than I blame my brother, Robbie, for going to Sweden at the end of the war instead of coming to Palestine with me. We had fought side by side in the resistance. I couldn't imagine us splitting up. But he had other ideas. 'I've had enough of this,' he told me. 'The Nazis have been beaten. I'm a man of peace now. Go to Palestine. Build Israel, if that's what you think your mission is. Spend the rest of your life fighting. Because that's what your life will be. Battle without end.' Was he right? Was I wrong? The question makes no sense. He got rich there. Is there something wrong with that? Of course not. Men make decisions and live with them. That's all."

"So why don't you tell Yoel that?"

"Because he must decide things for himself. He doesn't need my permission. I made my choice. I left my mother and father behind and my two little sisters. My grandmother as well. Mama begged me to stay, but I wouldn't. She had already sent your father to America with Uncle Shmuel. She couldn't bear to lose me, too. But I went to the resistance anyway. And I never saw any of them again. I live with that every day. I did try to save them, you know. We learned what was going on in the camps. The resistance primarily focused on sabotage against the Nazis, but we did manage to save some Jews. Not as many as we wanted to, but some. Not my family, unfortunately, and I live with that. Those were the choices I made, and I wasn't much older than Yoel is now. He has to learn to make his own decisions like I did. It isn't easy. What matters is not whether he flies fighters or commands tanks or performs surgery or runs off to America to be a millionaire. What matters is that he's man enough to live his own life as he sees fit."

"All right," Yakov said.

"And I hope you won't tell him about this talk," Marcus said. "I hope you'll do what I'm doing and allow him the opportunity to be that man."

■ ■ ■

How strange, Yakov thought on his way home from Marcus' office. To get such remarkably similar messages from both the boy's father and Blumenfeld, scoundrel that he was. There might be something in what they were saying. Perhaps it was time for him to keep his own mouth closed.

II

Naftali insisted that Yoel should clean his own room, but Yakov couldn't help himself. At least once a week he went in there to dust. Yoel's newest acquisitions had pride of place. His desk was stacked with the manuals required for his flight training, which he pored over from morning until night. Basically every moment he wasn't at school or the gym or on the beach playing volleyball for money against unsuspecting European tourists. That's how he and his friends earned their pocket money. His mother didn't like it, but Yakov and Naftali didn't see much harm, especially since most of the tourists were Germans and Swedes who could well afford such contributions to the local economy.

Front and center atop the bookcase was the trophy he'd won at the Mr. Israel contest. Propped next to it was a photo taken just after the contest. In it he looked uncannily like Cooper.

■ ■ ■

Of all the things he and Naftali had done for Yoel over the years, this was the hardest. And paradoxically, it entailed doing nothing at all. Yakov supposed lots of parents went through this stage—keeping their mouths shut, letting adult decisions be made by young people who weren't really adults yet, crossing their fingers behind their backs. It was for Yoel's good, after all. But to Yakov it seemed like sending the boy out on a tightrope without a safety net.

How had Mom and Dad managed to seem so fearless in the face of it?

■ ■ ■

"No," Naftali said. "You will not rush out of here with only a protein shake in your stomach. You'll sit down and eat this breakfast that Yakov has made you."

"I don't want to be late," Yoel protested.

"Late?" Naftali shook his head. "You could stay for lunch and still not be late."

"He's right," Yakov nodded. "And I've made all your favorites."

"If I eat all that, the plane will never get into the air," Yoel said.

"Very funny. Besides, it's not all for you."

"You're serious about this," Yoel said.

"How often do I tell you what to do?" Yakov asked. "Really?"

"All right," Yoel relented, sitting down at the table. "Fair enough."

"We know it's your solo flight," Naftali said. "We know how important it is to you. All we want is for you to take a few moments to realize how important you are to us."

■ ■ ■

"Are you frightened?" Naftali asked.

"I fear no man," Yakov said. He couldn't take his eyes off the small airplane taxiing slowly down the runway.

"Because you don't quite seem yourself today," Naftali said. "Don't worry. Yoel will do fine. Jossi Austerlitz is the best flight instructor in the Middle East. He consults with air forces all over the world. If he says Yoel's ready to solo, Yoel's ready to solo."

"It's not that," Yakov said.

"What is it then? Naftali asked. "The maintenance workers? Contaminated avgas? The aircraft itself? Air traffic control?"

"None of those," Yakov said. "It's the bastard hiding out in the bushes with a shoulder mounted ground-to-air missile launcher."

OCTOBER, 1994

"Wakey-wakey."

"Huh?"

"Out of bed, FitzMerlin. You're coming with us."

"I beg your pardon?" Rupert asked, sitting up. The alarm clock on his bedside table read two-thirty.

"Pull up that sheet, man. You're not decent."

"What you get, Robson-Jones. Taking a man unawares in his boudoir."

"Perhaps, but please keep yourself covered."

"How am I supposed to make myself decent if I'm wrapped in a sheet?"

"That's your affair, I'm sure," Robson-Jones sniffed. "Now shift it. We're wasting time."

"What's it about?" Rupert asked, pulling items of clothing out of the wardrobe with one hand and keeping the sheet in place with the other.

"Somebody's been a very bad boy," Robson-Jones said. "Very bad indeed. And until we know exactly who, your whole section is to be held in custody."

"I say."

"Control's orders," Robson-Jones said, fending off any possible appeal. "Direct from HQ. Signal came in less than half an hour ago. Top top secret. Burn before reading."

■ ■ ■

The only surprise was the timing, Rupert mused, shivering in the chill of the drab, dimly lit cubicle. It was a part of the embassy he avoided at all costs.

Straight out of the Lubyanka, which, come to think of it, was disconcertingly close to hand. Rupert walked past it at least once a week in his meanderings around Moscow. Its exterior appearance was surprisingly non-threatening, belying its fearsome reputation as vortex of the Gulag. He had been setting off signal rockets about Mortenssen for two months. And now, with him due to go on leave, this indefinite delay. Unless the pace picked up, he'd miss his flight. Even in the midst of a crisis, things in London moved at a glacier's pace. No surprise there. What was that old thing about God's mills grinding slow but exceedingly fine? He probably had the quote wrong.

■ ■ ■

"Found this bag in your flat," Robson-Jones oiled, bursting through the door like a KGB interrogator with the smell of blood in his nostrils. "Like to tell me about it? Or should I just draw an obvious and incriminating conclusion?"

"Check the residency log," Rupert said. "I officially went on leave at midnight. My flight was booked eight weeks ago. About to miss it, if you must know."

"Advance planning," Robson-Jones nodded. "Shows premeditation if you ask me."

"Listen, man," Rupert said, "only reason this particular balloon went up is the whistle I've been blowing lately. You should be thanking me. Really."

"Could be," Robson-Jones agreed. "Could also be that all those distress flares were just an exercise in shifting blame. Misinformation, in other words. Nobody's ready to commit just yet. Either here or in London."

"Oh, please."

"Seriously," Robson-Jones said, "just now you should be considering your position very carefully, my dear. Best to come clean while mummy's still in a forgiving mood."

"That's rot," Rupert said. "And what's more, you know it's rot. I think you're just having your jollies, wanking around like this."

"You'd know about wanking, FitzMerlin," Robson-Jones said, "if anyone would."

After exhausting those pleasantries, Rupert then had to unpack his painstakingly packed bag and account for every single item in it—not one of them the least bit incriminating, let it be noted—while one of the embassy staff took photos of it all and Robson-Jones kept notes. He was a lefty, and as he wrote some of the ink rubbed off onto the sides of his fingers. This cheered Rupert. Robson-Jones was enjoying the situation far too much. But he was within millimeters of spoiling his shirt cuff.

Once the contents of the bag had been photographed and catalogued, an embassy employee Rupert didn't recognize came in, swept the whole lot, bag included, into one of those black plastic bin liners and left.

"Not going anywhere any time soon," Robson-Jones said. "So you might as well relax."

"Could I at least have some tea?" Rupert asked, "and perhaps a book?"

"Tea, certainly," Robson-Jones nodded. "A bun or two as well, I should think. Kitchen staff might run as far as a sausage roll. Not sure about that book, however. Have to run that request by the ambassador himself, what? Might be the makings of an offensive weapon. Or an implement of suicide for that matter."

"Death by a thousand paper cuts?" Rupert suggested. "Spare me."

"A thoroughly desperate man might get up to anything," Robson-Jones mused. "The mind boggles."

"You've spent too much time at theatre," Rupert said, "enjoying the works of one Tom Stoppard is my guess."

■ ■ ■

"I've brought your things, FitzMerlin," Barnstable said.

"Oh, right," Rupert said, looking up from his book.

"A little rumpled, I'm afraid. And I'm to say that you're required to dress for travel."

"Travel?"

"Don't ask," Barnstable said. "Even if I knew I wouldn't tell you."

"Travel," Rupert said. "Well, presumably that at least means leaving this cell."

"It's hardly a cell, FitzMerlin."

"Somehow," Rupert said, "a quotation from Shakespeare seems called for at this point. 'King of infinite space.' Isn't that how it goes?"

"I'd start dressing if I were you," Barnstable suggested. "You'll be called for yourself in no more than five minutes, unless I miss my guess. And the security boys won't take kindly to it if you're not ready when they arrive. Might make you stay. Or trade you to the Russkis for someone Control actually wants back in London."

II

The destination wasn't London. Rupert could tell that much, even though there were no windows in the fuselage of the RAF jet they'd bundled him into at Sheremetyevo. Blindfolded, yet. He knew it was an RAF jet from the smell alone. Their destination wasn't anywhere on a map, he didn't expect, though he'd timed the flight by his Breitling and Scotland seemed the most likely. He wondered what depredations that wristwatch had suffered in the course of their investigations. Surely the neutrality of a Swiss product should have been respected, but he had his doubts. Scotland meant one of the outlying stations. Likely to be cold. Highland Scotland, in his experience, was the one place on earth with a less hospitable climate than Moscow. He hoped the interrogation wouldn't be too strenuous. He couldn't imagine they thought he was behind the whole thing. But that Mortenssen was such a clever cuss there was no telling what lengths he might have gone to to frame Rupert.

Cavendish to the rescue?

Not bloody likely. Not this time. Rupert had missed the boat on that one. When Cavendish said the service had deemed him temperamentally unsuited, he was telling the truth. Rupert had figured that out while still in training. All his fantasizing was just that. No, he was on his own. It might get ugly.

■ ■ ■

It was a rough landing. He wondered if the pilots had been instructed to alarm him in that manner or if it was inevitable given the weather—stiff crosswinds on approach, from what he could tell—and the terrain. With mountains in all directions, their approach had been a challenging one. He noted this as he stumbled down the folding metal stairway to the tarmac, the weight of his bag nearly taking him over the flimsy rail at one point.

A rough landing at night. Whatever runway lights there were had been extinguished before he was allowed out of the plane. A Land Rover was waiting, its headlights glaring harshly. A Land Rover without a roof and him in this lightweight wool suit.

Not a uniform in sight except for those two on the flight deck. Just sinister types in dark jumpsuits. Right out of an over written novel about spies. God help him.

■ ■ ■

"Control wants you out of sight," the duty officer explained, pouring tea. "Sugar? Milk?"

It was as good a story as any.

"Neither, thanks."

"And nowhere near London, needless to say. That's all I'm allowed to tell you. You're not under lock and key here."

"That's good," Rupert nodded.

"At least not technically," the man continued. "But should you decide to foot it, you'll find the terrain extremely challenging. And the weather."

"I noticed on our way in."

"Indeed," the man nodded, "and you're a very long way from anywhere. You'd have to be more desperate than I'm guessing you are to try it."

"It's a fair cop," Rupert said, in a disastrously bad cockney.

"It's not for long," the man assured him. "At least I shouldn't think so."

■ ■ ■

209

There were no interrogations. Rupert would have welcomed an opportunity to tell his side of things. But the security guys were tough cookies. He didn't regret being exempted from their attentions. Five minutes in their hands and he'd probably be prepared to sell out his own mother. God help him—some hero.

■ ■ ■

Days passed. Suddenly it was three weeks. He'd been due to meet Cavendish in Paris on the third day of his leave. He hoped somebody had bothered to get him word. Thinking about it more carefully, he decided he wasn't sure about that. Perhaps a worried Cavendish wasn't such a bad idea. Not that Cavendish would be able to do anything. Meanwhile the weather turned yet more frightful. He stared out the barred windows of the cottage at the falling snow. Scotland, jewel of the arctic.

He had run out of reading material. They furnished him with paper and biros and he tried his hand at poetry. That proved too confessional, so he attempted short fiction instead. It was abortive but time consuming. The ideal pastime for an exile of his type, in other words.

■ ■ ■

They had taken all his clothing on arrival, giving him several of the same dark coloured jumpsuits everyone else wore. Then one morning when he stumbled out of the bedroom, there was his bag sitting on the kitchen table, along with a note.

"Dress for travel," he muttered. Going on four weeks since they'd taken him from his bed in Moscow. His leave was all but over. Wouldn't it be comical if his next stop was back at the embassy?

III

It wasn't. He turned the key in the sticky lock and stepped into his Chelsea *pied a terre,* nostrils twitching at the smell of stale air, careful to avoid treading

210

on the piles of mail on the floor. Mostly advertising circulars, he was certain, but he'd go through them carefully anyway. Advertising circulars were sometimes utilized by the service in ingenious and unpredictable ways. The last thing he'd anticipated was arriving home and finding the flat undisturbed. By all rights the security people should have gone over every square inch of it for evidence of his guilt or otherwise.

■ ■ ■

One couldn't simply drop out of sight as Rupert had without people remarking on it. Except that was the case. When he walked into his gym the next morning, nobody batted an eye. He should have arrived from Paris weeks ago for the remainder of his leave. He'd called and sent messages arranging this meeting and that and then hadn't shown up for any of them. Since joining the service, his movements had been erratic at best. He supposed by now people were accustomed to his standing them up. And even before that, come to think of it, when he'd still been a student. Yes, he'd had terrible manners about that sort of thing. One couldn't expect to get away with it indefinitely. Still, his sudden reappearance should have occasioned more reaction than it did, he thought. Perhaps they'd all been warned not to notice it.

On reflection, he could only hope that was the case. The possibility that he was socially insignificant was more than he could bear.

■ ■ ■

Over the next couple of weeks everyone was apparently too well mannered to mention the suicide in Moscow recently of his superior, Frogmaxtedd, the assistant cultural attache. Apparently, Mortensson was as innocent as Rupert was. That fiendish Frogmaxtedd had managed to induce each of them to implicate the other.

■ ■ ■

"I still have no idea what happened," Rupert said, buttering a scone. Outside the dining room windows, an indisputably English rain was falling on the streets and rooftops of all too recognizable Bloomsbury. How he longed for a glimpse of Cavendish bounding up to the club entrance and shaking himself under the portico like a huge, wooly dog before coming inside. A Newfoundland or such.

"My dear boy," Ned Westerleigh twinkled, "you signed your articles and left the employment of the Her Majesty's security services, either for good or until such time as your services are once again required and you are recalled to the colours. You sat quietly while some anonymous bureaucrat reminded you in the sternest possible terms that you're a signatory to the Official Secrets Act and bound to carry information vital to the security of the realm to your grave. Information absolutely trivial as well. Such are the fiats of our masters. Surely you remember all that."

"Of course," Rupert nodded. "It's the rest of it."

"Oh, that," Ned nodded. "Well, it seems that you blew the whistle on the gravest security breach at the Moscow residency in living memory. That makes you a hero. It also makes you an embarrassment. Thus, you couldn't be allowed to continue to serve."

"I suppose," Rupert said, "but it leaves one feeling rather at loose ends."

He didn't mention that Cavendish had left for a new posting in Hong Kong just hours before his return. That had been the icing on this particularly noxious cake.

"Of course it does, my dear. But try not to be so down in the mouth about it. The stories I could tell you. Except that I can't, of course. Suffice it to say some of the very best men ever, individuals of the highest possible caliber, have had their careers in the service cut short for even less. In some cases their entire careers consisted of a solitary op. There's no dishonour in your situation at all, young Rupert."

"Can't seem to get interested in anything," he mused.

"There's a chap I think you should go see," Ned said. "Before you leave I'll give you his card. Ring him up tomorrow as well. Tell him to expect to hear from you."

"Dare I ask?"

"You are," Ned said, "as I am, a loyal Wykehamist. But really, there's no harm in Eton."

"Peregrine was educated there," Rupert said. "If you can call it that."

"You can't blame him on the school," Ned said. "I was at his christening, you remember."

"Actually, I don't," Rupert said. "Too young at the time."

"Of course," Ned said, "but let me assure you, it was evident even at that tender age that he was a bounder."

"That early?"

"Absolutely," Ned nodded. "So really, he's not Eton's fault."

"Suppose not."

"One hears that the school is definitely on the up. The very best people are sending their sons there nowadays."

"Ha, ha."

"That's better," Ned smiled. "I was almost afraid you'd lost your sense of humour."

"And what does any of this have to do with me?" Rupert asked.

"Schoolmastering can be a highly satisfying career, I'm told."

"Me?" Rupert laughed. "Surely you're joking."

"Not a bit," Ned said.

"Then you've lost your mind," Rupert said.

"Just see Stevenson," Ned said. "Let him be the judge of it. If I am wrong, you'll certainly be free to tell me so."

"Oh, all right," Rupert said. "I suppose."

"Keep your charming little *pied a terre* for weekends and hols," Ned said. "Couldn't be better located for a youngster of your interests. And Richmond during the week."

■ ■ ■

"Honestly, Reyerson Minor," Rupert boomed, "is that absolutely, positively the best you can do?"

"Sorry, FitzMerlin, sir."

"Who can assist him?" Rupert looked around the room at their faces, terrified, fascinated, anything but bored. The scene was strikingly familiar, even though the actual setting was brand new to him. Such must be the fate of all novices to his new profession. You apprehended the surroundings with your adolescent self, but you had to perform your duties as though you were an adult.

Silence.

"You, Quagg?"

"Sorry, sir."

"You, Forbes-Lytton?"

"Sorry, sir."

"Indefensible, I call it," Rupert stormed. "I've a good mind to send every last one of you to the Head to explain yourselves. Do you have any idea what it's costing your parents to have you here wasting your time like this? Of course you don't. You're all as ignorant of that as you are of everything else."

Quaking, they were. He'd never get used to it. Unless, of course, he continued channeling Cavendish. Cavendish would know exactly how to pull it off.

SEPTEMBER, 1995

"Money?" Yakov asked.

"Check," Yoel nodded.

"Tickets? Passport?"

"Check and check."

"You're sure you don't want me to drive you?" Yakov asked. "It's no trouble, really."

"I don't want you to drive me," Yoel said. Blumenfeld had been particularly insistent on it. Arrive at Ben Gurion by taxi. And not just any taxi. A particular taxi which would be waiting in a particular location at a specified time. And here was Yakov threatening to fuck it all up.

"Leave him alone," Naftali said. "He's not twelve years old."

"I know," Yakov nodded. "I know."

"Then act like you know it," Naftali laughed.

"It's all right," Yoel said. Blumenfeld had been just as fussy earlier that afternoon. And for similar reasons. Yoel understood what it meant, and thus it didn't annoy him.

"Thirty days leave," Yakov said. "How I envy you."

"You've got leave coming up yourself," Yoel said.

"Not for another six weeks."

"Still."

"I said, leave him alone," Naftali said. "Next thing you know you'll be inviting yourself to go along."

"Certainly not," Yakov said. "He's ready to fly solo."

"He's been flying solo for years," Naftali said.

■ ■ ■

The taxi picked Yoel up at the specified location at the exact time—checkpoint one. The traffic on the way out to Ben Gurion was as chaotic as usual. The security posts couldn't have been more efficient if they'd been staffed by Germans. Yoel fought off his impatience. The stops had all been built into his schedule. Still, *fighter pilot on leave. Off on an adventure.*

■ ■ ■

The 747 was enormous. Yoel had flown on one before, but not since joining the IAF. The F-4 he had recently qualified on was a toy compared to this behemoth. A lethal toy, to be sure. If a craft like that was not lethal it had no purpose. In the modern world, most flying machines were conceived not for the sheer, delirious joy of taking to the sky, as if that couldn't be purpose enough in itself, but with clearly defined, almost purely utilitarian objectives in mind. Such as killing people on one hand, or, in the case of this Boeing, transporting several hundred of them several thousand miles at high speed. And in a level of silence and comfort that only emphasized the murderous barbarity of the F-4 Yoel nevertheless thought of as his trusted friend.

If he wasn't careful, he'd end up as philosophical as his mother, the renowned poetess. That wouldn't do at all. Philosophy, Blumenfeld insisted, was a distraction. And distractions were potentially fatal. Yoel must aim for a life without distractions. Around him, the cavernous cabin was gradually filling. It seemed improbable that so many people intended to fly from Tel Aviv to Los Angeles on the same day. The practical explanation, that if you insisted on traveling on the "national airline" your choice of destinations was limited and Los Angeles might be an obligatory stop on the way to anywhere in western North America, still seemed insufficient to account for all those faces, pairs of shoes, handbags, magazines and newspapers, and assorted other paraphernalia as the payload accumulated.

■ ■ ■

Yoel's seat mates were a mother and daughter, middle aged and late teen respectively, named Wilson. They couldn't have appeared any more American if they had draped themselves in the Stars and Stripes. He had seen enough American television to recognize many of the clichés they embodied. He assumed they also represented others he was unaware of. They practically belonged in some sort of museum display of their species. Mrs. Wilson informed him that they were from a place called Tucson. She described it as a desert city, but apparently the Arizona desert was very different from the Sinai though she wasn't capable of explaining exactly how. During her monologue the daughter grinned and stared. Yoel knew what that meant. He got stared at lots. More, really, than made him comfortable. Mrs. Wilson also explained that they were Methodists, hence their visit to the Holy Land. From her comments, Yoel gathered that this term denoted some sort of Christian sect. He didn't know much about Christians except that Israel was more or less constantly overrun with them. They represented a crucial source of income. The national economy depended on them, and since he was a servant of the nation, it behooved him to behave as cordially as possible so as to encourage them to return again and again. Or at least encourage them to encourage their friends and relations to make similar pilgrimages. He understood that their presence was a source of profound annoyance to the more religious of his countrymen. Still, he didn't find them objectionable on those grounds, and he had enough relatives in America not to find them especially mysterious or obnoxious. They were just out of touch enough with real life to be mildly comical. Yoel's own upbringing included both Brit and Bar Mitzvah but not much else in the way of religious observance, though he invariably fasted on Yom Kippur and ate latkes for Hanukkah. Otherwise, his particular tribe was ruthlessly secular. The Luxembergs and his mother's family, the Schlesingers, could best be described as politically Marxist and culturally Freudian. That made them typical of their class of Israelis, though the nation liked to think of itself as a classless society.

■ ■ ■

The takeoff made him nervous. He never liked takeoffs except when he was at the controls himself. He felt the same way about landings, but in this case the landing was sixteen hours in the future. Plenty of time to worry about that later. He might even sleep through it.

■ ■ ■

"Lieutenant Luxemberg," the stewardess smiled. She spoke Hebrew with a Northern European accent. She had been flirting with him with just the right combination of enthusiasm and professional detachment since he boarded. He knew the Wilsons had noticed it.

"Hello, again," he said.

"Captain's compliments. He invites you to visit the flight deck."

"My pleasure," Yoel said, unfastening his seat belt.

"What did she say?" Mrs. Wilson asked. "Is something wrong?"

"Just a message for me," Yoel said. "I'll be right back."

He followed the stewardess up the aisle toward the front of the aircraft. The air was smooth. The giant wings were steady as granite. The Boeing seemed to hang motionless in the sky. This was what his older brother Rafi had given up his career in the IAF for. These days he piloted airliners between New York and Honolulu. But as they flew on into the west, it all reminded Yoel more and more of the busses going up and down Dizengoff Street.

The stewardess knocked on the cockpit door. It opened from inside.

"Captain Zimmermann," she said. "This is Lieutenant Luxemberg."

They stepped onto the flight deck.

"Welcome aboard, Lieutenant," the captain said, smiling up at him from his seat at the controls. "I flew with your brother in '73."

The Yom Kippur War. Rafi had shot down a couple of MiG's. Yoel was born during the hostilities.

"I guess you guys all opted for more spacious offices," Yoel said, looking around the cockpit.

"You got his sense of humor as well as his looks," Zimmermann laughed.

218

"I bet he never had your pectoral development, though," the co-pilot said. He spoke Hebrew with an American accent. "I saw you at the World Championships in Shanghai last year. You took fourth in the light-heavies."

"Sixth," Yoel said. "But thanks for the promotion."

"Samra here competes in the middleweights," Zimmermann said.

"Really?"

"Once or twice," the co-pilot shrugged. "Local shows only."

"Local in New Jersey is nothing to sneeze at," Zimmermann insisted. "New Jersey is what? Larger population than Israel?"

"I guess," the co-pilot nodded.

"Here, Luxemberg," Zimmermann nodded. "Take a seat and keep an eye on Samra while I have a small break."

"I couldn't," Yoel said.

"It's perfectly safe," Zimmermann laughed, "as long as you don't switch off the autopilot."

He climbed out of this seat. He was taller than Yoel expected.

"Go ahead," he said, motioning Yoel to take his place at the controls. "Later we'll talk about how this view compares to the one from an F-4."

■ ■ ■

"Will this be your first visit to the United States?" Mrs. Wilson asked.

Around them, the stewardesses were clearing the dinner service. Earlier, when Judy Wilson realized that Yoel was Israeli and presumably unlikely to convert to Methodism she had lost interest in him and retreated to the refuge of her book and earphones. She even ignored her dinner, dreaming presumably of a cheeseburger instead. Yoel would love one, too. But they weren't available on the national airline. In Yoel's case, cheeseburgers weren't taboo due to Jewish dietary law but because of the demands of his abdominals.

"I've been several times in the past," Yoel said. "I have relatives in the States."

"In Los Angeles?" Mrs. Wilson asked.

"In San Francisco," Yoel said. "And New York. I'll be renting a car."

II

At the car rental agency, the clerk's eyes said "come fuck me right now on the floor behind this counter," but Yoel knew that for all their flirtatiousness American women were basically prudes and the message was thus a false one. With Israeli girls, you didn't receive mixed signals. The answer was always clear whether it was yes or no. Whenever he visited the States, everything seemed overly complicated. But complication wasn't the true problem. Ambiguity was. Yoel had no patience with it.

"Ah, here it is, Mr. Luxemberg." Her smile grew brighter. She batted her eyes almost frantically. "I'm so sorry for the confusion. Someone seems to have filed your reservation paperwork in the wrong stack. I certainly hope this delay hasn't inconvenienced you. Now if I could just see your driver's license and credit card."

Yoel handed them over.

"Oh," she said, looking alarmed. "Oh, I'm sorry. I didn't realize. I'm afraid I'm going to have to speak with my supervisor."

"Is there a problem?" Yoel asked.

"No," she said. "I'm sure there's no problem. It's just that I'm new here. And I'm not sure—I think in my training they said something about international driver's licenses, but I can't remember what it was."

■ ■ ■

The Pontiac was electric blue. A convertible, yet. It wasn't at all what Yoel had reserved or budgeted for. The manager, a nervous young man, insisted on a free upgrade because of the mixup over Yoel's reservation and the delay caused by the clerk's unfamiliarity with company procedures. But the manager's slightly bloodshot eyes told a different story entirely. It was a story that featured Yoel's shiny hair and broad shoulders. More American ambiguity. . .

■ ■ ■

It was evening in Los Angeles, but back in Tel Aviv it was nearly sunrise. Yoel tried to sleep on the plane, but Mrs. Wilson's nerves kept her awake and her wakefulness kept Yoel from resting. It made him miss his F-4 fighter, which was a single seat aircraft. He had reserved a hotel room just outside the airport grounds, and once the Pontiac keys were in his hand and his bags were stowed in the trunk, he wasted no time getting there.

III

As a tourist, Yoel wasn't supposed to care that Highway One wasn't the fastest route between Los Angeles and San Francisco. He was supposed to put the top down—since he unexpectedly had one that you could do that with—and cruise along, stopping here and there to take in the sights. As a tourist, he wasn't supposed to wonder if anyone was observing his progress. That silver Volvo that followed him for miles and miles outside San Luis Obispo, for instance, even stopping at the same service station. When he finally got a look at them, the people traveling in the Volvo reminded him of the Wilsons. He memorized as many details about them as he could. Blumenfeld would want to know everything. As a tourist, nothing was supposed to matter but the road itself, the farms and villages alongside it, and the mighty Pacific, which gave no impression of doing anything but living up to its name under a cloudless sky on a perfect day that could as easily have been April or July or October.

All those miles of beaches where no rocket had ever fallen. All those towns and villages where no suicide bombing had ever taken place. All those people going about their business. The only things they ever needed shelter from were the sun, the wind, and the rain. Other people might envy Americans their big houses and flashy cars, but Yoel knew better. What they had that he wanted was peace.

■ ■ ■

They had space, as well. The sheer size of the country was astonishing. Just this journey from Los Angeles to San Francisco, short by American standards, was by far the longest one Yoel had ever taken by road. Hundreds of miles. Far longer than the greatest dimension of his homeland yet less than half the length of California, itself a mere fraction of the United States. Flying gave a false impression of distance. You didn't see the landscape creep past like this. You got into your plane at one point and disembarked at another. Everything below you disappeared. It might as well not exist. Time, rather than distance, was the measure of your journey. But this was different. Every foot you traveled was apparent outside the automobile. Every feature of the landscape demanded your attention. *This is your planet,* it declared. *See how small you are.*

Small, yes. And alien in Yoel's case. You could speak the language fluently. You could be related to some of the inhabitants. But those things didn't mean you belonged there. Of course the larger question was could a man like Yoel truly belong anywhere? But as a tourist, he wasn't supposed to spend his precious vacation time pondering larger questions.

■ ■ ■

As a tourist, he was supposed to be intent on preserving memories of his adventure, so he dutifully stopped every so often to take photographs. There were plenty of things to aim his camera at. It was a new camera, purchased for him immediately prior to the trip by Naftali. It was, Yoel understood, a very expensive camera with all the latest features, and he knew that the shots he was taking didn't warrant that level of sophistication. Naftali would have known how to take advantage of the advanced capabilities Yoel couldn't figure out how to be impressed by. It was a shame, really. Still, Yoel knew what kind of photos his friends and family would expect to see. He made sure to include the Pontiac in many of them, because his fellow pilots back at the air base would certainly be impressed by that. If he didn't give them plenty of shots of that car he'd never hear the end of it.

He couldn't help feeling that the car, like the camera, was wasted on him. But as a tourist, he knew such a thought was unworthy.

■ ■ ■

Just as he—irrationally, of course—began to despair of ever reaching his destination, he emerged from a last fogbank and there it was. He had visited the city several times before. Naftali and Yakov considered it their spiritual home and, he supposed, expected him to feel the same way about it. It was analogous to the way devout Jews all over the world felt about Jerusalem. Men like Naftali and Yakov were members of their own sort of diaspora. He had never gone so far as to declare himself a member of that club, but he'd never denied it either. There would be a time for him to take his stand, if a stand were to be taken, at some point in the future.

But regardless of what the city represented or didn't represent, as a tourist he couldn't help being impressed. And that afternoon it seemed particularly ravishing.

■ ■ ■

Yoel's cousin Cooper and his boyfriend Griffin lived in a building that wouldn't have been out of place in Tel Aviv. It was modern and unadorned, a tall, sand colored box, wide in one dimension and remarkably slim in the other. The broad side faced the bay, though at a distance of about a kilometer. Perhaps it was more than that. Yoel wasn't particularly skilled at estimating ground distances. He found a parking space not too far down the block from the main entrance. Leaving his bags in the car and the car securely locked, because while there wasn't the possibility of suicide bombers to contend with there was, according to his relative here, a shocking amount of petty street crime, he presented himself at the concierge desk in the lobby.

"Yes, Mr. Luxemberg," the nervous young man nodded. "I have a note right here. I'm to issue you their spare key and send you on upstairs. Mr. MacDonald should be getting in from work any time now. Oh, and I'm supposed to tell you not to worry about walking the dogs. He'll do that when he comes in."

■ ■ ■

The elevator doors opened and there was Griffin.

"Surprise, surprise," he laughed.

"What surprise?" Yoel asked, stepping inside.

"Right," Griffin said, rolling his eyes as the doors closed again and the elevator headed upward. "You Luxembergs take your uncanny timing for granted."

Griffin was Yoel's cousin-in-law. There was something of the bookworm about him. He reminded Yoel of a man constantly in search of his missing eyeglasses. It wasn't that he squinted or anything like that. It was simply that his face looked naked without glasses on it, ideally glasses with tortoise shell frames. He was extremely good looking but in a way that didn't call attention to itself. It wasn't until you looked at him a second, third, or even sixth time that the effect made itself clear. Once you'd seen it, though, you'd never be able to forget how adorable he was. His dark red hair was conservatively styled and always perfectly groomed. The crisp dress shirts and sharply creased trousers he wore to work begged someone to rip them off him and mess up that hair thoroughly prior to fucking him until he screamed. Yoel suspected that Griffin experienced such treatment at Cooper's hands on a regular basis, but that was based on his understandings of his cousin. Griffin's demeanor gave no clue as to what might or might not go on between them behind closed doors. He was that most paradoxical of creatures: there was nothing effeminate about him but he was all too certainly an exclusive bottom. He was quiet, invariably considerate, and, at least to Yoel, totally inscrutable. The one clue available to Yoel came on the rare occasions when he heard Griffin play piano. He was classically trained just like Yoel's cousin, Ariel Schlesinger. When he was at the keyboard there were hints of the turbulent and vivid inner life Yoel would have expected as a prerequisite to an existence as Cooper's partner.

"Where are you parked?" Griffin asked as the elevator halted and the doors slid open.

"Not far," Yoel said.

"You relax while I walk the dogs," Griffin said. "When I get back, we'll go pull your car into the garage."

"The garage?"

"Cooper has a listing in the building that the owners have already moved out of. You'll be parking in one of their assigned spaces."

"I'll come with you to walk the dogs," Yoel said. "Sixteen hours on the plane yesterday and then all day in the car today. I need to stretch my legs."

"Suit yourself."

■ ■ ■

"How long before Cooper gets in from work?" Yoel asked.

The Labradors, "exhausted" by their walk, lapped nosily at their water bowl.

"Several hours yet," Griffin said. "Are you hungry? I'll be glad to fix you something."

"I was thinking of heading to his gym," Yoel said. "Do you know if he arranged guest privileges for me?"

"Just tell them who you are at the desk," Griffin said. "Not that they'll be in any doubt about it. But you won't want to drive over there this time of day. You can use my MUNI pass."

■ ■ ■

No matter what time of day you showed up at Cooper's gym, one or more of his buddies would be there. Of course, Yoel only knew this from half a dozen visits over the years, but each time he'd been greeted like a conquering hero. Sometime over the year since his last visit, framed copies of his three magazine covers had gone on display on the same wall with several of Cooper's. Yoel never saw the resemblance himself, but he was used to being told they were like twins separated at birth. Or in this case, by a generation.

■ ■ ■

There might be eighteen years between Cooper and Yoel, but you couldn't tell it looking at them side by side. Cooper could easily have been a few months short of his thirtieth birthday rather than his fortieth. Yoel had noticed that a great many gay men in San Francisco shared this youthfulness. Certainly the climate, damp, cool, and devoid of extremes for the most part, played a role in this. Tel Aviv's climate, in contrast, was no respecter of complexions. Then, too, gay men here seemed to take obsessive care of themselves. The money they spent on it must be staggering. But Griffin insisted that the explanation was both simpler and more elemental.

"Look at your father," he said as Cooper finished up in the bathroom prior to their departure for dinner. "Born in 1922, right?"

"Yes," Yoel nodded.

"Making him seventy-three years old. But when we saw him in Israel last year, he didn't look a day over fifty-five. Simple genetics, that's all. Count your lucky stars. You Luxembergs cashed in at that particular sweepstakes."

■ ■ ■

"How was the gym?" Cooper asked, steering through the narrow streets in the Bentley sedan he borrowed from his real estate agency when he needed a vehicle with a back seat.

"Everyone there is very friendly," Yoel said. So friendly, in fact, that he'd made a detour to a particularly hospitable meathead's apartment post-workout.

"Glad to hear it," Cooper said. "Bet you worked up a hell of an appetite."

It was as if he could read Yoel's mind.

■ ■ ■

"The grilled swordfish," Cooper said. "And hold the pasta side dish."

They were at Cooper's favorite Italian restaurant in North Beach.

"Substitute grilled vegetables for the pasta?" The waiter asked.

"What are you serving tonight?" Cooper asked.

"Our usual mélange," the waiter said. "Or for an extra dollar I can give you asparagus."

"You liked the grilled asparagus the last time you had it," Griffin said.

"I did?"

"You did," Griffin nodded.

"Fine," Cooper said. "The asparagus."

"And for you, sir?" The waiter turned to Yoel.

"What he's having," Yoel growled. He liked the way his growl made the nervous, pretty young guys of San Francisco even more nervous.

"Very good, sir," the waiter smiled. "And the usual for you, Griffin?"

"You know me too well," Griffin laughed.

"What's the usual?" Yoel asked.

"Pasta carbonara," Griffin said.

"Can you believe it?" Cooper demanded. "His metabolism is so fast he can eat that poison and his abs are still as sharp as yours and mine."

"That's monstrous," Yoel laughed.

"File it under 'life is not fair'," Griffin smiled.

■ ■ ■

"Early curfew for you tonight," Cooper said, handing the Labradors treats to celebrate their humans' return from dinner. "Have to look fresh for your photo shoot tomorrow."

"Right," Yoel said. The photo shoot, as much as his "vacation", was the cover story for this entire trip.

"I'm off to bed myself," Griffin said. A high school teacher, his days began ridiculously early. "I put fresh towels in the guest bedroom for you, Yoel."

"You put fresh towels in there earlier," Yoel said.

"House rule," Griffin laughed. "Fresh towels every time you shower."

"Better service than at the Ritz," Yoel growled.

"I'll come tuck you in in a few minutes," Cooper said.

"Who, me?" Yoel asked.

"Asshole," Cooper laughed.

■ ■ ■

Yoel heard the shower go on. He crawled out of bed. He crept into Cooper and Griffin's bedroom. Griffin was lying on his back. Yoel climbed in beside him, stroking himself.

"What are you doing?" Griffin murmured, half asleep.

"Sssh," Yoel hissed, covering Griffin's mouth with his hand and easing himself between Griffin's legs. "It's all right. I won't hurt you."

Quickly he forced himself through the tight opening. Griffin's ass was wet and sticky inside. He and Cooper apparently didn't use condoms. Well, they wouldn't. Not with each other, at least. Griffin began to respond, and Yoel intensified the force of his attack. He'd dreamed of this all the way across the Atlantic. All the way up the coast in the shining automobile.

He woke up. The apartment was silent. The dream began to dissipate. In the bed next to him, one of the Labradors snored quietly.

■ ■ ■

The last time Yoel posed for Lance Garrison he had been paired for one session with a friend of Cooper's from New York, Eamonn Lannaghan. They had met before. Eamonn had won the first bodybuilding contest Yoel ever attended. He had sons Yoel's age but didn't look nearly old enough. He was as amazingly constructed as Cooper was but had a quintessential all-American look, with smooth sandy hair and sparkling gray eyes. Yoel thought immediately of the Captain America comic books his brother, Avi, had been hoarding since their boyhood. As they posed together, Yoel developed a clear understanding of how a man's physique might continue to evolve as he aged. Apparently age twenty-three—or even thirty-four—didn't have to represent the peak of his development either in terms of size or refinement. It was a lesson Blumenfeld had tried repeatedly to teach him. But until Yoel encountered a man who embodied the reality of it and experienced the phenomenon so intimately and existentially as he did in front of Lance's camera, he had thought of Blumenfeld's musings as his old mentor's perennial pep talk to himself: a sort of valedictory address on the part of a man who was ambivalent about his own advancing age. Yoel had been wrong in that assumption, and the realization changed everything. As he pulled into a parking space up the block from Lance's studio that morning, he wondered what lesson might be in store this time.

■ ■ ■

The first two days, they did solo work only. Lance wasn't the only photographer Yoel had ever worked with, but he was by far the finest. He put Yoel at ease immediately, and he knew how to organize a shoot for maximum efficiency. There was hardly any wasted time or effort. Every time Lance's camera ran out of film, his assistant had a second one loaded and ready. The assistant was a ridiculously good looking young man who paid Yoel no attention whatever.

Europeans, Yoel knew, thought nothing of a straight male photographer who specialized in the male physique, but here in America it was totally different. People who knew Lance only through his work assumed he was gay. Yoel thought it was extremely interesting that Lance didn't appear bothered by this.

■ ■ ■

The third day of shooting, Lance paired Yoel with a guy he recognized from the gym. His name was Owen, and he worked there as kind of a gofer. He was always wiping something down or carrying a stack of towels toward the shower area or showing new members around the facility. He was exactly Yoel's height but was thirteen or fourteen kilos lighter. His blond hair, honey colored skin, and slimmer but exquisitely chiseled physique made for a decided contrast to Yoel's black haired, exotic, massively sculpted appearance. One of Lance's gifts was knowing how to pair models who complemented each other so perfectly.

Yoel couldn't help wondering if Owen had a boyfriend, though he knew Lance disapproved of fraternization until shooting sessions completely wrapped.

IV

"It feels like you just got here," Griffin complained, watching Yoel stow his bags in the back of the Pontiac.

What was it with him? Cooper was as tough as nails, while this one was a walking bundle of vulnerabilities. By any reckoning at all, he ought to be in shreds. Once again, Yoel marveled at how much tougher he was than he appeared.

"Don't be a stranger," Cooper said, leaning in through the driver's side window.

Yoel felt they probably always would be.

■ ■ ■

The passenger side door opened.

"Good morning," Yoel said.

The young man pushed the seat back forward and shoved a couple of bags into the back seat. Then he got into the car and fastened his seat belt. He was Yoel's age. He had Yoel's coloring and haircut. He was Yoel's height and stocky enough that from a distance the illusion might be convincing. At least so went Blumenfeld's thinking.

"You know the way to the airport from here?" he asked.

"Sure," Yoel said. He'd studied the map the night before, but he'd been very careful not to mark the route on it. Blumenfeld would have been proud. He signaled, checked his rear view mirror, and pulled out into traffic. San Francisco was the only place he'd ever been with traffic as chaotic as Tel Aviv. Traffic in New York was bad, sure, but somehow more disciplined than this. He didn't see how Cooper and Griffin stood it. He'd only driven a few blocks since leaving their building, and already he was in the mood to kill at least a dozen of his fellow motorists.

"Your flight leaves in two hours," the young man said. "KLM to Amsterdam Schipol. Your name is Ilan Mostkowitz. You are a university student. There are eyeglasses in the backpack. You'll need to wear them at all times. They're the same ones you're wearing in the passport photo."

"Where am I from?" Yoel asked.

"Cape Town."

"Isn't my haircut wrong for a university student?"

"You keep it short because you spend much of your time surfing. It's easier to take care of that way."

"There's surfing in Cape Town?"

"There's excellent surfing around Cape Town," the young man laughed. "World famous, actually."

"Better than Tel Aviv?"

"You're joking, right?"

"Am I?" Yoel asked.

"Trust me," the young man said. "Cape Town has terrific surfing."

"If you say so."

"Are your pockets empty?"

"Yes."

"Completely?"

"Yes," Yoel repeated.

"Good. Pull into that service station at the corner."

"O.K."

"We switch over there. I drive the rest of the way."

"Then why did you ask me if I knew the way to the airport?"

"Don't ask questions," the young man said. "Take the big bag into the restroom with you and change clothes. Down to the skin, you understand?"

"I have no sentimental attachment to this underwear," Yoel said. "Rest assured."

"Socks as well. But those sneakers are O.K. Everyone in the world is wearing that brand these days."

■ ■ ■

"Did you take photos?" the young man asked. He was driving American style, with one hand on the wheel and the other out the window. They were no more than five minutes from the airport.

"Two rolls on the drive up the coast," Yoel said. "Another roll here in the city. I reloaded the camera this morning before I left my cousin's house. And there are six more rolls of blank film in the camera bag."

"Good," the young man said. "I won't have to stop to buy more for a couple of days, at least. How much cash are you leaving me?"

"Three hundred."

"So much?"

"My cousin and his boyfriend mostly paid for things."

■ ■ ■

"This passport looks genuine," Yoel said, staring at the photo of himself. He remembered having it taken wearing those glasses.

"It is genuine."

"But."

"And you are Ilan Moskowitz, right?"

■ ■ ■

"I'll drop you right at the terminal entrance."

"Thanks, Yoel," Yoel said, trying it on.

"My pleasure, Ilan," the young man laughed.

"Don't wreck the car, please," Yoel said. "I don't want that on my record."

"Don't worry. It'll be filthy but unmarked when you drop it at JFK."

"See that it is," Yoel growled.

"Sure, Ilan. Want to check those pockets one last time?"

"All I've got in my pockets is what you've given me."

"I have to ask."

"Sure, Yoel," Yoel said.

■ ■ ■

It was another 747. This time there was no Mrs. Wilson and Yoel/Ilan spent most of the flight asleep.

■ ■ ■

"Are these seats taken?"

"Please,"Yoel said. "Join me."

Around them, the train car was filling up. The girl was tall and blond. Her boyfriend was shorter and quite stocky. He had Yoel's coloring and haircut.

"I'm Eva," she said, sitting down across from Yoel while her boyfriend stowed their bags next to his in the overhead rack. "Eva Steinberg. My boyfriend's name is Ilan Moskowitz."

"Nice to meet you,"Yoel said. "Where are you two from?"

"Cape Town," Eva smiled. "Ilan's a student at the university and I'm an airline stewardess. Although I'm not sure it's completely accurate to introduce Ilan as a university student, since he seems to spend most of his time skipping classes to go surfing."

"It's true," Ilan said, sitting down next to Eva.

"I can hardly keep you out of the water, can I, baby?"

"She says I'm going to sprout gills sooner or later. I'm sorry, but I didn't catch your name."

"You have to excuse him," Eva laughed. "He's a terrible listener. Baby, he said his name is Jiri Mustonen. He's from Helsinki. He's a graduate student there."

"Oh," Ilan said. "What's your field?"

"Aeronautics,"Yoel said.

"Bet you hate traveling by train," Ilan said.

"It's not so bad,"Yoel said. He wondered if his accent sounded Finnish. He had no idea what a Finn speaking English should sound like.

"Still, it's a long ride to Munich," Ilan said.

"Speaking of which," Eva said, "looks like we're about to pull out."

■ ■ ■

"Do you mind?" Eva asked, reaching across and slipping off Yoel's glasses. "I've been wondering how Ilan would look wearing these."

"Of course,"Yoel said.

"Hold still, baby," she told Ilan, placing the glasses on him. "Let me have a look at you."

■ ■ ■

"German border's coming up," Ilan said. He was still wearing the glasses.

"We'll need our passports."

He stood and pulled their backpacks down from the rack. Yoel noticed how casually he handed over the "wrong" one. The switch was made.

V

"Jiri, over here."

He looked around. He'd been on his own ever since Munich airport, where Ilan and Eva left him to catch their flight to "Cape Town". He'd traveled on to Istanbul by himself. Over at the exit to the terminal, a chubby, dark haired woman was standing beside a cart heaped with luggage. She waved at him. He sauntered in her direction, responding to her obvious anxiety with a show of unconcern.

"Jiri," she said when he was five feet away. "We lost sight of you. You really shouldn't wander away like that."

He hadn't seen her in the line at immigration or at the baggage carousel, but that didn't mean anything.

"Sorry."

"Leave him alone, Brit," the man next to her said. "He's an adult, after all."

"An adult who'd wear mismatched socks if he didn't have someone like me looking out for him," she fumed.

"Matching socks today," Yoel smiled. "I can pull up my pants legs if you want to check."

"Sheer dumb luck, Max," she said. "That's how this one gets through life."

"That's a skill in itself," Max said.

"I don't know about that," Brit complained.

"Don't mind her, old man. She's a nervous traveler."

"That's a skill in itself," Yoel laughed.

"Here, why don't you put your luggage on the cart," Max said. "No telling how far it is to the car rental place."

■ ■ ■

The Renault rattled off down the street. Yoel watched it disappear into traffic. The people at the bus stop ignored him. He'd have thought that the hassle getting "his" luggage sorted out from Brit and Max's would have caused some curiosity. But the people on this bus line were apparently used to the antics of tourists.

■ ■ ■

They had shown him pictures. Slides, actually. He had sat in that darkened room in Tel Aviv hour after hour viewing slides that he now recognized had covered each stage of the route from the airport into the city center. Everything he saw outside the bus windows matched one or another of those recollected images. How many times Blumenfeld had shouted at him to stay awake, to maintain focus. At the time, he had obeyed Blumenfeld out of respect. But now the task was being validated existentially with each building they passed, each street sign, each square and each statue.

■ ■ ■

The apartment was on the top floor of the building. And of course there was no elevator. It wasn't that kind of building, or, for that matter, that kind of neighborhood. The apartment itself was as spartan as could be. The furniture, what little there was of it, was shabby. Kemal was a construction worker from the provinces. He had a pretty wife or girlfriend back home. Or at least he had the picture of a pretty girl in a frame on a small table beside the narrow bed. The little clothing stored in the wardrobe was exactly what Yoel would have expected: cheap, simple, well used but not quite to the point of being worn out. The tiny refrigerator was empty save for half a dozen tubs of plain yogurt and two cans of tuna. Kemal's diet was extremely stringent. On one wall of the living room hung a framed photo of a young bodybuilder posed triumphantly with a small trophy. Yoel remembered the picture being taken the year he won the Junior Mr. Israel title.

■ ■ ■

The gym was two blocks away from the apartment. A gym was a gym regardless of what city it was in. Yoel wandered inside and felt immediately at home, even though he didn't speak a word of Turkish.

■ ■ ■

"Excuse me."

Kemal had just emerged from the entrance to the gym. He kept walking.

"Excuse me."

The voice was louder this time, but Kemal pretended not to realize he was being spoken to. They'd shown him pictures of the man. Lots of them. They hadn't shared any biographical details. Kemal didn't need to know anything but what the man looked like. He'd seen the man come into the gym. He'd felt the man's eyes on him during his workout. *"Don't approach him,"* they had said. *"Let him come to you." "What if he doesn't?" "Don't worry. He will. Don't make any of it easy for him."*

"Excuse me." Now the man sounded a little desperate, and his words were accompanied by a soft tug on Kemal's elbow. He turned.

"Excuse me," the man said a fourth time. "Do you speak English?"

"English? No. A little," Kemal said. The man looked older in person than he had in the photographs. There were a few silver strands visible in the smooth blond hair. He had greased it into place that morning, but the day's heat and humidity were already starting to win their battle against those efforts. Immaculate minus, Kemal thought. The next thing he noticed were tiny wrinkles around the slightly bloodshot eyes. Then, like a camera pulling away from a tight closeup, he took in the expensively casual European style clothes, the onyx and diamond ring, the Rolex.

"A little English? Good," the man said. His smile was a nervous around the edges.

"You English?" Kemal asked.

"Australian, actually."

From the way the man said it, Kemal thought it was a lie. But he wasn't supposed to be able to discern a thing like that.

"Listen," the man said, "I'd like to talk to you."

"I not much English," Kemal said. They had told him that verbs were a tipoff. He should stumble over them, mangle both conjugations and tenses, omit them completely whenever possible.

"Is there somewhere we could go? I'd like to buy you a coffee."

"Coffee? You coffee? You go there." Kemal pointed up the block toward a café he had checked out earlier.

"Come with me," the man said.

■ ■ ■

It was as deluxe a hotel room as he had ever seen. He didn't have to pretend to feel awkward. The sensation was authentic. He wondered where they had concealed the cameras. He didn't know for a fact there were cameras. They hadn't said anything about cameras. But there had to be, obviously. What was the point of any of this if it wasn't observed? And presumably recorded?

"Why don't you put down your gym bag?" the man suggested. At the café, he had introduced himself as Andrew. Kemal sensed that this, in addition to his proclaimed nationality, was false. Kemal set his bag on the floor beside the entry to the bathroom.

"I saw you in the gym," the man had said during their prolonged verbal tango at the café. "I watched you working out. When you posed in front of the mirrors, I wanted to photograph you."

"Fotograf?"

"Camera. Take pictures."

"Ah. Kamera."

"Unfortunately, I left my camera at the hotel this morning."

"Hotel?"

"Yes," the man nodded. "My camera is at my hotel."

The hunger blazed in those bloodshot eyes. It made Kemal nervous to look into them.

"I'd be happy to pay you," the man said.

"Pay?"

"Give you money," the man said. "For the pictures."

They drank their coffee slowly. The man ate a pastry and then another. He offered Kemal one, but Kemal wasn't hungry. The man got out his wallet and put some money on the table, but Kemal knew it wasn't for him.

"Ready?" the man asked.

So here they were. The man moved around the hotel room turning on lights. He didn't open the curtains.

"Maybe you'd like to take your shirt off," he said, pantomiming what he wanted Kemal to do.

The man had done this kind of thing before. Obviously.

■ ■ ■

The next morning, he shaved, showered, fixed his hair. He used the unfamiliar products he found in Kemal's medicine cabinet. He went to more trouble than he thought Kemal would just to go to the gym, but they had told him not to worry about it. The man was an amateur. He'd notice the effect of these preparations, but he wouldn't question them. They'd given him a whole legend. He'd been worried about his construction worker persona. His hands were well calloused from the gym, but they weren't the hands of a manual laborer, and he worried that this would give him away. They made him a welder. A welder, they explained, would wear gloves at all times. In the event, the man didn't even ask Kemal that much about himself.

He wasn't even certain the man would show up at Kemal's gym a second time, but they had assured him he'd keep coming back until he got what he wanted. And what he wanted was more than photographs.

■ ■ ■

"You're very beautiful," the man said.

It was the third time they'd met. The second day, the man had asked Kemal to do his bodybuilding poses in the nude. Kemal allowed himself to be persuaded when the amount of money he was promised suddenly doubled.

"Really," the man said, advancing the film in his camera, "very beautiful."

Kemal hit a front double biceps pose.

"Sometimes I like to give beautiful young men pleasure," the man said. "With my mouth. You understand?"

Kemal moved into a front lat spread.

"I'll pay extra," the man said.

Kemal refused to think about the people operating the hidden cameras, or the other people back in Tel Aviv who would "analyze" the photos, or the use the photos would eventually be put to. He kept posing. The man set his camera on the bed. He moved toward Kemal.

"So very beautiful," he said.

■ ■ ■

Afterward, Kemal took a shower. The hotel room's bathroom was like a facility intended for ritual use in some temple. He could hear the shutter of the man's camera clicking over the sound of the running water.

■ ■ ■

There was a taxi waiting in front of the hotel when damp haired Kemal walked out the door. The driver was standing beside it.

"Get in," he said.

Those were the first words of Hebrew he had heard since leaving the plane in Los Angeles. He opened the rear door of the taxi and got inside. There was a familiar looking backpack on the seat.

"Where am I going?"

"The airport," the driver said, starting the engine.

He opened the backpack. He looked inside the travel folder he found there. There was a ticket to Frankfurt on Lufthansa. There was a Finnish passport. He opened it. *Welcome back, Jiri Mustonen*, he thought. *Nice to be you again.*

"Change clothes in a terminal restroom before checking in for your flight," the driver said. "Down to the skin, understand?"

"Sure," he said.

"Just leave that stuff you're wearing in the trash."

■ ■ ■

He fastened his seat belt. The A320 was crawling along the taxiway. He wondered if "Andrew" would show up at the gym the next day. He thought probably so. He'd done his best to give good value. He wondered how long Andrew would wait for Kemal. He wondered who Andrew would try to make friends with when Kemal didn't show up. He wondered who Andrew had waiting back home in Adelaide or Auckland or Ottawa or Manchester or Belfast or Glasgow.

It was a blackmail plot. It had to be. Nothing made sense otherwise. But of course it wouldn't be blackmail for money. Because he hadn't been employed by criminals. He'd been employed by the state. And the state, that state in particular, had to have nobler aims than mere money.

He looked at Jiri Mustonen's moderately priced Swiss made watch on his wrist. They were taking off on time. Time. He'd devote no more of it to pondering the myriad questions the past seventy-two hours brought to mind. He pulled the well-thumbed copy of *War and Peace* out of Jiri Mustonen's backback and pretended to read.

■ ■ ■

Coming out of passport control in Frankfurt, he collided with a tall blond girl who managed to switch travel folders with him so fast and unobtrusively he wasn't certain it had happened until he looked inside it.

Ilan Moskowitz was headed for Montreal on Air Canada. Complete with those tortoise shell framed eyeglasses. He was doing everything in reverse. But not in a mirror image of his previous trip. Istanbul to Frankfurt had been the rejoinder to Munich to Istanbul. Now Frankfurt to Montreal answered San Francisco to Amsterdam. It was a pattern that didn't look like a pattern. It was random but it wasn't. It would eventually get him back where he started from. That was the only true symmetry involved.

■ ■ ■

Ilan Moskowitz wasn't the type of men to waste time on metaphysical speculation. Nor did he devote himself to Russian literature. He passed the hours of the trip asleep.

VI

"Ilan."

He looked for the voice. He had just come out of customs and immigration.

"*Bienvenue a Montreal.*"

It was Blumenfeld. Wearing a yarmulke, of all crazy things.

"Uncle Jossi. What a surprise."

"Your Aunt Judit is certain you aren't capable of finding your own taxi, so here I am."

They walked down the concourse side by side schmoozing their heads off. Then suddenly they were going through a door that said No Admittance in both English and French.

■ ■ ■

241

"You realize, of course," Blumenfeld said, "that under ordinary circumstances we would never go to that much trouble over such a minor operation. We'd have employed a local and we'd have given him the impression that it was just garden variety blackmail."

"Of course," Yoel said. "I assumed it was some sort of audition."

"You could think of it that way," Blumenfeld nodded. "Or a training exercise."

"In that case," Yoel said, "how did I do?"

"It's not my place to judge that," Blumenfeld said. "Just as it's not my place to determine what happens next. Suffice it to say it's all under review by the proper authorities. I'm only here to give you your remaining instructions."

"Yes?"

"Your flight to Kennedy leaves in a little over an hour. You'll be met there. You'll drop your driver off at the ground transit center. You'll proceed to the car rental agency and turn in that chariot of yours."

"Sorry."

"No," Blumenfeld shook his head, "that was actually a nice touch. Then you'll contact your relatives to pick you up. Just like you originally planned. From here on out, it's your original itinerary. Four days with them in Manhattan and then El Al back home. The next time we see each other we'll be at our gym, just two muscleheads saying hello."

"Understood."

"Your job in the meanwhile is to forget everything you heard and saw since leaving your cousin's home in San Francisco. None of it happened. Not one bit."

APRIL, 1997

Except for a quick trip to Sydney a year earlier, Rupert hadn't seen much of Cavendish since his emigration. The news that his firm was bringing him back to the London office on a semi-permanent basis was like an answered prayer. And with the long vac just starting, Rupert's joy was practically boundless. He sauntered up the street in the late afternoon sunshine feeling that if not absolutely everything was right with the world at least the aspects of it most immediate to him were.

Cavendish. For nearly two decades now, that name, the mere suggestion of it, was all Rupert needed, really, to think of his life as worth living. Truth to tell, the separations had been of much greater duration than the times they spent together. That had been hard. Had been, truly, almost intolerable. Surely that was about to change. They were men now and finally about to be settled in sufficiently convenient proximity to each other that all might be satisfactorily regularized.

That was a word Cavendish had always approved of—regularized. A word and a concept. A place for everything and everything in its place. *Viz*—Cavendish's mighty organ at home and safely docked in Rupert's accommodating bum. What could be more regular than that?

■ ■ ■

"Your Lordship," the porter at Cavendish's club greeted him.

"Sorry, Protheroe," Rupert said, "but unless you're speaking ironically, I'm afraid you've mistaken me for someone else."

"Have I, m'lud? I don't believe so. Not in the habit of doing that sort of thing at all, I have to say. Certainly not this early in the afternoon."

"It's FitzMerlin, Protheroe. Plain old Rupert Fitz-Merlin. I'm only a 'hon' these days. And not strongly committed even to that."

"Really, m'lud?" Protheroe peered over the rims of his spectacles. "Mean to say, are you quite, quite certain of it?"

"Quite certain, Protheroe."

He stood at a kind of attention while Protheroe stared, wiped his battle scarred spectacles on his shirt cuff, replaced them on his repeatedly broken nose, and stared some more.

"Could have sworn you were that Fortescue pup, but now that I look more closely I see that you're not. My apologies, young man."

Fortescue, if indeed they were thinking of the same one, had been dead lo, these many years since that avalanche at Val d'Isere. Best part of a decade by now. And if that was indeed the Fortescue Protheroe was recalling, he'd been eight inches shorter and nine stone heavier than Rupert, so Protheroe's eyesight was a good deal more impaired than Rupert had been told.

"Not at all, Protheroe. Not surprised you didn't recognize me. Been absolute yonks since I darkened these precincts."

"As you say, sir. Now who is it you're here to see? As you're not Lord Fortescue, that is."

"Cavendish," Rupert said.

"Cavendish? To which are you referring? Cavendish Major, Cavendish Minor. . ."

Cavendish's grandfather and great uncle were both members, Rupert recalled. As well as Cavendish's father.

"Cavendish the younger, or Cavendish the youngest?"

"The youngest," Rupert nodded.

"Very sorry to have to tell you you're barking up the wrong tree, sir. Why, Cavendish the youngest decamped to Sydney quite a while back and hasn't been heard of since. Surprised you hadn't been informed of it, thick as the two of you always were. Still, that kind of knowledge must be awfully hard to come by behind the Iron Curtain, one supposes."

■ ■ ■

There was no telling how long they might have been at cross purposes there in the club vestibule. But just as Rupert was beginning to lose patience not only with Protheroe but with the traditional British men's club as an institution as well, not to mention the entire concept of ancient and revered—though almost inevitably dotty—retainers of said establishments, Cavendish (yes, *The* Cavendish of song and legend) sauntered in through the great portal and all was set right.

And almost the next thing Rupert knew, that mighty organ was roaring away happily in its accustomed location and at full volume.

■ ■ ■

"Heaven," Cavendish grunted as a last, exquisite dribble exited that favorite orifice and landed on Rupert's tongue.

"Mmm," Rupert agreed, swallowing languidly.

"Hope you're free for dinner, old chum," Cavendish said. "Seem to have worked up quite the appetite."

■ ■ ■

"You simply must insist on a different set of rooms," Rupert said, staring worshipfully across the dinner table at Cavendish. "Talk to the club secretary about it or whatever one does. Yours are positively uninhabitable."

"Truly rancid," Cavendish agreed. "Thing is, most of the club accommodations are worse. Place is rotten to the core. Surprised it hasn't fallen down around us."

"Well, then," Rupert said.

"Thanks, awfully," Cavendish said, reading his mind.

"Not at all," Rupert said. "Happy to oblige. Like old times, really. When we were training for the Games, what?"

"Great days, those," Cavendish mused.

"Long as you wish."

"Not too long, though," Cavendish said. "Awfully close quarters, couple of chaps our size. Really have to think about a place of one's own."

"No hurry."

"Still. Doesn't do to be living in one another's pockets."

Rupert, who'd been praying for years for just such an eventuality, didn't argue. If necessary they could go shopping for more commodious accommodations together. But no sense making such a suggestion at this point. Things went better when Cavendish thought he'd come up with ideas himself. It was just a matter of time and patience.

After dinner they collected Cavendish's things and installed him at Rupert's place.

■ ■ ■

"That you're reading?" Rupert asked, coming in from his jog to find Cavendish naked on the settee with a studious look on his face, as if perusing a scholarly paper on particle physics or recombinant DNA.

"Letter from Pips," Cavendish said, stroking his temples. "Old thing can't quite get the hang of infinitives."

"Really."

"And that's not the worst of it," Cavendish said. "Absolutely defeated by gerunds."

"Tragic."

"Indeed," Cavendish nodded. "Inattentive at school, most likely. Best one can make out, about to wind things up in Singapore. Headed in this general direction under full sail."

This was not good news as far as Rupert was concerned. Philippa Farquahr-Franklin had long been a highly determined aspirant to Cavendish's person. Even if there'd been nothing else objectionable about her, this alone would have made her inadmissible in polite society. But as the daughter of an earl, former (and not so former, at that) supermodel, and current entrepreneur of a particularly opportunistic, not to say downright sharklike, sort, she embodied many of Rupert's least favorite characteristics. This could mean nothing but trouble. His only defense, really, was to throw himself on the mercy of her astonishingly brief attention span. It had come to his rescue more than once in the past.

"Really," Rupert said, keeping his voice absolutely level.

"Chap," Cavendish yawned, "don't be like that."

"I didn't know I was," Rupert said.

"One reads your mind, don't forget," Cavendish said. "No need for it. Truly."

"The last time we discussed a certain person," Rupert said, "one was given to believe that there's enough of Cavendish to go around."

"Just so," Cavendish nodded. "Still holds true. So do be a good scout about it. Woman's basically harmless."

"So you say."

"It's true. Honour bright."

"We'll see," Rupert said.

■ ■ ■

The paparazzi had been alerted to Pippa's arrival at Heathrow via private jet, so the next morning Rupert was greeted in his *Times* by a shot of a sleepily grinning Cavendish handing her a couple dozen roses at the foot of the airstairs. This did nothing to improve his mood, though to be fair about it Cavendish was slumbering away in Rupert's own bed as he read the accompanying article. Cavendish hadn't mentioned that Pippa's return to London was intended to be a permanent relocation nor that the BBC had just signed her to do a weekly programme focusing on fashion and "lifestyle" matters. He'd assumed that just like all the other times, she'd be here today and off to Dubai or Nice tomorrow, leaving behind unimaginable messes to be cleaned up but a blessed silence in compensation. *In residence* implied a whole different order of potential distress. Something obviously had to be done, but Rupert had no idea what, short of the use of high explosives.

■ ■ ■

"Roops, darling, over here," Pippa brayed from halfway across the dining room. She was practically standing on her chair to signal him. Either Cavendish was in the gents', taking a call, on an inspection tour of the kitchen, or hadn't arrived yet. This was actually preferable. Rupert preferred to go through the obligatory burying of the hatchet ritual without Cavendish present. That way there were no witnesses and it was just Pippa's word against his. Since Pippa invariably overstated her case, Rupert came off rather well this way. Better than he might have, certainly.

"Yum," she declared as he arrived at the table. "What a lucky girl I am, to have the two best looking men in the British Isles luncheoning with me today."

"Oh?" Rupert said. "And who would they be?"

"Silly boy," she giggled. "One hears you've been quite, quite busy despoiling the local virgins of late."

"Does one?"

He'd never been able to decide whether this sort of remark was a kind of taunt, reflected wishful thinking on her part, or truly was an item of gossip—however inaccurate and unlikely—she'd accumulated somewhere.

"One does," she assured him, "from all quarters. You're to be congratulated. Scores of satisfied customers, my dear."

"In that case I shall have to be more careful covering my tracks," he said.

"Good luck with that," she said. "The local virgins are a particularly rapacious lot. Not to mention loquacious. Don't forget, darling, I was their generalissima once upon a time not so very long ago. They still look to me as a sort of role model."

"I'm sure they do."

"Ah, there's the lad now," she said, rising from her seat and waving. "Cavendish, darling. Over here."

II

"Ladies and gentlemen in the viewing audience, let me just say what a pleasure it's been to have two of England's premiere sportsmen on the programme this week," Pippa oozed at camera number two. "Don't forget that Kate Lange's new book about their triumphant return to Olympic glory in Atlanta last summer is now available from your local bookseller. And thanks so much, ladies and gentlemen, for tuning in."

She froze. Rupert counted silently to two.

"And we're off the air," the director intoned.

"There, my dears," she smiled, "that wasn't so bad, was it?"

■ ■ ■

"It's such fun, really," she said, bustling around the dressing room like a dervish. "Didn't you think?"

"Ripping," Cavendish said, stifling a yawn.

Rupert listened for a note of irony in that declaration but didn't detect it. His heart sank. The Cavendish he believed he knew couldn't have been taken in like that. Things were worse than he'd imagined.

"And wasn't Rupert absolutely brilliant?" Pippa enthused.

"Always is," Cavendish smiled. "One finds oneself depending on it, rather."

■ ■ ■

"More space at her flat," Cavendish muttered, folding things and placing them in his bag. "All there is to it, really. Not enough room here to swing a cat."

"I told you we should look for a bigger place."

"Too much bother, that," Cavendish said. "Have to move you, too."

"Anyway, with term starting soon, I'll hardly be here. You'll have the place to yourself."

"You're far too accommodating," Cavendish said. "Bound to get you into trouble sooner or later."

"But. . ."

"Only butt I'm interested in is the one at the junction of your long, stalwart legs, young Rupert."

It was the way Cavendish always got around him.

"Better this way," Cavendish said. "You'll see."

III

"Rupert, darling." Pippa's voice squawked from the telephone.

"Hello, Pippa. I'm afraid Cavendish isn't here just at the moment."

"Of course not," Pippa said. "He just left me. It's you with whom I wish to speak to."

"Oh?"

"Darling, the producers are wetting themselves. Our audience share is through the roof. You simply must agree to make another appearance on the programme. As soon as possible."

"Surely not," Rupert said.

"Whatever do you mean?"

"I can't imagine the citizenry of the United Kingdom want me invading their homes again. Ever."

"Well, imagine it, dear," Pippa said. "We'll speak of it when you luncheon with me next week."

Cavendish's criticism of her abuse of the Queen's English had been right on the mark. It bordered on criminal activity. "Luncheon" as a verb was just the tip of the iceberg. Those clouds of unnecessary prepositions flying around like shrapnel. Egad.

More telling, however, was that this continued to be the only criticism Cavendish aimed in her direction.

■ ■ ■

"Wouldn't you just die without asparagus?" Pippa asked, laying down her fork.

"It is rather fine today, isn't it?" Rupert smiled. No use picking fights unnecessarily. And what could be more unnecessary than an argument over asparagus? Futile as well.

"Darling, we must discuss your next appearance on the programme."

"I didn't know there was going to be one."

"Of course there is," she said. "Why wouldn't there be?"

"I can think of all sorts of reasons," Rupert said.

"And I can think of even more reasons why you should appear again," she insisted. "Not should, darling. Must."

Rupert decided it was probably best to at least give the impression he intended to cooperate. He continued to believe it would be a mistake to make an enemy of her. Better to let her make one of herself. Best of all, let Cavendish witness her doing it. How much longer could it be until she showed her true colours?

"What I have in mind is this," she said. "I've had rather a stroke of genius, you see. The kind I'm well known for. We'll kill two birds with one stone. We're going to do a Britain's Ten Most Eligible Bachelors episode, and you'll headline it. I know your willie is generally regarded as one of the most satiated ones in the British Isles, darling, but life isn't just about sex, you know. It's long past time we found you a bona fide girlfriend."

She pronounced "bona fide" as if it were a pair of trochees.

"You're not to be blamed for not having exploited your previous Olympic success in matrimonial terms, my dear. You were very young at the time. And Cavendish was too empty headed to think that far in advance, lunkhead that he is. Really, one finds him hopelessly self-absorbed. But now that you're rising thirty. . ."

"Really," Rupert said, biting his tongue.

"Just you leave everything to me," she smiled.

■ ■ ■

"What do you think?" Rupert asked.

"It's brilliant, Roops."

Every time Cavendish addressed him using this abysmal Pippa-ism, Rupert's heart fell.

"Spacious rooms," Rupert pointed out. "Views of the river. Two full bathrooms. And note the ridiculously oversized fridge."

"Saw it," Cavendish nodded.

"When I'm at school, you'll have the place to yourself."

"Thing is," Cavendish said, unable to look him in the eye, "not sure I should move back in with you just now. Pips is currently in a rather delicate state."

"Delicate state?" Rupert asked. "I *luncheoned* with her on Thursday. She's as delicate as a diesel electric locomotive. She's as delicate as that chum of yours that just won Mr. Olympia."

"Came third, he did," Cavendish said.

"I'm sure you take my point, in any case."

"Sorry, old chap," Cavendish said. "Didn't make myself clear. Pips is, as they say, *with child*."

"What?" Rupert was thunderstruck.

"Exactly," Cavendish said, a silly little grin playing about his mouth.

"But how can it possibly be yours?" Rupert asked. "You had that surgical procedure."

"Frightfully clever chap in Melbourne has made rather a speciality of undoing those things," Cavendish said, "for chaps who change their minds, don't you see?"

"I do," Rupert said. He didn't like what he was seeing, but he saw it perfectly well.

"Doesn't change anything, really," Cavendish said.

"Doesn't it?"

"Not if we don't want it to."

"What if Pippa wants it to?"

"Why should she?"

"Women do," Rupert said. "Inevitably."

"Let's not say anything anyone might regret later," Cavendish said, "shall we? Roops?"

JUNE, 1998

"Stop fidgeting," Eli said. "You're just like a little kid."

"He was always the hyperactive one," Eamonn laughed. "Could hardly keep him in his crib. His mother threatened to lash him down."

"He loves being talked about as if he isn't in the room," Liam said. "Has anyone noticed?"

"Shut the fuck up," Tory growled. "Every one of you."

"Or what?" Liam asked. "You'll sic Dad on us?"

"Very funny," Tory fumed.

"Victor Anthony," Eli snapped. "If you don't stand still, I'm never going to get this thing tied."

This thing was Tory's bow tie. Eli had already tied Liam's, Mick's, and Renzo's. He still had Eamonn's to do. If not for Eli, it was hard to imagine the Lannaghan men being sufficiently presentable for any occasion beyond the ordinary, much less Tory's wedding—T minus twenty minutes and counting. To be absolutely truthful about it, keeping this crew looking sharp, masterfully as he did it, was the least of Eli's contributions.

Yes, Eamonn thought, watching his husband wrangle his second son. If not for Eli. And here they were. The first wedding of one of the Lannaghan offspring.

■ ■ ■

Honest to God, Eamonn hadn't planned it this way. It just happened. For all he had known leaving Maribel alone with Liam and Tory that night on his way to

253

"play cards with the guys", nothing out of the ordinary was about to take place. Of course, you could hardly head for the tubs for a few hours of anonymous gay sex with that expectation. Not if you were Eamonn Lannaghan, twenty-three years old and as deep in the closet as it was possible to be. Just stepping into an establishment like that amounted to something about as extraordinary as being abducted by aliens. Yet he'd been going on these hunting expeditions often enough and for long enough that the whole thing, hot as it invariably turned out to be, was routine in its own way, and, for that matter, felt as mundane as any other aspect of his life. It had nothing to do with the scene he was leaving behind as he went down the stairs two at a time. It had nothing to do with his career as a firefighter. It had nothing to do with the guys at the gym, where his recently won bodybuilding trophies were prominently on display. It had nothing to do with Mom, Dad, his brothers, sisters, uncles, cousins, aunts, and grandparents. It was its own world, a place he visited most Thursday nights when he wasn't on shift and thought very little about the rest of the time. It provided him with exactly what he believed he needed. Going there gave him such total satisfaction that he didn't miss it when he wasn't there. Didn't even think about it, really. It was the perfect way for a guy like him to be gay. If that's what he even was, something he wasn't at all certain of. In any case, it was a place where you fulfilled your deepest sexual fantasies one night each week. Fulfilled them with as much passion and imagination as you were capable of; fulfilled them until you were so depleted you literally couldn't function any more right then. Afterward, you showered and went home. You walked out that door a few hours later and the rest of your life was completely unaffected by it. You left it behind until the next time.

It might not be the right solution for other guys, but it suited him perfectly.

■ ■ ■

He had first found his way there as a high school student, after overhearing one of his brother's friends talking about it. Several seniors from their school had been going there on weekends. They never set foot in the place, just stood around outside verbally harassing patrons as they arrived and left.

Sometimes the harassment went beyond insults and taunts. When Klaus-Peter heard about their activities, he used his star power as varsity quarterback to put a stop to it. "Not cool, guys," he said. "They're people just like everybody else. They're not doing anyone any harm. They're certainly not hurting you. Leave them alone."

This pronouncement, radical as it was for the time and place, was all it took. Either those classmates stopped what they were doing or stopped talking about it. Eamonn's charisma, embryonic at that stage, ran in the family. He witnessed his older brothers exercising it regularly. Not to mention his dad, uncles, and cousins. Making people do what you wanted and doing so with the least possible effort was his birthright.

■ ■ ■

The genie was out of the bottle. Sixteen year old Eamonn was astonished to learn that such a place existed. Once he comprehended that there was a place where men met for the sole purpose of having sex with each other, he couldn't get it out of his mind. He thought about it constantly. And, as a young man of action, the son and grandson of men of action, he couldn't merely think about it indefinitely.

■ ■ ■

Back then nobody wore hooded sweatshirts with baseball caps. But it was the best disguise Eamonn could think up. He took the fake I.D. his brother, Sean, had "lost" when he turned eighteen. Eamonn looked enough like Sean that it would probably work. He couldn't imagine a place like that was too particular. When he arrived, he quickly realized he'd been right. The man at the counter didn't even ask to see it. Eamonn stood in line long enough to figure out that nobody signed in using their real names, so he didn't either. He'd just read *Billy Budd* for English 11, so that's what he wrote in the register when it was his turn.

Up to then, Eamonn hadn't ever had sex. It wasn't for lack of opportunity. He was physically mature for his age, a Lannaghan trait. At school he was

255

regarded as a dreamboat—also a Lannaghan trait. Klaus-Peter and Sean had both cleaned up in high school and showed no signs of slowing down now that they had graduated and were sharing an apartment on the Lower East Side near the fire house where they were both assigned. Unlike them, Eamonn didn't take advantage of the attention, loads and loads of it, that came his way. He had been dating Maribel since sixth grade. And Maribel was a good girl in the time honored, Roman Catholic sense of the phrase. She was also worth waiting for. No question about it. With her looks and personality she drew plenty of attention herself, but she'd never given Eamonn reason to doubt her. And when she said no sex before they were married, she meant it. It wasn't easy, but Eamonn was determined to stay worthy of her. So he ignored all the other girls at school. And the ones from other schools who heard about him and made sure they met.

But what did sex with guys have to do with staying true to Maribel?

Nothing, as far as he could see. You couldn't marry a guy. You couldn't have a baby with him. Hell, you couldn't even date a guy. You couldn't do any of the things that made two people a couple.

You could, though, have sex. Apparently.

He couldn't see how there could be any harm in it.

So that night, although he'd never had sex before and couldn't imagine what men did together, he was adventurous of spirit, strong of body, and a dream on two legs.

■ ■ ■

The next Thursday night, it was easier. Not the sex part, which had presented no problem whatever during his first visit. Getting there had been the hard part. Working up the nerve to actually do it. Everything up until the moment that first guy touched him. A guy just a little bit older than he was. A guy who seemed surprisingly normal for someone about to do that.

That first touch—that was enough. Everything was simple after that.

■ ■ ■

Before long, Eamonn was a regular.

256

■ ■ ■

His senior year the place closed down. He had to go looking for another one. There were several closer to home than the one he finally chose on the southern edge of Chelsea.

II

"Hold still," Eli said.

Eamonn squared his shoulders and held his breath.

"There," Eli said. "That's straight enough for a convention of Rotarians."

"Thanks, Pop," Eamonn laughed.

"You're not too big for me to spank, you know," Eli grinned.

Except of course Eamonn was. It was the way he and Eli talked to each other in front of the boys. Even now, with the boys grown and everything out in the open, they played it this way.

"Seriously," Eli said, "try not to let it go crooked again until the reception at least."

"Roger," Eamonn said.

"He meant to say limp," Tory smirked.

"I did not," Eli fumed.

"Yeah, Dad," Mickey said. "Do as you're told. It's only fair. We have to."

"That's right," Liam said. "Eli's our boss, too. And everyone knows who to blame for it."

"Is it time yet?" Renzo asked.

"Quit fidgeting," Liam grunted. "You know how women are. It'll be a miracle if the bride is ready within twenty minutes of H-hour."

"Says the guy who's always primping," Renzo shot back. "You're at least as bad as Nancy is. Hours in front of the mirror before either of you can clear the front door, I swear."

"That's telling him," Tory laughed. "Some contest—who's going to hold up progress worse? My bride or my best man?"

■ ■ ■

Initially Eamonn didn't do much but have his cock sucked. It wasn't a problem that he didn't reciprocate. He was young and good looking enough that there were plenty of guys willing to let it go at that. He was getting bigger and stronger by the week, and his fear that he'd be recognized as underage quickly dissipated. After a few weeks, he figured out that jerking somebody off wasn't that different than handling his own equipment. And kissing turned out not to be a big deal either. Month by month his repertoire expanded, though he was never anything other than a top.

The guys at the new place in Chelsea were a younger crowd, more sexually adventurous, more—well, fun. Sometimes after sex Eamonn hung around just for the company. That surprised him at first. He'd never thought in terms of going there to be social, and he hadn't expected to have anything in common with guys like that, either. It didn't occur to him that this might have something to do with him. It was just that they were, at least some of them, cool guys. At least kind of cool. Cool enough for a few laughs after sex on a Thursday night. Nothing more than that. Not worth thinking about. Totally insignificant.

III

The best man and other attendants filed out, ready to take up their positions in the sanctuary. Tory's fiancée, Nancy, had decreed that bride and groom were both to be escorted up the aisle to be given away by their respective parents. Tory would march first.

"I can't tell you what it means to me that you want me to help give you away," Eli said, husky voiced.

"Cut that out, Uncle Eli," Tory grunted. "You're going to make me cry."

■ ■ ■

It seemed like the perfect arrangement. Having sex until he could hardly walk home once a week was just enough to keep Eamonn sane through late adolescence. It made it possible for him to be a gentleman with Maribel, and you couldn't put a price on that. It helped him discover things about his body that he couldn't imagine being able to learn otherwise. These were not arguments that he could have sold to his siblings, cousins, or teammates at gunpoint, so he didn't even try. The whole thing had to be a secret. Sometimes it made him laugh. Him, such an All-American guy, with a secret like that. It was ironic. And funny. But at the same time deadly serious. If people found out about it, it would mean trouble. He learned to appreciate the mental discipline keeping his mouth shut about it required. That, too, was part of becoming a man as far as he was concerned.

■ ■ ■

By the time he graduated from high school, he had developed the technique and reputation of a consummate sexual athlete. There were things he still wouldn't do. They were the things tops didn't do. He didn't think in terms of gay and straight. Those distinctions didn't apply in his case because as far as he could tell they were only relevant outside the walls of the "club", as it styled itself. The only categories that mattered were top, bottom, and switch hitter. Guys regularly urged him to experiment, to get in touch with his "feminine" side. He didn't bother to argue. He simply ignored them. There were plenty of opportunities for the kind of action he wanted. Some Thursdays he had sex with two or three men. Sometimes he participated in an orgy. Sometimes, though rarely, he spent the entire evening with one guy.

Whatever happened on any given visit, the result was the same. He fucked his way to near oblivion, showered, and left. By the time he was half a block away, he'd put the whole thing out of his mind.

■ ■ ■

He knew there were things he was supposed to be afraid of. The club might be raided at any time, so he took precautions; scoped out all possible escape routes. He might be followed there or followed home. He might catch a disease. Occasionally bad characters found their way into the club and fights or muggings ensued. He heard the same stories as everyone. It wouldn't be true to say they didn't bother him. But they never caused him to alter his plans. And his luck never let him down.

■ ■ ■

His months and years in the gym had results. He practically never encountered anyone at the club who was as impressive as he was. And as he matured, his looks ripened. He rarely encountered anyone at the club as handsome as he was. He had everybody he wanted. He had nearly everyone who wanted him. Nothing occurred to mar the perfection of his weekly visits and his ongoing oblivion the rest of the week. Nothing he experienced there made him question anything about himself or how he was living his life.

He made it through the academy and was sworn in, joining a long line of Lannaghans and their connections as a New York firefighter. He married Maribel the very next day. If the wedding night was something less than spectacular it was only to be expected, given the astonishing differences in their previous experiences. Prior to his wedding, he hadn't given any thought to how being married might alter his arrangements. He had seen no need to. And once he returned from the honeymoon, it seemed perfectly natural to keep on as before. He'd already trained Maribel to think of his Thursday nights as sacrosanct. She never even asked where he went or what he did. By the time he'd matured enough to realize how unusual her acquiescence was, it was too late to question it. Not even the birth of his first two sons, Liam and Victor Anthony (aka Tory), caused him to consider modifying his routine. It was as integral to his life as going to the gym, going to work, eating meals, sleeping.

IV

"Eli Danziger," Maribel said, allowing her cheek to be kissed by her husband's lover.

They were in the vestry, waiting while Tory suffered through a last session with the priest. Father Kilpatrick, though he seemed ridiculously young, was an old school priest. During preparations for the wedding there had been many "time outs" for counseling. Eli was of the opinion that this indicated some kind of crush on Father Kilpatrick's part, but Eamonn just thought the priest was an insufferable busybody like the priests of his youth had been.

Maribel was wearing that particular smile. Quizzical. A little ironic. Skeptical perhaps? Eamonn didn't know what it signified. He didn't know if Eli realized that Maribel only wore it in his presence.

"Mrs. Lannaghan," Eli said.

Their customary greeting.

"Ready for this?" Maribel said.

"Is anybody ever ready for these things?"

"Big doings, all right," Maribel said. "I can always depend on you to be philosophical, can't I?"

"Like the tide," Eli said.

"The phases of the moon," Maribel said.

It was excruciating watching the two of them like this. Over two decades now, and they'd spent ridiculously little time face to face. The number of words they'd exchanged would hardly fill a handful of typewritten pages. Eamonn had no idea from one minute to the next what they were preparing to say to each other. It could go anywhere—blow them all sky high or focus on nothing more significant than the weather. So far they'd elected to avoid anything resembling a confrontation, yet he could see it looming in both their eyes. It was like being an actor in a play everyone had a script for except him, with the climactic scene yet to come on stage.

Still they held their fire. Eamonn had depended on them to go along and get along for nearly a quarter century; to keep ignoring reality when in each other's company, and so far they hadn't let him down. Neither one had ever shown a sign of resisting. Or, more to the point, regretting. Still, they felt the load of it. That's what their eyes said. Could it last for another quarter century? 'Til death do them part? Could he ask that much?

"That dress," Eli said.

"You like it?" Maribel laughed without laughing. "You approve?"

"You're always exquisite," Eli said, shaking his head in wonder. "Your sense of style. You should have gone to work at *Vogue*."

"You should know about style," Maribel said. "Having a pal like Jill. She's here, I hope."

"Wouldn't miss it."

"With her girlfriend?" Maribel asked.

Eamonn held his breath.

"Who won't let Jill out of her sight," Eli said after a long pause.

"Smart woman," Maribel nodded. "Stray animals are trouble, aren't they?"

"A professor," Eli said. "Which makes her intelligence pretty unusual from what I gather."

"Thanks for taking charge of the menfolk for the occasion," Maribel said. "Wouldn't do to have them looking like unmade beds, which would have been the case otherwise."

"Anything to be of service," Eli smiled.

■ ■ ■

Nine years of Thursday nights. Hundreds of men. Perhaps as many as a thousand. Eamonn never bothered to count. Why would he? It wasn't a question of who he'd had sex with during his visits but what they let him do. How much pleasure they gave him. All those rides on the subway thinking about what he wanted to do that night. Not who he might meet, because it wasn't about the partner but the act. All those rides home afterward thinking about what he'd done, not who he'd done it with or to, because they were all faceless and the night was about the acts performed, the sensations he'd experienced. All those rides home while he savored them before locking them safely away.

■ ■ ■

There had been no indication that night as he shut the door behind him, went downstairs, stepped into the street, and headed for the station, that it was all about to change. He never thought about change. He recognized that it existed. He saw it in the constantly evolving cityscape, in the growth of his sons, in the sad decline of his great-grandmother. But his life would go on like this until. . .

Until it didn't.

He never thought beyond that.

■ ■ ■

He got there at the usual time. He signed in. Went to his usual locker. Undressed and put away his things. Cinched the towel around his waist. Headed off on the hunt.

■ ■ ■

He ran into a few other Thursday night regulars, signaling his greetings with a tilt of the head, a crooked grin, a "hey, bud". Nothing more than that. No handshakes. No names—never that.

■ ■ ■

Eamonn hardly ever encountered anyone as built as he was, or as handsome. But he did that night. They took one look at each other. Before they knew it they were in a cubicle together going at it.

Contrary to all expectations and appearances, the guy was stupefyingly bad sex.

■ ■ ■

That kind of thing happened sometimes. All those previous Thursday nights had left Eamonn philosophical about bad sex. It was no tragedy. The night was still young. The place was full of other guys. Satisfaction was still easily attainable by the time he had to head home. Eamonn left the guy drowsing and stepped through the door.

Down the corridor and around the corner at the end.

A guy about Eamonn's age was standing there looking, well, lost. That was the only way you could describe his expression.

There was nothing out of the ordinary about him. He was very nice looking but not quite handsome. He was just over medium height. There wasn't an ounce of fat on him, like he was a runner or something, but otherwise he wasn't particularly impressive. Just a guy.

Then their eyes met.

That's when everything changed.

■ ■ ■

It was like being born full grown at the age of twenty-five.

■ ■ ■

There was another night he'd never forget. He and Maribel were lying side by side in bed. They had just made love. The apartment was silent.

"Are you having an affair with Jill?"

Eamonn wasn't sure he'd heard the question at first. He was that close to drifting off.

"Jill?"

"Jill Wagstaffe," Maribel said.

"Of course not."

"Why 'of course'?" Maribel asked.

"I don't understand," Eamonn said. He'd never been so frightened.

"Why did you say 'of course not'? Why didn't you just say no?"

"What's the difference?" Eamonn asked.

"If you don't understand that. . ."

"What are we talking about here?" Eamonn asked.

"Every time I see that woman," Maribel said, "I can tell she's not being straight with me. She knows something I don't know. She's keeping something from me. Now what could that be, I wonder?"

"Maribel," Eamonn said. His heart was pounding. It might all be over in just a few more seconds. "Listen to me. I am not having an affair with Jill Wagstaffe."

"I don't have to be looking into your eyes to tell whether you're lying," Maribel said. "I hope you understand that."

It was true. Even here, lying on their backs in the darkness.

"It's Eli," Eamonn said.

"Eli?"

"That's right."

"Eli and Jill are having an affair? That makes no sense. Why would Jill think she had to hide that from me? No. It's something else."

"Eli and me," Eamonn said. They were the hardest three words he'd ever spoken.

"What?"

"Eli and I are the ones having an affair."

"You're joking."

"No."

"I don't understand. Are you saying you're gay? Because that can't be. I mean, didn't we just. . . ?"

"Yes," Eamonn said. "We just did. And I am gay. I'm also madly in love with the mother of my sons. But I'm in love with Eli, too."

"You can't be."

"But I am," Eamonn said. "You just said you could tell when I'm lying. Am I lying?"

Eamonn measured the silence by counting his heartbeats.

"Are you telling me you want to leave me to be with him?"

"No."

"Really?"

"Really."

"What are you saying, then?"

"I'm not saying anything," Eamonn said. "You wanted the truth, and I'm telling you the truth."

"How long has this been going on?"

"A while."

"He was at Mickey's christening," Maribel said.

"We'd known each other a few weeks at that time."

"Were you already lovers?"

"Yes."

"That long ago," Maribel said.

"Yes."

"How did I never figure it out?"

"I don't know."

There was a long silence. In the distance, Eamonn could hear a police siren. It didn't come any closer but it didn't fade away. It just went on and on.

"What happens now?" Maribel asked.

"I don't know," Eamonn said. "That's up to you really."

"What does that mean?"

"Just what I said. What happens next depends on what you decide."

"Will you break up with him?"

"If you ask me to," Eamonn said.

"You mean that?"

"Yes."

"Do you want to break up with him?"

"No," Eamonn said. "But I will. Just say the word."

"What happens if I do? Honestly? You keep on sneaking around?"

"I break up with him. You and I and the boys go on like before."

"But how can we?"

"We just do."

The police siren had finally stopped sounding. Now there was a helicopter. They said Manhatten was the city that never sleeps. But did any city ever sleep? Really? Would Eamonn ever sleep again?

"What do you want?" Maribel asked. She was speaking very slowly. Eamonn wondered if anybody else who knew her realized that the more emotional she was the flatter her vocal tone. Like now. Like this. She might be reading the stock listings out of the newspaper for all the feeling you could hear in her voice. Yet the feelings were there. He knew that like he knew about gravity. "If you could have anything in the world right now, what would it be? Think very carefully before you answer."

But Eamonn didn't have to think. He'd known the answer to that question for a long time.

"What I want more than anything," he said, "is for everything to go on exactly as it has been. I know that's asking too much. If it wasn't, we'd have had this discussion a long time ago. I guess I was just hoping. . ."

"There are two kinds of people who ask too much of you," Maribel said.

"Oh?"

"It's true. First, there are narcissists. Like my cousin Albertine. They ask too much of you because it's second nature to them. They ask for anything under the sun or even the sun itself because they think they deserve it. They honestly don't realize what they're doing to you by asking. Or if they do realize, they don't care."

"Sure," Eamonn said.

"Then there are the others," Maribel said. "They can't help themselves, either. But it's not because they're narcissists. It's because they know what they have to have to be happy."

"Which kind am I?" Eamonn asked.

"Well," Maribel laughed uneasily. "If you were a narcissist, you'd never ask that question. You'd say 'I'm certainly no narcissist', and that would be that. It's what makes this so hard. It's easy to say no to a narcissist."

So dispassionate. So in control of herself. That's what you got when you married a surgical nurse. They met any crisis head on. And with a self possession that seemed downright supernatural. There was no sign of what might be going on internally. Right now, Eamonn was broken hearted, on the point of bursting into tears at the enormity of what he had done and what he was asking her for. If he could only take back the last six years. But then he'd never have known Eli. And he couldn't turn his back on Eli any more than he could turn his back on her or the boys. That's why somebody else had to make this decision.

"If you could have anything in the world," he said. "Anything at all, what would it be?"

267

Again, he counted heartbeats and waited.

"I honestly don't know," she said. "I'll have to get back to you on that. Oops. That's Renzo. It's my turn."

"No," Eamonn said. "I'll go."

He spent the rest of that night holding his son.

V

"This is it," Tory said, squaring his shoulders in exactly the manner of his father.

The four of them were in the vestibule now, waiting for their cue. Inside the sanctuary, the organ played a piece by Bach that Eli had helped Nancy select. His fingerprints were all over the wedding.

"Yes, darling," Maribel nodded, offering Tory her arm.

She'd been a great mother. Eamonn couldn't think of a single thing to fault her for. The boys, his sons, had been the luckiest men on earth in that regard. And she'd make a fantastic grandmother when the time came. He only hoped his future daughters-in-law would appreciate her. That was treacherous territory, he knew. If things went well, Maribel would never get the credit for it. If they didn't, she'd get all the blame. That's how it went.

And what about those daughters-in-law and Eli?

■ ■ ■

What kind of wife had she been?

Any other man would have said perfect.

Eamonn would say perfect, too. But it meant something different to him than it could have to anyone else.

■ ■ ■

Hair grew luxuriant on Eli's chest and legs. Apparently it embarrassed him. He shaved it off the week they "officially" became a couple. Eamonn hated that. He didn't let Eli do it again. Eli suffered horribly from the stubble as it grew back in. Eamonn refrained from commenting on this.

Eli was Jewish. If you grew up in New York you knew all about Jews, except you didn't. What you knew about was their food, their holidays, their mannerisms, their slang. Yet there was something behind all that which seemed essential and unknowable. Eamonn realized that almost immediately. Jews were just like everybody else and at the same time completely different.

Eamonn had encountered hundreds of circumcised men by that point and never thought anything about it. They just weren't like him down there. But suddenly the difference was more than a mere anatomical detail, a choice some parents made different from others. In Eli's case it was something mysterious and profound. Eamonn liked that about Eli. He wanted Eli to be nothing like him. He wanted Eli to be nothing like Maribel. He wanted Eli to be Eli. He tried to explain it but was pretty sure it didn't come out the way he wanted it to. Eli was hurt but pretended not to be.

■ ■ ■

Eli's hair went gray prematurely and Eamonn wouldn't let him color it. Eli had two skin cancers, harmless ones, removed from the back of his neck. He fretted about the scars. He broke his ankle falling on the stairs to the Christopher Street subway station one rainy afternoon, and spent years trying—and eventually failing—to eradicate the almost imperceptible limp that resulted.

Eamonn adored those imperfections and all the others as they manifested themselves. Each one made Eli more real. The more real Eli was, the more real their relationship seemed. It took place in the shadows and on the fringes, silently and discreetly, unseen at first and later seen but ignored, yet it was as real as anything else about Eamonn's life. That's what the silver hair, the barely visible scars, the ghost of a limp, the ever accumulating artifacts of life and time, represented.

Year after year those gradual changes. They eventually added up to transformation, yet, paradoxically, Eli was the same as he'd been that night when their eyes first met in that shadowy corridor. Those eyes were the one thing that had never changed.

For that matter, Maribel might still be that girl in the front row in Sister Mary Rose's six grade class—the "good" class, the one all the smart kids were in. Eamonn never understood why he'd been assigned to that class. Grannie Lannaghan, probably, had intervened. She was a great one for laying down the law. There weren't many women in the parish who could give orders to the holy sisters, but Grannie Lannaghan was relentless. Eamonn hadn't thought of himself then, or ever, as one of the smart kids. He still didn't, though Maribel and Eli obviously were. But Eamonn had gotten everything he wanted out of this life. What did that say, if anything, on the subject of intelligence? Probably nothing. Probably it was all a question of grace.

VI

"Who gives this man in marriage?" Father Kilpatrick asked.

This was the moment of truth. Eamonn had no idea what was about to take place. He had tried to discuss it with Maribel, but she shut him down. She knew how to do it, though she hardly ever exerted herself that way. "*What are we going to say?*" "*I'll handle it.*" "*But Mar,*" "*But nothing. I'll handle it.*" He didn't ask her again. In spite of himself, he fretted. He wasn't good at not knowing what to expect. At wait and see. Her answer to him might mean anything. Her answer to the priest's question when it came likely meant everything. At the very least, a lost opportunity.

It wouldn't be long now. Eamonn felt Eli go stiff next to him. Head high, in that serene tone Eamonn remembered all the way back to sixth grade, Maribel spoke.

"His father, his step-father, and I do," she said. Her diction, as always, was everything the nuns could have demanded of a Catholic school girl. Her posture as well. She'd always been singled out as a model of deportment, Eamonn remembered. Plus, she'd never been a shrinking violet. She'd always stood up to whatever put itself in her way.

Out of the corner of his eye, Eamonn saw a single tear trickle onto Eli's cheek. Eli had waited a long time for a moment like that, with no promise it would ever arrive.

Eamonn took his hand and squeezed. Hard.

APRIL, 1999

"You'll love Dubrovnik," Blumenfeld said, sliding the passport and ticket folder across his desk.

"I certainly plan to,"Yoel said, opening the passport. "Finnish again?"

"We've been through that before," Blumenfeld said. "Finnish is one of the least spoken European languages. It gives you a perfect excuse to communicate only in English."

"I don't look Finnish,"Yoel objected.

"If it comes up, which it won't, what are you supposed to say?"

"My mother is Chinese,"Yoel said. "But nobody will ever buy it."

"Enough," Blumenfeld said. "Now don't forget."

"I know,"Yoel smiled. "Let her come to me."

■ ■ ■

Tel Aviv to London as Mark Spektor, South African mining engineer. He passed off that passport to a young woman who brushed up against him in the terminal.

London to Vienna as Jonas Van Dyke, Dutch sales representative. He passed off that passport to the boy who took his order at the schnitzel counter in the food court.

Vienna to Dubrovnik. Finally on the Finnish passport.

■ ■ ■

He initially saw her eating dinner by herself in the hotel dining room. It was his first evening there, and his assignment was to observe—nothing more.

271

She was very beautiful, but she was no longer young. In fact, she hadn't been young in quite a while. Yoel wasn't a teenager yet, for instance, when she could last have accurately described herself using that word. Still, she had somehow negotiated an armistice with the advancing years which left her in possession of sufficient of her powers that she could still turn men's heads. Apparently not her husband's, however. But it wasn't merely his money that made everyone so attentive to her. That was apparent.

Blumenfeld had told him he needn't anticipate difficulties. He had never been wrong about such things, but there was always a first time. Especially in this business.

■ ■ ■

Blumenfeld had said she spent her days at the hotel swimming pool. That's where he found her the next morning. He followed instructions and let her come to him. It was far easier than he expected. He had thought it might take several days, but it was as if she'd been waiting for him to show up. He didn't know if this was luck or a cause for suspicion.

■ ■ ■

"Excuse me, madame," he said with his sunniest smile. "You seem to have dropped this."

She couldn't have been more obvious about the maneuver, but she managed to appear surprised and flustered nevertheless when he placed the lighter in her hand. He thought that was charming.

"Why, thank you, kind sir," she smiled, accepting it from him.

It was Cartier. Like her, it was beautiful but a little the worse for wear. He suspected it had been dropped more than once before. Not that she seemed the clumsy sort. Or the sort to have to pick up men. She was probably accustomed to having them line up, and he was a little surprised that the competition hadn't shown itself. There were a couple of obvious "professionals" already on duty, but they hardly looked up from their reading. Blumenfeld had insisted he wear the skimpiest of swimming suits, so she couldn't accurately be described as undressing him with her eyes. Still. . .

"You must allow me to buy you a drink," she said. "To express my appreciation."

By sundown he was in her bed. Just like that.

■ ■ ■

"My husband arrives tomorrow," she said as he was pulling on his clothes prior to returning to his room the third night they were together.

"Oh?"

"I don't know what your plans were for your stay," she continued. From the sound of her voice, he thought she must have rehearsed this speech. He shrugged.

"I hate to ask it of you," she said, "but I'm afraid I can't face him with you still in the hotel."

"I'll leave first thing in the morning," he said.

"You don't know how grateful I am."

"Please," he said. "Don't think about it."

"I'd like you to have something to remember me by," she said, opening a drawer in the nightstand next to her. He saw the pistol there. He'd been told to expect it. She handed him a small gift box. "Please don't open it until later."

■ ■ ■

He didn't until he got back to his room. It was a Rolex. Stainless steel, but a Rolex.

Less than twenty-four hours later, he was back in Tel Aviv. During his debriefing, Blumenfeld told him he couldn't keep the watch. Even after that meeting, which he had hoped would answer some of his questions if only by implication and inference, he still wasn't certain the whole thing hadn't been a training exercise. Or perhaps some kind of test. Maybe the guys upstairs wanted to make sure he could fuck women. It would be just like them to obsess over that. As if he'd ever had a problem that way. It wasn't because he couldn't do it with women that he usually did it with men.

Her hunger for him had been disturbing. He fervently hoped it wasn't real. He wasn't comfortable with the idea of making someone feel like that. If she'd been acting, however. . .

II

"Geneva," Blumenfeld said. "You'll have to be extra careful. The Swiss. They're like the Nazis back during the war. Relentless. Hardly anything gets past them."

"All right," Yoel said.

It had been six weeks since his previous trip.

"Here," Blumenfeld said, pushing the Rolex across the desk at him. "She'll expect to see you wearing this."

"Really?"

"Perhaps expect is the wrong word," Blumenfeld said. "But it will send a message. The one we need her to receive."

■ ■ ■

He was contemplating the fountains and the lake when she found him.

"I can't believe it's you," she said.

"What a surprise," he said. He did his best to make it sound genuine.

"I didn't think I'd ever see you again," she said.

He heard tears in her voice.

"It's a miracle," she said.

■ ■ ■

"I'm sorry I can't stay longer," he said. "I'd rearrange my schedule if I could."

She was lying in bed watching him dress. It was his fourth night in Geneva. There had been no mention of her husband. There had been very little of anything except the two of them in bed. He was certain the room service waiters were scandalized.

"Of course," she said. Her voice broke on the words.

"Please don't cry."

"I can't lose you again," she sobbed. "You must give me some way of reaching you. I won't be able to stand your leaving otherwise."

He gave her the address Blumenfeld had arranged. The idea of Blumenfeld's people reading words meant for him gave him the creeps a little, but there was no help for it. The first thing that arrived for him there was a parcel containing a set of platinum cufflinks and matching shirt studs.

■ ■ ■

"You see," Blumenfeld said. "And you didn't think it was worth the follow-up trip. You told me to move on to plan B."

"Doesn't it seem too easy?" Yoel asked. What he meant was *how are you sure she's not playing us?*

"Underestimating yourself," Blumenfeld said, shaking his head. "An agent on an operation must believe in himself. He's dead otherwise. Don't forget it."

III

They met regularly after that. Paris. Naples. Santorini. London. Sometimes for two nights, sometimes for four nights. Never any more than that. There was a limit, apparently, to what her husband would stand for, though she never mentioned him. They met once a month, more or less.

Every time they parted, there was a gift. Each time he returned to Tel Aviv, he handed these over to Blumenfeld. Each time he got ready to see her again, Blumenfeld retrieved them from whatever vault they resided in. It was apparently crucial for Yoel to display them to her when they met.

In Geneva, she had said she was in love with him. In Paris, she said it didn't matter to her whether he was in love with her or not. She said she didn't see how he could be. He was too young. Too beautiful. And she was who she was. In Santorini, she said she didn't think she could live without him. He hoped she didn't mean it, but what he heard in her voice and saw in her eyes insisted it was true. He tried not to take it personally.

He didn't reassure her, but he wasn't cruel, either. He wasn't cruel by nature. At least he didn't want to think so. But the real reason was that being cruel to her wasn't in the plan. And he never begged off or made an excuse when she summoned him. He did everything he could to make her believe in him.

IV

"Cannes this time," Blumenfeld said. "The French Riviera. And her husband has become suspicious. You must be prepared for him to show up unexpectedly."

"Check," Yoel said.

■ ■ ■

"God, how I miss you when we're not together," she said.

He had never seen her so anxious. She seemed on the point of losing her mind. She had practically torn his clothing off in her desperation.

"Silly girl," he smiled, cradling her face to his freshly shaven chest. "I'm here now."

■ ■ ■

They got word to him the minute her husband's plane touched down. It was on the third night, just as he was leaving his hotel room to meet her for dinner. "*Don't worry*," his contact said. "*Just play it out to the end.*"

That's how he knew it was coming, whatever it was.

■ ■ ■

But who expects to be lying next to a beautiful woman after just having made love to her when her husband bursts into the room and points a gun? That kind of thing only happened in movies.

"My God, Ernst, what are you doing?" she shrieked.

He got that clearly enough, even though his Yiddish wasn't really up to deciphering the German she sometimes spoke.

"I could ask you the same thing, you stupid cow," her husband said. He answered her in English, presumably for Yoel's benefit. "And please to shut up before someone comes. I'll shoot him if you don't stop that screaming."

"Kill me instead," she begged.

"Don't be ridiculous," he said. "Do you think I want to spend the rest of my life in prison? An intruder raping my wife is a different story."

"What if I don't testify to the rape?"

"The facts speak for themselves," he shrugged.

But if that was going to be the story, Yoel was pretty sure he'd already have been shot. Blumenfeld had assured him that the man's terror of notoriety was his life insurance policy. At least for the first few moments.

The gun was pointed directly at Yoel's face. It was equipped with a silencer. Of course. Ernst could do it without making the least disturbance. But she'd scream. Even louder than she was screaming now. If Ernst really wanted to do it quietly, he'd have to shoot her, too. Yoel's instincts said move. Try to wrestle the gun away. Ernst was thirty years older than Yoel. And he was fat. And he smelled of drink. An attempt to disarm him might work. There was probably a better than even chance. But it wasn't the plan. Just like none of the other alternatives to "*just play it out*" were in the plan. If Blumenfeld—or more likely Blumenfeld's superiors—had miscalculated, Yoel was in terrible danger. He couldn't allow himself to dwell on it.

"Get out of bed, you."

The gun trembled. The barrel drooped slightly. The eyes were glassy and bloodshot.

"Don't listen to him, darling."

"Did you just call pretty boy 'darling'?"

It came out half a snarl, half a whine. Yoel couldn't recall ever hearing an utterance so decadent. The possibility of dying at the hands of a creature like this infuriated him. He couldn't allow himself to dwell on it.

"I think I'd better do as he says," Yoel suggested.

"Good idea. So you're not just a handsome face and a ridiculous collection of muscles."

Yoel pulled back the sheets. His nakedness couldn't be an embarrassment. He must make it a weapon. Thinking it was how he'd make it so. He moved slowly and carefully.

"Please don't hurt him," she sobbed. "Please. For the love of God."

"It is of no consequence to you, wife, what I do or do not do with this piece of trash."

"Please," she begged.

"I really thought better of you, you know. Look at him. He's a cartoon. I assumed sooner or later you'd latch onto someone. Or someone would latch onto you. That was a more likely scenario considering your age and my money. But I expected someone more, well—why don't we say spiritual? I never suspected you of being so shallow as to go for a Neanderthal like this, my dear."

"My clothes," Yoel said.

"You don't need to wear clothing to fuck my wife," the man said. "And you don't need to wear clothing to go for a walk with me. No sudden moves, all right?"

"Sure," Yoel said. "Whatever you say."

"Finally. Someone talking sensibly."

"What are you going to do with him?"

She was sobbing. She was near hysterics.

"None of your business," the man said. "You can rest assured, however, that you won't be seeing him again. At least not in this life. In hell—who knows? Nothing about that place would surprise me. Come along now, we're leaving."

The man shoved Yoel ahead of him toward the door to the corridor. Yoel could feel the muzzle of the gun against his bare back. Even now, he could probably turn the tables. Blumenfeld could hardly blame him under the circumstances. But it wasn't in the plan. He stepped toward the door. Behind them, he could still hear her sobbing and moaning the name she knew him by.

There was an explosion. He heard a scream. He smelled gunpowder. Closer to him he heard a grunt, and a heavy weight seemed to press down on him from behind. The screaming didn't stop. He felt warm stickiness splashing and trickling against his back. But there wasn't any pain. He wasn't sure what that meant at first. There were two more explosions. Then another. Then the door burst open.

Two men wearing black grabbed Yoel by the arms and began pulling him forward toward the door they'd just appeared through.

"Don't look back," the taller one cautioned him.

In Hebrew. He nearly fainted with relief, but it wasn't over yet.

The third and fourth men moved past them into the room.

The screaming hadn't stopped. As Yoel and his escorts moved out into the corridor, it followed them. The elevator doors gaped in front of them, and the men half carried him inside. Yoel heard her screaming even as the elevator started down.

"You're safe," the shorter man told him.

"We're sorry we don't have time to let you clean up," the other man said.

"It's a full twenty minutes to the airport," the shorter man explained, "and we're in a hurry. You can sponge off in the car."

■ ■ ■

Yoel could hear the jet engines running as the Mercedes pulled to a stop forty feet from the plane. He pulled the blanket tighter around himself.

"Careful on the stairs," someone said.

Then he was inside the cabin. And there was Blumenfeld.

V

"You know you were never in any danger," Blumenfeld said.

"I do?"Yoel had gone into the washroom and cleaned up as best he could. One of the men had wiped his back, but he still felt sticky. He smelled blood all over himself. He didn't know if he would ever feel clean again. They had brought him a change of clothing—an aircraft mechanic's jumpsuit. Even with it unzipped to his navel it was too tight on him.

"Of course. He would never have shot you in the hotel. Think of the complications. And before he could have taken you anywhere, our men would have stopped him. We had men right outside the door, you know. We had listeners in the room next door."

"Maybe."

"No maybe about it."

■ ■ ■

"How did he find out about me?"Yoel asked.

"How does a man like that know his wife is having an affair?" Blumenfeld asked. "Any number of ways."

"Yes,"Yoel said. "But how did that particular man find out about me?"

"I know what you're asking," Blumenfeld nodded. "You want to know if our people tipped him off. In order to move things forward. Try not to think about it from a personal perspective."

"How am I supposed to do that?"Yoel asked.

"I can't answer that question," Blumenfeld said, "because the answer is different for everyone who's ever been operational."

"Right."

"We had to control the situation," Blumenfeld said, "in order to achieve our objective. And that meant controlling how and when he found out about you. If we had left it up to chance, you'd have been in even greater danger."

■ ■ ■

Yoel could have ended up dead. But he hadn't. The outcome had very little to do with Blumenfeld's efforts. That fact had to be faced. That he was here

280

in this airplane instead of lying cold on a mortuary table was more accident than anything else. If Yoel had believed in God, he might have found his survival easier to take for granted. Blumenfeld wanted him to consider the matter from an operational perspective. But perhaps it was best not to think about it at all.

■ ■ ■

Perhaps it wasn't too late to go back into the IAF.

Would he be allowed to?

Would they even take him back?

■ ■ ■

"Just so you know," Blumenfeld said, as the plane leveled off somewhere out over the Mediterranean, "he was one of the richest men in Central Europe. And he's been funneling twenty to twenty-five million a year to terrorist organizations. That's American dollars, you understand. When terrorist rockets are fired into our country, there's a good chance his money paid for them."

"And he had to be stopped," Yoel said. "I get it. But like that?"

"We have policies. We do not engage in political assassinations."

"What do you call that?" Yoel asked.

"An unfortunate domestic incident."

"A technicality," Yoel snorted.

"But a crucial one," Blumenfeld said. "People die, sure. We orchestrate all kinds of scenarios. But always under the cover of deniability. And as often as we can arrange it, not actually at our hands."

"And that's supposed to satisfy me?"

"Whether it satisfies you or not," Blumenfeld said, "it's our creed. Over a hundred fifty millions he's supplied to our enemies over the past few years and no end in sight. I'd have happily shot him down in the street. But if an Israeli does such a thing, it only hurts our cause. You know how it works."

■ ■ ■

"Did you know she kept a loaded gun in her nightstand?"

"Did you?" Blumenfeld asked.

"Certainly,"Yoel said. "I almost went for it."

"Good thing you remembered your training instead," Blumenfeld said. "A sudden move like that and he probably would have killed you."

"Right."

"Her maid has been working with us for years," Blumenfeld said. "There's not much about her we don't know. We know about her husband's two mistresses. And that he beat her regularly. We have access to her psychologist's notes. They make harrowing reading."

"So you manipulated her into killing him."

Blumenfeld shrugged.

"You used me to manipulate her into killing him."

"It was just a matter of time before tragedy struck," Blumenfeld said. "Surely you recognize that."

Yoel did. But he was nowhere near ready to admit it out loud.

"And when that terrible event finally occurred, who was to say that she wouldn't have been the one who ended up dead? But if we directed the scene. . ."

"Rationalization," Yoel said, looking out the plane window into the darkness.

■ ■ ■

"She'll never see the inside of a cell," Blumenfeld said. "Not with her psychiatric profile and history. And certainly not once the authorities have seen the video we shot of the incident from the next door hotel room. French intelligence have had their eyes on him, too. God knows they're no friends of ours, but they'll think of his death as an out of season Christmas gift. And this time tomorrow, she'll have checked into an exclusive rest home in Switzerland."

OCTOBER, 2000

"You should come," Cooper said. "It's time."

"Oh, sweetheart," Griffin said. "I'm so sorry."

"Do what we talked about." Cooper's voice was steady as a rock—a bad sign. Cooper was a master of histrionics. When he got quiet like this it meant his internal climate was in absolute turmoil.

"I remember," Griffin said. "Book my flight into La Guardia. Taxi directly to Sloan-Kettering. I'll call you when I've got the arrangements made."

"Good," Cooper said. "Even Ike's coming."

"Got it."

■ ■ ■

Griffin's mother-in-law, Shoshonnah Freitag Luxemberg, had received her cancer diagnosis seven years earlier. At the time she'd been given three to six months to live. The additional time had nothing to do with medical advances and miracle cures. Practically nothing was known about the variety of endometrial cancer she suffered from. There weren't enough patients in the world for the profession to pay much attention. Her survival all that time was a testament to one thing only—her incredible determination. Griffin had never seen anything like that will to keep fighting. It was a lesson he planned to carry through whatever life remained to him. Two weeks ago she'd been told that there was nothing left to do but say her goodbyes. In a characteristic response, Shoshonnah had nearly burned down the doctor's office. The kind of goodbye being suggested wasn't in her vocabulary.

■ ■ ■

Cooper had been in New York for a week, leaving Griffin discombobulated. He managed to keep the household running and himself employed, but he wasn't sure how. The dogs got exercised and fed. The laundry got done. The bills got paid. Ordinarily the most conscientious of cooks, he subsisted on frozen dinners and binged on junk food. It wasn't pretty. Heaven help him in case of widowhood or divorce. But he managed.

After Cooper called, Griffin went on a kind of automatic pilot. He arranged for the dogs to stay with their littermates and cousins at the Bentley-Romanovsky's place, got his plane reservation made, left word for the security desk downstairs to hold the mail, called for a substitute teacher, and wrote a week's worth of lesson plans and emailed them to the secretary and his colleagues Cameron and Craig on the time honored belt-and-suspenders principle.

He packed. He scheduled a taxi pick up for the airport run.

■ ■ ■

Times had changed. Used to, Tristan or Big Steve would roll up in the Land Rover, the dogs would hop aboard, and all Griffin had to do was wave good-bye. Big Steve was long dead. Nowadays Tristan was married to Nick. They had three teenagers in the house, and pick up and delivery was a thing of the past. Three Labradors in the back of a Mini-Cooper was a lot, even with the seat folded down. But they were used to "togetherness" and they were happy travelers. It wasn't a long drive out to St. Francis Wood. Stefano and Nick, Jr. took the dogs in hand almost before Griffin pulled up in the driveway.

"I left a message on Nick's voicemail," Tristan said. "I'm sure he'll call Cooper as soon as he gets it."

"Thanks," Griffin said. "How much longer is he due to be in Chicago?"

"He's hoping to come home on Tuesday," Tristan said.

"I'm sure the boys miss him."

"Like Jarheads miss their drill instructor."

"Right."

That's the kind of dad Nick was.

"She's had a long fight, hasn't she?"

"Interminable," Griffin nodded.

"He'll get over it,"Tristan said. He'd lost his own mother to cancer.

"We'll see," Griffin said.

"When's your flight?"

"First thing tomorrow."

■ ■ ■

The predawn chill woke Griffin up. He could have waited in the lobby. Standing out on the sidewalk wouldn't make the taxi come any sooner.

■ ■ ■

Ordinarily Griffin read Thomas Pynchon on the plane. But ordinarily he was on vacation when he flew. This was the opposite of a pleasure trip. He'd chosen something "light" this time. Or had it chosen for him: his boss Louisa swore by this author. The woman next to him was traveling with a nine year old boy. They were obviously Jewish, and obviously New Yorkers. The boy had a copy of *Treasure Island* with him. The woman was reading Kitty Kelly's biography of Nancy Reagan. A few pages into his book, Griffin wondered if either of them might be willing to trade.

■ ■ ■

It was the perfect late autumn afternoon, warm and sunny. Manhattan was at its best on such an afternoon. In San Francisco they called that kind of weather "summer", and it occurred for a few days a year at best. Griffin called Cooper from the airport to announce his arrival. The taxi driver was unusually cooperative, depositing him at the main entrance to the hospital and expressing what sounded like sincere appreciation for his tip. New York wasn't supposed to be so hospitable. Of course, that was the New York of stereotype and legend, not the New York Griffin knew as an adopted son.

Cooper had given him the room number. He felt conspicuous as hell wheeling his luggage through the lobby as though the place were a hotel.

■ ■ ■

Shoshannah was alone when he entered the room. Cooper had said Griffin would find everyone eating a late lunch in one of the waiting lounges, but Griffin had to see her first. During the flight he had tried to imagine the scene. But really, you couldn't. She was just a collection of lumps in the bed with a morphine drip attached. He knew that her condition had deteriorated markedly over the few months since they'd been together in Aruba last June, but it was still a shock. He could hardly recognize her.

He stepped to the bed. He stared hard at her, taking it all in, cataloguing the details, making himself a camera. Her forehead was dry and cool. It felt like paper waiting to go into a printer.

"I'm here," he sobbed.

No. That wouldn't do at all. She didn't want his tears. He thought back to every conversation they'd had during the years since she learned how sick she was. Even before she'd come clean about it to Cooper and him. No. No tears. Like always, she wanted him clear headed and strong. She wanted him equal to the future. Prepared to face it head on. Straight backed, feet planted. Ready. Well, he could at least pretend those things. For her he could do it. For her and for Cooper.

"So," he said, mastering the quaver. "Here we are."

Somewhere inside that morphine fog he knew she was listening. He chose his words carefully.

"Here's what I have to say to you," he said. "I know he's your youngest. Your baby. I know he's the one who gave you the most worry over the years, but that's all over. He's a man now. A man you can be proud of. And he's going to be fine. I'm taking over now. I'll do your worrying for you after this. And no matter what happens, I'll take care of him. That's my solemn promise.

Everything that's in my power to do, I'll do. You can rest easy. I'm here now and I'll be at his side until I'm gone myself."

■ ■ ■

The Luxembergs could face anything as long as they had properly fortified themselves by means of consuming copious quantities of Chinese takeout. Griffin followed the sound of their voices and the aroma of the food until he found them sitting around a conference table in a room that wasn't really a waiting area but that had been assigned them—or more likely they had commandeered—for the purpose. He stared in through the doorway for a long moment before announcing his presence.

Josh and his partner Andrew. Check.

Cooper's niece Genikayte and her swoonworthy husband, Emilio. Check.

Yakov and his equally swoonworthy husband, Naftali Goldman. They had arrived from Tel Aviv several days ago.

Cooper himself. Invincible. Invulnerable. Gnawing on a barbecue pork rib.

At the head of the table, Willi, the patriarch.

They didn't have a care in the world as long as they sat at that table eating that food. Griffin catalogued the dishes. Not a favorite was missing. Mongolian Beef. General Tso's Chicken. Spring rolls. Shrimp in lobster sauce. Barbecue pork fried rice. Shrimp Lo Mein—there could never be enough shrimp for this bunch. Crispy Duck. Griffin's mouth watered. There was food enough to feed them all and every nurse on shift besides.

■ ■ ■

"Ike's not here yet?" Griffin asked, looking down at the plate Cooper had served him.

"It's Shabbat," Josh snorted. "He can't travel until sundown."

"Since when?" Griffin asked. He was used to his in-laws' skepticism of religious observances. Not to mention their love of shellfish and pork products.

287

"Since he got too religious for his own good," Cooper said.

"And Cherie's not coming," Josh said. "It's too hard to travel with the little ones."

"They're eleven and nine," Griffin said. "Not babies."

"Of course it's all excuses," Andrew said.

"It's all bullshit," Cooper growled.

■ ■ ■

The others piled into taxis for the trip to the Luxemberg apartment on Riverside Drive, but Cooper said he needed to stretch his legs. Griffin hoped this really denoted a wish to reconnect with his husband after a week's separation, but when his in-laws were in the picture he took nothing for granted. He surrendered his luggage to Yakov and watched the taxis disappear, absorbed into the traffic that was the city's lifeblood.

"I hope you're O.K. with this," Cooper grunted.

"Six hours on the plane and you're not sure I want a good walk?"

"I mean all this," Cooper said.

"Who can be O.K. under these circumstances?" Griffin asked. "I'm here. That's what matters."

■ ■ ■

When you lived in San Francisco, it was easy to be jaded. But skirting the west side of Central Park as night fell was enough to make anyone a romantic about New York, Griffin thought.

"I can't believe it's come to this," he said. In his mind's eye, he saw the steady drip of morphine.

"It's a lot to get used to," Cooper said. "Turns out that even after we found out she was sick we all thought she was invincible."

■ ■ ■

"It's unbelievable that she kept it from us for so long," Griffin said. "By the time she got around to telling us, she should have been dead for two and a half years."

"Yes," Cooper nodded. "Even Rosie was in the dark."

"What a secret for Willi to have to keep."

"He's tougher than we realize," Cooper said. "At least, I hope he is."

"I keep thinking back to that period," Griffin said. "Everything that was going on. And how she had to have been seeing it so differently from the rest of us."

"Exactly," Cooper said. "You know, I'm really glad you're here."

"Where else would I be?"

"Spending the last week with her made me think a lot about how much I take for granted."

■ ■ ■

"Were you actually able to talk with her?" Griffin asked.

"A little," Cooper said. "Not enough, obviously. But she knew I was there. I told her you were coming."

"Good."

"That's when she finally agreed to let them increase the dose," Cooper said. "When everybody's reservations were confirmed."

■ ■ ■

"We met in first grade," Rosie Stern Wallach said. She and her husband Lou had brought over a pair of deli trays, but after all that Chinese the most anybody could do was nibble. She had also brought a plate of rugalach. Sighting it, Griffin threw his good intentions out the window.

"I was there the day she met Willi," Rosie said. "She was engaged to someone else at the time."

"Uncle Jerry," Josh nodded.

"That's right," Rosie nodded. "Jerry Fugelsang, who later married your Aunt Rivka. And did I ever tell you we were playing miniature golf out in New Jersey the night her water broke with you, Cooper?"

They had all heard these stories before, but Rosie loved telling them.

"'The baby's not due for five weeks yet'. That's what she told your father. 'It's perfectly safe for me to go out with Rosie'."

"Impatient bastard," Yakov laughed, grinning at Cooper.

■ ■ ■

"I wish Dad wouldn't come," Genikayte said. Tall, willowy, blond like her father and two older uncles, she took after her grandmother's family, the Freitags. "I don't want to see him."

"Come on, honey," Emilio said. "It'll take at least an hour and a half to get home, even this time of night. And you know we're coming back tomorrow."

"At least that horrible woman has the sense to stay home," Genikayte said. "I don't know why he thinks he needs to come and torture us."

"Honey, please."

■ ■ ■

"I know he doesn't look it," Josh said, "but Emilio's undoubtedly the most pussy whipped man his age in America."

"It's about to get worse," Cooper said. "Just watch. With Mom gone, she's going to be impossible. Poor fucker."

"I always think it's funny," Griffin said.

"That he's pussy whipped?" Naftali asked.

"That he couldn't look less like a human resources officer," Griffin said.

"Anything but that," Yakov agreed. "Personal trainer. Bicycle messenger. Nightclub bouncer. You name it."

"You left out fitness model," Josh said.

"It's one thing for you two to mistake his identity," Cooper said. "It's something else altogether for his wife to."

"Ike and Cherie should have done what the rest of us did," Andrew said. Cooper's nickname for him was 'the In-law With Opinions'. "If Gen and Emilio were determined to have an exclusively Christian wedding. . ."

"Which never made sense, really," Cooper said. "I mean, how hard could it be to find a minister and a rabbi willing to officiate a wedding jointly? This is New York, not Mississippi."

"Exactly," Naftali laughed.

"It was a big 'fuck you' to her whole family," Yakov said, "and there's plenty of precedent for that among the Luxembergs."

"The point is," Andrew said, "we all went to the reception. We didn't stay away completely. And we all wrote very nice checks. That's what Ike and Cherie should have done. We'd be past all the *tsuris* by now."

"You really think so?" Griffin asked.

"Of course," Andrew said.

"I doubt it," Cooper said, "knowing the parties involved. Between that girl and her mother, it's a duel to the death. Remember what Cherie did to her sister Melanie."

"Ancient history," Andrew scoffed.

"No," Yakov disagreed. "In families, some things are never over."

II

Ike flapped around the room like a disoriented pelican in search of a suitable landing zone.

"Where are the nurses?" he demanded. "Where are the doctors? Why isn't anybody doing anything for her? Running tests? Administering treatments?"

He had arrived from Boston that morning. On his way from the airport he stopped to check into a hotel. The rest of them had taken their time over brunch and still beaten him to the hospital.

"That all happened years ago, you idiot," Josh fumed, "and you couldn't be bothered to show up."

"What the hell are you talking about?" Ike asked.

"There's nothing more they can do for her, Ike," Yakov said. "She's been fighting this for years. But now it's the end."

"That's ridiculous."

"Your brother-in-law is a doctor," Cooper said. "Why don't you ask him?"

Griffin heard Willi out in the hallway talking to Lou Wallach. He wouldn't be in the same room with Ike.

■ ■ ■

"Don't let him near me," Genikayte begged.

"Gen," Cooper shook his head.

"I'm not speaking to him," she insisted. "Not until he apologizes to Emilio."

■ ■ ■

"Why don't we all gather at the bedside?" Rabbi Spektor suggested. She was Josh and Andrew's rabbi, from the gay synagogue. Shoshonnah and Willi hadn't been members of a congregation since Cooper left home.

"I'm not going in there," Willi said. "He threw away his daughter. And now he's letting my wife die with a broken heart."

"I'll stay with him," Naftali said, taking Willi by the arm.

■ ■ ■

Rosie took charge. She crouched, face right at Shoshonnah's ear.

"Darling, it's me, Rosie," she said. "We're all here. Everyone you love. You've fought long enough. Rest now. We're with you. You can go."

Griffin watched. The eyes didn't open. But something was going on. Just like yesterday, when he'd stood there pouring out his heart and making the most solemn promise of his life. She heard. There was no question about it. Through the pain and disorientation of that narcotic fog, she absolutely heard. She knew.

"Darling, it's all right," Rosie murmured. "Listen to me. It's all right for you to go."

■ ■ ■

A few last breaths and it was over. Rosie talked her through it, never letting go of that clawlike hand.

■ ■ ■

"I've never seen anything like it," Griffin murmured.

"How else could it have gone?" Cooper asked, squeezing his hand.

Griffin noticed that his eyes were dry.

■ ■ ■

"Why didn't anybody tell me what was happening?" Ike wailed from halfway down the corridor. "In God's name, why?"

Everybody ignored him. They had spent years trying to get through.

Griffin recalled listening to Cooper's end of hours and hours of telephone calls. Ike had been told. Ike had been warned. Ike had been pleaded with. Over and over again.

■ ■ ■

On the sidewalk in front of the hospital.

"Dad, you come with Andrew and me," Josh said.

"Andrew?" Willi looked around.

"He's gone to get the car."

"Let's walk," Cooper said.

Griffin nodded.

■ ■ ■

When they got back to the apartment, it was time for more takeout. Italian this time.

"I don't know what my grandparents were thinking," Rosie said, pulling flatware out of a drawer. "We weren't that big a family. But they bought that huge plot. Anyway, it's all settled. Shoshonnah will be buried there, and when it's Willi's time he'll go next to her."

■ ■ ■

"Joshua," Ike said, "Cherie wanted me to ask you about Mom's jewelry."

"What about it?"

Beside him, Griffin could feel Cooper about to erupt.

"Well, she was hoping. . ."

"Was she?" Cooper asked.

"Of course," Ike said. "Why not? She's the only daughter-in-law. Who else should get it? As I remember, Mom had lots of really nice things. Only stands to reason, as the owner of a jewelry store. And for that matter, there were all those pieces Nannie Freitag left her."

"Most of it's gone," Josh said.

"Gone?"

"Sold off," Josh said.

"Sold off? What for? It isn't like they needed the money."

"Where was she going to wear any of it?" Andrew asked. "Sitting under her palapa on the beach? You'd be crazy to travel with that stuff. Particularly to the Caribbean."

"But. . ."

"She gave a lot of it away," Josh said. "Mom had lots of friends. There's Rosie. . ."

"Of course," Ike said. "Rosie should have anything she wants to remember Mom by."

"And Rosie's daughters-in-law," Josh continued, "and there's Babbo and Fina, too."

"Who?"

"Mom's Italian friends," Cooper said. "Mrs. DeBellis and Mrs. Romine. I know you've met them."

"Right," Ike said. "Those two."

"And their daughers," Josh said. "Mom was really close to their daughers."

"And their daughers-in-law," Cooper nodded.

"She sent some very nice pieces to her relatives in Israel," Naftali said. "She was very generous with them."

"And don't forget the Fugelsang girls," Cooper said. "You know, Rivka's daughters-in-law."

And Genikayte as well, Griffin thought. She'd been given some very fine things of Shoshonnah's for her wedding and at each anniversary. But nobody was likely to mention that.

"Mom had lots of time to think about where she wanted it all to go," Josh said. "She made lists."

"And then there are a few pieces that Dad will want to keep for sentimental reasons," Andrew said.

"Well, certainly," Ike said. "But surely—I mean, I can hardly go back to my wife empty handed."

"You'll have to talk to Dad about that," Josh said.

■ ■ ■

"What's Yoel up to lately?" Cooper asked.

"We don't speak of it," Naftali said.

"Why not?" Griffin asked.

"Big scandal," Naftali said. "Really, you shouldn't ask."

"If you believe that crock," Yakov said, making a face.

"Why wouldn't anybody believe it?" Naftali asked

"What scandal?" Griffin asked. He'd been a big fan of Yoel's since first meeting him. Inevitable, really, since Yoel reminded him so totally of Cooper when they first met.

"Drummed out of the military," Yakov said, "for conduct unbecoming. A complete fabrication, of course."

"How is it a fabrication?" Naftali asked. "They had the incident on tape."

"It was staged," Yakov insisted. "Do you know how much easier it would have been to stage something like that than get it on tape accidentally? Yoel's not so stupid as to let himself be caught red handed."

"In any case," Naftali said, "the story is that he fell under the influence of that Blumenfeld scoundrel. Now he's working in an exclusive male brothel in Frankfurt."

"My God," Griffin said.

"Yes," Yakov nodded, "that's exactly what we're supposed to say if anyone asks about him. Truth, of course, is stranger than fiction."

"You don't believe it, apparently," Cooper said. "You probably think he's Mossad."

"Not another word," Naftali warned.

■ ■ ■

"Honey," Ike said, "I wish you'd talk to me. Come sit down for a few minutes before you leave."

"Emilio's far too tired," Genikayte said. "We've got to get on the road while he's still able to drive."

Griffin couldn't remember ever seeing such toxic body language from her.

■ ■ ■

"I'm not saying Ike doesn't deserve all this," Griffin said, "but it's painful to watch."

"Don't start feeling sorry for him," Cooper said, climbing into bed.

"I'm not," Griffin insisted, "I promise."

"You're too tender hearted is what it is," Cooper said, turning out the bedside lamp. "Mom loved that about you. But there's a time and place for it. Now go to sleep. Tomorrow's going to be a very long day."

III

The cemetery was way out in New Jersey. The hearse was already there when they arrived. Griffin and Cooper rode out from the city in the car Yakov and Naftali had rented. Naftali was surprisingly effective behind the wheel. Griffin recalled catastrophic traffic conditions in Tel Aviv, but Yakov had done all the driving during their visits.

The graves stretched into near infinity in all directions. So many dead. And on every headstone a Jewish name. Being married to Cooper—nonobservant son of the tribe that he was—reading about Jewish culture and history, thinking back on his Old Testament studies in college; none of it brought home the reality of this alien but oh, so familiar tribe like seeing all those names on all those headstones. Griffin almost felt irreverent, just showing up. Like an unworthy interloper.

"Good morning," the funeral director greeted them as they emerged from the car. "Beautiful day, isn't it?"

He handed Griffin a yarmulke.

■ ■ ■

Rabbi Spektor had brought her intern along. His name was Jason, and he looked like an Abercrombie and Fitch model. He had played a couple of seasons of major league baseball before attending rabbinical school, and his hair was almost as red as Griffin's.

"I visited with Shoshonnah many times over the last few months," he said after they'd been introduced. "She always spoke very highly of you. With great affection—you understand?"

"It was mutual," Griffin said, tongue tied as always when confronted with a hot young man. "I never knew my mother. Either of my parents, really. My father died before I was born and my mother a few hours after. Shoshonnah taught me what it meant to have a mother. The Luxembergs always treated me like a prince."

"That's exactly what she called you," Jason nodded, "a prince."

■ ■ ■

"Eli," Griffin said, "and Eamonn. I didn't know you'd be here."

"She was a great lady," Eamonn said, grabbing Griffin by the shoulders and engulfing him in an embrace very nearly as evocative as one of his own husband's, "had to pay our respects."

"It's true," Eli nodded. "I don't know if my mother would ever have been able to come to terms with having a gay son if it hadn't been for Shoshonnah's example."

"Three gay sons," Eamonn nodded. "And the straight one is the black sheep. You can't make shit like that up."

■ ■ ■

Gradually they all assembled at the gravesite. The heap of newly dug earth and the hole next to it seemed like a desecration among the beautifully manicured grounds. The great granite marker at the head of the plot proclaimed "Stern"—Rosie's family. She had arrived early and was acting as hostess.

■ ■ ■

In the moments of remembrance before the final prayers, Rosie told the story of how she and Shoshonnah met in first grade, the one about how they sneaked into the yearbook photos of all the clubs and organizations they weren't really members of their senior year in high school, and the one about the day Shoshonnah and Willi met. Everyone present had heard them at least once before except perhaps Rabbi Spektor and intern Jason.

■ ■ ■

Griffin shouldn't have been surprised. Willi and Ike had dropped single, genteel shovelfuls of earth onto the casket, but Yakov and Cooper grabbed the tools from them and went at it like they planned to fill the whole grave in a matter of minutes.

"Here," Josh murmured, holding out another shovel.

Griffin took it. The wood of the handle was rough against his hands. He remembered the sensation from his boyhood on the farm. He moved to the pile of earth and drove the blade into it. Next thing he knew, Eli was beside him, and they were matching Cooper and Yakov shovel full by shovel full.

■ ■ ■

Finally the moment Griffin had been waiting for arrived. How many years? Over half his lifetime. And never once? Not for a second? But now, with the mourners moving away from the grave and the words of the prayers a receding memory, came that loss of control he'd known he'd eventually witness. In all their time together, happy, fighting, or in bed, Cooper's preternatural reserve had never cracked. Within the fire there had always been that granite—not steel that the heat might soften, but stone. People didn't think of Cooper as emotional. Gregarious, yes. High spirited, certainly. But not like this. After all this time, Griffin still only knew it was in there by assumption.

Now it emerged. All the passion and turmoil. The anguished face. The sobs. The heaving shoulders, suddenly disarmed. The rock cracking before Griffin's eyes. This was what agony looked like on that face.

In that moment it wasn't Griffin Cooper turned to; wasn't one of his brothers, either. It was Eamonn's shoulders, the one pair as stalwart as his own, he leaned on; Eamonn's arms, the only ones present whose magnitude could compare to his, that closed around him.

Fine, Griffin thought. *Of course I'm not big enough for that job.*

It was over in less than a minute.

■ ■ ■

It wasn't anything to be jealous of, Griffin reminded himself. Cooper's action in turning to Eamonn for comfort had been as natural—and predictable—as sunrise. Instinctual, more than anything. How could you fault your husband for a thing like that? From the moment they first met, when those voices in Griffin's head had insisted that here was the man who, unlikely as it might seem, was his destiny, he had known he'd never be equal to certain tasks involved, certain demands which would be made of him. Day to day, it hadn't been a problem. He could do the mundane. He could meet the ongoing requirements. Fulfill the promises. The "love, honor, obey". The "in sickness and health". Even the "forsaking all others"—which really was the easiest of all. This was one of those instances, mercifully few over two decades and counting, when his inadequacy was brought home to him in the most unambiguous way. You just had to stand and take it. Your pain, in a moment like the one he'd just witnessed, was less than his—your husband's. That's what you reminded yourself of. Your grief was the grief occasioned by failure. His was the grief of loss.

It was his fault, not Cooper's. Certainly not Eamonn's. So any disappointment Griffin felt had to be in himself.

■ ■ ■

"He what?" Josh was dumbfounded.

Around them cars were filling up. Engines were starting.

"He has a three o'clock flight," Yakov said. "He says he needs someone to drive him to the airport at one."

"We'll barely get back to Dad's place by then," Josh said.

"I told him to get on his cell phone and call a car service," Cooper said. "I even gave him the number of the guy Dad always uses."

"He can't give her a full twenty-four hours?" Josh shook his head. "Not even that much?"

"I'll be happy to drive him," Andrew offered.

"You will not," Cooper snapped. "He can either make that call or miss his flight. People have been catering to that bastard all his life."

■ ■ ■

Back on Riverside Drive, the dining table was covered with deli platters. The sideboard bore rank on rank of champagne flutes. Cooper and Naftali poured out the Bollinger. Shoshonnah had always eschewed other labels.

■ ■ ■

"No, Rosie," Josh said, shaking his head. They were head to head in the kitchen. "Four nights is all. Tonight will be for old family friends and all the former employees. Tomorrow it's my crowd because they're all off on Mondays. Tuesday it's the Italians. They never feel they can let their hair down properly with too many Jews around. And Wednesday will be for anybody who shows up."

You're sure about this?"

"Absolutely," Josh said. "Nobody sits Shiva for a whole week any more. And don't worry about the food. People will bring. You order more trays, we'll just end up throwing too much away."

■ ■ ■

"Cherie and Ike blamed Mom," Cooper said.

"How was she responsible?" Naftali asked.

"She was the one person Genikayte would listen to," Cooper said. "They still think that if Mom had put her foot down, Genikayte would have given up on the idea. It would all have blown over and now they'd have a nice Jewish son-in-law and some nice Jewish grandchildren."

"That's ridiculous," Naftali said. "People don't choose. Life just happens."

■ ■ ■

"I was surprised none of the Fugelsangs came," Rosie said, shaking her head sadly.

"It's a long trip from L.A.," Griffin said.

"Everybody went when Rivka passed," Rosie said. "Shoshonnah, Willi, Josh, Andrew. And of course you and Cooper were there."

"San Francisco to L.A. isn't much of a trip."

"Still," Rosie said, "not one of them?"

"There have been hard feelings ever since Rivka passed," Griffin said.

"I know, but even so. She was their only aunt. They have nothing to do with their father's family."

"The boys blame Willi," Griffin said.

"I heard all about it," Rosie said, "but it had nothing to do with him. It was their mother. She kept telling Shoshonnah not to come. Shoshonnah was ready to book a trip—oh, I can't tell you how many times. But always Rivka said no."

"And then it was too late," Griffin said.

"It wasn't too late. You all got there before she passed."

"It was too late for the boys," Griffin said. "They'd already decided on the story. Their Aunt Shoshonnah had deserted their mother."

"Oy," Rosie said, "and I heard the daughters-in-law behaved terribly. Practically stripped the apartment to the bare walls."

"They even took some things that belonged to Al's first wife. That's how bad it was," Griffin said.

"It's a shame how funerals bring out the worst in people."

■ ■ ■

"She needs to have a baby," Babbo said. "Really. That's all it is."

"Settle her right down," Fina nodded. "Never fails."

"Don't you think?" Babbo asked.

"It's hard to imagine Gen as a mother," Griffin said.

"Of course it is," Babbo nodded.

"But motherhood changes a girl," Fina insisted. "You should have seen this one before her first came."

"I was holy terror," Babbo confirmed, "just a holy terror. Nobody could do a thing with me. Poor Gianni was at his wits end. He thought he'd gone and married a madwoman."

"Do you think they've even considered it?" Fina asked.

"I have no idea," Griffin said.

"'Cause we know she talks to Cooper all the time."

"True," Griffin said. "More than ever, since her grandmother went into that last phase. Three or four times a week at least. And that's just the calls I overhear."

"I would have thought they'd have a child by now," Babbo said. "At least one. You don't suppose there's anything wrong, do you?"

"Wrong?" Griffin asked.

"With Emilio, you know?" Fina suggested.

"Like a sports injury or something," Babbo said. "Every time you talk to him he's just back from playing soccer or just on his way out the door for a volleyball match."

"He swims several miles a day," Fina said, "and that can't be good for his you know. . ."

■ ■ ■

"Ike's leaving?" Willi asked. "So soon? Well, good riddance to him. He broke his mother's heart and now he can rot in hell. He should only do it under his own roof. With that woman."

"Dad, come say goodbye to him at least," Josh said.

"Let him come to me," Willi said. "I bet he's not man enough."

V

"What the fuck are all these shoeboxes?" Cooper demanded, emerging from the closet. Two nights sitting Shiva had driven him almost out of his mind. He had to do something more than eat and schmooze.

"Lottery tickets," Willi said. "Mom saved them. She knew she was going to hit it big eventually. She was going to charge off all those losses against that win. For taxes, you know?"

"Can you do that?" Griffin asked. "Oops, sorry. Stupid question."

"They go back years," Cooper said, staring at a bundle of stubs he'd pulled out of the first box. "They're in rubber bands. Each batch is dated. There's got to be seven—eight shoeboxes full."

"Right," Willi nodded.

"I don't know why you're surprised," Griffin said. "It's exactly the kind of thing she would have done."

JUNE, 2001

It was a very distinctive scent. The kind you never forgot. Rupert recognized it the moment he stepped into the empty elevator even though he'd left Moscow years earlier. He'd had a contact there, a minor functionary in the Ministry of Culture, who plastered his hair down with copious amounts of the stuff. Whenever they met, Rupert smelled Misha well before he saw him. In addition to its aggressive fragrance, the stuff was formulated to give the hair a high shine. Rupert recalled the blinding highlights that had danced off Misha's redolent locks. Misha had never been much good as a source, but he was certainly picturesque. In retrospect, it seemed obvious that the KGB had been using him as a provocateur. Apparently, Rupert was supposed to succumb to that scent and that shine regardless of what they were attached to. Eventually, Frogmaxtedd had fallen prey to a different honey pot altogether. But Rupert's career was over just as if he'd been the one who allowed himself to be seduced. There was a lesson for you.

"What the hell?" he muttered.

His bewilderment didn't dissipate until the elevator deposited him on the third parking level.

■ ■ ■

It was too unlikely to credit, he thought as he sat behind the wheel waiting for the cabrio top to go down. Where would anybody get that stuff around here? More to the point, who would want it?

■ ■ ■

By the time he got home from work, he'd about convinced himself he'd imagined the whole thing. But the minute he stepped into the elevator there it was again. Tenacious as it was, that scent couldn't have persisted all day.

■ ■ ■

He smelled it again in fitness center the next morning. He never used the fitness center in his building. He had a membership at gym over in Hillcrest. But the phenomenon had been bothering him all night, so first thing that morning he went on patrol of all the common areas. The pool deck, on the roof of one of the building's lower wings and overlooking the bay, was too open a space, of course, to hold a trace of the scent. But he had a look—or a sniff—out there anyway, just in case. There wasn't a hint of it in the business center or the library. But when he stepped into the fitness center, there it hung, clear and distinct in the tangy air.

■ ■ ■

Rupert had always wanted to live in California. His boyhood dreams shimmered with the sunshine off the water and rattled with the breezes through the palm fronds. In countless reveries, he steered his gleaming sports car along winding coastlines at sunset, the wind in his hair and the salt tinged slipstream caressing his bare forearms. He dined in chic restaurants with glamorous women and distinguished looking men—or vice versa—at neighbouring tables. Adventure followed hot on the heels of adventure, though their nature was sketchy and undefined, along those wide, palm lined avenues, beneath that serenely evocative moon. California. Land of dreams. The golden state.

Childish nonsense, of course. But a convenient excuse when the time came. A convenient excuse was exactly what Rupert required in the aftermath of Cavendish. Captain Smith must have known a similar feeling moments after striking the iceberg when it became inescapably clear that everything up to the point of impact had been a delusion. *Unsinkable? Bollocks, man. Only a fool. . .* Or consider if you will for a moment Don Quixote going up against those bloody windmills. That was Cavendish. Or rather, those scenarios were analogues for Rupert's whatever-it-had-been with Cavendish. Cavendish was just, had always been and would always be, Cavendish. No more and no less. Beauty wasn't truth, despite the poet's assertion. No matter how arresting it might be, it didn't automatically bear the burden of profundity and significance on its monumental shoulders. Cavendish the beautiful—yes. Cavendish the magnificent—no argument there. Cavendish the object of worship—undoubtedly. But Cavendish, the man to share your life with? To grow old alongside? Forsaking all others till death do you part—even unspokenly and ever so discreetly from the background? All of that twaddle had been in Rupert's head and nowhere else. Facts had to be faced. Cavendish forced him to. Perhaps someday Rupert would accept that it was the kindest thing Cavendish had ever done for him. Someday. Meanwhile—broken heart? Exile necessitated by disappointment in romance? *Rubbish, old man. Just living out a boyhood dream. Finally getting around to it, opportunity at last presented itself, no time like the present, not getting any younger, life's too short. . .*

An excuse. One everybody Rupert knew had marveled at when he communicated it but no one disputed.

A geographical cure was the only hope, really. From a distance of six thousand miles Rupert could admit it to himself. As he could admit to himself that strewing sexual favors the length and breadth of the Home Counties, winning Olympic medals, spying for Queen and Country, and abdicating one of Jolly Olde's most venerable and bizarre titles had been the exploits of a youth not so much misspent as misunderstood and thus insufficiently appreciated. Who else in history had gone to California, pot of gold at the end of the rainbow and worldwide centre for the manufacture and distribution of dreams, on a quest for reality?

■ ■ ■

Anywhere would have done, given his state of heart and mind at the time of embarkation. He could easily have thrown himself on the stern but tender mercies

307

of his guardian angel and distant kinsman, Ned Westerleigh, who apparently ran the City of San Francisco as a sort of hobby, complete with a clone of their old school where Rupert could have washed up with no effort involved on his own part. He had availed himself of Ned's assistance at the time of his Retreat from Moscow and his subsequent career was all the proof anyone could have needed of that man's astuteness as a mentor and competence as a guide. But this time he sensed that it would be too easy. Rupert's sorrow required not balm but cauterization. Purification through the pain of making his own way on the shores of the New World. Except for a stake to get him set up, those millions Pa had settled on him must be disregarded, their existence forgotten or at least ignored for the duration. A new home. A new job. New friends—had he ever had friends, truly? His boyhood alter ego, that gaudy, stereotypical disguise he inhabited, certainly did. Friends galore. But the new clear eyed, sober minded, authentic Rupert FitzMerlin? Not only would he have to make new friends, he'd have to figure out how such a thing was done. As for love, that had to be right out of the question while he reinvented himself.

■ ■ ■

He ended up in San Diego. Less frenetic by far than Los Angeles, more temperate and less daunting of terrain than San Francisco, and cosmopolitan enough to boast sufficient of the features of what Rupert regarded as civilization to make it a tolerable place of exile, it seemed the perfect locale for licking his wounds and Figuring Everything Out. He got a job at a school for fourteen to eighteen year olds—which the Yanks referred to as a high school—reasoning that teaching was the only serious enterprise he was any good at. The school was coeducational, which was jarring at first. And at second, third, and fourth, come to that. Rupert couldn't envision a time when the female of the species wouldn't bewilder him. And though it was a resolutely Anglican institution—the Yanks called it Episcopalian, but it was the same thing—it wasn't much like an English school. The parents were wealthy but for the most part not well educated by the standards Rupert was acquainted with, the students didn't seem worried at all about being admitted to university, apparently depending on their parents' connections to take care of that as they took care of everything else, and sports were ridiculously overemphasized yet at the same time not very well played, while "sportsmanship", a concept much revered in the institution's collective discourse and featuring prominently on its website and in its fancy brochure, was apparently little understood.

Rupert bought a flat—which the yanks called a condominium—in a tower block near the city's downtown district. It faced the bay and, because he had chosen quite a high floor, looked out across Coronado Island—which was actually a peninsula—to the Pacific. It afforded stunning views of the aircraft carriers moored alongside the island and the airbase located at its tip. Beyond, nestling in the shadow of Point Loma, the nuclear submarine base hid in plain sight. In other words, Rupert purchased a great spy's nest as well as a flat. Most of the flats in the building were owned by "investors" who rented them out, so most of Rupert's neighbors were tenants rather than owners. The building was greatly favored, for instance, by the young pilots who flew jets off those carriers when they were at sea. They were a handsome bunch, athletic, boisterous, and fun loving, and riding the elevators with them or encountering them in the mailroom, on the pool deck, or in the underground garage, they seemed like Old Wykehamists. Except for their rakish American haircuts and jarring American accents he might have known them at school.

He splurged on a Porsche in a shade of blue so dark it almost looked black in dim light and incidentally matched his eyes. Its interior was lipstick red, which made him laugh to think of how his London associates would react. He made a practice of never arriving at school with the cabriolet top up even in the most inclement of weathers, though by U.K. standards the term inclement sounded ridiculous when applied to anything San Diego had in its repertoire. He bought a membership in a gym in the city's gay neighborhood. He discovered the neighborhood's gay clubs. He tried to learn the art of dating, but there were tricks to it that put the KGB to shame. Gradually his previous life receded from memory, taking up a position a safe though not quite comfortable distance from every day reality.

■ ■ ■

And then that infernal scent intruded on his new, arduously assembled reality that afternoon on the elevator. For three days he endured it, doing nothing more in response to its ubiquity than that initial morning patrol. But obnoxious as it was, it tantalized him. And just as he was about to go into full investigative mode and track it and its user down, it came to him. He smelled it almost before the elevator doors opened. He was almost too surprised by it to step inside.

But he did.

The individual he saw there was not just the bearer of that scent. He was a revelation. The sleek, glistening locks, black as night and smooth as the ice of a hockey rink before the start of the match, were just the start of it. The face was ridiculously handsome. The eyes were icy too, glinting an unusual silvery blue. They were terrifying as well. And that breathtaking head was supported by a pair of shoulders as broad as Rupert's own, though the man himself was two or perhaps three inches shorter. The shirt he wore, one of those white, quasi military ones of the type favored by commercial aircraft pilots, was obviously not an off the rack number. The man's musculature was stupefying, yet that shirt fit him perfectly. It was obviously tailor made.

■ ■ ■

Rupert spent the rest of the day in near catatonia. The encounter had lasted for less than a minute. That was how long it took for the elevator to reach the second level of the parking facilities in the basement of the building, where the man got off. Rupert experienced an almost overwhelming impulse to follow him, but at the last possible instant his training prevented him. He rode on to the third level where the Porsche was parked. He sat behind the wheel for he couldn't have said how long trying to clear his head. He completely forgot where he'd been headed and what he had planned to do when he arrived there. Eventually he gave up, got out of the car, and went back upstairs.

■ ■ ■

Recalling that terrifying moment from the solitude of his terrace, he eventually calmed down enough to decipher its significance. The man was the most spectacular specimen of masculine beauty Rupert had encountered since Cavendish. Since the end of the Cavendish era, Rupert had known, at least hypothetically, that somewhere out there Cavendish's equal existed. Now that archon was no longer an abstraction. He breathed. A heart pumped blood through his veins. And by some inscrutable caprice of the fates he inhabited a space in shockingly close proximity.

■ ■ ■

All that being clarified, Rupert got back to business. The gym. That's where he'd been headed when the interruption occurred. When he got downstairs, his gym bag was still sitting in the passenger seat of the Porsche where he'd left it.

■ ■ ■

By the time he worked out and ran a few errands, his next step was clear. A man like that couldn't just show up out of nowhere and then disappear again without a trace. But since he was obviously a pilot of some kind, that's exactly what would happen if Rupert didn't take some steps. With those looks and that particular grooming agent in his armamentarium, the gentleman was obviously just passing through. But now that he had reawakened something essential in Rupert's nature, he couldn't be allowed to vanish without being known.

■ ■ ■

For a man of Rupert's training and experience it was the work of less than half an hour. Without raising the slightest suspicion among his neighbors or the building staff, Rupert completed his research. The copy of the rental agreement on file in the building manager's office told all. Slipping into the locked office like it was his own bedroom closet, he had the document out of the binder, into the copy machine, back into the binder and the binder back in its place on the shelf behind the manager's desk with the speed of light. Then he read. Space number in the basement garage. Flat number—two floors up from Rupert's, a one bedroom rented from an absentee owner. License number and description of vehicle, a white Jeep Wrangler. And a name. Bobak Aghazadeh. That explained the coloring and lean, angular features. Those cheekbones, that jawline. That heavy black beard shadowing the pale skin of that freshly shaven face. Persian father from the name, while a Russian or perhaps Ukrainian mother completed the picture. Rupert knew the story. Russia had more ethnic minorities than just about any other country on the planet. Persians were well up on the list. And Russian women found Persian men fascinating. You saw these mixtures in Moscow, Kiev—everywhere you went from St. Petersburg to Vladivostok. That lineage—and Rupert would have placed a sizeable bet on the accuracy of his hypothesis—explained everything.

And the man wasn't passing through. He had signed a six month lease. He was a flying instructor. He worked for a school out at Gillespie Field, north and east of the city.

Rupert had time.

II

They sent Ned Westerleigh. This surprised Rupert, though it shouldn't have done. Nobody ever retired from the service. Personnel were simply "de-activated". And once they were, they all lived with the knowledge that unlikely as it might be they could just as easily be reactivated at any time and for any purpose, no matter how momentous or trivial, it might occur to some shadowy figure in London to enlist them for. For that matter, rumors of Ned's retirement had been merely that—rumors. They didn't throw receptions for that kind of thing or banquets at the end of which gold watches were bestowed on loyal retainers while all assembled rose from their seats at table and applauded prior to singing "God Save the Queen".

Rupert hadn't known for certain they would send anybody, or when. It was a shot in the dark, nothing more. But there Ned was one afternoon when Rupert emerged from his gym, sitting at an outdoor table at the taqueria across the street, big as life. Which meant that they'd placed Rupert under surveillance for long enough to chart his comings and goings. He had bargained on this. They wouldn't resort to a contact *en clair*—explicit and out in the open—because whoever he'd been watching might easily have noticed it and started watching him. They'd do it like this. Choreographed and using covers. So there Ned was, except he wasn't Ned Westerleigh at all. Ned Westerleigh would never have worn that garish Hawaiian print shirt or paired it with those baggy madras walking shorts. Ned Westerleigh would have known not to wear those black knee socks with those hideous Birkenstocks or to top off his ensemble with that wide brimmed straw hat. He couldn't have been more conspicuous if he'd set off emergency flares. So no—definitely not Ned Westerleigh. Which, in turn, meant that Rupert wasn't Rupert. He hoisted his gym bag and set off toward the Porsche, parked on the other side of the street just past the taqueria. He sauntered along aimlessly with a totally uncharacteristic, loose limbed, slouching gait that disregarded his professional training, athletic accomplishments, rigorous education since age eight, and centuries of English history and tradition, and waited for Ned's signal.

"Hulloa."

There it was. Rupert walked on, apparently oblivious. Lost in thought.

"You there. Derek? Derek Trent?"

Derek Trent. Rupert hadn't used that one since before Moscow. Like the elephant, Ned Westerleigh never forgot. Derek Trent was quintessential Essex Man, the platonic ideal of the dim but affluent suburbanite. Not particularly bright and utterly conventional. So be it. He turned, taking care to look befuddled and maintaining that abysmal posture.

"Gosh. George. George Winterbottom. As I live and breathe. And here, of all places."

"Not half as surprised to see me as I am to see you, old man."

Inactive as they might be, they were handling it superbly. Two Englishmen abroad, encountering each other unexpectedly. Derek's putative family were *nouveau classe moyenne*, which necessitated certain adjustments to his accent and diction. George Winterbottom, he recalled, was from Yorkshire, which entailed even more radical modifications. Where were the BBC casting directors when such sublime powers of improvisation were on display?

"My boy, you must join me."

Derek consulted his watch, squinting.

"Why yes," he said, ooching the last few paces and flopping into a chair at George's table. "What in the world brings you here?"

"The weather, I should think."

"Yes," Derek nodded. "Lovely day. That's about all we seem to have here. Never thought I could get bored with such a thing, but every now and then."

"Indeed," George Winterbottom said. "And me, sitting here attempting to determine just exactly what a fish taco is. Concierge at the hotel insisted I try them. I suppose he'll be disappointed if I return unenlightened."

"There will be a quiz, what?"

"Just so."

"They're quite delicious, actually," Derek said. "Sort of a local speciality."

Their sarabande continued. They did how's your family and the general state of Jolly Olde. They did George's feckless niece Hermione, who had more or less left poor Derek at the altar and was now repenting of her sins at length, having recently been unceremoniously dumped by her second husband, Rog. "Can't trust those flash boys," George grumbled. "Turn your back for an instant and they're up to trouble." They did the long running feud between George's wife Hilda and the officials of the local chapter of the Women's Institute in the Surrey village where the couple lived now that George was retired from The City. By that time the fish tacos had been disposed of and in the unlikely event anyone was listening in on them, said individual must surely have died of boredom.

Not that there had been any sign of watchers.

"Now my boy," Ned Westerleigh said, altering his volume without altering his body language, which Rupert knew was one of the hardest tricks to pull off. "Suppose you take me through it."

Rupert did. Every last detail. No omissions, no emendations, no elaborations, no embroidery. Just the facts. You could safely do that with Ned because

Ned was the body and soul of British discretion and by Ned's lights there were no character flaws, no peccadilloes, and no embarrassments either minor or monumental on the part of professionals engaged in their duties whether official or, as in this instance, on their own initiative. The worst there could be in their line of work was error. Objective error. One wasn't humiliated by making an error. At least no sane man was. One simply learned from it, corrected it if possible, and went on. Except in this case, apparently, Rupert had made none.

"So either the subject is a KGB field agent," Rupert said, winding it up, "has delusions of being a KGB field agent, desires to entrap a KGB field agent, or merely wishes others to believe him to be a KGB field agent."

"Just so," Ned Westerleigh said.

"And I wondered if someone might want to come round for a look at the chap. Second opinion kind of thing."

"Exactly," Ned nodded. "Except I shouldn't think they'll bother."

"Backwater like this," Rupert nodded. "Even with his flat looking out over those aircraft carriers. Submarine base in easy range of a good pair of binoculars."

"It's not that, my boy," Ned Westerleigh said. "It's not any of the explanations you're thinking of. Budgetary worries. Likelihood of giving offense to the Cousins—major one, that. Top floor infighting. General inefficiency and uselessness. Collapse of the empire. None of those things. They don't need to take another reading because the old hands recall clearly that you were one of the best they had at the time. If the top floor possessed any sense whatever, you'd never have been deactivated. You'd have been promoted. They'd have made room for you in London. Running agents of your own by now, I shouldn't wonder. No, they won't send anyone for a look-see because there's nothing more to find out about this fellow here on the ground. If you didn't see something it wouldn't have been because you missed it. It could only be because it wasn't there."

"Thanks," Rupert said. Even if it wasn't true, some impulse had caused Ned to say it. And Ned was no pushover, so, well. . . "thanks ever so."

"Now I'm going to relay this information to our associates. And in doing so, I'm taking it out of your hands. Completely, you understand?"

"Yes."

"Off your shoulders," Ned said. "Out of your hair. Any and all anatomical metaphors, you understand? No more keeping an eye on the chap. It's not your business any more, whatever happens. Or doesn't happen, as the case may be. Under no circumstances will you do anything at all. You may or may not be an inactive member of an organization that doesn't exist in the first place. And has never been active on these particular shores. Very important, that part. Cousins are big on the national sovereignty thing, right? Which means that you keep yourself to yourself and you mind no one's business but your own."

"Understood."

"You shouldn't expect to hear anything about the outcome of any further investigation which may or may not take place regarding this or any other matter."

"Right."

"And finally I'm to caution you that you signed the Official Secrets Act once upon a time and each and every one of its provisions remains in force, more or less until the end of time and certainly well beyond your expected or even unexpectedly protracted lifespan."

That Ned certainly had a turn of phrase.

◼ ◼ ◼

Rupert couldn't make himself go cold turkey. He tried. For several days he resolutely ignored Aghazadeh's presence in his general vicinity, difficult a proposition as it was. But that scent wouldn't leave him alone. On the elevator. In the fitness center. Lingering in the mail room. Hanging in the air of the garage. It taunted him. He couldn't help himself. He had to continue his surveillance.

But in deference to Ned, when at last Rupert fell off the wagon he did it in the best possible style. He assumed the persona of the lovesick poofter he was trying his best not to be in actuality. Whoever the man was in reality, he'd certainly be able to distinguish the bumblings of a clumsy suitor from genuine tradecraft. Rupert could have his cake and eat it as well. Pretending to be an idiot homosexual who couldn't possibly pose a threat to operational security while continuing to stalk that spectacular man. Ned the proxy for Control would chide, but Ned the incurable romantic would applaud from the wings.

SEPTEMBER, 2001

Bobak took a last glance at himself in the mirror. He hated the smell of that infernal stuff, but his handlers insisted he use it on his hair. In the event his cover as a simple flight instructor was penetrated, the secondary legend—deactivated KGB operative recently defected to the west—had to hold up. Real professionals wouldn't have been fooled, but there was a general consensus that he wasn't dealing with real professionals this time. His handlers cautioned that this only made the subjects more dangerous, and he took this as self-evident. He went to great pains over the care and feeding of the legend they had provided, exactly as instructed. Right down to this slick, pungent detail. God only knew who thought these things up. All Bobak knew was he never wanted to meet the man.

One final swipe of the comb. The look itself wasn't bad. He had to admit it. But that reek. He wasn't sure how he'd ever eradicate it once the time came that he was permitted to.

He had filed his most recent report just a few hours earlier. He never received any response beyond the standard "message acknowledged". He hoped his sense of urgency was communicating itself between the lines of those innocuous code phrases. Something big was up. His subjects were more agitated than at any time during the months he'd spent watching them. Things were obviously approaching the boiling point. He hadn't been ordered to, but he was already preparing to "self-extract" so that the minute the order came there wouldn't be a wasted second. And really, how hard could it be, with the Mexican border just a few miles away?

The one fly in the ointment was that infernal Englishman who lived two floors down. He was too interested in Bobak by half. The reason for his interest was clear enough, big old poofter that he was. There wasn't anything dangerous about it. It was distracting merely. If he hadn't been Bobak, if he'd encountered the gentleman when he wasn't on an op, he might have considered the opportunity. Because, really, the Englishman wasn't that old. And he was presentable enough. Bobak had to admit that there was something rather seductive about being lusted after that obviously and fiercely. Actually, it wasn't Bobak who had to admit that. It was the guy he'd been before Bobak even existed. Back that far.

That was the problem exactly. He wasn't even supposed to remember that there had been a time when he wasn't Bobak. Drat that Englishman, with his long legs and floppy blond hair and famished eyes. Bobak wasn't sure whether it was the man himself or just the idea of being desired like that that was more intriguing.

■ ■ ■

He drank his protein shake while he dressed. He drafted his morning report, encoded it carefully while the set tuned up, keyed it in, confirmed that the encription device was on and operating properly, and sent it. The confirmation signal came through almost immediately. That wasn't always the case. Sometimes he waited for as long as an hour to hear that beep come back. Sometimes the delays made him wonder if his handlers cared as much as he was supposed to believe they did. He never got any feedback other than that beep, but no news was good news.

■ ■ ■

He checked and rechecked his "extraction kit." It went everywhere with him these days, and not an item could be omitted. Better to be obsessive compulsive about it beforehand than sorry afterward. That's what the trainers had always told him. His natural inclinations took over when they weren't around to nag him. And every time he left the apartment, even if it was just to go downstairs for the mail, he set his security apparatus on the front door. It wasn't meant to keep anyone out. It merely informed him if there had been an intruder.

■ ■ ■

In the parking garage, the Englishman's space was empty. He taught at a posh private school, and classes were finally back in session. That had taken a lot of pressure off Bobak. He'd spent weeks with that one shadowing him, showing up in the fitness center in the middle of his workout more than once. Even following him into the shower that one morning. He'd obviously been on Bobak's tail for a while at that point. The Englishman had never used the fitness center in the building before that. He went to a gym over in that neighborhood where all the other poofs congregated. And the stalking wasn't restricted to the building where they lived, though that would have been bad enough. Bobak had been followed to work at least once during late August. That Porsche couldn't have been more conspicuous. But now that school had started, the Englishman was far less in evidence.

■ ■ ■

The Englishman was a type. That was all. He reminded Bobak of his very first op. He'd served as the bait in a honey trap. The subject was a businessman from Sydney. Bobak had never forgotten the silky shine of that smooth, blond, Anglo/Australian head of hair bobbing in and out, in and out at his crotch. His current Englishman had exactly that hair. It was apparently a cliché in itself.

■ ■ ■

Sooner or later, this operation would end. They always did. Then, however briefly, Bobak would get his life—and real name—back again. He couldn't wait to hear someone call him Yoel.

■ ■ ■

The San Diego climate was a great one for flying. Almost as good as back home, really, and without the perpetual threat of terrorist activities or other disruptions. That climate must have been the reason the military had established so many facilities in the region during the 'thirties and 'forties. Several hundred days per year of clear flying weather. Perfect for training. Bobak's—no, that other guy's—own particular brand of paradise. And really, he could get used to the rest of it—the beaches, the city, the friendly people, as well. Make some friends. Open his own flying school instead of working for somebody else. Not that he was shopping for a new home. But he couldn't help thinking about it from time to time.

He pulled out of the garage just before sunrise. The light cloud cover would disperse well before his first scheduled lesson of the day. He might take the Beechcraft up for a short run beforehand. Yes. That's how he'd steady his nerves.

His subjects weren't early risers. They never arrived at the field before eight a.m. More than once, Bobak had considered following them when they left after their day's lessons, but his handlers had forbidden it. He assumed they had other watchers in place for that. He got the impression that this was a fairly high priority surveillance, so it stood to reason. And God knew there were plenty of his compatriots living in the area. It wouldn't have been hard to staff other phases, other locations.

■ ■ ■

He had just parked the Beechcraft and was chocking the wheels when he saw them roll in, driving that nondescript Toyota. He checked his Breitling. Yes. Three minutes after eight. As usual.

SEPTEMBER 10, 2001

Griffin stood to the side while Josh stowed his bag in the back of the Mini-Cooper. Josh didn't like to be helped with his luggage. Or anything else, really. This was a Luxemberg family trait, as Griffin knew all too well. It was best if you stood back and let them get on with things. Griffin didn't like driving the Mini-Cooper. It was too new and too powerful. Its automatic transmission made him feel as if he was being abducted. He was quite certain it had tricks up its sleeve. He much preferred his own car, a thirty-six year old Porsche. But he had to admit that for errands like this, or taking the dogs to the vet, or when a back seat was necessary, it was far more practical. That was how Cooper justified the expense of owning three cars.

"How was the flight?" Griffin asked.

"Fine," Josh said. "A little bumpy over Chicago, but that's all."

In Luxembergoise, "a little bumpy" connoted service items bouncing off the walls and ceiling of the cabin, women screaming about impending death, and flight attendants strapped white-knuckled into their jump seats. After one particularly harrowing flight to the Caribbean, Griffin complained about turbulence only to have Cooper look at him as if he'd lost his mind and ask "what turbulence?" After that, Griffin never mentioned rough air again. He kept his terror to himself. He had come to realize that his husband's family was among the most intrepid travelers on the planet. His mother- and father-in-law had weathered hurricanes, earthquakes, cruise ship engine room fires which sent everyone into the lifeboats, political upheavals in more than one hemisphere, and various food- and/or waterborne diseases in the course of their globe-trotting and spoke of these experiences as far less momentous than a hand of poker that hadn't turned their way in the casinos that were their chosen places of worship. Losing at cards was the only true catastrophe according to their worldview. Anything else could be endured. In widowhood, Willi Luxemberg continued to live by this ethic. Griffin assumed that the privations suffered by the Children of Israel in the desert had inured his in-laws' subset of God's Chosen to any and all vicissitudes of travel.

"That's good," Griffin said, climbing into the driver's seat. "How's Andrew?"

"Fine," Josh said. "He'll be here on Thursday."

Griffin had long since given up trying to deconstruct Josh and Andrew's domestic arrangements. If it had been him, he'd have just waited the extra two days and traveled in the seat next to Cooper. But just as Josh and Andrew maintained separate addresses, one in Manhattan and the other in New Haven due to Andrew's professorship at Yale, they flew separately. At least on domestic flights. Internationally was a different matter, and one they seemed to assume required no explanation, being self-evident. They explained their practices with regard to domestic travel as being based on their chaotic work schedules, but Griffin couldn't help seeing something more sinister in it. Still, it wasn't his business. And it seemed to work for them. His in-laws were nothing if not pragmatists.

"And Dad's doing well?" Griffin asked. "He certainly seemed chipper when we saw him in Vegas over Labor Day Weekend."

"He misses Mom terribly, of course," Josh said. "What with his health issues and his grief, certain people didn't expect him to survive this long without her. But yes. He's adapted remarkably well."

"Certain people" referred to Rosie Stern Wallach, the late Shoshonnah Luxemberg's best friend from first grade to her deathbed, now almost eleven months past. At the graveside, Rosie had pointed to the space next to Shoshonnah's and proclaimed that it would surely be occupied within a year. As far as Griffin was concerned, Villem Luxemberg's continuing survival was predicated on his decades-long determination to prove Rosie wrong if not actively thwart her intentions. His health issues included a prostate gland stuffed full of radioactive pellets, a missing kidney due to an aggressive strain of cancer that nevertheless hadn't recurred in over a decade, and a blown out sciatic nerve that would have put a lesser man in a wheelchair. He made do with a cane, a credit card that racked up a staggering number of bonus miles, and an extensive repertoire of wisecracks.

"How's school?" Josh asked. "New year off and running all right?"

"Fine," Griffin said.

"The usual chaos, in other words," Josh said.

"Exactly."

■ ■ ■

"I'll come with you," Josh suggested, watching Griffin leash the dogs.

"Are you sure? Cooper will be here any minute."

"I need to stretch my legs," Josh said. "And I could use some air. The San Francisco air is so different from what I'm used to."

Yes, Griffin thought. Anything to avoid being in a room with his younger brother without a referee present.

■ ■ ■

Griffin was well aware that New York, or at least the Borough of Manhattan, was the center of the universe. Two decades plus married to a native of the island had left him in no doubt of it. But in his day to day existence he rarely gave thought to that essential truth. San Francisco, the city that had for all practical purposes taken him in as a refugee, claimed the entirety of his affection, though he could certainly admire other places. This was true during the forty-five or so weeks of the year when he wasn't visiting his in-laws and they weren't visiting him. New Yorkers might decry San Francisco as provincial, though Josh and Andrew had never done so in Griffin's hearing (and they didn't even approve of the outer boroughs, much less the areas of New Jersey and Connecticut in commuting distance) but Griffin still felt a little geographically defensive when in the company of any member of Cooper's extended family.

Of course, if New York was that great, one of their friends once told Griffin in a clumsy attempt to soothe him, Cooper could have moved back there at any time during the last quarter century. And hadn't. And in fact showed no sign of ever wanting to. But Griffin had visited The Big Apple often enough to know the truth of the matter. It was the center of the universe and always would be. At least until the Chinese took over the world. Then, presumably, the center of the universe would be Shanghai. By then Griffin and Cooper and everyone they knew would be dead and it wouldn't matter. But even then New York would still outrank everywhere else. San Francisco, however much he might adore it, would always be eclipsed by Babylon on the Hudson.

■ ■ ■

"So by the time the pathology report came back on Karla's biopsy, Jill had done all the homework. Staging and grading of breast tumors, state of the art treatment protocols, best legal strategies to employ in the event the insurers refuse to cover some treatment or other, you name it," Josh said. "She was all revved up to be the tireless and supportive caregiver/advocate. Andrew insists that she was actually a little disappointed when the growth turned out to be benign."

"That's a terrible thing to say," Griffin said, "but unfortunately, it's funny at the same time."

"You know Jill," Josh shrugged.

And Griffin knew Andrew.

■ ■ ■

That afternoon something magic happened, just for a moment. Josh stopped in his tracks and gazed over the rooftops and past the towers of downtown toward the glistening waters of the bay and Alcatraz in the distance.

"Amazing," he muttered. "It's like Venice, St. Petersburg and Dubrovnik all in one. It makes perfect sense that the two of you live here."

The Labradors wagged their tails and flashed goofy smiles as if in agreement. Griffin's heart skipped a beat.

A similar scene took place at least once every time Josh visited. It redeemed both him and this city of sanctuary in Griffin's eyes.

■ ■ ■

When they got back from walking the dogs, Cooper was in the kitchen rinsing out the blender carafe. There was a protein shake mustache on his upper lip.

"Hey, Josh," he said. "You got here."

The brothers hugged. It was a lackadaisical hug totally uncharacteristic of Cooper in any other circumstances but typical when it came to greeting any of his brothers.

"Still living at the gym, I see," Josh said. "Must be awfully quiet for Griffin around the house."

"He manages," Cooper said. "Besides, somebody has to keep all the twenty-something gym rats in check."

"Can't have them running amuck," Josh laughed. "I'm sure the ones here are just as bad as the ones in New York. Chelsea is crawling with them these days. You practically have to wear a gas mask to ward off testosterone fumes when you walk down Eighth Avenue. I'd say you're just the man for the job."

"While you've got all those cute chorus boys to terrify and intimidate," Cooper said. "For all practical purposes it's the same thing. Except you get paid for it while I'm just a community volunteer. Speaking of which, how did closing night go? Triumph or fiasco?"

"Both," Josh grinned.

Josh had embarked on a Broadway career fresh out of college. After over a decade he hadn't advanced beyond chorus boy status, and with his joints starting to give out and his look not as "fresh" as that of the competition he was forced to Do Something Drastic. Most guys in his situation ended up selling insurance or real estate if they hadn't managed to break into the soaps or marry an heiress in the meantime. But Josh wasn't through with the theatre. He went back to school and got a master's degree in stagecraft. He started back at the bottom and over the last fifteen years had become one of Broadway's most sought after stage managers. He worked with geniuses and charlatans. He worked with the notorious and the celebrated and with individuals so obscure as to be practically invisible. He worked on blockbuster hits, Tony winners, and flops which became legendary after their closings. He worked on revivals of beloved classics and on the most unlikely and "experimental" of Off-Off Broadway efforts. Anything, really, as long as the project interested him or somebody he knew and liked or at least respected was involved with the production. In all that time, he'd never been out of work except when he wanted to be. And when he wanted to be he didn't sit around. Luxembergs abhorred inactivity with even greater fervor than nature abhorred a vacuum, so when he wasn't working he still worked—he temped in the financial district. There he amassed a reputation similar to the one he enjoyed in the theatre community. He was a genius at organization, he was indefatigable, and in the execution of his duties he never took no for an answer. Every time he left to do another show, his employers du jour begged him to stay.

■ ■ ■

"The critics loved the show," Josh said, sipping his wine.

They had adjourned to the terrace. The fog already obscured most of the view and it was as chilly as January, but Josh didn't seem to notice and Cooper didn't care.

"I read the reviews online," Griffin nodded.

"Unfortunately the audiences found the show incomprehensible," Josh continued. "Which was only reasonable, to be fair about it. I mean, most of the time I didn't understand it myself. The cast was devastated, of course. They were really committed to the work. And the backers were practically suicidal."

"Six months isn't that bad a run," Griffin said.

"It should have done better," Josh said.

"The glamorous life of the theatre," Cooper said without a trace of irony. "So what's next?"

Josh named a financial services company. It wasn't household name but highly respected among people who knew about such things

"When do you start?" Cooper asked.

"Monday after next."

"Where are they located?" Griffin asked.

"They're in the World Trade Center," Josh said.

"Easy commute for you," Cooper nodded. "Just jump on the Number One train at Christopher Street and you're there in no time."

■ ■ ■

Griffin settled himself in the back seat of the Mini-Cooper. When they had guests Cooper insisted on being behind the wheel, and Josh's legs never got any shorter. Whenever Cooper and Griffin visited New York, Josh's husband Andrew insisted on choosing the restaurants. "Tonight we're going to our favorite Serbian restaurant," he'd say—or Italian, Japanese, Tex-Mex, whatever—and lead them on foot and by subway to their destination, explaining all the while what made the place so special and telling them what they should order there. When Josh and Andrew came west, Cooper didn't give the restaurants any advance billing whatever. Conversation that took place en route tended to be about how the Giants were doing, work, or everybody's most recent vacations.

Cooper's renowned parking karma was working full time that night. It wasn't that North Beach was unusually deserted. Cooper just had a gift when it came to finding an empty space within half a block of any given destination. The phenomenon had been apparent ever since he got his license. Any more it only occasioned comment from new acqaintances.

■ ■ ■

Cooper had grilled swordfish with no sauce and only nibbled at his pasta side dish. Josh ordered veal. Griffin had his favorite fusilli carbonara. He believed that this restaurant prepared the carbonara by which all other carbonara was to be judged, though he'd never have said so aloud. He feared it might lead people to conclude that he was unsophisticated. Cooper skipped dessert. The waiter knew better than to ask him. Josh and Griffin split a piece of the house specialty, light as a feather lemon cake doused with zabaglione.

"What a terrific place," Josh enthused as they left.

"We like it," Cooper said.

Once again, Griffin felt validated.

■ ■ ■

"He put her on the speaker phone," Griffin said. "The conversation almost curled my hair."

"The thing is," Cooper said, "Genikayte watches too much television. Chat shows, my God. You know how fucked up those people are. Oprah is bad and everyone else is worse. It's warped the girl's expectations. And to Griffin's dismay, she's become fluent in psychobabble."

"I know," Josh said, making a face.

"She was feeding me this line about how her marriage is hopelessly broken," Cooper said. "I asked her what she based that assessment on. 'Does he cheat on you?' 'No, Uncle Cooper.' 'Does he drink too much?' 'No.' 'Does he take drugs? Run up your credit cards? Spend too much time out with the boys? Beat you? Threaten to beat you? Is he verbally abusive?' I went down the whole list. I watch daytime television too. Occasionally. Always by accident, right? By the time she'd excused Emilio of every infraction I could mention you'd have thought she had the perfect husband. 'So what's the problem?' 'I want to be treated like a wife,' she said, 'not a girlfriend.' What the hell is that supposed to mean?"

"The time before that," Griffin said, "she said Emilio is 'emotionally unavailable'."

"I'm sure he is," Josh said. "At least in the sense she means it. Most straight men are, when you come right down to it. Women of previous generations didn't consider that it made them bad husbands. They took it for granted. They learned to depend on it, actually, and find the emotional support they needed in their friends. Not to mention their mothers and sisters. They were all in the same boat, so it really wasn't worth complaining about. But at the same time, there's no question that Emilio spoils her. He does all the cooking, all the cleaning, all the laundry. He pays the rent and utilities and buys the groceries out of his paycheck. Car payments and insurance, too. All she has to do with the money she makes is go shopping."

"Exactly," Griffin said.

"And this is the thanks he gets," Cooper said. "She's looking for any excuse to leave him."

"Poor bastard," Griffin said.

"All I know," Josh said, "is that she's been lost since Mom passed. Mom could talk to her. Aunt Rosie tries, but she gets flustered and just ends up making things worse. Andrew says it's because she never had a daughter."

"Mom never had a daughter, either," Cooper pointed out.

"If Mom had heard her talking like that," Josh said, "she'd have told her she was full of shit and that would have been the end of it."

"I think she's just bored," Cooper nodded.

"You think she needs to have a baby," Griffin said.

"That, too," Cooper nodded.

■ ■ ■

"Anything new with Eli?" Cooper asked.

Griffin held his breath. Bringing the subject up was always risky. It amazed Griffin that a disagreement like the one over Eamonn could last that long. Still, you never knew how Josh would react when you mentioned Eli's name. So Griffin never did. But that didn't stop Cooper, who considered the whole disagreement ridiculous.

"Eli's Eli," Josh said. "What can I say? He never changes."

"And neither do you," Cooper said.

"Nanny Freitag always said people don't change, really," Josh nodded. "They just get more so."

"She could have been describing herself," Cooper said.

"That doesn't mean it's not true," Josh said.

■ ■ ■

"Well, gentlemen," Griffin said, "I hate to break up the party, but it's a school night."

"Right," Josh said, checking his watch, "and it's nearly midnight in New York. Think I'll turn in, too."

"There are fresh towels in the guest bathroom," Cooper said, going for the remote. "Let me know if there's anything else you need."

SEPTEMBER 11, 2001

This was why Maribel never let Eamonn or the boys ride motorcycles. Several of her brothers, brothers-in-law, cousins, nephews, and even a couple of nieces did. They had for years now with no serious consequences, though there had been too many close calls to count. But none of the men who lived under her roof or had grown up there rode. Or ever would, if she had anything to do with it. Because of things like this. The young man on the operating table had at least been wearing a helmet. That, undoubtedly, was what saved his life—so far. His long-term survival wasn't assured at this point, but he was still breathing. His heart was still beating. His brain was still functioning. Plasma was still going into him. In other words, his condition was stable. But he'd lost a kidney. His spleen was within minutes of being lifted out of his abdominal cavity and placed in a surgical tray for eventual disposal. After that, several feet of his small intestine would be removed. The lacerations to his liver had already been repaired. His ruptured bladder could probably be saved.

"Internal injuries." The public heard those words and had no idea of the carnage they signified. If the young man was lucky enough to leave the hospital on his own two feet—and the orthopedic surgeons wouldn't get a look at him until tomorrow at the earliest—at the very least his life would never be the same. And he was the same age as Lorenzo, her youngest. Twenty-three.

So no motorcycles. Riding one in Manhattan was like holding a loaded gun to your head and inviting random passers-by to pull the trigger. Eventually someone would. Then you'd end up here. Or dead.

Beside her, Dr. Altschul hummed as he worked. Something from Wagner, presumably. She didn't recognize it, but she knew he was devoted to Wagner.

It seemed a little strange to her that a Jewish doctor should be so passionate, not to mention single minded, about Hitler's favorite composer, but that was Dr. Altschul all over. He was a walking collection of contradictions. His love of Wagner was the least of them. Those contradictions made him typical of his breed. Maribel knew a thing or two about trauma surgeons. Over a quarter century of close observation guaranteed it. She had worked with some of the finest. Young, old, fat, thin, male, female (not many of those, of course—the specialty was still a boys' club), and representing a multiplicity of races and creeds, they were nonetheless a clearly defined species. Savants, basically. Brilliant at what they did in the O.R., but beyond that it was a crap shoot. They beat their wives. Drank. Gambled. Terrorized their children and, to Maribel's dismay, nurses and other staffers. Held to the most bizarre imaginable political philosophies or religious beliefs. Dedicated their time off duty to hobbies so esoteric she sometimes had to read about them online and then often wished she hadn't. Their quirks weren't all questionable, of course, but they were invariably picturesque in the extreme. She couldn't imagine what kind of person could be friends with a trauma surgeon outside working hours. But she didn't judge. Except for the work they performed with her at their elbows, she was as blind to them and their foibles as that statue of justice.

"There, Mom," Dr. Altschul said, passing her the used scalpel. "Now we move on."

He called her mom. God help her.

■ ■ ■

"You studied with my mom."

"That's right, Dr. Altschul," Maribel said.

His mother, the legendary Roberta Steinberg Altschul, had trained two generations of R.N.'s in her specialty. You couldn't walk into an O.R. in the whole tri-state area without encountering at least one of her former proteges. It was Dr. Altschul's first day on shift at St. Vincent's and Maribel had just been introduced to him. The younger staffers were hyperventilating, but Maribel knew better. That skin was too perfect, as was that hair. Those muscles bulged outrageously inside custom tailored scrubs that, improbably, matched his blue eyes. Stunning as he was, it was all too calculated. Either he was a character in a movie or he was something else. Maribel had two something elses in her immediate family. Her husband and her youngest son. Three something elses if you counted Eli, which she knew she was supposed to do though he was more nondescript than attention grabbing. In any case, she knew all about the variety of something else she suspected Dr. Altschul was an example of. She really should write a book on the subject. A how-to manual was probably more in her line than a field guide. *The Care and Feeding of. . .* In any case, the younger staffers, all but Joey Rindone and Salvador O'Donnell, were doomed to disappointment.

"Great to meet you, Nurse Lannaghan," he said.

"Thank you, doctor," she said. "Welcome to St. Vincent's. And how is your mother? I haven't heard anything of her in years."

"Stage four ovarian cancer," he said. His grin didn't waver, but there was a flash of something, the anticipation of loss, Maribel presumed, in those brilliant eyes. There and gone. Just like that. But she knew she hadn't imagined it. It was clear as lightning in a night sky. Suddenly he seemed actually human. That was a good sign. Too many of his colleagues were lacking in that department. They might be skilled technicians, but their human deficits kept them from being particularly good doctors as far as she was concerned.

"She really should have had them removed when she had the hysterectomy. Most women go that route."

"I'm so sorry," she said. She had gone that route herself. Occasionally she regretted it, but not when she heard a story like this.

"She was determined never to do what Dad told her," he said.

"I remember," Maribel said. The Altschuls had been notoriously ill matched. Maribel knew about that first hand, too. But in her own case, ill matched hadn't resulted in a terrible marriage. Perhaps that should be the topic of her second book. *Opposites Attract* oversimplified the case. *Strange Bedfellows*—that was more like it.

"He was particularly insistent that time," Dr. Altschul smiled. "With predictable results."

"Sometimes we pay too much attention to what other people think," she said, "even when we believe we're not."

"Her in a nutshell," he nodded. He went on to name the hospice facility. It was near where Maribel lived.

"She loves having visitors," he suggested.

"I can't believe she'd remember me."

"Oh, but she does," he insisted.

And she just might, Maribel thought. The woman's memory had been as legendary as everything else about her.

■ ■ ■

So she went later that week. She took a bag of grapes. When Maribel was Roberta Steinberg Altschul's student, there had been a running gag about bringing grapes to hospital patients, so the grapes were an ice breaker, a nod to their past as much as they were actual fruit. The other reason was that she couldn't imagine facing her former professor empty handed. Unwanted fruit could easily be disposed of, so there was no danger of waste. Maribel knew what stage four cancer patients looked like, and there was no surprise waiting for her when she entered the room.

"Lannaghan," the figure in the bed croaked. "How badly is that boy of mine misbehaving?"

"Not at all, nurse."

"You're lying. You must be."

"No," Maribel laughed.

"A leopard doesn't change its spots," Steinberg Altschul said. "Says so in scripture. At least my scripture. I don't know about yours."

"Ours, too," Maribel said.

"Well that boy has spots, believe me. He takes after his father. He has spots on top of his spots."

"I hadn't noticed."

"Sit down. And call me Roberta. I see you brought grapes. I guess I really did train you well. But how did you know huge black grapes like that were my favorite? That rotten pup Dar tell you?"

"I swear, he's not rotten," Maribel said.

"But he is a pup," Roberta said. "Barely house trained. The problem with him is the problem with all of them. They keep getting younger all the time. We stay the same, of course. But they get younger."

■ ■ ■

"How long do you have?" Maribel asked. She'd been there long enough by then and their conversation had been sufficiently frank that she felt she could ask.

"When I was diagnosed," Roberta said, "they told me I had three to eight months. That was four years ago. So really, who the hell knows? Not long enough. That's what matters."

■ ■ ■

"Don't come again if you don't want to," Roberta said as Maribel was getting ready to leave. "I hate it when people feel obligated."

"Of course I'll come again."

"Promise me one thing," Roberta said.

"What?"

"Look out for Dar. He's the kind of boy who can go haywire in a hurry. Too smart—brilliant, really. And so good looking. He's ridiculous. I have no idea how that happened. If his father had been that good looking I'd never have divorced him. I wouldn't have had the will power. I'd have had to kill him instead. Trouble finds boys like that, you know. Bad trouble."

"I'm sure he's. . ."

"You're a mother, Maribel. You have boys. I hear your Liam is specializing in surgery."

"He is," Maribel said.

"You know how it is. Anyway, it's the reason I insisted Dar join the staff at St. Vincent's. I knew you were working there. Not just working there, but in the same department. You'll see him every day. Please."

"Of course."

■ ■ ■

A couple of days after Maribel's hospice visit, Dr. Altschul found her in the break room.

"Mom says you have a gay son," he said.

"That's right," Maribel nodded.

"Well, now you have a gay nephew, too. Mom's orders."

But he never started calling her "aunt". The week after Roberta's funeral was when he started calling her mom. Only in surgery. The rest of the time she was Nurse Lanaghan. He never stopped being Dr. Altschul to her. She refused to take liberties.

He lifted the spleen free. She had the tray waiting.

■ ■ ■

Renzo's gym was open twenty-four hours a day. Located in the heart of Chelsea, it was a kind of gay ground zero. Lots of the guys went there only to show off and hook up. For them, the place might as well be a stage set. Thank God they were a later crowd. Renzo didn't have to work very hard at avoiding them, though he did enjoy window shopping from time to time. That generally required an extra visit, given how little overlap there was between his and their schedules. They might not be hard core gym rats like he was, but some of them were certainly hot. Still, he was far too serious about working out to want to waste time every day shouldering them out of the way in order to use the equipment they were posing with while they flirted and preened. That wasn't the only problem. Their chatter ruined his concentration. Their cologne made it hard for him to breathe. And their approaches—"spot you, big boy?"—made him feel like a piece of meat. That wasn't always a bad thing. Often enough, a piece of meat was exactly what he wanted to feel like. But they didn't need to be so blatant about it, and it would be nice if they didn't presume so much.

It wasn't a gay thing exclusively. Renzo had been to the gym in Soho where Liam worked out. That one was way more straight (or less gay, which he knew was how he was supposed to think of it) than Renzo's gym but just as much of a meat market. Obviously, there was a double standard at work. Gays who slept around were promiscuous. Straight women who slept around were sluts. But straight men who bagged everything in sight were just being guys. Except for the ones who were good enough at it to be designated studs. It was a sign of how little the culture had progressed, regardless of the sexual revolution of his parents' era. Renzo had expounded on this theme at Mom's house on Sunday when he and his brothers were all there for their weekly dose of roast beef and scalloped potatoes. The ensuing argument had been, as were their typical fraternal dustups, loud but not particularly fierce. He wondered what Dad and Eli would have added to it if they'd been there.

He could have found another gym, of course, but this one was so convenient to his apartment that he hated the thought of going somewhere else. And the gay men of the New York Metro Area had embraced gym culture so avidly and comprehensively that he'd probably have to go well past the outer boroughs to find an establishment offering substantially less in the way of distractions. It was easier to adjust his schedule. And what was wrong with an early morning workout? That morning, the gym was unusually deserted. Tuesdays were ordinarily livelier, even at that hour. He'd be able to think back through the material for his exam later that day while he worked out. There were only three other guys present. One of them wouldn't sleep with Renzo, Renzo wouldn't sleep with the second, and the third one didn't sleep with anyone. So they were all able to ignore each other and get down to business.

Third year law school moved fast. It reminded Renzo of his first year in that respect. Second year was apparently the outlier. Third year was such a challenge, in fact, that by the second week of term his six a.m. workout became this five a.m. one. A fellow gym rat had burned him a disc informally titled "Wagner's Greatest Hits". It was fabulous workout music. He inserted his earphones, hit play, and started his stretches.

■ ■ ■

"All right now," Dr. Altschul said, interrupting his whistled rendition of "Ride of the Valkyries," "let's close."

"Yes, doctor," Maribel said.

337

■ ■ ■

Geni loved to sleep in until the last minute. Her husband was the opposite. If Emilio wasn't ten—or better yet fifteen—minutes early leaving the house in the morning, he considered himself behind schedule. And when he was behind schedule he became agitated, something he preferred to avoid, though she found it comical. Emilio's proactive approach to life prohibited it, though in his case "proactive" was just a self-help book eupehmism for obsessive compulsive behavior. Geni wouldn't dream of complaining of it, however. His compensation and overcompensation made mornings heavenly. She could luxuriate, the cats curled up in bed with her, while he bustled. And Emilio bustled like Pavarotti sang opera. Like Jeter played baseball. He was the Donald Trump of puttering. Just thinking about it exhausted her. He packed their lunches to take to work. He set out food and water for the cats and cleaned their litter box. He organized his briefcase for the day even though he'd done the same just before bedtime. He checked his messages, though he'd done that just before bedtime, too. He organized his work clothes neatly in his gym bag. His razor and toiletries went in there as well. Geni couldn't remember the last time he had showered and shaved at home on a work day. While she rode the train into Manhattan, he'd be finishing his workout and getting ready for his day as a human resources officer. She had no idea what that entailed. When he tried to explain to her what he did in the course of a normal day, she nearly fell asleep. Sat in lots of meetings, apparently. Conducted lots of interviews and investigations. Completed paperwork. Occasionally he had to give depositions. It was hard to imagine. He was anal retentive enough to do paperwork. And patient enough to endure meetings. She recognized that. But he was just so physical. The idea of him in an office at all was absurd. He was twenty-nine going on eighteen, and he always would be. He should be an iron worker or a commercial fisherman.

That was it. A commercial fisherman. Gone from home for weeks at a time. Of course the cats would miss him. And Geni really didn't enjoy housework. She'd have to hire someone to come in.

After work, while she shopped before catching her train home, Emilio would be off swimming or playing volleyball or soccer. Her single friends, who sometimes dated his single friends, insisted that he was a demon on the hockey ice. She'd never seen him on skates and couldn't imagine it. She knew he hated restrictive clothing, and getting him into a hockey uniform seemed impossible. Whatever it was he played on any given day, he was exhausted by the time he got home. She never saw him eat anything except energy bars. He washed them down with protein shakes. She lived on salads, bowls of soup, microwaveable entrees. They never sat down at the dining table together. She wasn't sure why they even had one. She might as well give in and let him put a pool table in its place like he'd been asking to. By the time they crawled into bed later, they would barely have exchanged a dozen words all day long. She couldn't remember the last time they'd had sex. Thank God. It meant she never had to explain why she still wasn't pregnant. She loved having sex with Emilio. It was about the only thing she still liked about him. But she loved it so much that sometimes thinking about it convinced her she was still in love with him. And she couldn't have that any more than she could have his children.

■ ■ ■

Eli could have set his watch by the young Englishman. Their first encounter, months ago now on a morning when Eli had left home ten minutes earlier than usual on a whim he still couldn't explain, had permanently altered his morning routine. That morning he rounded the last corner of his route from the West Village, and standing in line to buy coffee had been this vision. Tall, broad shouldered, lanky, he looked like he belonged in the pages of a magazine modeling high end men's suits. That thick, smooth textured, perfectly groomed blond hair—Eli was knocked flat on his ass without so much as a look at the man's face. Eli, who didn't drink coffee and would never have considered buying it from a cart on the street if he had, became an addict on the spot. He fell into line behind that magnificent stranger without conscious thought. When his turn came, the young man ordered his coffee in an accent so exquisite that Eli could imagine him tutoring members of the royal family in elocution. Every vowel perfectly formed. Every consonant immaculately articulated. The tone just husky enough to make it ineffably sexy. All this Eli apprehended from behind. Then, having paid and, Eli noted, left a generous tip, the vision turned. After a lifetime of moments just like that which turned into bitter disappointments, Eli's fantasies at last were fulfilled. That face kept the promise implied by everything else. It defined the word handsome while at the same time making it inadequate. Though, it had to be said, it did so with a Slavic cast to the features, particularly evident in the cheekbones and exotically shaped eyes—brilliant, blue, amazing—that didn't entirely coincide with the accent. Eli was smitten in a way he couldn't remember being in decades. Not that he had any intention of acting on the feeling, and not that the young man would have given him the time of day in any case. It was just a feeling. A feeling that had persisted over the changing seasons from late winter until this morning. It had nothing to do with Eamonn. It had nothing to do with any aspect of real life. Yet Eli found that few minutes of fantasy every morning profoundly moving.

"You're back," he said.

"Oh, hello," the young man turned and smiled.

"How was the trip?"

"Place is absolute heaven on earth. Can't imagine why it's not better known as a destination. Ravishing beaches. Fabulous climate. People almost too friendly to credit."

"So I've heard," Eli said.

"You haven't been?"

"Never," Eli said.

"Makes no sense," the young man said. "If it were on the Mediterranean, the whole world would flock there."

"Perhaps it's too close to L.A.," Eli suggested.

"I suppose that's it," the young man said. "Only one thing I didn't entirely like about the place. Final approach to the airport. Absolutely appalling landing. Truly. You come in from the east right across the city. Tall buildings just off the wingtips. Seems impossible nobody's ever run into one of them. Horrible accident waiting to happen. Unimaginable catastrophe, but there it is just waiting outside the airplane windows."

"Really."

"Must give the flight crews fits."

"And your—brother, was it? That you went there to visit? He's doing well?"

"Brother, yes," the young man nodded. "Flourishing."

By that point they both had their coffees. They joined the crowds streaming down the sidewalk toward the towers.

■ ■ ■

Renzo stepped off the train and headed for the exit stairs. Castle was widely regarded as one of the toughest professors in the entire law school. This morning's exam would be the first of the term in his class, and Renzo knew he only had one opportunity to make a good impression. So he didn't waste time stopping to smell the flowers or any of that bullshit. When he reached the street he was already at a trot.

■ ■ ■

Peregrine nodded at the man as he stepped off the lift and the man raised his hand in a small motion of salute. The lift doors closed and Peregrine continued upward. It was the kind of relationship that could never happen in London, where people resolutely minded their own business and even your closest associates lived lives you knew little or nothing about. This man, still and probably forever nameless, shared a daily ritual with Peregrine, one in which a small but nevertheless real connection had formed. They were of different generations and that was far from the only difference between them. The man was probably Jewish and presumably gay. Jewish because the great majority of men of his generation working on the upper floors of this building seemed to be, so it was a statistical probability at the very least. And gay? That appeared certain from the great care he took over his appearance, the perfectly groomed silver hair, the carefully tended skin. Not to mention the money he spent on clothing and shoes. Americans were good at spending money but shockingly bad at knowing what to spend it on. Gay men, Peregrine had observed, far exceeded their countrymen in their astuteness in that regard. It wasn't that they spent more money on clothing and shoes. What they spent, they spent more wisely. They had good taste rather than expensive taste. Back home, this wouldn't have been a marker of sexual orientation but of social class. Aside from this there were the man's manners. Heterosexual American males basically had none beyond the superficial minimum which made their sports and business dealings possible, while this man's were exemplary. So yes, Peregrine knew, or thought he knew, a great deal about the man. But what did amount to, really?

Any morning Peregrine chose he could turn the conversation in whatever direction he wished as they walked together from the coffee stall toward the building. He could ask any question that occurred to him and the man would certainly answer it. That was the kind of good manners he possessed. And Americans thought nothing of that degree of intimacy. Indeed, they took it for granted. But of course Peregrine wouldn't do that. An Englishman didn't. He might live here now, but until the day he died he'd think of himself as an Englishman. Every morning those lift doors rang down the curtain on one of their tiny scenes. It was like *Rosencrantz and Guildenstern,* Peregrine mused. All the important action of the drama took place on some other stage.

■ ■ ■

At his desk, Peregrine dashed off a quick email to Rupert reporting his safe arrival in Manhattan and offering thanks for his brother's hospitality. He hadn't been completely honest with his coffee buying partner. Rupert wasn't truly flourishing. Oh, he was in the finest of health. Bright eyes, glossy coat, tail carried high. And those ridiculous muscles. Those got bigger every time he saw Rupert. He must spend all his time away from school at the gym. But that was just the surface. Beneath it all, he seemed hideously adrift. And preoccupied almost to the point of catatonia. Of course none of it was Peregrine's business. He certainly wouldn't mention his misgivings to their parents when they visited from London later in the month. But it was worrying all the same. In that condition, Rupert might do foolish things with his money. Peregrine knew that he had been extremely abstemious up to now, financially speaking.

But that money had to last Rupert's entire lifespan and hopefully be subsumed back into the family fortune after his death. As much of it as possible, in other words, must be preserved. And that required a Rupert in somewhat better fettle mentally and emotionally than Peregrine had observed during his visit.

■ ■ ■

"Ladies and gentlemen, this is the captain. We apologize for this traffic-related delay. Things are backed up getting out of here this morning. The good news is the tower tells me we're now third in line for takeoff clearance, so just bear with us a little bit longer and we'll have you on your way to San Francisco."

Finally, Cavendish thought. His connection on to San Diego was already tight. If there were any further delays, he might miss it and have to rebook. And with Rupert waiting. Of course after waiting for over two decades, Rupert wouldn't complain about a few extra hours. Not the long-suffering Rupert.

■ ■ ■

Geni pulled into her regular spot in the park and ride lot. She hoped the trains were running on time today, because she was behind schedule. Or, to put it accurately, she was more behind schedule than usual. Her reputation at the office as barely on time on the best of days had earned her a couple of meetings with her supervisor recently. The next one would probably result in a formal reprimand. Not that she cared. She just didn't appreciate the drama. She got her work done. That's all that should matter.

Midtown Manhattan was a long ride from New Jersey, but she had a new book that Aunt Rosie had sent her.

■ ■ ■

"What the hell was that?" someone asked out in the hall.

"Sounded like some kind of explosion."

343

Eli took a deep breath. It wasn't just a loud noise. The building had actually moved, rocking back and forth for several seconds. He'd been in earthquakes before, though never in Manhattan. That's what it felt like.

A moment later the alarms started sounding. What had Eamonn told him all those times? Get out immediately? But was it that simple? How did you get out from this high up in the building? If the explosion had been above them, it would be easy enough. Just go down the emergency stairs. It would take a while from seventy floors up, so you couldn't waste time. But you'd eventually get there. On the other hand, if the explosion had been below them, it could be tricky. You'd have to figure out which stairwell, if any, was blocked and take one of the others.

Even as he was thinking through all this, Eli was on the move. Briefcase. Jacket. Keys. Cellphone. Everywhere he looked, people were standing around looking confused.

"Come on," he said. "There's no time to lose."

He was out the door and in the corridor before he knew it. A crowd had gathered at the elevators.

"Ladies and gentlemen," a security man said. "Please go back to your offices. There's no need to panic. There's been no order to evacuate the building. You'll just cause problems by trying to leave."

Meanwhile, the alarms continued to sound.

"This way," Eli shouted. "The elevators aren't safe. We have to head for the stairs."

He pulled open the door and stepped onto the landing. The stairwell was empty. He looked over the railing. As far down as he could see, it was clear. Above was another matter. There were unidentifiable noises drifting downward. And a smell of burning. Something was terribly wrong up there. He stepped back through the doorway.

"Anybody going with me, I'm leaving now," he said. He didn't wait to see if he was being followed.

■ ■ ■

By the time they finished the procedure and the patient had been taken to recovery, Maribel felt like she was ready to drop. It was always like that after a long operation during the middle of the night. You ran on adrenaline until you didn't have to any more. Then you felt like you'd run into a brick wall. Or, more accurately, like a brick wall had fallen on top of you.

Poor young man. But he'd been lucky. You could live a normal lifespan without a spleen. You could live without a few feet of intestine. Thousands of people were walking around on only one kidney. It was a lot to endure, but she'd seen much worse. She'd seen people die on the table. Dozens of them. And this patient had drawn the very best trauma surgeon in Lower Manhattan. If she'd had any doubt about it before, she didn't now. Dr. Altschul's talent was uncanny.

"Come on, Lannaghan," he said, pulling off his surgical mask. "I'm buying you breakfast."

■ ■ ■

"You've got to eat more than that," Dr. Altschul said, glancing at her tray.

"I won't sleep if I do," Maribel said. "This just has to get me home and into bed. I'll have a big lunch in the late afternoon."

"Two poached eggs and hot tea isn't enough," he insisted. "You're eating for two these days."

"What the hell are you talking about?" she demanded.

"Don't worry," he laughed. "I know you're not pregnant. It's just I'm two weeks out from the Mr. Tri-States contest, and if I'm going to avoid competing as the lightest super-heavy in the contest I've got to lose a few more pounds. Two-twenty is the upper limit for heavyweights. I'm sure you know all about it, given your family connections. So you're eating everything I'm not allowed to have right now. Here, take this cheese Danish."

■ ■ ■

She was just taking her first bite of the Danish when the P.A. squawked out a code.

"Good thing you're here to translate," Dr. Altschul said. "I have no idea what that one is. If I'm not careful, hospital admin is going to revoke my privileges."

"General disaster," she said, getting up and grabbing her tray. All over the cafeteria, people were moving toward the exits. "All available personnel to E.R."

"You've worked these before," he nodded.

"Drills," she said, though this wasn't the whole truth.

The P.A. continued its summons.

"This doesn't seem to be a drill," he said, following her. "Any guesses?"

"Hotel or school on fire. Derailment on the subway. Plane crash," she said, heart sinking further as she named each grisly possibility. "Staten Island Ferry capsizing. Natural gas explosion. Take your pick."

■ ■ ■

When Eamonn stepped out of the shower, he saw the blinking light on his cell phone. He was supposed to keep the ringer on at all times, but it was so annoying the way it went off at the most inconvenient moments. He dried his hands and picked up the fool thing. He pushed what he hoped was the right button for voicemail and held the phone to his ear.

"Sweetheart," Eli said, "there's been some kind of explosion here in the building. I don't know any details, but I'm on the emergency stairs heading down. It seems to be all clear below. I think whatever's wrong must have been above our floor. I'll call again when I get outside."

Good man, Eli. Better to be safe than sorry. Eamonn imagined the scene inside the tower. People would be confused. And confused people did stupid things. But Eli had been listening all those times when Eamonn talked about the necessity for speed in exiting a building. He pushed the button again and listened to the next message.

"Dad, it's Mick. Something big is going on at the World Trade Center. Bad fire on one of the upper floors of the north tower. We're about to head down there. Get up here to the station as soon as you can. Or meet us there."

The time stamp said five minutes ago. He'd never get to the house before they pulled out. But there was an engine company a few blocks from Eli's apartment. He'd report there. If it was something big, they'd get the call, too. And they'd have spare equipment he could sign out.

■ ■ ■

Ned Westerleigh was an early riser. He was already finishing his full English breakfast when Oliver brought him the telephone. Outside, San Francisco looked as gloomy as London in December. It was Kaminsky calling from New York. He was an attache at the Polish mission to the U.N. He'd just been out jogging, and he'd witnessed something astonishing. Something he thought Ned needed to hear about. Kaminski's call was the first of what became a stream and then a torrent.

■ ■ ■

"I'm taking Lannaghan with me," Dr. Altschul said. "We'll meet the team at O.R. Two."

"But I want Lannaghan," Dr. Patel insisted.

Just what Maribel needed. To be fought over by two surgeons. What woman didn't dream of that?

"Want to wrestle me for her?" Dr. Altschul laughed. "Didn't think so. Come on, nurse, let's go."

"Yes, doctor," she said.

"Un-fucking believable," he muttered, breaking into a trot. "Who flies a plane into a skyscraper?"

"Are you all right?" she asked, matching his pace.

"Sure," he said. "Why wouldn't I be?"

"You just seemed rattled for a moment."

"Crazy situation," he said. "That's all. Totally unexpected, right?"

"Of course," she said, not believing him. He didn't get rattled. Something was wrong.

"I'm fine," he said. "Just stay with me. It's likely to be a busy day. You're my good luck charm."

"Right."

■ ■ ■

For the first several floors, Eli had the stairwell completely to himself. He would have felt foolish about this flight if not for Eamonn's constant insistence that it was always best to err on the side of caution. Regardless of how much ridicule Eli might encounter after the fact, Eamonn would approve and congratulate him. As he reached the sixties, people began to join him on the trek downward. One woman had left her office because her boss absolutely forbade it. "And he's a dick, so I told him he's a dick and left. He'll probably fire me when I get there tomorrow." One man's wife had a weird premonition a few days earlier, which she reminded him of over breakfast. She regularly had premonitions and never once had one come true, but the man said he'd never hear the end of it if he didn't at least pretend to take her seriously. The general consensus was that some failure had occurred to the building's infrastructure. A second woman joined them, and she was certain that a boiler had exploded. Eli wasn't sure there even were boilers at the World Trade Center, but what did he know? Another man with them had a brother-in-law who was a city building inspector. According to him, there were several thousand things that could go awry in a building like this.

It was on about the fifty-second floor that Eli first heard talk of an aircraft striking the building. He had a vision of something small, a single engine Cessna or Piper for instance, spattering itself against the tower like a bug against a windshield. He wondered what it must have looked like from the street. A man behind Eli mentioned that back in the 'Forties a B-25 had hit the Empire State Building in the fog. Several people had died. It was the first spoken hint of mortality, though Eli suspected that others had been thinking of it, as he had.

■ ■ ■

Twenty minutes on the phone while simultaneously checking his emails and Ned had his game plan in place. He keyed in one last telephone number. Volk answered on the first ring.

"Gas up whichever one of your Benzes you're driving today," Ned said without preliminaries. "We're headed south."

"Check," Volk growled.

"You might want to bring Maier along."

"Already alerted him that we'd be hearing from you," Volk said. "We'll pick you up in twenty minutes. Should we be prepared for overnight?"

"I shouldn't think it'll be necessary," Ned said. "But just in case."

■ ■ ■

"Ladies and gentlemen," Professor Castle said, "pens down. Please pass your test booklets forward."

Renzo had been reading back through his last essay. Definitely B+ work. Maybe better than that, depending on what kind of mood Castle's grader was in. She was a sharp African-American woman from Mississippi. Nothing got past her. When she was grading, the gulf between B+ and A- was as wide as the Amazon.

"Hey, Renzo," Sarah Farrar said next to him.

"Huh?" he asked, turning on his phone.

"Let's head to the library."

"Check my messages first," he grunted, following her out of the lecture hall. Eli's number was the first one that came up.

"Renzo." Eli's voice crackled with emotion. "A plane has hit the World Trade Center. People are evacuating the building. I'm on the emergency stairs. Soon as I get outside, I'm on my way to the apartment. I'm not sure the trains will be running, so I may be on foot. I'm going to pick up the dog and head for your place, if that's all right. Lower Manhattan's going to be a mess all day. Call me."

"What is it?" Sarah asked.

He told her.

"My God," she said.

"They've hit the second tower," someone yelled. "This is no accident."

■ ■ ■

They had heard about the second impact on their radios when they were still several blocks from the staging area. But Eamonn's first glimpse of the scene stunned him like nothing he could remember. Those huge towers with thick smoke billowing out of them. He'd seen lots of crazy things in his time, but this dwarfed them all.

"Jesus," the guy next to him muttered.

"Leave Him out of this, will ya?" the guy across from them grumbled.

It wasn't real. It couldn't be. Hollywood did stuff like this, but only with smoke and mirrors. Nothing Eamonn knew of in the whole world could. . .

But that was only because he wanted to think so. The engine groaned to a halt. They started clambering off it, grabbing their equipment as if it was any other call. How many hundreds had he been on over the years? This was different, but thinking about it that way could paralyze you. Even kill you. One step in front of the other, they trotted down the street toward the catastrophe.

■ ■ ■

The train emerged from the tunnel and then halted.

"Holy shit," someone in the front of the car said. "Will 'ya look at that?"

Geni looked. And gasped. A huge plume of smoke towered over Manhattan.

■ ■ ■

Who could she call? She had to call someone. The train had been sitting for twenty minutes now. There had been no announcement. The smoke over Manhattan looked angrier by the minute. And nobody on the train had been able to get a call through to the city.

350

■ ■ ■

As they continued their trudge down the emergency stairs, Eli couldn't help thinking of the blond young Englishman. Had he possessed the presence of mind to head downward, or was he one of those stoic types who kept his upper lip stiff and his hands on the wheel regardless of circumstances? Or worse, was he trapped on one of the highest floors? Because they were beginning to hear terrible rumors about conditions up there.

Each landing they reached brought not just additions to the ranks of the evacuees, but direr news. By the time they had descended as far as the thirties, rumors about aircraft had become certainty. And Eli's imagined light plane had turned into a 737 with dozens of passengers aboard. But how could such an accident happen?

When they encountered the first of what would quickly become scores of firefighters ascending the tower, Eli peeled his eyes for familiar faces.

■ ■ ■

"Chaps," Cavendish said, "this young man and I are the largest ones here. We're obviously the men for the job. I'm absolutely confident that a galley cart, appropriately propelled, can take down the cockpit door."

■ ■ ■

His cellphone chirped. Cooper opened one eye and looked at the clock on the nightstand. Who the hell would be calling this early? He grabbed the phone and peered at the display. Genikayte. Sure. She liked to call from the train on her way to work in the city. She was even worse than her late grandmother about the time difference. She actually thought it was later in California than in New York.

"Gen."

"Uncle Cooper. Turn on your T.V."

"Huh?"

"I'm on the train. We're stopped. Manhattan's on fire. We can't get any calls in. Turn on your T.V. Tell me what's going on."

"Hold your water," he grunted. He pulled on gym shorts and padded down the hall to the den. The remote was right where he'd left it at two a.m. He turned on the set and found CNN.

"Holy shit," he said.

"What is it?" she asked.

"You're not going to believe this," Cooper said. He took a deep breath and got ready to explain.

■ ■ ■

It was unbearably hot in the room, and the air was rank and hazy. There hadn't been many of them in the office when the plane hit, and there were even fewer now. Peregrine wasn't sure where the others had gone. He had ranged all over their floor of the building checking out the emergency stairwells, which were all blocked by the fires below. If he had left the office right after the impact, before the fires had a chance to spread, he might have made it. But there was no sense of urgency at the time. Now that the situation was clear, it was too late. There literally was no way out. And only a fool could continue to believe that help was on its way. They were all going to die.

There was still so much he hoped to do. More polo. More yachting. He'd been planning to begin flying lessons in October. How ironic, given what was about to happen. And he'd cut his short list down to three, Mai-Margit, Britt, and Lena. He was definitely planning to propose to someone by the end of the year. Except now he wasn't. He imagined the slow parade of years, the stages of his life yet to be lived, the sons fathered and reared, the title succeeded to, the estate managed, the career built. All a dying dream. Scenes imagined over and over in cinematic detail, but soon to flicker out like shadows at high noon. Misfortune and untimely death had cursed every generation of the FitzMerlins since the eleventh century. What an idiot he'd been to consider himself immune from it. That oaf Rupert had been the smart one after all. How Peregrine hated that he was about to become part of that ancient legend instead of creating one of his own.

He gave his desk a last tidying up. Of all the actions he'd ever performed this was by far the most futile, but he invested it with as much meaning as he could. Everything would be perfectly in place when he turned his back on it. That final glimpse of serenity and order would accompany him on his journey. As he worked, the babble around him receded to a hum. Some were praying. Some were cursing. Anderson was curled up underneath the conference table moaning. To each his own.

Rupert. Peregrine had never had any use for him. And their crazy, drunken mother. He'd never had any use for either of them. Everything he'd done in life he'd done with the intention of proving those two wrong or thwarting their intentions. It had been a crucial mistake. He'd have done everything the same way, with one exception of course, but it all would have been purified if his motivations had been clearer, more focused on his own judgments and less on resisting those fools. Even this morning, walking down from his flat in Soho, he could have called Pa and set everything in motion. He had no need, really, of the title or the estate. He'd undoubtedly have been happier in the long run doing as Rupert had done. But that hadn't been an option for the simple reason that Rupert had selected it. What a fool he'd been, Peregrine thought.

No need to delay any longer. Soon this last choice would be taken from him, the choice of whether to suffocate or burn or fall through space. His last act before stepping away from his desk was to hit "send".

"Chaps," he said, though he was sure they were all lost in their own final musings and not a soul was paying attention, "chaps, I'm just stepping out."

It was just like they said in *Rosencrantz and Guildenstern are Dead*, he thought. Every exit was an entrance somewhere else.

He moved slowly among the maze of desks, filing cabinets, credenzas, conference tables. Soon he reached the far end of the room. He looked back for a brief instant. Nothing there had anything to do with him now. He moved through the jagged opening that marked his exit, or entry as the case might be.

■ ■ ■

Their progress slowed to a crawl as they descended the last few floors. By then they knew everything, or at least believed they did. Hijackers. A 767 with perhaps hundreds on board. And a second one crashing a while later into the south tower. Eli stepped out of the stairwell into a world that would never be the same. A world of chaos, noise, and an indescribable smell of burning which he had almost been able to ignore inside the building.

■ ■ ■

"They've hit the Pentagon as well," Volk said as Ned climbed into the back seat.

"Yes," Ned said.

The Benz was Volk's pride and joy, a 1971 600 model in showroom condition. There were much newer cars, obviously; more technically advanced ones. But Volk insisted that the Benz 600 of the 'Sixties and early 'Seventies represented a high water mark in automotive evolution. He swore it was the finest large sedan ever produced. Thus, he had a trio of them in perfect repair ready for his use at all times. Today's was the midnight blue with the red leather and zebra wood interior. Ned appreciated it for its spacious back seat. And because driving it kept Volk happy, and Ned needed Volk happy today. Because a happy Volk was a Volk at the peak of his powers, and Ned had no idea what they might be facing.

"Morning, Ned," Maier chirped from shotgun position.

"Maier," Ned said. "I wasn't sure you'd be available at such short notice."

"I'll call in a few cancellations while we're on the road," Maier said.

"I hate to disrupt your business."

In "civilian" life, Maier was one of the city's most celebrated hustlers. A date with him started north of the four figure mark. A week of his company had been known to go as high as six.

"Nonsense, Ned," Maier laughed. "A day or two off always stimulates demand. As in supply and. . ."

"He's thinking of retiring anyway," Volk growled in his central European accent.

"Really."

354

"I'm always thinking about retiring," Maier laughed. "But Volk hasn't made me the right offer yet."

"I'm sure that Volk is in a position to meet any possible demand on your part," Ned chuckled.

"It's not the money, Ned," Maier said. "It's the terms. If he wants to make an honest twinkie of me, there are certain things I'm going to have to insist on."

"How much of a hurry are we in?" Volk asked, accelerating past a line of city buses.

"Seventy-three mile an hour cruise," Ned said. "Our objective probably won't be a high priority target for anyone else until much later in the day."

He certainly hoped that was the case. It should be if Rupert had followed instructions and left well enough alone. That was no sure thing. Ned had already left multiple messages on his voice mail insisting he stay the hell away.

"You have intel to that effect?" Volk asked.

"No," Ned admitted. "Just a hunch as to the Yanks' current hierarchy of misery and ire."

■ ■ ■

When Griffin got to school, Alberta Drummond was directing traffic in the faculty parking lot. There was no end to her eccentricities. In fact, as they went, this one seemed fairly innocuous. She appeared agitated, but as a retired Marine Corps Drill Instructor and the school's ranking assistant principal, consternation was her more or less perpetual state. He simply pulled into the space she indicated—not his habitual one, though they weren't assigned—and chalked the phenomenon up to her highly developed instincts to control and regimentation.

"Still driving this windup toy, Griffin," she rumbled as he unfolded himself from the driver's seat of the Porsche. "Must be as old as you are."

"Not quite."

"Looks like it," she said. "Anyway, news flash: faculty meeting in the library prior to the beginning of classes."

"O.K." he said. "What's it about?"

"You haven't heard?"

"Heard what?"

"Jesus, Mary, and Joseph. That's right. You refuse any and all contact with the outside world prior to leaving home in the morning. Well, it's World War III, boyo, so grab your balls with one hand and cover your ass with the other.

■ ■ ■

They were on the freeway headed south within minutes. Maier had his headphones on and was listening to *Sunset Boulevard* in his native German. Volk preferred silence when he drove, which suited Ned perfectly. He had more calls to make. Lots of them.

■ ■ ■

The projection screen in the library was running when Griffin walked in. He couldn't believe what he saw. He thought immediately of Eli, who worked on the seventy-eighth floor. Griffin couldn't remember which tower, though from the visuals that obviously didn't matter. He felt terror grip him. Eli. And Eamonn, who must surely be on the scene. And Eamonn's two firefighter sons. And Eamonn's brothers and nephews. So many Lannaghans and their tributaries on the force. Not to mention serving with the NYPD. Griffin offered up a silent prayer for their safety.

■ ■ ■

Out on the street, hundreds of firefighters waited to go up into the buildings. Hundreds of police officers shouted at the evacuees to clear the area. Eli searched in vain for Eamonn, Tory, Mick, any familiar face. The police were stern and impatient. There was nothing Eli was qualified to do to help even if they'd allowed him to stay. He headed north. Greenwich Village seemed a continent away.

■ ■ ■

"So you'll confiscate all cell phones," Louisa said, "as the students enter your classrooms. Labeling them as you do so with the painter's tape Alberta will issue you as you leave here. We'll send runners with boxes to your classrooms to collect them, and students will be able to retrieve them from the assistant principals' office at the end of the school day."

"Is this absolutely necessary?" Yolanda Pangilinan asked. She was second-in-command in the counseling department and, Griffin knew, a raging enabler. "Our students are bound to feel insecure and threatened. Isn't is better for them to be able to contact their parents for emotional support at a time like this?"

"No, it is not," Louisa said. "I'm not going to have them on their cell phones all day talking to their parents and friends and siblings and reporters and drug dealers. All of them stoking each other's paranoia. This is a school. And unless and until the district releases us, school is in session."

"Here's what you should tell any student who objects to surrendering his or her cell phone," Alberta barked. "A cell phone signal can be used to detonate an explosive device remotely. It's possible for a casual phone call, such as a student might make to her grandmother, to accidentally access the same frequency a terrorist is attempting to use to blow up a building."

"That's impossible," Rik Eisenstadt objected. "I for one am not about to use a flimsy pretext like that to support your fascist takeover of this school."

Rik was chair of Social Sciences, an only minimally reformed student radical from the 'Sixties. Griffin groaned inwardly. Emergency faculty meetings always brought into focus the ordinarily concealed craziness and vapidity of his colleagues.

"Unlikely, yes," Alberta said. "But not impossible. And I, for one, refuse to take the risk of allowing our students to put us all in danger. Under circumstances like these."

She was a great believer in using the power of circumstances to get her way.

"Very well said, Alberta," Louisa said. "And besides, I won't have students sharing information as to conditions inside the school today. No good can come of that. Any information that goes out needs to be issued through my office. Nobody's happy about what's going on. We just have to get through it."

■ ■ ■

The train finally started moving again. Geni stared out the windows at the cataclysm across the river. All around her people were pointing, speculating. It was the worst thing she'd ever witnessed.

■ ■ ■

The instant the rumbling started, Eamonn knew what it meant. The waiting was over. Here, weeks short of retirement, his luck had run out.

It might have ended on any one of hundreds of days stretching back to his earliest years with the department, in hundreds of different places around the city. There had been too many close calls to count. Probably more than his share. All he remembered of any of them was the fear—always the fear that his time had come. Now it had. With that certainty came, strangely enough, the absence of fear. It was inexplicable but it was true. No fear but sorrow. He'd never felt anything like it. Somewhere above him, either one floor higher or thirty, Mickey was already dead or about to die. There was nothing Eamonn could do for him. They were both helpless. His thoughts shifted to the others, Liam, Tory, Renzo, Lisa and his grandchildren to be. They'd go on now without him. Sooner or later they'd forget him. He'd be a smile in a photograph they'd hardly ever look at.

Most of all he thought of Maribel and Eli. What would it be like for them? All these years Eamonn had tried his best to do right by both of them. As if that were even possible. But if there was one thing life had taught him it was that he wasn't a superman. The lesson would have destroyed him if he hadn't learned it incrementally. Despite his intentions, he'd let his wife and his husband down countless times and in countless ways. Would either of them have gone down this road with him if they'd known where it was leading? It was too late now to ask. Too late to explain once again. Too late to make it better. He'd made mistake after mistake. Year after year they accumulated. His mistakes meant that neither of them had lived the life they truly wanted. Only he had done that. But the truth was he'd never stopped loving either of them. He could only hope their memory of that would be enough.

The noise was deafening now. The world seemed to be shaking itself apart. The building

■ ■ ■

The headmaster's voice faded away in a barely perceptible hiss of static. She was referred to as the headmaster because to say headmistress would be sexist and politicaly incorrect, but to Rupert this absurdity seemed worse. And what a thing to be thinking about just now, with the students staring in amazement and the classroom uncharacteristically silent.

Rupert had known, when he first heard about the attack, that there was a good chance Peregrine was in the building when the plane hit. All Rupert could hope for now was that his offices were on a floor below the crash site and that he'd had the presence of mind to evacuate quickly. Now this email taunted him. As recently as forty minutes ago Peregrine had been alive. But Rupert couldn't bring himself to open the message. The subject line offered no clue. That in itself was a clue. If one had escaped, wouldn't one acknowledge that up front?

And what of Cavendish? With flights grounded all over the country, there was no telling when Rupert would have news of him.

He clicked on the mouse. The message opened.

"Mr. FitzMerlin?"

"Yes? What is it?"

"Are you all right, sir?" Jackson asked.

"Of course, boy," Rupert said. "Why wouldn't I be?"

"You've been staring at your computer ever since we came into the classroom. Shouldn't you take roll?"

Seven words. Peregrine had always been terse. But seven words seemed like pitifully few under the circumstances. *No way out. I intend to jump.*

Shakespeare could hardly have done better, Rupert thought.

■ ■ ■

The subway was still running. Nobody seemed to know how far south it was open, but Renzo figured he'd find out. The northbound trains that came through the station while he waited on the platform were crammed.

■ ■ ■

When the call came to return to the airfield Bobak was out over the water, flying parallel to Sunset Cliffs. Johnny was terse over the radio, but Johnny was always terse. He said come back "toot sweet" and since he was the boss, Bobak didn't question it. He turned the Beechcraft into the sun and began a gradual climb.

■ ■ ■

The train pulled into the station and the doors opened. None of the passengers moved.

"Ladies and gentlemen," the P.A. sounded. "Service inbound to Manhattan has been canceled for today. This train will not be proceeding beyond this station. Passengers inbound must make alternate arrangements."

Geni had been half expecting this ever since speaking to Uncle Cooper, but what was she supposed to do now? She'd been trying to get a call through to Emilio for over an hour, with no luck. He knew she got off her train at the World Trade Center every day. What he didn't know was how late she actually arrived there. That had been her secret for several months. For all he knew, she might have been on the spot when everything happened. He must be worried sick.

Nobody'd better hassle her about tardiness ever again. It had probably saved her life.

■ ■ ■

"Toot sweet," Bobak muttered to himself, taxiing up to the hangar. "*Tout suite.*"

360

Johnny stepped out of the office and flashed him a thumbs up. He wasn't smiling. Bobak cut the engine and killed all the switches. He unfastened the belt and swung open the door.

"No more flying today," Johnny announced as he emerged from the cabin.

"What do you mean? We've got a full schedule of lessons."

"Big terrorist attack on New York and Washington," Johnny drawled. "They flew airliners into the World Trade Center and the Pentagon. No telling how many other aircraft are on their way to how many other targets. Nationwide no fly order going into effect. No more flying today and God only knows when we'll be able to go back up."

"You're joking, right?"

But Bobak knew better. His surprise was for show. For when somebody came around asking Johnny questions about him. This was what Bobak had tried to warn them about. He hadn't known any details, of course. But those bastards he'd been observing all these months had to be in on it. Arabs taking flying lessons here in the U.S. instead of in their own countries. Who didn't see a threat there?

"Got the T.V. on in the office if you don't believe me. All hell's busting loose. For all I know it's the end of the world."

"Hardly that," Bobak said, unzipping his jumpsuit to the waist.

"See for yourself," Johnny said.

■ ■ ■

"Headin' home?" Johnny asked.

"Actually," Bobak said, "might check out the surfing."

"You would," Johnny laughed. "Sometimes I think you like surfin' better than flyin'."

"Maybe you're right."

■ ■ ■

Geni finally reached Grandpa at his place on Riverside Drive.

"It's Gen," she blurted the second he picked up.

"Where are you? Are you all right?"

"I'm out here in New Jersey. The train never got into the city."

"Thank God."

"Grandpa, have you heard from Emilio?"

"As a matter of fact, yes. He's frantic, as you can imagine. He wanted to go into the city to look for you. I told him he should go home and wait instead. I don't know what he decided. You know how he is with unsolicited advice. Almost as bad as you."

■ ■ ■

When Renzo got off the train in Chelsea, he heard the news that the north tower had fallen. Thousands of people must still have been inside. The fear that had been gnawing at him suddenly burst free of his control. He stood on the sidewalk, paralyzed, thinking of everyone he loved who must be on the scene. Dad. Tory. Mick. Uncle Sean. Uncle Martin. Uncle Klaus-Peter. All the cousins. Any one of them might be trapped in what had to be a mountain of rubble. He imagined broken bodies. Rivers of blood. All he wanted to do was scream.

Instead, he began to run. Eli might have gotten to the apartment by now. Renzo couldn't do anything for the men down at the disaster site, but Eli and Beowulf would need him.

■ ■ ■

Bobak kept a spare board in one of the storage rooms at the back of the hanger. He pulled it out, careful not to look like he was in a hurry. He had everything else he needed with him.

"Where you headin'?" Johnny asked.

"Probably Windansea," Bobak said, laying a false trail for when those guys finally came asking questions. Windansea, miles from his actual destination.

"All those rich La Jolla assholes there," Johnny complained. "Doesn't matter how good the surfin' is if you have to deal with them."

"Look at me," Bobak laughed, switching into his thickest accent. "I fit right in, can't you tell?"

■ ■ ■

"Cooper."

Buzz never got rattled. His voice over the phone betrayed no emotion whatever. All those years teaching high school English before changing careers must have given him nerves of steel.

"Yes, Buzz," Cooper said, hitting the mute button. On the screen, the north tower was collapsing. Again. In the next room, Josh was trying to get a call through to Eli.

"I've just had a call from Ned. He's asking me to open a member account in his name with the San Diego Association of Realtors. Also a subscription to a lockbox service down there. Know anything about it?"

"Nope," Cooper said. On the screen, an airliner was crashing into the south tower. Again. "Just charge it all against his next commission draw."

"All right," Buzz said. "You coming in to the office today?"

"Probably not," Cooper said. "Unless you think I need to."

"I really don't see the point," Buzz said. "In fact, I was thinking of heading home myself."

"It's fine with me if you want to close the office," Cooper said. "I can't imagine any worthwhile leads are going to walk in off the street today."

■ ■ ■

Maribel tried not to think about what was going on down there. There wasn't a thing she could do to help them anyway. Her attention was needed here. There was a patient in front of her. Dar Altschul's steady, dexterous fingers did their dance before her eyes, and she responded with moves of her own. That had to be her focus. Imagined scenes of what might be taking place in another part of the city had to be forced back out of her consciousness. Lives were in the balance here just as surely as they were there.

She had never been one of those women who went weak in the knees at the least sign of trouble. She'd had to be tough, resourceful, serene. She'd had to stand up to anything and everything, and she couldn't stop now. But how she longed for a pair of strong arms to bear her up.

■ ■ ■

Bobak steered the Jeep onto the freeway heading south. Traffic was always light southbound at that time of day. He couldn't tell if the events of the morning had any effect on it at all. Just moments after he pulled away from the field his "abort operation" signal came through on the radio, but he'd already known. No time to get back to the apartment and sanitize. Just go. He'd known it would be like this when the time came, or at least that it might be like this, so he was prepared. He didn't bother calling his handlers for an escape route. They'd either give him instructions similar to the ones he'd made up for himself or other ones, almost certainly less efficient and more risky.

■ ■ ■

There was no sign of Eli and Beowulf when Renzo got to the apartment. He turned on the television. The south tower was collapsing in a cascade of dust, debris and smoke. Knowing the news folks, they must be rerunning that footage continually. It seemed impossible that anyone could have survived. It reminded him of a scene from a Hollywood blockbuster. It couldn't possibly be real. He must be stuck in a nightmare. That was the only possible explanation. He stared at the set, working out in his head the route Eli would take from Greenwich Village. It was a long way, walking a small dog on a leash. Renzo could only imagine the chaos on the sidewalks. He changed into a pair of shoes that would be better for walking. His bicycle was down in the trunk room. He'd grab it and go to meet them.

■ ■ ■

Bobak steered the Jeep into a parking space. Anyone watching would think he was just another surfer. He changed into his wet suit, careful not to appear to be in a hurry. He strapped the backpack on, hoping that wasn't too conspicuous. He took the board under his arm and headed down the sand. The beach was deserted. It was the last stretch of beach in the Continental United States. Yards away the U.S. ended and Mexico began. The border fence was patrolled, but three quarters of a mile down the beach, where he'd step back out of the water, there was no security at all. The Americans were desperate to keep people out of their country but the Mexicans didn't much care who entered theirs. At least not from the north.

■ ■ ■

Renzo heard Beowulf before he spotted either of them in the crowds trudging up Eighth Avenue. That yelp was as distinctive as could be. The minute he was in range, he scooped the terrier up from the sidewalk and received a face full of kisses.

"Are you all right?" he asked Eli.

"No," Eli said. "I can't stop thinking about your father and brothers."

"I know," Renzo said. "Let's get to my place."

■ ■ ■

The student aide walked up to Griffin's desk and handed him three pink slips. He scanned them. These students were the first, but they wouldn't be the last. He'd been expecting it since Louisa's first announcement on the P.A. system just minutes after school started. He didn't understand why parents would bring their kids to school and then take them right back out again. Sure, the situation in New York was bad. But that was three thousand miles away. And did people really think a little known high school on the opposite end of the country from the World Trade Center was a prime target?

Apparently they did. Why did he bother being surprised?

"Aguilar. O'Connell. Nakamura," he called out their names. "You're going home. Don't forget your stuff."

■ ■ ■

"I guess there's no point telling you not to turn on the television," Renzo said, filling a bowl with water for Beowulf.

"Why wouldn't I?" Eli asked.

"What good is watching?" Renzo asked. "Listening to all those idiots babble. Nobody can do anything more than speculate right now."

"Hand me the remote, please," Eli said.

"Really," Renzo said, "I wish you'd go in the bedroom and lie down."

■ ■ ■

At a luggage shop on one of Tijuana's main shopping streets Bobak bought a medium sized, totally nondescript suitcase. The shop next door yielded a pair of shoes. Halfway down the block he bought two changes of clothes, a belt, underwear and socks. He paid cash for all his purchases—American dollars.

■ ■ ■

In all his planning, Bobak had never been able to decide whether to fly or take a bus. Attempting to board a plane seemed riskier. Nobody paid much attention to bus passengers, but there could easily be surveillance at the airport. On the other hand, the bus trip from Tijuana to Mexico City took thirty hours. That exponentially increased the risk of pursuit. Anywhere along the route, police could stop the bus and take him into custody. He had no reason to think he was being pursued. But that might change at any time.

Yes, that was the crucial factor. Time. He needed to get to the embassy in Mexico City as fast as he could.

■ ■ ■

366

This was the fourth student aide to enter the room so far. Griffin took the pink slips. At this rate, there would be no one left on campus by the end of third period.

"Chang," he called out. "Ferelli. Pangilinan. Washington. Rodriguez."

■ ■ ■

"Where are you going?" Eli asked, pressing the mute button. On the screen the towers fell incessantly. The scene alternated with ones of planes flying into skyscrapers.

"South," Renzo said. "See how close I can get."

"They're saying all of Lower Manhattan is locked down," Eli said.

"I know this city like the back of my hand," Renzo said. "I'll find a way."

"Be sure to check in regularly," Eli said.

"Anything you want from the refrigerator, feel free."

■ ■ ■

An hour and ten minutes after climbing out of the water, Bobak was standing in a line to buy tickets at the airport. So far, the Mexican government hadn't followed the lead of the Yanks and Canadians and shut down their airspace. Since he climbed out of the water on Mexican soil, nobody had taken a second look at him. If anyone had, he'd have flashed his fake French passport. Some lucky Mexican had already taken possession of his board and wetsuit. It might be days before anyone alerted the Imperial Beach authorities about his abandoned Jeep. From what he would tell, he'd gotten away clean. With any luck at all, he'd be in Mexico City in a few hours. Once he arrived, he wouldn't try to leave the airport. He'd contact the embassy from there. Let them come to him.

■ ■ ■

"You doing O.K., Lannaghan?"

"At least as well as you are, doctor."

"Nice backup on that one," he grinned.

Maribel didn't like the look of him. His eyes were too bright. He was trying too hard. She was sure she looked even worse.

"Let's go see what else they've got for us," he suggested.

She didn't argue.

■ ■ ■

No matter what route Renzo tried, the streets were closed. Officers turned him back wordlessly. Everywhere he looked, people were heading away from the site. It amazed him that they hadn't gotten any farther than this. Dusty, dazed, bedraggled, some obviously in need of first aid, they made him think of newsreel footage from World War II Europe. Sirens keened in all directions. Ash and bits of paper fell like snow. The sidewalks were covered. The gutters were full.

■ ■ ■

They pulled up in front of the building at exactly 1:30p.m. San Diego was sunny, warm, and more than usually somnolent that afternoon, as if its residents had missed out on the day's drama.

"All right," Ned said. "You're a couple shopping for a luxury condominium and I'm your realtor."

"That'll be a stretch," Maier snickered. In one of his most recent video appearances, he'd played the bottom half of a gay couple out shopping for luxury condominiums. The ultimate scene had featured dual anal penetration, Ned recalled, something at which Maier was an internationally recognized expert.

"Don't go getting ideas," Volk growled, locking the Benz.

■ ■ ■

"It's the toilets, senor," the flight attendant smiled. "Both of the toilets in tourist class are clogged. If the maintenance crew in Guadalajara cannot fix them quickly, we may have to wait for a replacement aircraft. Of course, the airline will try its best to rebook passengers for whom the delay is critical."

Clogged toilets? Bobak supposed the toilets on an airliner could become clogged. But to the extent that an "emergency" landing was necessary? It didn't seem very likely. There were toilets in first class. Why would the airline go to such expense only to preserve the class system? The Mexican Secret Service must have been alerted by the Americans. That was the only possible explanation. He could expect to be taken into custody as soon as they set down.

■ ■ ■

Ned introduced himself at the security desk in the lobby.

"Afternoon," he said, handing the young man his business card. "My name's Westerleigh. I'm here to show my clients unit 809. It's on lockbox, I believe."

Thank God there was so much unsold inventory in San Diego at the moment. Any building you wanted to inspect was accessible if you were a credentialed real estate agent.

"Certainly, Mr. Westerleigh," the young man smiled. "If you'll wait here, I'll bring the box out to you."

"Thanks, my good man," Ned said, accentuating his dotty Brit persona. "I called the listing agent earlier. She said the unit is vacant."

"That's correct, sir."

■ ■ ■

"Where are you?" Eli asked.

"A pay phone in Soho," Renzo replied. "There's no cell phone service down here."

"Your Uncle Klaus-Peter checked in. He wants you to call him."

"Did he leave a number?" Renzo asked.

"Have you got something to write with?"

"I'll remember it," Renzo said. "Just give it to me three times in succession and I'll remember it."

■ ■ ■

They spent just long enough in unit 809 for Ned to leave his business card as verification of their visit. The elevators in the building were equipped with surveillance cameras, so they had to take the emergency stairs to the nineteenth floor. When they got to 1902, Ned noticed the tiny pieces of wood wedged between the door and its frame—just as Rupert had described them. That was the detail that had aroused Rupert's suspicions in the first place. Those chips would fall to the floor the minute the door was opened, giving the occupant warning that someone had entered in his absence. An intruder who didn't know the trick would never know the sign he was leaving. Only a highly specialized intruder would be wise to the gambit and re-set them.

"Old KGB trick," Volk muttered.

"Indeed," Ned nodded. "Our chaps are trained not to use it."

"What do you mean *our?*" Maier grunted. He was on his knees, already at work on the locks. "We're all freelance these days, aren't we?"

They made short work of the place, leaving no evidence of their visit. They found no transmitter, no laptop, no camera equipment, none of the paraphernalia which would indicate an operative in residence, just everyday signs of a male occupant. Probably not American, going by the contents of the medicine cabinet.

"Chap's already gone," Ned said.

"Right," Maier nodded. "He either left as soon as he heard about the attack or had some kind of advance warning of it."

"He knows what he's doing," Volk said. "When the Americans come, they won't find anything."

"Better check his parking space downstairs just to be certain," Maier said.

They closed the apartment. The wooden wedges came with them in Ned's pocket. In the event the operative returned he'd have his warning. In the event others got there first, that tiny bit of evidence would be gone. They took the emergency stairs back to the eighth floor so as to give the impression that they'd never left unit 809. They reboarded the elevator there. A quick visit to the parking levels was a reasonable enough detour. Ned made a great show of locating unit 809's designated parking space for the surveillance cameras. It was empty.

■ ■ ■

"And now, gentlemen," Ned said as they strode away from the security desk, where he had returned unit 809's keys to the lockbox, "I believe it's time for a late lunch."

■ ■ ■

"*Damas y senores, su attencion por favor.*"

Finally, Bobak thought. Surely this was their call to reboard the aircraft, not merely another explanation for the delay.

Clogged toilets. Unbelievable. But no one had paid him the least attention as he stepped into the terminal earlier or as he sat in the departure lounge. He was still a free man.

■ ■ ■

As promised, the officers at the checkpoint on Hudson Street let Renzo through. It took only minutes from there to find the place. Uncle Klaus-Peter was Dad's oldest brother. He'd climbed higher in the FDNY ranks than any Lannaghan in history. He was filthy with soot and ash, and he carried the scent of destruction. It was probably ridiculous at this point to wish he didn't smoke. But the irony of seeing him take drag after drag off that cigarette made Renzo want to cry.

"I was stationed just outside the main entrance to the south tower."

"Right," Renzo said.

"I saw Eamonn come out of the lobby. I motioned him over."

"How did he look?"

"Like your father on a very tough day," Klaus-Peter grunted. "What do you think?"

371

"Sorry."

This was what came of rejecting family tradition and going to law school. Renzo's male relatives never missed a chance to take a dig at him.

"He asked me if I'd seen Mickey come out. I told him what I knew—which was only my best guess, you understand?—that Mickey and his buddies were still somewhere up in the forties or fifties. Honest to God, kid, I tried to stop him."

"Nobody could have," Renzo said, imagining his father turning and going back inside.

"Wasn't more than five, six minutes later the whole place came down."

■ ■ ■

"Very well, gentlemen," Ned said. The three pointed star was pointing northward again. "I didn't fill you in on this matter beforehand because I wanted your unbiased impressions. If you wouldn't mind too much, I'd like to hear them now."

"What we have, apparently," Maier said, dropping like lead weights the fey mannerisms he'd exhibited during their lunch, "is a Mossad agent operating in the United States, though such a thing isn't supposed ever to occur."

"There are precedents," Volk grunted.

"Rumored ones only," Maier insisted. "He's set himself up in a perfect location to monitor the movements of the American aircraft carriers which home port here, flight operations at North Island, other vessels of the fleet based at National City, and even the comings and goings at the submarine base at Point Loma. *From his living room.* It takes your breath away."

In another life, Maier had been a defense analyst for the *Kriegsmarine* based in Hamburg. His knowledge of the matters he was referring to was encyclopedic.

"It would be astonishing," Volk agreed, "except that such activities on the part of an Israeli operative make no sense in themselves. His government can access better intel through official channels than he can provide them."

"Exactly," Maier said. "His presence here is only comprehensible if we assume that he's not here to spy on the American Navy but on someone else who is spying on the American Navy. A terrorist cell, for instance."

"And that assumption also explains the legend implied by the tradecraft he's using," Volk said. "He wishes to give the impression that he's a KGB operative or better yet a KGB defector. Defector's my favorite hypothesis."

"Leaving us with one question only," Maier said.

"What's that, my boy?"

"How you learned of him in the first place, Ned."

"Several months ago," Ned said, "an inactive agent of an unnamed British intelligence organization contacted London Centre with a story of a KGB operative living two floors above him in a condo building close to the waterfront in San Diego. They asked me to come along for a look see—in a completely unofficial capacity, you understand—and I did. The expat agent was, as it happened, a distant cousin of mine, a young man I helped recruit for the service in the first place. So it only made sense that I should be the one to contact him. Especially living close as I do."

"Gave you cover, too," Volk grunted. "Distant relative stuff."

"Inactive?" Maier asked. "Inactive how?"

"Moscow," Ned said. "The Frogmaxtedd debacle. Cousin Rupert blew the whistle. Blew it and blew it and blew it some more. And was ignored until the whole thing exploded in spectacular fashion. They tried to pin the whole thing on him, but then Frogmaxtedd's mistress came forward and Frogmaxtedd killed himself. Rupert ended up totally exonerated but deactivated nonetheless."

"Because as we know," Volk said, "when it comes to whistleblowers in British intelligence, no good deed goes unpunished."

"Too right," Maier laughed

"At any rate," Ned said, "I met with Rupert and debriefed him and passed my observations along to London Centre."

"But that's not all you did, is it?" Volk asked. "You Limey traitor, you."

"Please bear in mind that at no point in the proceedings did anyone at London Centre speak those magic words 'Official Secrets Act', so I felt perfectly within my rights."

"The spirit, Ned," Maier said. "Not the letter."

"But the Official Secrets Act is written in letters," Ned said. "There's nothing spiritual about it. So, based on the story Rupert told I contacted Blumenfeld in Tel Aviv."

"The legendary Blumenfeld," Volk grunted.

"Never one to worry about the spirit or the letter of anything," Maier said. "Ultimate pragmatists, those Israelis."

"Turns out, the U.S. Navy angle was a red herring," Ned said. "Chap was keeping tabs on a cell of terrorists who were taking flying lessons."

"Jesus," Maier exploded.

"Blumenfeld's people alerted the Yanks," Ned said. "And the Yanks seem to have done bugger all with the intel."

"Typical American arrogance," Volk growled.

"In the light of today's events," Ned said, "it's pretty certain the Yanks are going to want to speak to our chap fairly urgently."

"But they have to find him first," Maier said. "And our Ned decided to help him cover his tracks."

"He'll be holed up in the Israeli Consulate in L.A. by now," Volk said, "or more likely, he crossed into Mexico."

"The Mexicans haven't closed their air space," Maier said. "He's probably halfway to Mexico City by now, heading for the Israeli embassy."

■ ■ ■

"It's me," Renzo said. He'd waited in line for twenty minutes to use the pay phone. There was an even longer line behind him.

"Where are you?" Eli asked.

"Tribeca. I just spoke with Klaus-Peter," Renzo said. "I'm afraid the news isn't good."

"I've been watching television all afternoon," Eli said. "I've got a pretty good idea."

"Dad and Mick are missing," Renzo said. "That could mean anything at this point."

"Right."

"Listen," Renzo said, "I'll pick up some takeout on my way back."

"You know," Eli said, "I think Beowulf and I are heading home. I appreciate your hospitality, but we need to be in our own space."

"I'll bring the takeout to you there," Renzo said. "What sounds good?"

"Absolutely nothing," Eli said.

"I know," Renzo said. "But we have to eat."

■ ■ ■

Geni watched in the rear view mirror as the attendant replaced the gas cap. As far as she knew, New Jersey was the last place in the developed world where you didn't have to pump your own gas. In fact, self-service was illegal. People looked down their noses at the state, but was there anything less civilized than self-service gas stations?

"Anything else for you today, ma'am?"

She hated it when they called her ma'am. She wasn't nearly old enough for that.

"No, thanks," she said.

"That'll be twenty dollars."

She handed him her credit card.

"Sorry, ma'am," he said. "Machines are all down. Cash only."

"Really?"

She rummaged in her purse and finally came up with a ten, a five, three singles, and eight quarters.

"Crazy day, huh?" he mused.

"No kidding," she said.

"See you again soon," he said.

She hit the window button and shut him back out. After finally making it back to the park and ride lot, she'd spent most of the day driving around. Ordinarily, she'd have gone shopping to calm down, but she knew that wherever she went people would be talking about it. In the stores, there would be banks of televisions tuned to the coverage. It would make her want to scream.

Somewhere out there she knew Emilio was looking for her. Probably frantically. That's how he did everything. She felt bad for him, but really it was his own fault. You married a girl like her, you got what you got. She didn't change for anybody. She should go home. She should figure out a way to get word to him that she was safe and put him out of his misery. She knew the event was supposed to bring her to some epiphany—to make her appreciate him more. To want to be a good wife for a change. So far it was having the opposite effect. All she could think of was that being married to Emilio was wasting her life.

■ ■ ■

When Griffin came in from school, Cooper and Josh were sitting on the sofa in the media room as if they had taken root there.

"Don't worry," Cooper greeted him, grasping the remote like it was a weapon. "The dogs have been walked twice."

"I never worry," Griffin said, hoping a quote from his late mother-in-law might lighten the atmosphere. He should have known better. They didn't even register it. He turned to Josh. "I expect you've been on the phone all day."

"Not that it's done much good," Josh said. "Nobody south of Times Square seems to have cell service at this point. And the landlines are hopeless. All the circuits are jammed."

"Surely you've been able to get through to someone," Griffin insisted.

"Dad's fine," Josh nodded. "So is Rosie, over in Fort Lee. And I was able to speak to Andrew briefly. He said New Haven's like a ghost town. But no word from anyone else. Eli works in the north tower, you know. He was almost certainly there at the time."

"But ten or fifteen floors down from the impact zone," Cooper said. "So we're hoping he got out."

"Right," Griffin nodded. He'd spent the entire day mentally going over the list of names. At the top were Eamonn and his two sons. It was already obvious that New York's firefighters had paid a fearsome toll.

■ ■ ■

"What's the word from the hospital?" Eli asked.

Renzo turned. Eli looked ten years older than he had earlier in the day.

"Mom should be out of surgery within the hour. I can't believe they'll let her go in on another procedure after this one no matter how bad it is around there. She went on duty twenty hours ago."

"You'd better get over to St. Vincent's," Eli said. "She'll need you."

"I hate to leave you on your own," Renzo said.

"Eventually you'll have to," Eli smiled. "You can't babysit forever."

"But. . ."

"No arguments, Renzo," Eli said.

■ ■ ■

"Emilio?" Geni called into the darkness. "Are you here?"

There was no answer. She stepped into the apartment and closed the front door behind her. One of the cats rubbed against her leg.

■ ■ ■

It was after nightfall by the time the flight landed in Mexico City. Bobak took his time exiting the plane. There was nothing to be gained by looking as if he was in a hurry. He sauntered up the jetway like he hadn't a care in the world. He didn't rush to the first pay telephone he saw on the concourse. He walked past three of them and stopped at the fourth.

When making his purchases in Tijuana earlier, he had paid in dollars but insisted on receiving his change in Mexican currency. He fed coins into the telephone and made the first of the sequence of calls it would require to identify himself to the personnel at the embassy.

■ ■ ■

Elaine O'Rourke, the hospital administrator, was waiting for them when they came out of surgery.

"Dr. Altschul, Nurse Lannaghan," she said, "I understand your procedure was successful."

"A cakewalk," Dar said.

It had been anything but.

"The two of you have been on duty for over twenty-four hours. I'm sending you home."

"We can stay if you need us," Dar said.

"No," O'Rourke said, shaking her head, "you two are done. I don't want to see either of you on site for forty-eight hours at least. And I'm sure Nurse Lannaghan would appreciate it if you didn't speak for her."

"Sorry, Lannaghan," he grinned.

"Sorry, yourself," Maribel laughed. "You're as bad as any one of my sons."

"You raised them," he said.

"Incidentally, nurse," O'Rourke said, "there's someone waiting for you in the lounge."

"Who?" Maribel asked.

"Lorenzo," Mrs. O'Rourke said. "Your youngest, right?"

■ ■ ■

"It'll be O.K." Dar said, squeezing her hand.

"I don't know what you're talking about."

"Come on," Dar said, "I'll walk with you."

"That isn't necessary," Maribel said.

"Of course it is."

"I'm not helpless," she snapped.

"This isn't about helpless," he said. "You're terrified. You've been worried all day. It's only natural."

■ ■ ■

In the lounge, Renzo was watching the television with the sound turned off. He looked up, and in that instant she knew what he was there to tell her. He readjusted his expression immediately, but she'd seen what she'd seen. He couldn't take it back. It wasn't any worse than she'd been imagining all day. Whatever details he'd come to share with her, it couldn't be any worse than that.

"Mom," he said, lumbering across the room toward her.

"Baby," she choked as his arms closed around her.

"I love you," he said.

"This is Dr. Altschul," she said, stepping out of the embrace. "Dr. Altschul, my son Renzo."

"We've met," Dr. Altschul said.

She couldn't begin to decipher the look that passed between them. Or maybe she just didn't want to.

"We go to the same gym," Renzo said.

Perhaps that was it. Perhaps it wasn't any of her business anyway.

"Thanks for delivering me," Maribel said.

"You're welcome," Dar said. "Good seeing you, Renzo. Anything I can do to help?"

"Maybe you'd sit with us for a minute," Renzo said.

"Sure."

"What?" Maribel asked. "You've got news so bad you think I may need medical attention?"

"It's not all bad news, Mom," Renzo said. "Uncle Sean, Uncle Paddy. Uncle Beto, Uncle Miguel, Uncle Martin, Uncle Klaus-Peter, Cousin Sam. . ."

"Enough with the list," she said.

"Everybody safe and accounted for," Renzo said.

"Except?"

"Mick," Renzo said. "And Dad."

She felt Dar's grip on her elbow tighten.

"I see," she said. It would have to be those two. Her two. Well, good for her sisters-in-law. And her cousins. She was grateful for their good fortune. Truly she was. But she didn't want to live a single minute longer if her husband and her baby were gone.

"Not dead, Mom," Renzo insisted. "Nobody's saying they're dead. At this point they're just listed as missing. There are hundreds of guys down there digging through the rubble. They'll be pulling people out all night."

"All right," she said. "So we wait. We wait and we pray."

"Sure, Mom," Renzo said. "Anyway, I'm here to take you home. Aunt Yenny and Aunt Lucy are going to be staying with you."

"How are we getting there?" Maribel asked. "I can't face the train right now."

"There are plenty of taxis out front," Renzo said. "North of Fourteenth Street, things are just like normal."

The idea of life going on just a few blocks away seemed obscene.

"Nonsense," Dar said. "I've got my car here. I'll drive you."

"Thanks," Renzo said, "but we couldn't ask you."

"You're not asking me," Dar said. "Didn't you hear me? I offered."

■ ■ ■

"Thanks so much for the ride," Maribel said, getting out of the car. "Now go home and get some rest. You may think you're Superman, but moms know best."

Renzo was already on the sidewalk.

"I'll wait for Renzo here," Dar said. "He'll need a ride to his place. And we just live a couple of blocks from each other."

"I won't be long," Renzo said. "I'll just see her inside."

■ ■ ■

As the hours drew on, the news only got worse. Eli's ears ached from waiting for the telephone to ring. There had been nothing since that call from Josh earlier. Meanwhile, his certainty was like freshly poured concrete—growing more solid by the minute. It seemed impossible, but it seemed inescapable. How could it be that he would never feel those arms around him again or hear that deep growl of a voice speaking his name?

All day watching those images on the television screen. Planes crashing into buildings. Billowing smoke. Blizzards of debris falling out of the sky. Towers collapsing. Cascading destruction. It all mirrored perfectly what he felt going on inside him. It was the slow motion end of the world. It never stopped. Would it? Would he ever sleep again? Would the pain ever lessen? Even the tiniest bit?

Eamonn. The sound of that name, unspoken except in his heart, was like a scream. It deafened him to everything else in the universe.

A quarter century seemed like long time until you were looking back at it.

■ ■ ■

The nighttime streets looked no different from usual. Renzo had spent all day expecting things that didn't happen and being dumbfounded by everything that did. It felt like being turned inside out. In the driver's seat, Dar was like a stranger who'd stopped to pick up a hitchhiker but at the same time like a friend you knew so well neither of you had to speak. It couldn't be both, but which was it? After this day, would anyone be capable of certainty again?

It was fatigue, sure. They were both punch drunk. But it wasn't entirely that. Things really were different than they had ever been. They had witnessed the impossible in a way that called into question the whole concept of impossibility. Renzo felt that new reality deep inside himself. They were in a changed world. Everything looked the same but they couldn't assume that anything meant what they thought it did.

■ ■ ■

Once Dar turned off the engine, the parking garage was silent. It was almost as if the world had stopped turning.

"Thanks for the ride," Renzo said. "And for looking out for Mom all day. I can't thank you enough. She seems as solid as granite. But nobody can be expected to stand up to a thing like this."

"You got a minute?" Dar asked.

"Sure," Renzo said. "What's up?"

"Like you to listen to something," Dar said, pulling his phone out of his pocket and pressing some buttons.

"*Dar, it's me.*"

It was a man's voice.

"*I guess you must be in surgery or something. I was hoping I wouldn't get your voicemail. Anyway, by the time you get this you'll surely know what's going on. The plane apparently hit several floors below us here, and all the emergency stairways are blocked. At first there were rumors about a helicopter rescue from the roof and some people from our office headed up there, but the access was locked. I don't think they could bring in helicopters anyway, because of the fire. . .*"

"My God," Renzo said. "Who is that?"

"*I can't see any way out.*"

"Sssh."

"*Dar, I'm sorry it's ending like this. I wanted to do this apology right, you know? Like over a nice dinner or something. I'm sorry I slept with Trent. And Monte and Rick and all those other guys. I know you never wanted an open relationship. I should have at least tried to give you what you wanted. I'd give anything for another chance to make you happy. I hope when you think of us you'll. . .*"

"His name was Axel," Dar said. "He worked for Cantor Fitzgerald. We had six months."

He sounded so calm, Renzo thought, speaking in the past tense. What kind of will power allowed for something like that?

"*Dar, I really do love you. Please remember that.*"

"Feels more like six days, really."

"When did you first pick up this message?" Renzo asked.

"About eleven a.m." Dar said.

"Fourteen hours ago," Renzo said. "And you didn't say anything to anyone, did you?"

"We were kind of busy," Dar said. "You do what you have to do. People depend on that. Your Mom knows how it works."

"Right," Renzo said. "But. . ."

"At least somebody knows now," Dar said. "Hey, what're you doing?"

"Putting my number in your phone," Renzo said, pressing the tiny buttons. "Anything you need, you call me, O.K?"

OCTOBER, 2001

The new guy at Renzo's gym was as choice as could be. Short cropped blond hair, honey colored skin, eyes like the sky on a summer day, and the ripped body of a gymnast. If Renzo didn't hit on him somebody else would, probably before the guy had a chance to finish his workout. This was Chelsea, not Omaha. People moved fast. Not that Renzo needed the additional motivation provided by competition when a guy was that cute.

"Hi," he said, squaring his shoulders. "I'm Renzo, and you're new here."

"Hello," the guy smiled, offering his right hand. "My name is Horst."

He had a strong grip. Renzo met too many guys who shook hands like girls. It wasn't necessarily a gay/straight thing, except for when it was. Did that mean this guy was straight? The German accent was unmistakable. Renzo hadn't been expecting it, but given the guy's looks it wasn't exactly a surprise.

"Horst," Renzo smiled. "Nice to meet you. I had a great-uncle named Horst."

This was not a line. Renzo's grandmother's oldest brother had been named Horst.

"Really?" Horst asked. "What was he like?"

"I never met him," Renzo said. "He died outside Stalingrad."

"I'm named after my grandfather," Horst said. "He was taken prisoner by the Russians at Riga. He spent over ten years in Siberia."

"Wow," Renzo marveled, "but he got out?"

"Yes," Horst said. "He and my grandmother still live in Lubeck. But tell me, Renzo. You don't look German."

"German and Irish on my father's side," Renzo said.

"And your mother? She is Italian?"

"Puerto Rican."

■ ■ ■

"Your body fat is obviously quite low," Horst said, "but you must weigh at least one hundred kilos."

They were in the showers now, standing beneath neighboring heads. In Renzo's experience European guys were extremely cool about such things. He still hadn't figured out if Horst was gay or just European.

"About that," Renzo said. Closer to one hundred five, actually, but he didn't want to come off as narcissistic. "And you must. . ."

"Must what?" Horst asked.

"See the view of Eighth Avenue from my apartment," Renzo said. He wasn't sure the gambit would go over, but nothing ventured, nothing gained.

"Really? It is a nice view?"

"Parts of it," Renzo said.

■ ■ ■

"You know," Renzo said, on the sidewalk in front of the gym. "I'm kind of hungry. You want to grab something to eat first?"

"So does that make this a date?" Horst asked.

"As opposed to what?" Renzo asked. "A zebra?"

"As opposed to going to your apartment right now and having sex," Horst said.

"The sex," Renzo said, "would kind of be for dessert."

"I like dessert very much," Horst said, "but best after dinner."

■ ■ ■

When they got to Renzo's place, the first thing he saw was the blinking light on his answering machine. Normally under the circumstances he'd have ignored it until later. But Mom and his brothers had instituted a strict regime since the attacks. All family members were now required to stay in touch at all times. He had no idea why whoever it was hadn't called on his cell.

"Make yourself comfortable," he said. "I just have to check this."

Horst walked over to the bookcase.

"So many German books," he said, pulling one off the shelf. "You didn't say you spoke German."

"I have a master's degree in German literature," Renzo said.

"Really?"

Now that Horst was standing in Renzo's living room looking at Renzo's things, he was hotter than Renzo had realized at first. Or even at the restaurant, if that was possible.

"Really," Renzo nodded. That damned answering machine light. Who needed that kind of distraction?

"So you do what? Teach in a university?"

"At the moment I'm attending law school," Renzo said. He pressed the button.

"*Renzo, it's Liam. Family meeting tomorrow at Mom's. Seven p.m. Tory and I will bring takeout. You pick up beer. You know what everybody likes. Also, Mom wants you to make sure Eli's there. No excuses.*"

"You look troubled," Horst said. "Perhaps I should go."

"No," Renzo said. "You absolutely shouldn't go."

"But what is it?"

Renzo's grandmother had taught him that you could never pull the wool over the eyes of a German. So—face the music.

"Lots of New York City firefighters in my family. Uncles. Cousins. Dad. My brothers Tory and Mick. Seventeen in all."

"*Lieber Gott*," Horst said. "Is everyone safe?"

"All but two," Renzo said. "Dad and Mick are still missing."

"And your mother wants a meeting tomorrow night," Horst said.

"It might be news," Renzo nodded, "but after four weeks it won't be good news."

"I should go," Horst said.

"No," Renzo said. "Don't. Please."

"Maybe," Horst said. "But who is this Eli? Your boyfriend?"

"You wouldn't be here right now if I had a boyfriend," Renzo said.

"No?"

"Absolutely not," Renzo said.

"Ex-boyfriend, then?"

"More like an uncle," Renzo said. It was too much to explain right now.

Horst screwed up his face like he wasn't used to thinking so hard. He was so cute like that Renzo could hardly keep from grabbing him.

"I believe you're telling the truth," Horst finally said.

"Good," Renzo said.

"Because that's what you want me to believe?"

"Because Eli really is like my uncle."

"*Like* your uncle."

"Come here," Renzo said. But actually Horst was already as close as he needed to be for Renzo to start unbuttoning his shirt.

■ ■ ■

"Lufthansa, huh?" Eli grunted. "And newly transferred here? I thought all the airlines were cutting back."

They had met in midtown, where Eli's firm rented temporary office space. Their former headquarters wasn't even rubble at this point. More like dust. Now he and Renzo waited for their train with about half a million other New Yorkers.

"A bunch of their senior staff at Kennedy have asked to be sent back to Germany," Renzo said. "He's replacing two of them."

"Where did he transfer from?" Eli asked. "Frankfurt and Munich are their big European hubs, right?"

"Riga," Renzo said.

"Riga?"

"His grandfather was captured by the Red Army there in 'forty-four. Horst heard stories about the place and wanted to see it."

"You can see it in an afternoon or two," Eli said. "Your father and I did. You don't need to move there. What happened to the grandfather?"

"Spent over a decade in the gulag."

"If he survived that long, he was very lucky," Eli said. "Or very tough."

"Both, I expect," Renzo said. "Lives in Lubeck these days. Likes to take Horst sailing on the Baltic."

"If the two of you spent that much time exchanging life stories," Eli said, "and had dinner first, that was no trick."

"Who knows?"

"Oh, I think you have a pretty good idea."

"Right."

"Seriously, Lorenzo."

"Dad only called me that when he was annoyed," Renzo said.

■ ■ ■

"Manicotti," Renzo said, surveying the dining table. "Lasagna. Fettucine Alfredo. Sausage and peppers. An antipasto consisting entirely of cheeses and cured meats. Gee, thanks, everybody. Not a thing here I can eat. Just think what Dad would say."

"There's canned tuna in the fridge, dear," Maribel said. "In spring water, just like you always bought it when you were living at home."

"Only one person in the world I can depend on," Renzo grumbled.

"Some people don't even have that," Tory pointed out.

"I thought you and Nancy were trying to patch things up," Renzo said.

"Trying isn't the same as succeeding," Tory said. "And nobody better say 'I told you so'."

■ ■ ■

"Eli, there's something I need to say to you," Maribel said.

Renzo recognized her tone. His ears pricked up. He felt like Eli's terrier, Beowulf.

"Should we step onto the terrace?" Eli asked.

"It's something I'd like everybody to hear," Maribel said.

"Mom?"

"It's all right, Liam."

"If you're sure," Liam said.

"Believe me," Maribel sighed. "Eli, it's time we put this thing to rest. Past time, really. You're the man Eamonn loved. I'm the woman he loved. There's no point in ignoring reality, right? And time to end this tug of war with Eamonn as the rope. So I'm declaring peace. And no more elephant in the living room."

"You acknowledged it years ago," Eli said.

Renzo recognized Eli's tone. There were several decades' worth of tears in it.

"Not in so many words, I'm afraid," Maribel said. "Not so that everybody understood that I'd made my peace with it. Eamonn knew. But not anybody else, I'm afraid. I left it too ambiguous, anyway. So there it is. In front of God and these witnesses."

"All right," Eli said. "Thank you."

"We get it, Mom," Liam said.

"Yes," Renzo nodded.

"Mom," Tory said. "What's with all these past tenses? 'You're the man he loved.' Really?"

"Please, darling," Maribel laughed. "I've spent the last thirty years working in operating rooms. You think I can't face the reality of my husband's death?"

"He could still be. . ."

"Tory, stop. No, he can't. Any more than Mick can. Sorry, Lisa."

"No, Maribel," Lisa said. "You're right. I've known since the day after it happened that I'll never see him again."

"And that your baby will never know its father," Maribel nodded.

"What baby?"

"You're no actress, honey," Maribel said. "Hold onto your day job. I know about the baby. We all know. You don't have to keep putting off the announcement to spare our feelings. Mick told me he was getting ready to propose to you. And it wasn't because you were pregnant. He had no idea when he first told me his plans. Honest to God. Men are so stupid sometimes."

"Jesus, Mom,"Tory said.

"He did?" Lisa asked.

"Last time we talked," Maribel nodded.

Renzo recognized the tone. Mom wasn't necessarily telling the truth. Or rather, she was telling the truth but skirting the facts. As a law student he wasn't supposed to admit that was even possible, but he'd have done the same.

"I wish he'd told me," Lisa said.

■ ■ ■

"Bottom line—the remains they found are definitely Mick," Liam said.

"They're sure?"Tory choked.

"There's no question," Liam said.

"DNA doesn't lie," Renzo said. "We all gave samples, remember?"

"I'm satisfied there's no mistake," Maribel said, "which leaves the question what do we want to do?"

"Not what do we want to do, Mom," Renzo said. "What do you want to do?"

"I think at the very least you should also be directing that question to the mother of his child," Maribel said.

"Sorry, Lisa," Renzo said.

"It's all right," Lisa said. "I had no idea why Maribel wanted me here to-night. The girlfriend."

"The fiancée," Maribel insisted.

"How can I be the fiancée if he never proposed to me?"

"I told you, dear," Maribel said. "He was going to. Next time he saw you. Or at least as soon as he had the ring. We're not going to argue about it. No more arguments in this family. And no more pretending. You're my daughter in law. You're carrying my grandchild. Eli's—hell, Eli, I have no idea what you are, but you're family, get it? You will both always be part of this family."

■ ■ ■

"So we're all agreed," Liam said. "No funeral for now. We wait and see if they find any of Dad's remains."

"Not past Thanksgiving," Maribel insisted. "We're not letting it go any longer than that. I can't do it. Not even for Eamonn. He doesn't show up by then, we're having his funeral without him. We'll bury their coffins side by side."

■ ■ ■

"Are you all right?" Renzo asked.

He and Eli were on their way back to the subway station.

"Why wouldn't I be?"

"Who the hell do you think you're talking to?" Renzo laughed.

"I know I deserve that."

"Uh huh."

"Does she really forgive me?" Eli asked. "Do you think it could be that easy after all this time?"

"I knew you missed the point," Renzo said. "What you heard tonight was her telling you there's nothing to forgive. How could any of us blame someone for falling in love with Dad? Kind of a miracle there weren't dozens of you. Male and female."

■ ■ ■

"When are you going to call Horst?" Eli asked.

Renzo really didn't want to have this discussion, but it was Eli. It would be like trying to shut Dad down.

"Who says I'm going to?" Renzo asked.

"Now it's my turn," Eli said. "Who the hell do you think you're talking to?"

"I just feel strange about it," Renzo said.

"Strange? You mean guilty."

"All right."

"Why?" Eli demanded. "Life has to go on. It's what Eamonn would want. It's what your mother wants. All of us moving forward."

"Sure."

"Nobody's saying you have to marry this guy," Eli said, "but I hear it in your voice when you talk about him. Something happened last night."

"I don't know what you're talking about."

"Call him, you little bastard."

OCTOBER, 2001

"Note for you, sir," Greenberg said.

For an Anglican school, there were certainly a lot of Jewish students enrolled. A good thing, too. They certainly raised the tone, academically speaking. And Greenberg, a ferocious rugger, couldn't have been more adorable. Rupert's soft spot for rugby players had only intensified since his arrival in the States, where they were a much rarer species. In the U.K., playing rugby was a more or less unconscious choice for a man of a certain physique and social class. Here, it required real commitment.

"Thanks, Greenberg," Rupert smiled.

The note was from the headmistress. Macheteing his way through her ornately Victorian prose, he eventually identified her point. Would he please drop by her office? The school's anglophilia was ubiquitous, obsessive. Was ridiculous, really. Like a fervent twelve year old's desperation to maintain a belief in Santa Claus. Still, instead of simply scrawling 'O.K.' and handing the note back to Greenberg, Rupert quoted Hamlet: "*I shall in all my best obey you, madam*", signed off with "*yr. obt. svt.*", and initialed his response "*RFM*" in his fanciest, most florid hand. There. The sensibilities of his fellow prisoners having been honoured, he handed the note back to Greenberg.

"Off with you, boy."

■ ■ ■

The hero worship started pretty much the minute Rupert stepped on campus his very first day. He was an Olympic champion, albeit in a sport most

395

Americans decried as unmanly at best. Still, Olympic medals were Olympic medals, though Rupert resolutely refused to bring them to school for show and tell. Then, too, he was an aristocrat, and no one, it seemed, had greater reverence for the British aristocracy than Yanks, who hardly understood a thing about it. Perhaps such profound ignorance was a prerequisite to their worshipfulness. Recent events, of course, had only added to his luster. The whole school knew about Peregrine, who had leapt into eternity from the ninety-somethingth floor. They knew about Cavendish (if only as Rupert's partner in Olympic glory) on that ill-fated plane that went down in Pennsylania. There were rumours, unsubstantiated but tantalizing and certainly true to the man's character, that Cavendish had been one of the first to die, his throat slashed with one of those box cutters as he tried to Put A Stop To the hijackers of his flight. Poor Greenberg had practically been quivering as he handed Rupert Dr. Ainsley's note.

The dears meant well. Every solitary one of them. Rupert had to admit that. They had no idea how unworthy he felt of their reverence.

"You're to go right in," the head's secretary told him, a look of profound sympathy on her face, as if he was about to face a firing squad.

■ ■ ■

"I had no idea," Dr. Ainsley said, "when Mr. Westerleigh called to arrange this visit, that you two were related."

Ned had been at the funerals, but other than the requisite greetings and condolences, nothing had passed between them. His sudden appearance in the headmistress' office must Mean Something.

"Chair of the Board of Governors of St. Dunstan's," Dr. Ainsley breathed.

"That he is," Rupert smiled. "As well as my noble kinsman. Great to see you, Ned."

"My boy."

■ ■ ■

"So I'll leave you in Rupert's all too capable hands for the campus tour," Dr. Ainsley said.

"So very obliged," Ned smiled.

"And you must let me know if there's any way at all in which I or my staff can be of further service to you."

"I shall indeed," Ned assured her. "I shall indeed. And many thanks."

■ ■ ■

"You old string-puller," Rupert chuckled, as they descended the stairs from the administration building. "Or should one say leg?"

"All in a day's work," Ned said.

"Is that what this is?" Rupert asked. "Work?"

"Sometimes work is a pleasure," Ned said.

"Ah yes," Rupert said. "The old Westerleigh charm. You know what Mum said after the funeral, don't you?"

"How would I?"

"She called you 'the finest man in England'. I reminded her that you've been expat lo these many years, but she wasn't having a bit of it. 'That Ned Westerleigh's the finest man in England. Hands down'. She meant it as an implied criticism of my father, you can be sure."

"Charming woman," Ned said.

"Tragically confused, of course."

"Still, one can't help but appreciate her regard."

"Certainly."

By now they were well away from the buildings and out of earshot. The groundskeepers didn't work this late in the afternoon.

"I assume you've some sort of news for me," Rupert said. "Am I being reactivated?"

"Not exactly," Ned said.

■ ■ ■

"We're not having this conversation, you understand," Ned said.

At this point they'd walked so far they were out of the line of sight of any campus building, Rupert noted. Ned was taking no chances.

"Burn before reading," Rupert nodded.

"Just so. And even if we were, I wouldn't be telling you anything official. I don't know anything official. That's the official line, at least."

"Right."

"Good lad. It seems that the individual you called to our attention was indeed an operative."

"Blimey."

"In the service of a power indefatigably friendly to the west but at the same time notoriously independent."

"Mossad?" Rupert asked.

That wasn't much of a guess. It was the only possibility that fit Ned's description.

"You know I can't tell you."

"Mossad," Rupert nodded.

"He attempted, through his own service you understand, to alert the Cousins to the activities of certain individuals here."

"Several of the hijackers did their flight training at Gillespie Field," Rupert nodded. "All over the local news."

"As you say," Ned nodded. "Chap was surveilling them, as the Cousins put it. Passed info of the most inflammatory sort on to his people, who passed it on in turn. The Cousins, as they are often wont to do, chose to ignore the warning."

"Almost as if they wanted the plot to succeed," Rupert said. "One can only guess at their motivation. Hoping for a provocation. Gave the baddies plenty of rope to hang themselves with and in the process tragically misjudged the potential severity of the event."

"Your words," Ned said. "Not mine."

"Understood."

"At any rate, said individual has now fallen off everybody's radar. Not that he was on anyone's but yours. The Cousins had no knowledge of him and his people went to every possible length to disguise the source of the information they forwarded. But you know what I'm getting at. Now the Cousins are frantic to get their hands on him—whoever he might be, as he's still a hypothesis from their perspective—for 'debriefing'."

"You said off everybody's radar?" Rupert asked. "Even his own chaps'?"

"No idea. They're not talking. They're furious with the Cousins and in no mood to be cooperative with anyone who might be cooperative with DC."

"As well they should be," Rupert said. "I know it's my adopted country these days, but I sometimes think these yanks would sell out their own mothers for the right price. Or the right ideology, more like."

"Only some of them would," Ned said. "Some of them truly are men of honour."

"There's that in their favour," Rupert mused.

"Anyway, his own people are notoriously independent."

"You said that."

They had to be Mossad, Rupert thought. His recalled perceptions of the man, or rather his own inferences based on those perceptions, were rearranging themselves dramatically.

"They're not about to hand him over."

"Lord, I should hope not," Rupert said.

"And our boys never knew anything more about him than what you provided."

"I see."

"Have you seen any sign of him? Since the attacks?"

"Certainly not," Rupert said. God only knew he'd looked. "First thing I did when I got home from school that afternoon—checked out his flat. Completely untouched. Like he'd just gone out for the day. But one can tell, can't one, when the bird has flown?"

"Yes," Ned nodded.

"Felt like that," Rupert said. "Kept watch as best I could, but work, you know? By the end of the week, the place had been cleaned out. No idea by whom. But professionals, definitely. You could have performed surgery in there."

■ ■ ■

"Now for the bad news," Ned said.

"Let me guess," Rupert said. "Moscow all over again?"

"In our work as in no other," Ned said, "the dictum 'no good deed goes unpunished' takes on the force of Holy Writ. Might as well be the Eleventh Commandment. So yes. You've stepped in it, I'm afraid."

"How badly?"

"What the Cousins hate even more than the enemy is the friend who shows them up. Which you did. But good."

"Am I to be deported?"

"It certainly looked like it might go that way."

"Bloody hell."

"I said *looked*," Ned said. "*Might*."

"So what's to happen?"

"Negotiations were tricky," Ned said, "but a deal has finally been struck. You're being allowed to finish the academic year here. Then you'll relocate to San Francisco. There you'll be under the watchful eye of yours truly."

"You vouched for me," Rupert said. "Gosh, Ned, thanks awfully. I don't think I could stick it back in Jolly Olde. In fact, quite sure I couldn't just now."

"All contingent, young Rupert," Ned said, "on your keeping your nose absolutely immaculate. Pristine, do you hear? Otherwise one can be of no further assistance."

■ ■ ■

"My boy, just let me say it once more," Ned said. "I'm so frightfully sorry for your loss."

"You always considered Peregrine a bounder," Rupert said.

"I haven't altered my opinion as to that," Ned said, "but please don't think it makes my condolence disingenuous."

"Sorry, old man. Not what I meant at all."

"I didn't suppose you did," Ned said.

400

"Can't help but hold myself a little responsible," Rupert said. "I should have tried harder with Peregrine."

"You can't mean that you believe in the curse of the FitzMerlins."

"Certainly not," Rupert said. "Just—he needn't have been in New York on the day. Might have prevented that somehow. Keep telling oneself one must try harder next time. But of course, no next time in prospect. Should somehow have stopped the other thing, as well."

"Cavendish on that flight to San Francisco," Ned said. "Pippa believes you summoned him."

"Did she say that?"

"Implied," Ned said. "Nothing more."

"One has a difficult time imagining Pippa implying anything."

"Toned herself down for the sake of the boys, one supposes," Ned said.

"Right," Rupert said. "So is that what he told her? That his trip was my idea?"

"Who knows? I shouldn't think so. Grown surprisingly perspicacious in her old age. Or suspicious, at least. Nothing more to it than that."

"Motherhood, I suppose," Rupert said.

"Perhaps," Ned nodded. "My own mother was of the opinion that no woman truly knew her husband until after the divorce was final. Since she eventually had three ex-husbands she may have been onto something."

"Should have tried harder there, too," Rupert said. "Might have worked out differently."

"He wanted sons," Ned said. "Nothing in the world trumps that."

"So I've heard," Rupert said.

"Mustn't blame yourself. Couldn't be helped."

"I didn't summon him, you know. One knew of the divorce, certainly. But one made no assumptions based on that. More likely to have been Pippa's idea than his. At least so one believed. And he gave no indication what he had in mind subsequently. Of late, we'd hardly spoken. I had no idea he was coming until I got the email that morning. By then he was already on his plane. Or en route to the airport at least. Impossible to have stopped him, even if one had wanted to."

"Did you answer his email?"

"What?"

"Did you tell him not to come? Or at least, would you have?"

"Old man, please."

"You don't have to tell me. Still, best be honest with yourself at least. The divorce was already final. He was a free man. No one could blame you."

"Is any man with an ex-wife and children really free? Ever?"

"Probably not."

"Besides, the email was totally noncommittal. 'Headed your way. Hope you can put me up for a few days'. Only that. Could have meant anything. Or nothing. Now one won't ever be certain. In a way, that's the hardest thing."

■ ■ ■

They had the sort of dinner in the sort of restaurant that befitted expatriate kinsmen of a certain class indulging in a brief reunion. The meal, Rupert didn't have to be told, was cover. Just in case they were being observed. It was the remotest of possibilities, but Ned left nothing to chance. And Rupert shouldn't, either. That was the message Ned was sending. They were living through the most paranoid of times. There seemed no lengths the Cousins wouldn't go to. And the Cousins weren't the only players, at least potentially. "Inactive" was a designation highly revered by bureaucrats but generally accepted as meaningless by every other inhabitant of that shadowy corner of the planet. So be on your guard, Rupert.

Their conversation over dinner couldn't have been more innocuous. Rupert insisted on paying the check. Then Ned drove off in his rental Buick in the direction of Lindbergh Field. He wasn't even staying the night.

■ ■ ■

Pippa had been far too friendly at the funeral. She must finally have figured something out. Had Cavendish bared his soul in the course of their harrowing dissolution? Had he left a diary? Had any one of hundreds of possible witnesses

402

to his carryings-on with Rupert over the years finally gotten up the nerve to approach her? None of those things seemed likely. Cavendish was not the type to make such a confession. For that matter, it was all but impossible to imagine Cavendish deciding there was anything to confess. Cavendish the diarist? Preposterous. Or at least nearly so. And the witnesses must surely assume that by now Pippa knew everything already and simply didn't care. Didn't she pride herself on being the most jaded woman of her generation?

Perhaps it was intuition, though Pippa seemed congenitally incapable of such a thing. Or of empathy, as far as that went. But she knew something. Or thought she did. How else was Rupert to explain her elaborate cordiality? She had always gushed over him and always insincerely, but their encounter at the funeral had been nothing less than the performance of a diva. Too over the top even to warrant the description. A new one was required, but Rupert wasn't up to the task of formulating it.

Perhaps the fact that Cavendish had been on his way to see Rupert that day was the only evidence she needed. *The one person he simply had to see the minute I wasn't his wife any more was. . .*

The more Rupert thought about it the more he was drawn to that explanation. She'd been the picture of the glamourous widow that day, he recalled. Widowhood still—despite the sophistication of the times—carried a cachet that divorce couldn't match. Rupert expected she'd spend the rest of her life referring to Cavendish as her late husband rather than her ex. With the decree just hours old when Cavendish left England on his fateful journey, Rupert didn't see how she'd be able to resist the temptation.

The two boys were gorgeous. Tiny copies of their father. Looking at them standing in front of their father's casket had been torture. Recalling them there still was.

■ ■ ■

Rupert's flat, a mausoleum of late, felt even colder and emptier than when he'd left for work that morning. He didn't bother turning on lights. What he needed from the bedside table he found by touch. He then retraced his steps and went out onto the terrace. The view across North Island to the slumbering Pacific was as evocative as ever. He sat looking into the gloomy distance. Somewhere the man was out there. Rupert knew who he was, finally, but had no name to call him. He had vanished as completely as anyone could on this planet of seven billion or so. If even the Yanks couldn't locate him, he was truly lost.

On that afternoon in the flat upstairs, Rupert had taken great care not to touch anything. No fingerprints or DNA did he leave behind for the investigators he had to assume would eventually arrive. One thing only felt the pressure of his fingers, and it left the flat secure in his pants pocket. Now he unscrewed the cap and sniffed the contents of the metal tube.

NOVEMBER, 2001

Cooper lunged from his seat into the aisle.

"Stop," Griffin pleaded. "Don't."

"Someone has to," Cooper snarled over his shoulder.

The airliner lurched.

"You! American! Back in your seat!"

But Cooper moved up the aisle toward the hijacker. A woman screamed. The knife blade gleamed in the cabin lights.

Griffin woke. Beside him, Cooper snored softly. On the floor around the bed, the Labradors slumbered undisturbed. Again. Every night since it happened. There was no telling how long it would take him to get back to sleep.

■ ■ ■

"The dogs will be fine," Cooper said.

"I know."

"You always get like this when we leave them."

"I know," Griffin said. He was glad he had the dogs for an excuse. He wasn't crazy about Cooper figuring out how terrified he was. He'd never been what you could call a good flier, but this was the worst. That damn dream. Every fucking night. And their trip getting closer by the day. Until the day became tomorrow.

"You're all packed, of course," Cooper said.

"Yes."

Griffin packed light and packed quickly. Cooper packed comprehensively and painstakingly and took forever.

"Go on to bed," Cooper said. "I'll be in as soon as I'm finished."

His clothes for the trip were neatly arrayed around the guest room. He refused to get luggage out before the dogs were in the kennel. He believed packing upset them and didn't want them seeing any evidence of the process.

"Your alarm is set?" Cooper asked.

"Yes."

■ ■ ■

At the last possible moment, Cooper stepped off the elevator. Griffin had been shivering on the curb for a good while as the cabby sat behind the wheel fidgeting. It wasn't that Cooper was late. Cooper was never actually late. He was always just in the nick of time. It made cabbies antsy, and co-dependent Griffin felt responsible.

"Money?" Cooper asked. "Tickets? Passports?"

"Everything," Griffin said. "You?"

"Check."

■ ■ ■

The line inched forward toward the security checkpoint. It was all new, different, faintly menacing. It reminded Griffin of flying out of Tel Aviv. Except not really. In Tel Aviv, even the two year olds understood the protocols and followed them efficiently. Griffin's fellow citizens seemed totally flummoxed. It would be a miracle if anyone actually boarded a plane that morning.

■ ■ ■

"You're being very brave," Cooper muttered, fastening his seat belt.

"What?"

"I know you're terrified. There's no need. Think about it. You're much safer flying today than you would have been two months ago when everybody was still in denial about the threat."

So Griffin had been transparent after all. He tried his best, but as always Cooper saw through him. Why did he bother?

"Seriously," Cooper said. "Calm down."

That was a Luxemberg for you. Their fearlessness wasn't mere bravado. It was a triumph comprised of one part rational thinking and one part indefatigable optimism. Or looked at another way, pragmatism taken to the last reasonable extreme. Any further and they'd have been foolish. As it was, they were merely irrepressible.

■ ■ ■

Hours later, after a transcontinental flight unmarred by incident or turbulence, Manhattan appeared off the left wing. So far nobody looked like they were considering taking over the airliner, except for a grandmotherly type who obviously disapproved of the parenting skills of everyone on board accompanied by a small child. Griffin looked out at his first glimpse of gaping emptiness in what had been a familiar skyline.

II

Except for that absence, the city appeared completely normal. Surreally so, it seemed to Griffin, who had spent countless hours over the past weeks staring at images of Manhattan *Agonistes* on the television screen. As they emerged from the tunnel, all the familiar sights and sounds unfolded around the taxi. It was as if the whole thing had been a nightmare and Griffin was finally awakening.

"This is good," Cooper told the driver.

They got out of the cab. The driver wrestled their bags out of the trunk.

"We'll catch the train at Christopher Street," Cooper said.

"Right," Griffin said.

"Dad would have sent a car for us," Cooper said. Willi was a great patron of livery services.

"This is better," Griffin said. Nothing told him he was in Manhattan like descending the stairs to a subway station. It made him feel as intrepid as a mountaineer on the lower slopes of Everest.

"I thought so," Cooper smiled. "So tell me. Which way is Christopher Street from here?"

"This way," Griffin said, heading down the sidewalk.

"Very good," Cooper laughed, "for an out-of-towner."

■ ■ ■

Willi Luxemberg still lived in the family apartment on Riverside Drive where he and his wife had raised their four sons. Griffin never felt as much like a foreign presence in Cooper's life as he did when he stood looking up at the façade, which had actually appeared in a few movies and television shows. That's how evocative it was. And how alienating.

"Home, sweet home," Cooper said, an ironic smirk on his face.

Griffin wondered what they'd find upstairs. On their last visit the previous Christmas, nothing had changed since Shoshonnah's death except that her closet was empty. Was the entire apartment a time capsule, or had Willi started to move on?

■ ■ ■

"I don't know why you wouldn't let me send a car to pick you up," Willi said.

"We wouldn't have gotten here any faster," Cooper said. "Not at this time of day."

"It's not about that," Willi said.

Griffin had no idea when his father-in-law had last availed himself of public transportation. Probably not since the 'Sixties. Perhaps longer ago than that. Public transportation was something you left behind as soon as you possessed the resources, apparently.

"What else would it be about?" Willi demanded.

"Griffin loves riding the subway," Cooper said. "It's one of his favorite things about coming to New York. It's so different from MUNI."

Griffin squirmed. What Cooper said was true, but he'd just as soon not have it broadcast. He believed his in-laws already considered him too eccentric for Twenty-first Century life.

"Sure," Willi said. "I forgot. Riding the subway is a big deal for Griffin. I forget everything these days. Even that he's not a New Yorker himself, in which case he would know better."

Except he wouldn't. Griffin never tired of riding the MUNI. Stepping onto a MUNI car gave him a sense that life was worth living. And that he was actually someone approximating the man he aspired to be.

"He's practically a native as it is," Cooper said. "You should see him navigate."

"You're a good boy, Griffin," Willi smiled. "I could use a few more like you around here. This lunkhead. . ."

"Oh, Cooper has his uses," Griffin laughed.

"Good for moving furniture, right?" Willi nodded.

■ ■ ■

Josh and Andrew arrived carrying bags of Chinese takeout. Based on years of observation, Griffin had concluded that sitting down together and feasting on Chinese takeout was the minimally observant Jew's equivalent of Holy Communion.

"Pass the barbecue pork ribs," Cooper said.

It was like a priestly incantation to begin a ritual.

■ ■ ■

"What time is the funeral tomorrow?" Willi asked.

"There's not actually going to be a funeral," Andrew said. "Just a simple graveside service."

"What time is the simple graveside service going to be?" Willi asked.

"Joshua and I will meet you up here. We'll all drive to the cemetery together. We'll need to leave by ten."

"But what time is the service?" Willi insisted.

"It's at eleven," Griffin said.

"Finally someone who knows how to answer a simple question," Willi grumbled.

"Eleven," Josh corroborated.

"You sure we can make it all the way out there in an hour?" Willi asked.

"Why not?" Andrew shrugged. "Traffic's not so bad on a Saturday."

"Big crowd there, I expect," Willi said. "Two dead firefighters. Parking will be a nightmare."

"Cooper will be in the car with us," Josh said.

"What's that supposed to mean?" Willi asked.

"You won't need to worry about parking."

III

It was like being an extra in a movie, Griffin thought. He understood why it had to be the way it was, but the clichés still dismayed him. The long lines of firefighters looked ready to, well, fight fires rather than bury two of their fallen comrades.

"I know what you're thinking," Cooper murmured.

"What am I thinking?"

"Please," Cooper insisted, "just because it's all theatrical like this doesn't mean it's inauthentic. I know how displays like this bother you. But try to remember it isn't about you."

Fair enough, Griffin thought. This wasn't about him. Thus it wasn't accountable to his aesthetic sensibilities or his opinions. It was about Maribel, the boys, the whole family. It was about how you turned personal misfortune and tragedy into something everyone involved could think of as noble. As having meant something. The worst tragedy of all wasn't what had happened that day in lower Manhattan but the possibility that the event hadn't been important. If you couldn't believe in the nobility of the men, if you couldn't believe in their deaths as a sacrifice, what did you have to remember? Rubble? Smoke billowing across the sky? A million sheets of charred paper raining onto the streets? Crushed bodies? Nobody wanted to be reminded of horrendous details like those. Or to be forced to imagine the terror, the screams, the unseen moments of agony in those offices and stairwells, those bodies plummeting to earth. They wanted to believe that it all had a larger significance, to think of the people who had lost their lives as heroes. That was what they could stand to remember. This morning, like so many others since the attack, was about New York and how New Yorkers wanted to commemorate that terrible event. And how, indeed, did you commemorate the unthinkable? The incomprehensible?

You gave it a familiar shape. You translated it into something people could get their heads and hearts around. The shorthand for that was, Griffin had to admit now that he thought about it, the careful selection, orchestration, and portrayal of clichés. And the participation of those present in familiar rituals. The long lines of men in uniform, the tears shining on their tough guy faces betraying the vulnerability behind all that macho symbolism. The bagpipes keening "Amazing Grace", a call to faith and an antidote to despair. The solemn looking politicians clumsily simulating emotion beyond their ability to articulate and stumbling over their prepared remarks in a vain attempt to bestow a civic blessing that was ultimately inadequate to a moment of such profundity. Despite the regalia of patriotism on display in every direction, death and pain transcended notions of nationality and politics. The images, not the words, were what people could grasp. Those images were the ones they expected at such a moment. Those sights and sounds permitted, even facilitated, authentic grief. Leave questions about iconography and metacognition to the academics. Leave your cynicism in your other pants. Forget about analysis for now. Better yet, forever. Put on a play that expressed what the audience wanted to believe. That's what rituals were—what they had always been since the time everyone lived in caves.

■ ■ ■

A tearful hug for Eli. Manly handshakes for Liam, Tory, and Renzo. A kiss on the cheek for Maribel and another for Lisa, now visibly pregnant. How could they stand there like that? Hour on hour, as the mourners filed past, offered homespun consolation, platitude upon platitude?

Could Griffin do what they were doing if the men in the graves included Cooper? He'd have died himself rather than mourn unworthily, but where did you find such strength? Where did such dignity come from?

■ ■ ■

There was to be a private luncheon for close family. It wasn't possible to grab another moment with Eli before the long procession of black limousines snaked out of the graveyard. The hordes of other mourners followed.

"We'll see him tonight," Andrew said. "At Talbot's."

■ ■ ■

Talbot Kleinbaum was Eli's first cousin. One of the first men to approach the production of gay pornography from a modern, entrepreneurial perspective, he'd started out as a trust fund baby out for a lark but because the enterprise was, from his standpoint, more experiment than necessity, just got richer and richer. Cooper referred to the phenomenon as the sixty-ninth corollary to Murphy's Law: people made money in inverse proportion to their practical need for it. Griffin didn't really see the point of all that cosmetic surgery, but a guy like Talbot was going to spend his money on something, whether it was art of questionable aesthetics, twinkies of ambiguous orientation and questionable character, or drugs of immaculate provenance. For all his profligacy, Talbot was a notorious tightwad. But he was capable of overwhelming generosity from time to time. Thus, he was the obvious host for a gathering such as this.

The tradition had been born of necessity in the early days of AIDS. So many dead sons were taken by their grieving families back to their hometowns in Iowa, Mississippi, Wyoming, and New Mexico, where they were buried

412

in the accustomed manner beside great-grandparents, veterans of forgotten wars, children dead of epidemics—all the historic mortalities known to humankind. But in this instance, unfortunately, it left their authentic identities as gay men unacknowledged and unmourned and their real friends, their families of choice rather than biology, with no way of marking their passing, of staking a claim, as it were, to those memories, those lost lives, those submerged biographies. It wasn't something to be taken lying down, and gays and their allies hadn't. But it could only be subverted remotely. You couldn't stop the families from doing what they did. You could only celebrate an alternative kind of memorial. You got together, told your stories, cried your tears, and remembered your friends as they had truly been. You raised your glass not to the small town sissy who "just never found the right girl" but to the sharp tongued terror of the dance floor. You released balloons in the name not of the closeted high school librarian but the after-hours toast of Greenwich Village—the drag queen of the western world. You hugged and wiped away the tears of the widower, not the "special friend". So what if families disapproved of the men they'd become when they got to the big city? So what if families insisted on keeping secrets out of their own embarrassment? So what if small minded straight people wanted to avoid reality at any cost?

That had been nearly two decades ago, but gay and straight mourners still found it difficult to coexist peacefully. It was easier just to ignore each other at the funeral and then go on to the "afterparties" separately.

■ ■ ■

The distinction between the two groups had never been absolute, however. And in this case that truth was embodied in the person of Eamonn's youngest son, baby faced yet as monumental of physique as his father, the divine Lorenzo "Renzo" Lannaghan. If he hadn't existed, the gay community would have had to invent him. That's what an iconic figure he was. Griffin remembered him long before he attained that status, however. He remembered a black haired, hazel eyed three-year-old with a grave expression and a precocious vocabulary. In these two details, he had changed surprisingly little.

413

"Dad always said you and Cooper were the ideal gay couple," Renzo told Griffin after releasing him from an honest to God, old school "Hug of Death."

"He was an amazing guy," Griffin smiled, mortified at the compliment. "We'll miss him terribly."

"I know," Renzo said. "He's leaving a big hole."

"So you're in your final year of law school?"

"That's right," Renzo nodded. "I'll graduate next spring, if Dad's brothers don't kill me first. They're not sure what's worse. That I'm planning to be a lawyer or that I'm gay."

"But your father. . ." Griffin said.

"They still think he was just going through a phase," Renzo said.

"Gay isn't a phase."

"Not that," Renzo smiled. "They were perfectly happy ignoring the fact that he and Eli were lovers. They didn't see any need to object to it. Dad couldn't really be gay because look—he married a woman who could have made it as a fashion model, he fathered a bunch of sons who were all good at sports, and he was a bona fide hero of FDNY. And for that matter, Eli wears suits to work every day and makes lots of money. Since Jews are hopeless at law enforcement and fighting fires, what else should he be doing? If Dad was going to mess around with somebody on the side and it wasn't going to be a woman, Eli was perfect. You could take him anywhere and nobody would know. See, in their book, gay still means interior decorator, chorus boy, fashion designer, or hairdresser. And since Eli didn't lisp, could at least talk sports intelligently, and knew when to keep his mouth shut, it was easy to ignore what they wanted to ignore. What got their goat was that Dad didn't talk me into taking up the family trade. That's his unforgivable sin."

"Liam's a doctor," Griffin pointed out.

"Firefighters and police officers believe in the medical profession," Renzo said. "They depend on doctors when they're injured in the line of duty or when their wives and children get sick, and the potential for these things is constantly on their minds. Lawyers just mean trouble. Usually very expensive trouble. Or trouble that results in perpetrators going free or unworthy plaintiffs cashing in."

■ ■ ■

"You finally got your wish," Andrew said.

"What are you talking about?" Josh asked.

Beside him, Griffin could sense Cooper fuming.

"You never approved of Eamonn," Andrew pointed out.

"I approved of him just fine," Josh said. "I thought he was a great guy."

"You hated him as Eli's husband," Andrew said.

"He wasn't Eli's husband," Josh said. "That's the point. He never stopped being Maribel's husband."

"If you two don't shut the fuck up," Cooper growled, "I'm going to punch your lights out, one after the other. Then I'll help Talbot's husbands drag you downstairs and lay you out on the sidewalk."

■ ■ ■

"It's a damn shame is what it is," Talbot told Griffin.

"What is?"

"I could have made him a superstar," Talbot said. "Just like I could have made that husband of yours a superstar."

"Not everybody wants to be that kind of superstar," Griffin said.

"Maybe not," Talbot said, "but the gay community never has enough icons."

"The gay community doesn't seem to have anything but icons," Griffin said.

"Not the right kind," Talbot said. "Drag queens. Fashion designers. Chorus boys. Those aren't icons any more than a monkey swinging from the trees is an icon. We need icons who are real men."

"And having sex on camera makes them real men?" Griffin asked.

"It's not what they do on camera," Talbot said. "It's what they look like doing it. There's plenty of gay porn featuring nellie types."

"But it doesn't come from your studio," Griffin said.

"Damn right," Talbot said. "Keeping up a hypermasculine aesthetic is our mission."

"It's certainly made you lots of money."

"But it's not about the money," Talbot insisted. "It's about being faithful to my vision. And that vision isn't about porn, really. It's about how I believe gay men need to see themselves. As essentially men."

"Is it true that the biggest checks you ever sign are to 'straight appearing tops' who agree to bottom on camera?" Griffin asked, just to be argumentative.

"Sure," Talbot nodded, "but that's not merely iconography, it's economics as well. Supply and demand. The audiences go crazy for that kind of scene."

"Right," Griffin said, "so essentially you think it's a damned shame that the gay community never got a chance to watch Eamonn taking it up the ass."

"Among other damned shames, yes," Talbot said.

■ ■ ■

"Griffin darling," Jill Wagstaffe said, "perhaps you can explain to me how I end up in these predicaments."

She had arrived accompanied by her lesbian ex-lover, her soon to be ex-husband, and her new girlfriend.

"What predicaments?" Griffin said. "Every time I see you you seem to have the world by the tail."

"I may indeed give that impression," Jill said, "but. . ."

"Spare me the one about the 'tears of a clown'," Griffin laughed. "It's a lousy opera."

■ ■ ■

"He writes short stories," Josh said.

"Renzo?" Griffin asked. "I know."

"In German," Josh said. "He publishes them in German literary journals."

"My friend Scott works as a literary translator," Griffin said. "He's over there lots. It's apparently turning into a minor phenomenon. He says the Germans are finally starting to take an interest in their own diaspora."

"Yes, but look at him," Josh said. "You wouldn't think of him as a genius, would you?"

"Why not?"

"Oh, you would say that," Josh complained. "You're one yourself."

"What are you talking about?"

"I've heard your recital tapes from the old days. And that Ph.D. you got in your spare time. For no better reason than you were starting to get bored, apparently. And you've stayed married to my brother for over twenty years. If that doesn't make a man a genius I don't know what would."

■ ■ ■

"I feel so stupid," Griffin said.

"Why's that?" Eli asked.

"I can't think of a thing to say."

"Thank God," Eli said. "I'm up to here with homilies and epigrams. One more piece of well-meaning advice and I'll be ready to throw somebody off the terrace. I'm just glad you and that big lug are here."

"Who?" Griffin asked. "The transcendently stalwart Renzo?"

"Him, too," Eli said.

■ ■ ■

"Hardly any of these people really got him," Cooper complained, looking around the room.

"You're right," Griffin said. "You, me, those two guys over in the corner from his gym. And Renzo and Eli of course."

"It would be pointless to try and set the rest of them straight," Cooper said.

"Like teaching a pig to roller skate," Griffin nodded. "The point is, it's probably more important to be remembered accurately by a handful of people than to be idolized by thousands."

"Is it?" Cooper asked. "Is that really the point?"

IV

Regardless of the circumstances, Griffin's in-laws were ruthlessly pragmatic. Learning the date of Eamonn and Mick's funeral, they calendared a ceremony of their own for the next day. The fact that a Christian funeral more or less couldn't be held on a Sunday while Jewish cemeteries were closed on Saturday dovetailed the two events perfectly. The fact that there was no hard and fast rule about when an unveiling was supposed to take place only made it simpler.

■ ■ ■

Shoshonnah had been buried in Rosie Stern Wallach's family plot in a cemetery in New Jersey. And now, a little over a year since her passing, it was time to visit the spot again, to pull the gauze back from the grave marker and reveal the polished black surface, the simple inscription.

A year ago when they buried her here, the towers had still stood proudly. A year ago, no one had imagined a day like the one when they fell. Things like that shouldn't have happened, just as women who loved life so passionately shouldn't die before their time. Three score and ten years, sure. She'd only missed that by a few weeks. But Nanny Freitag had lived to nearly a hundred. Shoshonnah's family tree was full of people who had lived well into their eighties and nineties. She should have had that kind of time herself. Should have seen great-grandchildren born. Should have laughed with Cooper as his black hair shot through with silver. Should have explored the globe with her beloved husband for another decade or so before having to slow down. Should have finally hit the long anticipated big one in the casinos.

Sometimes the imperfection of the world was more than Griffin could bear.

"I never knew my own mother," he said when it was his turn to speak. "Shoshonnah taught me what a mother was."

■ ■ ■

The usual suspects were all present. Rosie Stern Wallach and her husband, Lou. Rosie's three sons and their wives, though Rosie's grandchildren were otherwise engaged. Shoshonnah's close friends, Babbo and Fina, and their husbands, who reminded Griffin of low level Mafiosi though he wasn't even allowed to think it because of its possible similarity to reality. Several of their sons and daughters, who were all stereotypically east-coast Italian and whom Griffin could never keep unraveled in his mind, so thoroughly entangled were the two families. A handful of former employees of Luxemberg Jewelers, now long closed. And, escorted by Jill Wagstaffe and the magnificent Renzo, good old Eli.

■ ■ ■

Genikayte and Emilio stood hand in hand looking down at the marker. Genikayte's wish had been granted. Her father and mother had stayed away. Griffin couldn't look at the two young people together without imagining a collar and leash around Emilio's neck. That marriage would be over the day Emilio decided he'd had enough. And Genikayte wouldn't shed a single tear over it.

■ ■ ■

"Maribel and the boys send their greetings," Eli told Willi. "They really appreciated it that you were there yesterday."

"It's great to see you, son," Willi said. "Shoshonnah always referred to you and Eamonn as sons number seven and eight. Five and six were Naftali and Griffin here."

"I know," Eli said. "I remember. She was always very kind to us. Eamonn appreciated it so much."

■ ■ ■

"I'll be coming to San Francisco for a visit soon," Renzo said.

"You'll stay with us, of course," Cooper said.

"I wouldn't want to put you out," Renzo insisted.

"Don't talk nonsense," Cooper growled. "You're family. You'll stay with us. As long as you want and whenever you want to come. And if there's any way you can stuff that one into your luggage. . ."

"Whole reason for the trip," Renzo said. "Get Eli out of New York. Get him some perspective on what his life can be now."

"We're depending on you," Griffin said. "Please take care of him for us."

"Done," Renzo nodded.

V

Knowing that Cooper wouldn't be content with spending just two days in the city, Griffin had taken extra days of personal leave so they could stay through Monday and travel on Tuesday. Once in New York, Cooper would need to see as much of the city as possible just to be assured it was still there. As searing as the televised images of the tragedy had been for Griffin, they were worse for Cooper. He was a true son of Manhattan. The attack had been like a knife to his own heart.

■ ■ ■

The subway would have been faster, but you couldn't see what Cooper needed to see from underground. They took buses and they walked. The weather was cool but sunny. The city, all but that devastated few blocks of it, was recognizably itself. The people still swaggered. The swagger had been transformed, however. Happy-go-lucky before, it was now defiant.

■ ■ ■

Griffin ticked off the landmarks. He knew the list. He knew the route Cooper would take from one to the other as if he'd planned it himself. They were medieval pilgrims, feeding their souls by visiting holy sites.

■ ■ ■

They reached the fire station just before nightfall. The façade was plastered with photographs, greeting cards, posters crafted by school children. All these weeks later, people were still bringing flowers. American flags were ubiquitous. Mournful looking teddy bears stood watch.

■ ■ ■

"I know you guys," a voice came out of the twilight.

Griffin turned. A tall young firefighter regarded them from an open doorway.

"You were at the funeral Saturday."

"I'm Cooper Luxemberg," Cooper said. "This is my husband, Griffin MacDonald."

"Patrick McGinley," the young man said. "You're the guys from San Francisco. Eamonn talked about you lots."

"He was a great man," Griffin said, barely able to speak.

"They all were," McGinley said. "They're all missed."

"You haven't been with the department long," Cooper said.

"It shows?"

"You can't be more than nineteen," Griffin said.

"Twenty-three," McGinley grinned. "Guys younger than me died that day."

"Right," Cooper said.

"You know," McGinley said, "I'm not sure how to put this. I've never said it to anybody. But when Mick died it felt like part of me died, too. I know he was straight and had a girlfriend, but. . ."

VI

Tuesday morning Renzo picked them up in Liam's Audi.

"Shouldn't you be at the gym?" Cooper asked, watching his bags being loaded into the trunk.

421

"Already went."

"School then," Cooper suggested. "Or walking Eli's dog or something."

"You guys came all the way to honor Dad and Mick," Renzo said. "Least I could do."

"Shoshonnah as well," Griffin said.

"Mrs. Luxemberg was like a third grannie for us," Renzo said. "And a lot more fun than the other two."

"All her surrogate grandkids say that," Griffin said.

"We could have taken the train downtown and then got a taxi out to Newark," Cooper said.

"What he means is 'thank you'," Griffin smiled.

"Sure," Renzo nodded. "You could have booked a shuttle. Willi could have called his usual driver. There are all kinds of ways to get to Newark. This is what Dad would have wanted."

"That's a very convenient excuse," Cooper said. "I expect you'll be trotting it out lots."

"For as long as it works," Renzo grunted. "And don't worry. I actually have a driver's license."

"I'm sorry my husband is so insistent on being obnoxious," Griffin said. "We really do appreciate the ride."

"Obnoxious," Renzo snorted. "He's being a New Yorker is all."

"See," Cooper said.

"Thing is, Dad and your mom were two of a kind," Renzo said.

"How do you figure that?" Cooper asked.

"Who do you know that was determined as those two to ignore any limits people tried to set for them?"

■ ■ ■

This was the new normal, Griffin thought as he stood in line at the security checkpoint. Empty spaces in a skyline and in your heart. Jagged, razor sharp edges where there should be smoothness. And these endless lines whenever you wanted to get on a plane.

DECEMBER, 2001

In addition to tragedy, Eli thought, there were monstrous ironies in the event. Eamonn and Mick were heroes who had given their lives attempting to save others. At the "temporary" office his firm now occupied in midtown, Eli was a hero for having been the first to run away. His example in beginning the evacuation at the first sign of trouble had prompted others to do the same. That timely and prudent reaction had saved lives, according to his bosses, though Eli couldn't manage to see it as anything other than an act of craven cowardice. Once he'd made the initial suggestion, he was out the door. He hadn't even stayed long enough to see if anyone was following him.

But they had been.

"I told the other secretaries," Alicia Jefferson said the first morning they had assembled in their new quarters. "I said, 'Mr. Danziger already left. And he's got lots of friends in the fire department, so he knows what to do at a time like this. Now, I don't know about you girls, but the company doesn't pay me enough to risk my life for it.' That's what I said, so help me Baby Jesus."

All day long, working at his shiny new, terrifyingly unfamiliar desk, Eli received a steady stream of visitors expressing their gratitude. Even as they'd been making their exits, the building P.A. system was encouraging everyone to stay in place. Following his example had saved them. He was embarrassed to the point of mortification by this attention. But his bosses insisted on a ceremony. Not in his honor specifically, of course. They billed it as "moments of remembrance, reunion, and renewal," but his role on the day received prominent mention.

When he described the event and his reactions to it to Renzo afterward, the response he encountered surprised him. Renzo saw no irony in the situation at all.

"How many people did your firm lose?" he asked. "Wasn't it no more than a handful?"

"Two," Eli told him. McGillicudy and D'Agostino. Two fratboy junior account men. They'd been obnoxious fuckups, but their ineptitude shouldn't have meant a death sentence.

"Two," Renzo nodded. "Out of several hundred employees in the office at the time. And on a floor that high. How many others might not have left in time if you'd waited?"

"There's no way of knowing, of course," Eli insisted.

"Here's what I do know," Renzo said. "You're very senior in that firm. People look up to you. It would have been different if one of the secretaries had been the first to leave. Or an intern maybe. Nobody would have paid any attention. But when it's Eli Danziger heading for the exits people take notice."

■ ■ ■

Eli replayed his last moments with Eamonn over and over. They'd been totally inconsequential. Somehow that made the memory sting even worse.

■ ■ ■

Eli knew he was supposed to remove Eamonn's toiletries from the medicine cabinet, but he couldn't bring himself to do it. Eamonn had never completely taken up residence at Eli's apartment, but he kept one of everything there for when he spent nights. Eventually, after one of Renzo's visits, Eli noticed that it was all missing. At first, he was furious. A few days later, he realized the depth of his gratitude at Renzo's thoughtfulness.

■ ■ ■

During the weeks after Eamonn and Mick's funeral, Eli found himself becoming obsessed with the young Englishman he'd met at the coffee cart each morning. His last glimpse of the man, a businesslike nod through the narrowing gap as the elevator doors were closing that morning, tantalized him. They had never exchanged names. Eli mentioned it to Renzo. He was confiding a lot in Renzo lately. Too much, really, but Renzo never complained. Renzo seemed to take it for granted, actually.

"The British Embassy issued a list of U.K. citizens killed or missing," Renzo said. "It's well over a hundred, I believe. But based on age and sex you can pare that down. Then it's just a matter of doing google searches. If you can't identify him that way, then he probably made it out."

■ ■ ■

That's what Eli wanted, of course. To verify that the young man wasn't among the dead or missing. To know that, though they'd almost certainly never meet again, the young man's loved ones weren't going through what Eli was. A few days later, Eli found what he was looking for in an archive piece from the *New York Times*.

Peer's Son Feared Dead in Twin Towers Attack

Peregrine FitzMerlin, son of Lord FitzMerlin of Langemere and Routhenedge and heir apparent to one of Britain's most ancient titles, is missing and presumed killed in last week's terrorist attack on the World Trade Center. FitzMerlin, 33, was employed at Cantor Fitzgerald, whose offices in the North Tower were located above the impact zone. The death toll among Cantor Fitzgerald employees is in the hundreds. In emails which FitzMerlin sent to several individuals including his brother, Rupert FitzMerlin, during the moments prior to the tower's collapse, he expressed his intention to jump from the building. As yet, no remains have been identified.

Peregrine Olaf St. John Andreas Benedict FitzMerlin was born in London on April 1, 1968 to Gawain Claude Risely von

Osterwald und Langebacke FitzMerlin and his wife, Britta (nee Jegelevicius). Gawain FitzMerlin succeeded as the 27th Lord FitzMerlin on the death of his father Percival Nils Joachim Ethelbald, 26th Lord FitzMerlin, in 1994. Peregrine became heir apparent to the title at that time, his older brother, Rupert Lars Petro Ingebrit (b. 1966) having previously renounced his claims to the title and lands. Peregrine is survived by his parents, his brother Rupert, his brother Crispin (now heir presumptive), nephews Archimedes Janusz, Viktor Lars-Olaf, Sven Gregor, and Markus Pavel, as well as numerous cousins and uncles. . .

As evocative as this information was, it seemed inconclusive to Eli, who needed something more substantial by way of identification. He found it in the London *Times*, which was more subdued in its tone but provided what for Eli was the telling detail: the older brother Rupert was identified as a resident of San Diego. Eli recalled his last conversation with the young man, in which they had discussed his recent return from a trip to visit his brother there. Based on Rupert's name and location, it took Renzo only moments to provide Eli with an email address.

■ ■ ■

That year Hanukkah began almost exactly two weeks before Christmas. Eli's sisters and cousins took turns hosting. There was an event to attend each night and woe be to him, especially this year when the entire tribe was determined to "cheer him up", should he skip one of the gatherings in preference to another. He distributed his usual greeting cards, checks included, to his nieces and nephews and the handful of great-nieces and nephews as well. They were all on their best behavior, very careful to mention how much Eamonn was missed. Most of them even managed to sound sincere. He supposed they were. It was more and more difficult with each passing week to keep his cynicism in check.

"Oh, Eli," his sister Hannah sniffed. She hosted the first night. "I so hope you don't feel we weren't welcoming enough of Eamonn all those years. We did try, you know."

He tried to be a better man than he actually was, but only briefly.

"It doesn't really matter what I feel," he told her.

"Oh?"

"At this point, the only thing that matters is what he felt," he said.

She looked alarmed for a moment.

"He thought you all were terrific."

He ate latkes and played with dreidels until he felt seriously overdosed. Maybe next year would be easier.

■ ■ ■

He spent Christmas Eve at the grand gathering of the Lannaghans. Eamonn's parents were still alive and remarkably spry. He knew Eamonn's German mother had always been more troubled that he was Jewish than that Eamonn was in a same sex—not to mention adulterous—relationship, but she never failed to treat him cordially and this year was no exception.

Flanked by Maribel and Renzo, he distributed his usual greeting cards. These featured a shepherd boy on a hillside surrounded by his flock and gazing up at a single star. The Lannaghans preferred cash, which was much easier for his bookkeeping.

"God, Eli," Eamonn's brother Klaus-Peter sobbed, unleashing gusts of whiskey breath in his direction, "you're the best, you know that? The God damned best. The way you took care of our baby brother—you, too, of course, Mar—I can't help gettin' weepy thinkin' about it."

Maybe next year would be easier. Or just maybe there wouldn't be a next year. Maybe Eli would go to Hawaii instead, for instance.

■ ■ ■

Eli joined the Luxemberg clan, Willi, Josh and Andrew, and Genikayte and the divine Emilio, for their traditional Christmas Day observance: a movie, followed by Chinese food in their favorite restaurant near Rockefeller Center. The movie was the big blockbuster of the season, which they had all avoided

427

seeing so as to save it for the big day. Geni sulked throughout the meal and Emilio exhausted them all with his clumsy but endearing efforts to cheer her up.

Afterward, Eli stood with Willi on the sidewalk out front while Andrew and Josh went to get Andrew's car.

"Christmas just isn't the same any more," Willi said. "Not with Shoshonnah gone. You're the only one in this crowd who understands how it feels, Eli."

■ ■ ■

By New Year's Eve, he was finished with holiday cheer. Cousin Talbot was hosting his usual bash, of course. And Josh and Andrew invited him to dinner. Jill Wagstaffe called requesting his services as her escort for a posh do on the Upper East Side. They all warned him in the sternest possible terms against playing hookie. But that afternoon, he pled the onset of flu symptoms. He had already laid in a goodly supply of takeout. He refused to turn on the television. When it finally got late enough, he took Beowulf for a walk and unplugged the phone the minute they got back in the door.

He tossed Beowulf an extra ration of Milk Bone, booted up his computer, and sat down to send that email he'd been putting off.

Hello, he wrote. *We haven't met, but I knew your brother, Peregrine...*

He meant it to be the last goodbye except for the one he didn't think he'd ever be able to say.

■ ■ ■

For such a short message, it took a ridiculously long time to compose. He looked it over a final time and hit send. Then he went off to bed, where Beowulf was already waiting. He lay awake for a long time wishing there would be a miracle. The only one he could imagine—the only miracle worthy of the name—was waking up one morning to find Eamonn lying next to him and realizing that the whole hideous thing had been a nightmare.

■ ■ ■

Each year, Eamonn greeted the new year the same way. "The best is yet to come," he would say. "Just wait and see."

He'd been right every time but the last.

FEBRUARY, 2002

Honest to Pete, the cabbies of Manhattan were psychopaths. This pedestrian had been rolled onto the hood, bounced off the windshield, and landed on the pavement before being run over by a rear wheel of the taxi. Dr. Patel was about to finish the splenectomy. Then they'd be ready to close.

Maribel said "honest to Pete" these days, not "honest to God." She didn't even think "honest to God". God was on probation. He had a lot of explaining to do. She refused to take Him seriously as long as He failed to prove that He wasn't one of the bad guys. So far He'd shown no sign of an intention to talk her out of her newly discovered skepticism. For Him everything was apparently business as usual. This, she thought, must be what Jews felt when they thought of the Holocaust. If He was everything people said, why hadn't He stopped it?

■ ■ ■

When Maribel got out of surgery, Dr. Altschul was waiting for her.

"No, doctor," she said, ignoring the bright eyes and Technicolor smile. Resolution was her middle name when it came to men like Dr. Altschul. Literally. She'd made it the first of her New Year's resolutions, and so far she'd kept every one. "I'm very sorry, but I can't help you today. I've already done a double shift. I'd only put your patient at risk."

"Relax," he grinned. "I just want to buy you breakfast."

■ ■ ■

"How was the Caribbean?" Maribel asked. She couldn't even bring herself to speak the name of the island.

"It wasn't quite everything I might have hoped for," he smiled. This time that smile was toned down substantially. That's how she knew it was genuine. Everybody smiled like that these days. You saw a smile like that and you required no further explanation. Only small children and the deranged smiled like in the old days. He looked at least five years older lately. Still breathtaking, just not so juvenile. His actual age, in other words. She liked him better this way, but there was no telling how it played in the clubs.

"I expect it wouldn't have been," she said.

"Still," he said, "I suppose the trip was worth it. If only because it wasn't as bad as I was anticipating."

"That's something," she smiled.

"It's a great deal, I think."

"I believe you were very brave even to try it," she said. "I couldn't have faced revisiting the setting of my honeymoon."

■ ■ ■

"What is it you're not telling me?" Maribel asked. He had offered to drive her home, and she hadn't been able to say no. Still a sucker for a pretty face. You'd think she'd know better by now.

"You're just like Mom," he laughed. "I couldn't keep secrets from her, either."

"So?"

"I've given two weeks' notice at the hospital," he said.

"Oh?"

"I'm enlisting. I'll go into the army as a captain, and I'm shipping out to Afghanistan pretty much the minute I put on my uniform."

"You know I'm supposed to talk you out of something like this," Maribel said.

"You promised Mom," he nodded.

"That was our agreement," she nodded. "However, I'm not going to try. You're at least as stubborn as any of my male relatives. And that's saying a lot."

"I have to do this," he said.

"I know," Maribel said. "For that matter, she knows."

"Those bastards in Washington are hell bent on taking us to war," he said. "Afghanistan isn't going to be the last of it. It's barely even a down payment. They've got a comprehensive plan for the Middle East. Lots of boys are going to get shot up so Bush and Cheney can get their rocks off, and someone's going to have to put them back together. That's where I come in."

"It'll be dangerous, of course," she said.

"At least as dangerous as getting out of bed one morning and going to work in a tall building," he nodded.

■ ■ ■

Maribel didn't know if Dar and Renzo compared notes at the gym or if they'd come up with their theory independently. They believed that the government had been expecting the attack. There was ample intelligence beforehand, Renzo insisted, and her own reading on the internet seemed to confirm it. The powers that be hadn't tried to stop it because they wanted a pretext for a general conflict in the Persian Gulf. Bush I had left the job unfinished at the end of Desert Storm and now Bush II had to go in and redeem the family honor. When advised of the threat, Bush and Cheney put out the word that terror attacks shouldn't be stopped, just monitored. They were depending on the American public's gullibility as much as its patriotism. But they were also making dangerous assumptions about the enemy. "You've seen one terrorist fanatic, you've seen them all" was apparently the mantra in effect at the White House. A rookie mistake if there ever was one—underestimating your adversary. As far back as Roman Catholic elementary school, Maribel had known better. Trust the shadowy men who actually ran America to get it wrong. Their wives could have told them, but men like that didn't listen to their wives any more than they had to. When the time came, of course, the attack was much worse than Bush, Cheney, *et al* expected. There wasn't supposed to be such horrific loss of life. There wasn't supposed to be such devastation. Their banker buddies would never have agreed to such economic disruption. American political culture being what it was, none of this signified defeat, just miscalculation. And deniability. Above all, that. Because when had an American politician ever been held accountable for anything that mattered?

Thus spake her youngest son and her "adopted" one. For all she knew they were right. It wasn't that hard to believe. In fact, it was almost impossible *not* to accept Renzo's explanation. The media ridiculed any and all conspiracy theories, and the ones the media mentioned were indeed ridiculous. CIA operatives hadn't hijacked those planes. The whole thing hadn't been staged by the NSA with help from George Lucas and Steven Spielberg. Aliens from distant planets hadn't been involved nor had the Knights Templar, the Freemasons, or the Trilateral Commission—whatever that was. But Renzo and Dar were no wild eyed loonies. They were intelligent, well informed young men and their theory made perfect sense. So much sense that when the experts were ruling things out, they didn't even address possibilities such as the ones Renzo and Dar raised. That, as far as Maribel was concerned, was as close to definitive proof as anyone should need that her young men were correct.

That's why she'd lost her husband and son. Not because of a bunch of crazed loonies hiding out in the desert and dreaming grandiose dreams of bringing the west to its knees, but because a bunch of Republicans wanted to play macho games and a bunch of bankers were worried about oil prices. It almost made her ashamed to be an American. Except if she was sure of anything, it was who the real Americans were.

■ ■ ■

"I get it," she told him. "Really."

"I knew you would," Dar said.

"Join the Army. See the world," she said. "That was their recruiting slogan when I was a girl. You'll come over for dinner before you leave. We'll gather the tribe. You're one of ours now."

■ ■ ■

So that was Dar's way of putting things right, she thought later that night while emptying the dishwasher. At least on the limited scale any individual was capable of doing so. Use his skills—near supernatural ones, she recognized—to save lives the "bad guys" on both sides of the conflict were all too ready to squander. She understood the impulse and she could certainly respect it. She couldn't imagine his mother, formidable as she was, would have been able to talk him out of it. But the thought of it terrified her. A field hospital seemed to her a perfect target for rocket attacks. And that was just for starters.

II

"Maribel?"

"Artie," she smiled. She had arrived at the restaurant early. She wanted to watch his entrance. She knew him the instant he stepped through the door, though she couldn't say how.

He slipped out of his coat and hung it over the back of his chair before sitting down across from her. He did this methodically.

"You look exactly like your photo."

"You sound surprised," Maribel said.

"Most of the women on that website apparently haven't had a picture taken in the last twenty years. I'm thinking it's some sort of cult."

The website was a highly specialized one for widows and widowers of the Twin Towers. She already knew his wife had worked for Cantor Fitzgerald, just as he already knew about her husband and son.

"I have nothing to hide," she laughed.

Artie apparently thought he did. He hadn't posted a picture of himself. He had chosen the *photo available on request* option. She didn't request. She'd had enough masculine pulchritude to last a lifetime. It came with too many complications. Or maybe she wanted to avoid comparisons with her late husband. And this was what she got. He was chubby and he was bald. He dressed expensively but nondescriptly. He reminded her of a veteran sofa that had been banished to the rumpus room. A little threadbare, but you couldn't wait to sink down onto it. The twinkle in his eye, however, struck her as unnervingly familiar. It didn't seem possible that you could go on a website and come up with someone so perfect on your first attempt. Perhaps God did exist and She was a middle aged female contemplating the prospect of a solitary old age.

"Well, it's certainly a pleasant surprise," he said.

"Thank you," she said. "It's nice to meet you, too."

"Your posting didn't say anything about a job," he said. "What is it you do?"

"Guess," she said.

"Television anchorwoman," he said. "You've got that look."

"Oh, Artie," she laughed. "Those women are such idiots. They don't give a thought to what comes out of their mouths."

"Sorry," he said. "I'm not really good at this."

She almost asked "good at what?" but didn't want to embarrass him further.

"Try again."

"All right," he said. "Fashion consultant."

"Ouch," she said. "That's even worse. I'm an O.R. nurse attached to the trauma unit at St. Vincent's."

"Jeez," he said. "Brains, too."

She knew she was beautiful, of course. She was used to bowling men over, even at her age. It wasn't so long ago that the producers of Jill Wagstaffe's soap had tried to hire her. She promised to consider it. Not because she was interested in beginning a career in acting but because she wanted to gauge Jill's reaction. That had been instructive, to say the least.

"All right," she said. "I showed you mine, Artie, now. . ."

"Oh," he said. "I work on Wall Street."

"I was leaning toward clergyman," Maribel said, making it up as she went. "Presbyterian, most likely."

"My last name's Shapiro," he said.

"Just goes to show you can't judge a book by its cover," she laughed.

"That's for damned sure," he said, finally giving her an honest to Pete smile. "What's good here?"

"Dear Artie," she said. "I wouldn't dream of patronizing you. But I come here specially for the lox and *schmeer*. Though I believe the matzoh bry is also very highly regarded."

■ ■ ■

"This was very nice," he said.

They were on the sidewalk out front. There was an icy breeze coming up the Hudson. It made her feel like a girl again.

"I had a great time," she agreed.

He shuffled his feet. It wasn't that cold. She sensed his uncertainty. He didn't think he was in her league.

"I hope I didn't make you late for your appointment."

"Not at all," she said. "It's just two subway stops and a five minute walk from here."

"That's good."

"My next day off is Tuesday," she said, taking the bull by the horns and giving Artie a quick kiss on the cheek. "Let's do this again."

III

"Thank God you're here," Masai Nakawatase said. "I never understand a word the doctor says."

In Maribel's day, you waited nine months. When the baby finally came, it was in the form of surprise package and stranger. The new technology of obstetrics had taken lots of the guesswork out the process, but also, Maribel thought, lots of the fun. Lisa was having twin boys. Their heads were currently visible on the screen of the ultrasound unit.

"And look," Dr. Schoenstein said, sounding like a tour guide on the Circle Line, "those are the legs."

"It's not as mysterious as it seems," Maribel said. Masai and Lisa were like peas in a pod. If Masai was any indication, Lisa was going to be the perfect daughter-in-law. That would be a nice change after Tory's wife, Nancy, who was a perfect nightmare. What a catastrophe that marriage turned out to be. Maribel had bit her tongue thousands of times during their courtship, so now she was in no position to say "I told you so." It was a lesson she had learned from her mother in law.

"Well, in my day. . ." Masai began.

This was the clue for the two grandmothers-to-be to dissolve in giggles.

IV

"The forecast for Tuesday is sunny," Helga Lannaghan said. "With a high in the fifties."

"Is it?" Maribel asked, squeezing lemon into her tea.

"I checked," Helga nodded. "I always check the forecast."

Against my work schedule, Maribel thought. She knew she wasn't supposed to be impatient with her mother-in-law, but it was getting more and more difficult. Still, she came at least once a week for tea and pastries. Helga Lannaghan was many things. Master baker was one of them. Ignoring her bossiness was the price you paid for perfect strudel.

"So I was thinking, you know."

"Do I?" Maribel asked. "Know what?"

"Klaus-Peter is off that day as well," Helga said. "I already asked him to drive us out to the cemetery."

"Oh."

"Of course," Helga said, "if you're still not ready. . ."

V

Maribel surveyed the contents of the refrigerator with satisfaction. It was going to be a nice dinner party. Renzo would bring his own food, of course. He wouldn't subject his abdominals to her lavish cooking. On the other hand, Dar's abdominals were about to become property of the Department of Defense and thus to have to follow orders. So Maribel needn't alter her menu planning in deference to either her youngest son or the guest of honor. The rest of her brood, with the possible exception of mother-to-be Lisa, presented no problem at all. They'd eat what she put in front of them. They'd even like it. Her heterosexual sons didn't have the imagination not to, and Eli's manners were too good to allow any dissent on his part. The sleep she'd lost over the years in anticipation of entertaining. Eamonn had been right to try and talk her down all those times. Now that she was over it, he was in no position to know. The new world they all inhabited was chock full of ironies of that sort.

Maribel wished Dar wouldn't leave. Surely there must be a way he could get out of his enlistment. But she wouldn't try to talk him into or out of it. If there was one thing her life had taught her it was that people must be allowed to make their own choices. That was the only way you maintained relations with them. You either refused to interfere or you found ways to interfere without anyone realizing it. And in Dar's case, she was still too low on the learning curve for the second. She only wished she knew something about gay matchmaking. The look on his face the last time he'd been over for coffee and they watched Renzo and Horst loading the dishwasher together had broken her heart.

◼ ◼ ◼

Artie was waiting for her at the entrance to the park. He lived somewhere here along the west side, though he hadn't yet identified for her his building or even the street. Whatever his address, it meant money. He might not be seriously rich, but the location required a higher degree of affluence than she'd ever dreamed of enjoying. The idea made her nervous. She hoped she hadn't given him the wrong impression.

"There you are," she said, pecking him on the cheek.

"Mar," he smiled. "Punctual as Big Ben."

"Honestly," she laughed, "every time we meet you look like you weren't expecting me to show up."

His smile turned sheepish.

"I'll never stand you up, Artie," she said. "I'm not that kind of girl. If I decide I'm not coming, I'll call."

"Sure," he said, staring at the ground.

"Seriously."

"O.K."

"What?"

"You're the only woman I've ever known who truly understands the concept of comfortable shoes. It must be your career."

"You sweet-talker," she laughed.

"Shall we?" he asked, offering her his arm.

■ ■ ■

Honest to Pete, Maribel thought, watching Dr. Banerjee make her first incision. The bicycle messengers of Manhattan. . .

APRIL, 2002

I

People kept telling Eli it was time to move on, but it wasn't as simple as they made it sound. Move on, sure. But didn't you have to have something to move on to? Eli still had his job. He still had his apartment. He still had Josh just downstairs. He had his faithful terrier, Beowulf. Basically he had everything except what mattered most. What all those concerned friends and acquaintences meant, of course, was "find a new boyfriend." But how the hell did you do that when you were over fifty years old? When your hair was gray—though his friends all referred to it as silver—and your abs, sharp as they might be for a man your age, would never be mistaken, even in the most flattering light, for those of a ripped, satin skinned thirty year old?

Most recently even Maribel had started in on him. She was dating a man who'd lost his wife in the attack. He had grown children and even a couple of grandsons—toddlers. He was sweet, funny, and kind, and Maribel was guardedly optimistic. Straight survivors of the catastrophe had formed support groups and constructed networks. Surely gay survivors had done the same. Eli should look one up. And by the way: there was no time like the present. Well, more power to her. If she had met someone nice that way, someone who understood the feelings and was prepared to share the day to day struggle, why the hell not?

But Eli wasn't sure he wanted somebody like that. It sounded like settling. He'd given up too much in the past for the sake of his late husband to consider such a compromise at this point. Really, he wasn't sure he wanted somebody at all. What he wanted, of course, was the one thing he couldn't have: Eamonn back. On any terms.

■ ■ ■

The city was ravishing that spring, as if in rebuke to the attackers. "You can scar me," it seemed to be saying, "but my essential beauty can never be obscured." Or maybe that was only what Eli wanted to believe. That underneath the superficial damage the city was actually unscathed. He desperately wanted to believe that. And in an effort to preserve the illusion he absolutely refused to go farther downtown than his own block of Hudson immediately south of Barrow. People he knew went to view the site. Maribel and the boys went— not that they were boys anymore, of course—and came back somber. Renzo reported that the experience was "moving", whatever that meant. But Eli didn't want to be moved. He wanted to be allowed to go on pretending that nothing had changed. That sooner or later the nightmare he was trapped in would dissipate and everything return to its rightful place. Seeing the site in person, as opposed to viewing second hand images, would, he sensed, destroy that possibility forever.

■ ■ ■

One thing had changed, however. And Eli didn't have the heart to resist it. Beowulf now slept in the bed with him. Beowulf had been a birthday gift from Eamonn three years back. Eli had never thought of himself as a dog lover, and the gift seemed a strange one at first. That few pounds of wiry, dark gray brindle coat wrapped around the militant alertness of a Doberman and the majestic self-possession of a Saint Bernard had seemed as cryptic as a yeti. Eli couldn't imagine what Eamonn was thinking of. Cute, yes. But what did a dog like that need with a man like Eli? "He'll let you know," Eamonn said in response to the question.

He had known what he was talking about. Beowulf communicated his faith in their new relationship by taking it absolutely for granted from the first instant. Eli found this strangely reassuring. Being taken on walks by the little dog several times a day, being reminded to keep food and water dishes topped up and the treat jar stocked gave his life a meaning it lacked whenever Eamonn wasn't around. And overnight, Eli, who had lived in the neighborhood for over a quarter century, went from invisible to a minor celebrity. People constantly stopped them on their walks to wish Beowulf good day or ask his opinion of things. And before long they began including Eli in their conversations as well. It was like being a papal bodyguard or lady in waiting to a queen. Beowulf took for granted that he was the monarch of that quarter of Greenwich Village, and people regularly made inquiries as to his biography. Most frequently they asked if he was a Scottie, but as far as Eli was concerned there was no resemblance. A Cairn, once Eli read up on them, seemed as distinctive as could be.

Since his earliest puppyhood Beowulf had never shown any interest in sleeping in the bed. Not even on nights when Eli was alone in the apartment. Which was most nights. Five or six of them each week. Eamonn set him up with a luxurious and very expensive doggie bed and Beowulf occupied it like a potentate. Except for a few moments each morning just after Eli's alarm went off, when the little tyke hurtled "onboard" for a serious cuddle, the bed was reserved for humans.

Then, the night of September 11, he staked his claim. When Eli came into the bedroom to lie down that night, the little dog was already curled up on Eamonn's side of the bed, his back against Eamonn's pillow. Eli had spent most of the day on the telephone with one or another of the Lannaghans as they all tried to convince themselves that Eamonn and Mick would show up safe. But Beowulf believed—or somehow knew—otherwise, and Eli took it as a sign.

■ ■ ■

Over the next few days it became apparent that Beowulf believed he had been ordained. No longer was he Eli's second string guardian angel. Now that entire load was on his shoulders. But the tilt of his head and the attitude of his tail when he stared at Eli conveyed his confidence that he was up to the challenge.

II

There was a small park near the apartment, but they only went there when the weather forced them to. Beowulf preferred, and Eli seconded his choice, a "members only" dog park a few blocks farther away. For a monthly charge, they had the privilege of swiping Eli's key card at the gate and gaining admittance. Beowulf could romp off leash on beautifully maintained grass surrounded by privacy hedges and security fencing, under the watchful eye of the matrons who ran the place with surprisingly gruff voices and icy, tight jawed glares. Eli was terrified of them, but Beowulf insisted they were a necessary evil and essentially benign, and he was probably right. Dog owners had been banished from the grounds for minor infractions of the rules, or in a few cases merely because they seemed capable of committing such infractions at some undetermined time in the future. Dogs were allowed somewhat more latitude. Playfulness was encouraged because, as Eli had heard one matron say, "Dogs will be dogs", but there were limits. The dogs themselves seemed to know where the lines were drawn. The paramount concern appeared to be safety. For the dogs at least. Eli could certainly appreciate that. Beowulf was generally what Eli thought of as friendly but slightly aloof, preferring diligent explorations of the grounds to socializing. That Saturday morning Eli was mildly surprised to see his dog in the company of an unfamiliar Yorkie, a silverback sporting a similar coiffure to Beowulf's, i.e., a rather butch, rugged looking cut. When it was time to go, Beowulf seemed genuinely sorry to say goodbye to the little chap, who followed them nearly to the gate before turning back.

■ ■ ■

"Those two are certainly devoted to each other," Mrs. Van Schuyten said the next Saturday. She was one of the reigning matrons of the park. Everything about her proclaimed her identity as an affluent New Yorker of a certain age, roughly a decade older than Eli but ruthlessly maintained.

Thirty feet away Beowulf and the little Yorkie wrestled on the grass.

"No kidding," Eli said. "My boy hates leaving when that little guy is here. I practically have to carry him out the gate. I wish I knew who his little friend belongs to."

"You don't know?"

"No idea."

"Zephyr lives with us," Mrs. Van Schuyten said. "Us" meant Mrs. Van Schuyten and her two Havanese, Duchess and Daisy, acknowledged royalty of the establishment.

"I didn't realize."

"He's only been with us a few weeks," Mrs. Van Schuyten explained. "He was my son Erik's dog."

Eli noticed her lip quivering slightly.

"Oh?"

"Erik worked for Cantor Fitzgerald."

The firm's offices had been located on some of the floors of the Twin Towers most isolated by the attack. The death toll among their employees was horrendous.

"Oh," Eli said. "I'm so very sorry."

"It's been difficult," Mrs. Van Schuyten said. "He was my youngest. His older brothers worked in the building, too. Thank God they had no trouble getting out. My grandchildren are very fortunate."

"I understand," Eli said.

"Do you?"

Eli felt a single tear leak down his left cheek.

"You do," Mrs. Van Schuyten nodded. "Who was it?"

"My friend was a fire fighter."

"Friend?"

Eli nodded. He couldn't speak. That first tear had been joined by others.

"Oh," she said. "That kind of friend. Erik was gay. He didn't have a friend like that, I'm sorry to say. I'm afraid he wasn't a very happy person. His father and I were as supportive as we knew how to be, but apparently that wasn't enough."

Eli still couldn't speak. The dogs had ranged closer. Their play sounded blood curdling, but that was terriers for you.

"The young man I see here with you sometimes? Very athletic looking? Very handsome?"

"He's the son," Eli said. "The youngest of four boys. One of his brothers was also lost."

"I'm so sorry. How long were you and the father. . . ?"

"Since before the two younger sons were born," Eli said. "It's a long story."

■ ■ ■

Thursdays had been Eli and Renzo's dinner nights since Renzo started law school. He was now getting ready to graduate. Eli would pick up Chinese takeout on his way home from work and Renzo would arrive a while later with precooked chicken breasts, which he would warm up in Eli's microwave, or canned tuna, which he would drain and dress with unsweetened non-fat yogurt. They'd watch television or just talk. Since Eamonn's death, the evenings had taken on an almost religious significance, though they rarely spoke of Eamonn or Renzo's brother Mick. Eli knew that Renzo was serious about his new boyfriend when he brought Horst with him one Thursday night. Horst looked like the type for chicken breasts or tuna but turned out to be devoted to Chinese takeout, which was terrific because Eli always bought too much and then had trouble disposing of the leftovers.

The chemistry between Renzo and Horst was unmistakable, but it was Horst and Beowulf who had fallen in love at first sight. Horst spoke German to the little dog and then provided the dog's "responses" in a gruff but squeaky voice that somehow captured Beowulf's personality perfectly. Renzo understood the "conversations", of course, and sometimes joined in. Eli's Yiddish had never been strong and was really rusty at that point, but he managed to get the gist of what Horst and Beowulf "said" to one another. Mostly this consisted of stories of Beowulf's secret life while Eli was away at work all day. His neighborhood friends, whose moms and dads were also off making a living, dropped by to play cards, drink, smoke cigars, tell stories about chasing "tail", and generally celebrate dogs' day out. Eli wasn't used to thinking of Germans as humorous people, and Horst seemed particularly serious minded otherwise, but Eli loved this zany side of his stepson-in-law—or whatever it was Horst was turning into before his eyes.

■ ■ ■

They had a long spell of truly atrocious weather. Beowulf didn't take kindly to being cooped up but equally hated going out in it, even decked out in the little New York Yankees and Rangers slickers that Renzo was always buying for him. It was a full two weeks before they saw Zephyr and Mrs. Van Schuyten again.

"You told me that Zephyr has been with you for a few weeks," Eli said, hardly knowing how to frame his question.

"Yes," Mrs. Van Schuyten nodded. "At first he went to live with my mother-in-law. It wasn't the best arrangement, but she insisted on it. She used to breed Yorkies and felt that qualified her to be his new owner. But then recently she had to give up her apartment."

"That's too bad," Eli said.

"Actually, it was overdue. The last couple of years were nerve wracking. I was sure she'd burn down the building she lived in. Or poison herself. She loves her new place. We didn't say anything to her about what kind of establishment it is when we moved her in there. She seems to have concluded that she's on an extended stay at an exclusive resort."

"My grandmother reacted that way," Eli said. "At least at first."

"Yes," Mrs. Van Schuyten said. "It's a blessing, really, that stage when they're confused but still happy. And she apparently doesn't remember Zephyr at all. For that matter she hardly remembers me or my husband. Some days she believes she's aboard a cruise ship and refers to him as her cabin steward."

"Well, lucky for Zephyr you were able to take him."

"It would be," Mrs. Van Schuyten said. "The board of our co-op has bent over backwards to be nice about it. But they're beginning to be impatient. The by-laws are very specific. No more than two dogs per apartment. My husband

447

is inclined to just pay the fines once they start coming, but I'm not sure I think that's the best solution."

III

"I have no idea why she would want me there," Eli said.

"You're family," Renzo said. "Mom wants us all to meet this guy. Liam says it's about to get serious."

"How the hell is she planning to explain me?"

"Who says she has to explain you?"

"Come on, Renzo," Eli said. "You know better than that. There's no precedent, is there? 'This is my late husband's boyfriend?'"

"Mom knows her boyfriend better than you do. For all we know he has all kinds of gay connections."

"As in 'some of my best friends are. . .'" Eli made a face.

"Stop agonizing over it," Renzo said. "Mom's not taking no for an answer and neither am I. Horst will be there, too. If there's any possibility of this guy becoming our stepfather, he's going to have to deal with us all exactly as we are."

■ ■ ■

So Eli showed up Sunday night at Maribel's apartment. Liam was there with his latest Barbie doll clone. When you were a handsome young doctor, there was apparently an endless supply of young women like that available to you. Tory was there solo. His and Nancy's most recent attempt at a reconciliation had failed. Lisa was big as a house. She was having twin boys and looked as if she might go into labor at any moment, even though the due date was still three weeks out.

"Ah, here you are," Maribel greeted him.

"You probably have plenty here to drink," he said, handing her the carrier bag, "but I picked up a couple of bottles just in case."

"Thank God," she laughed. "None of my sons has decent taste in wine. And I'm too cheap to buy the good stuff only to have them guzzle it like Koolaid."

"Where's the guest of honor?" Eli asked.

"Out on the terrace with Renzo and Horst. And before you get any ideas about going out to rescue them, you need to know that Artie has a couple of gay nephews. And an old roommate from college he's still buddies with. So relax."

■ ■ ■

That wasn't the most surprising thing about Artie, however.

"It's great to finally meet you, Eli," he said when they had a moment to themselves. "Maribel assured me her family wouldn't so much as blink at a Jewish boyfriend, but it's certainly good to have another member of the tribe in the room."

"The Lannaghans are an equal opportunity bunch," Eli laughed. "Irish, Puerto Rican, German, gay, straight, Asian. . ."

"Asian?" Artie raised an eyebrow. "I might have to draw the line there. But I'm not sure who you're referring to. I didn't notice anyone here fitting that description."

Lisa's last name was Nakawatase. She might sound like Manhattan, but she looked like Tokyo.

"Very funny," Eli said. "It had occurred to me you might just be pretending to be Jewish, but with a sense of humor that terrible, there's no question you're genuine."

"There you go," Artie laughed, slapping his back.

■ ■ ■

"It's so nice tonight," Horst said. "We should pick up Beowulf and go to the park."

"You two must have better things to do on a Saturday night," Eli laughed.

"It's a great idea," Renzo said. "That place never closes, does it?"

"Open all night," Eli said.

"Good," Horst said. "Let's go."

449

"And no post mortems of the evening," Renzo said.

"None?" Eli asked.

"All right," Renzo said. "Just one. That was Mom laying all her cards on the table. She wanted Artie to know exactly what he'll be getting if he decides to take things farther. Her gay son and son-in-law. Her half-Japanese grandchildren-to-be. And you, Eli."

■ ■ ■

Eli thought they might have the park all to themselves. They almost did. The only other dogs present were Zephyr and the two Havanese, which presumably made the gentlemen in evening clothes Mrs. Van Schuyten's husband and son.

"Edward Van Schuyten," the older of the two said, extending his hand.

"Eli Danziger," Eli said. "And these are my stepson, Renzo, and his boyfriend, Horst."

Renzo had recently insisted that "stepson" rather than "nephew" was how Eli should refer to him. Eli wasn't used to it yet.

"This is my oldest son, Edward, Jr."

Everyone was pleased to meet everyone. The Van Schuytens were the type of straight men who always made Eli a little self-conscious. He stood up straighter, stiffened his jaw and wrists, and took care how he enunciated when in such company. Renzo and Horst, however, went on holding hands as if it was the most natural thing in the world.

"And this must be the famous Beowulf," the older Edward said, bending down and scratching the proffered muzzle. "My wife doesn't generally approve of any dogs other than her own, but this little fellow has stolen her heart."

"And I have to confess," Eli said, "I have a real soft spot for Zephyr,"

"He's a magnificent little beast, isn't he?" Mr. Van Schuyten agreed. "Erik wasn't a good judge of people, I'm afraid. But he really got it right with that guy."

"For a fleabag he's not bad," the younger Mr. Van Schuyten said in a private school drawl, "but if you're not careful, Dad, he's going to get you evicted."

"They'll have to deal with my attorneys first."

"I thought they already had," the younger Mr. Van Schuyten said. "Weren't papers served?"

"Early innings," his father said. "I'll bankrupt the board over it, if necessary. And call in the tabloids. Can you imagine what they'll do with the story? That face on the front page of the *Post* under the headline *'World Trade Center Orphan Threatened with Homelessness'*? I won't have anyone forcing me to give up your brother's dog. Now, will you look at those two play? You'd think they were littermates."

"They're quite devoted," Eli said.

■ ■ ■

"What were those men talking about?" Renzo asked when they finally headed toward home.

"There's a limit on the number of pets per unit in the Van Schuytens' building," Eli said.

"You mean there's trouble over Zephyr?" Horst asked.

"I don't think it's that serious," Renzo said. "Who'd go up against a guy with a jawline like that?"

IV

"Hello."

"Eli, Henry Frankel here. We met at Josh and Andrew's Seder."

Eli had been dreading this call, which somehow seemed inevitable.

"Hello, Henry. Of course I remember you."

"I hope you don't mind. Josh gave me your number."

Eli did mind. He minded a lot. But it wasn't Henry he blamed.

"It's fine," he said.

"The thing is, I've got Yankees tickets for Thursday night next week. Andrew told me you're a baseball fan. I was hoping you might join me."

There would be hell to pay if Eli turned him down. On the other hand, the consequences of saying yes might be nearly as dire.

"I'd like that, Henry."

"You would?" Henry sounded surprised.

"Sure."

■ ■ ■

Eli regretted saying yes almost immediately, but he couldn't bring himself to call the date off. Henry was nice enough, he supposed, although it had been a little tedious listening to Henry's story of nursing his partner, Jacques, through his final weeks. Eli already knew as much about lung cancer as he ever wanted to from watching Aunt Layne die of it. Yes, Henry was nice enough, but Eli did wish that men his age wouldn't color their hair. Having gone gray in his late twenties, he understood the impulse. He'd been on the point himself, but Eamonn put his foot down and that was the end of it. Even now, Eli couldn't consider it. He got wanting to look as young as you could. But it always looked so fake. It seemed almost as pathetic as wearing a toupee.

■ ■ ■

"Tell me honestly, Eli," Maribel asked over the top of her menu, "what did you think of Artie?"

"He wasn't quite what I was expecting."

"You mean he wasn't anything like Eamonn," she said. "I know. Balding. Paunchy. Stereotypically Jewish."

"I hadn't noticed," Eli said.

"Right," Maribel laughed. "The thing is, I've done the superhero thing already. And I'm not shopping gene pools these days. Artie is gentle and considerate. He makes me laugh."

"So he is like Eamonn after all," Eli said.

"In the ways that count," Maribel nodded.

"Is it serious?"

"Who knows? It's nice just as it is. If something more is in store for us, that's fine. But I'm not holding my breath."

"One day at a time," Eli nodded.

"Like you know anything about that," she scoffed.

"I'm told it's the secret recipe for happiness," Eli chuckled.

"Happiness is such an overused word, don't you think?"

"No," Eli said. "Why would you say such a thing?"

"I think what people are really hoping for is contentment," she said.

"I'm not sure people think of contentment and happiness as different things," Eli said.

"Perhaps not," Maribel said, "but happiness seems like so much work."

"What did Artie think of all of us?"

"He said he thinks I'm a very lucky woman," she said. "And I suppose I am."

Her pager started to vibrate. She checked the message.

"Lisa," she said. "I'd better head for the hospital."

"I'll come with you."

■ ■ ■

It was a fast labor, especially for a first time mother.

"Damn that girl," Maribel said on the elevator up to the room. "I was in labor for several days with Mickey."

Eli remembered. He and Eamonn had only been dating for a short time when Mick arrived. At the time, he certainly hadn't been thinking about greeting Eamonn's grandchildren decades later.

"It's just not fair," Maribel said.

"I think you have to give her a break for presenting you with your first grandchildren."

"I wonder what she's going to name them," Maribel said. "I won't have any dead family members being memorialized that way. She promised me she wouldn't, but when a girl's just given birth she's not necessarily thinking clearly."

"Would it be such a bad thing?"

■ ■ ■

The babies looked like their father at that age. Eli remembered newborn Mick vividly. But they had heads of thick black hair.

■ ■ ■

"Remember," Maribel instructed. "You're going to list Michael David Lannaghan as the father on the birth certificate. Masai, don't let her forget."

Masai Nakawatase, Lisa's mother, taught tenth grade English to the children of the plutocracy at a private school on the Upper East Side. Lisa's father worked on Wall Street. They were Episcopalians. Eli didn't know why he thought that was funny. He supposed he must be a tiny bit racist.

"I'd like to name the older one after you, Eli," Lisa said.

"With your permission, of course," Mr. Nakawatase said.

"I'd be deeply honored," Eli said, "but I can't imagine why you'd want to do it."

"Oh, I think I can explain," Lisa said. "You and I enjoy similarly ambiguous positions in the Lannaghan tribe."

"You're going to throw that up to me for the next fifty years, I suppose," Maribel snorted. "That makes you as real a daughter-in-law as it's possible to be, marriage license or not."

■ ■ ■

"She's bound to marry some time," Eli said, as they rode the elevator back downstairs. "You can't expect to hold her hostage just to ensure your access to Mick's sons."

"Eli, Eli," Maribel shook her head, "surely you know me better than that by now."

"Do I?"

"Of course you do," Maribel said. "She'll marry just as soon as she's ready. Which will be a few months to a year after I pick out the guy."

"You're going to pick out the guy?"

"Well I'm certainly not leaving it up to Masai," Maribel said. "I mean she's very nice, of course. But I can't imagine who she might come up with. Besides, I'm already working on it."

"Huh?"

"I've made a list."

■ ■ ■

Episcopalians were not very restrictive about who was allowed to serve as godparents. Eli had learned all about the Roman Catholic rules involved back in Mick and Renzo's infancies. In comparison, the current situation seemed downright anarchistic. Lisa asked Renzo to be godfather and her sister Kimiko Morgenstern to be godmother. Kimiko had converted to Judaism as a matter of conviction. She hadn't even met her husband-to-be at the time. As a minimally observant Jew, Eli was invariably skeptical on the topic of conversion, but in Kimiko's case he had to admit she was not only sincere but knowledgeable enough to have made an authentic choice. It was fascinating. Her husband, Steven, was an air traffic controller who worked out of Newark. That didn't seem very Jewish. But he attended the christening wearing a yarmulke. So he was apparently more Jewish than Eli.

■ ■ ■

Renzo looked less like Eamonn than any of his brothers. Liam, for instance, was practically the image of his father. But unlike the others, Renzo had taken up bodybuilding. That's where his resemblance to his father was most apparent. A somewhat different head, but sitting on top of the same body. For Eli's money, he was the most attractive of the bunch, including the score or more of male cousins. That afternoon he was so handsome it hurt to look at him.

"He loves you, Eli," Horst muttered, standing next to him in the sanctuary. "They all do. Don't forget that."

■ ■ ■

As always with the Lannaghans and their many tributaries, it was the party afterward that mattered. The Nakawatases were a small family, based out of an apartment Chelsea. Maribel's parents were still in the family home out in Queens, complete with lush back yard. They hosted the celebration.

■ ■ ■

How many times had Eli stood under the huge trees in that backyard sipping wine and nibbling hors d'oeuvres while listening to snatches of gossip from all directions and savoring the beauty of everyone present? This addition to the gene pool provided by the Nakawatases would only sharpen and refine what had already been ridiculously photogenic. The twins, Eli and Tetsuo (for Lisa's uncle who had died on Okinawa), were stunning babies. Jill Wagstaffe, who was absent that afternoon due to multiple bookings, was already insisting that an agent be hired to represent them. Identical twins, she said, were a potential gold mine in casting terms. If you had a role for an infant or toddler, you needed to hire twins because of the child labor laws.

Eden had its serpent, and today's gathering boasted Andrew Rubenstein.

"We heard your date with Henry went very well," he gloated.

"Sorry," Eli said, "I must have missed something. Was that a date? I thought it was the Yankees versus Boston."

"Eli," Andrew shook his head and actually went so far as to shake his index finger. Sometimes Eli didn't know how Josh stood being married to him.

"Didn't I tell you not to bring it up today?" Josh chastised. "He'll only get his back up."

"You shouldn't be so particular, Eli," Andrew said. "You're not getting any younger, you know. Henry's got a great job. His apartment is bigger than yours and on a better street."

"Better than Hudson Street?" Eli laughed. "No such thing."

"You know better than that," Andrew said.

"Hon," Josh protested, "leave him alone about it. You promised Henry you wouldn't interfere."

"How come he never promises me anything like that?" Eli asked.

■ ■ ■

"The attorneys have stopped trying to talk sense to Edward," Mrs. Van Schuyten said. "They've simply refused to proceed any further in the matter."

"Really," Eli said, watching Beowulf and Zephyr pretend to kill each other. The christening party was still going on for all he knew. At a certain point, he simply had to get out of there. It was wrong that Eamonn wasn't there glorying in his new grandsons. Everybody felt it, of course. But nobody there felt it the way Eli was feeling it. Only one creature in the cosmos was capable of that kind of empathy. Beowulf had given him that certain look as he'd come in the door that said everything Eli was feeling. Ten minutes later they were here. Zephyr had been waiting at the gate as if by some canine form of telepathy.

"The fact of the matter is that no matter how sympathetic the members of the board are to our predicament," Mrs. Van Schuyten continued, "they can't make an exception. It would mean setting a precedent, and they don't dare. The litigation alone would bankrupt them. And of course, if the board is bankrupt, we're all bankrupt by association."

"What's going to happen to Zephyr?" Eli asked. The prospect of Beowulf losing his new friend was almost as painful as Eli's loss of Eamonn. He didn't know how the two of them would face it.

"Nothing for the moment," Mrs. Van Schuyten said. "I know better than to try to change Edward's mind at this point. He's out shopping for new attorneys as we speak. But it won't be long until he gives up. I've already resigned myself to losing the little fellow. And it's going to be a bitter pill, I can tell you. He's the last thing we have of Erik."

"Of course," Eli nodded.

They stood for a long moment in the twilight. The Havanese surveyed the rampaging terriers with serene disdain.

"Eli, dear, I have no idea as to the nature of your living circumstances," Mrs. Van Schuyten said, "but is there any way you might see your way clear to helping us out?"

V

"I had a really good time tonight," Henry said.

They were at the Roxy Deli in Times Square sharing a post-show slice of cheesecake. Henry was attractive, funny, considerate. He'd make somebody a great boyfriend. It was a shame, really, that Eli was allowing him to waste his time like this. Still, he had to make an effort. He'd never hear the end of it if Henry gave Andrew the impression that he hadn't at least tried.

"Sondheim never lets you down, does he?" Eli mused, trying his best to ignore the unnatural shine off Henry's hair, which had just been in for a tune-up.

"That's for sure," Henry agreed.

The moment grew awkward. Eli wondered what he else was supposed to say, if anything.

"Listen," Henry said, "you're a hell of a nice guy. Handsome, too. But really, Eli, there's no chemistry between us, is there?"

"Honestly?" Eli asked.

"Honestly," Henry nodded.

"I'm sorry," Eli said, "but there's not."

"Thank God you get that," Henry said. "I know Andrew's all hot to play matchmaker. But I just can't see us together. I told Josh before I ever asked you out that I thought it was a waste of time."

"You did?"

"I'm very sorry about this," Henry said. "I thought maybe they were right and I did need to try something new. And the way they described you—well, you really are wonderful. But the truth is you're just not my type."

"There's no need to apologize," Eli insisted.

"But I'd hate it if you thought I was rejecting you," Henry said.

"Aren't you?"

"Eli, you're just not old enough. Why, you're almost the same age as me. It would be like having sex with one of my brothers."

■ ■ ■

"Are you still speaking to me?" Josh asked.

"Stop acting pathetic," Eli said. "Every time you roll out that act, I understand why you're a stage manager these days."

"Ouch."

"You deserved that," Eli said.

"Double ouch," Josh laughed. "Would it help if I promise never to do it again?"

"Not really," Eli said. "Seeing as you're not really the guilty party. And there's no possible way you'll ever get Andrew under your thumb."

"I've already told him I'm not going to help him any more with this project."

"Listen," Eli said. "I get it. You two just want me to be happy. And in Andrew's book the only way that can happen is if I find a new husband. But maybe that's not the answer."

■ ■ ■

"Oh, good," Mrs. Van Schuyten said, rushing up to them in the lobby. "I wanted to catch you before you went up to Edward's office."

"And good morning to you," Eli laughed. If he let it, her anxiety could rub off on him.

"Renzo, Horst," she said, looking at them closely, "what gorgeous suits. Are they Hugo Boss by any chance?"

"Yes," Horst nodded.

"I knew it," Mrs. Van Schuyten nodded. "Erik never wore any other label. He had dozens of Hugo Boss suits. All either navy or charcoal. It used to drive his father crazy. 'what's wrong with brown?' he'd ask. As if there's anything right about a brown suit. Honestly."

"We both needed suits for the christening," Renzo said.

"Well, you look like a thousand dollar an hour attorney if I ever saw one," she smiled.

"Speaking of attorneys," Eli suggested.

"Yes," she nodded. "That's what I wanted to talk to you about. And it's a good thing you're here, Renzo. Edward has no idea you're still in law school, you know. He's under the impression that you've already graduated and been admitted to the bar. He assumes you're representing Eli."

"He does?"

"I may have led him to believe that," she smiled.

"In that case, it's all true," Renzo said, squaring his shoulders.

"Good man," she said. "The thing is, the adoption contract they've drawn up is ridiculously fierce. But that's for Edward's benefit, not yours. Our attorneys want to get this thing over with, believe me. But they've got to put up a good show or Edward will smell a rat. And that rat's name is Estelle Winwood Van Schuyten, yours truly. I'd go in there and object to several of the provisions if I were you. If not a full half dozen. Anyone looking at Beowulf knows Eli's capable of looking after a dog properly."

"I'll advise my client accordingly," Renzo said.

"Excellent," she nodded. "Oh, Eli, it makes me so happy to think of little Zephyr moving in with his best friends. You won't desert us at the park, I hope."

"Don't worry," Horst said. "We won't let him."

■ ■ ■

"Erik called me," Mr. Van Schuyten said, "as soon as he realized he had no chance of getting out of the building. My secretary said he was on the line, but I couldn't imagine what he needed to talk to me about. We practically never spoke. He and his mother were very close, but I might as well not have existed."

"Edward," Mrs. Van Schuyten protested, "that's hardly fair."

"To him or to me?"

"Both, I presume."

"He believed I disapproved of his lifestyle," Mr. Van Schuyten said. "Even I know better than to call it that. Sexual orientation isn't a lifestyle, is it, Eli? It's an identity."

"Sure," Eli said.

"I loved my son," Mr. Van Schuyten said. "That's the point I'm trying to make. And whether Erik figured that out at the end or not, I couldn't tell you. I hope and pray that he did. He said he was calling me because he didn't want to upset his mother. I had no idea what he was getting at. Just then my administrative assistant came in. She'd arrived at work late because of the chaos on the subways. She was hysterical. Between her and Erik, they filled me in. He knew he was about to die and he was terrified. Who could blame him?"

"Darling," Mrs. Van Schuyten said, "you don't have to put yourself through this."

"I want Eli to understand," Mr. Van Schuyten insisted.

"He does," Mrs. Van Schuyten said. "Renzo does as well. Renzo's father was a firefighter. So was his brother."

"It's all right," Renzo said. "Let him tell it. It helps to tell the story. Nobody knows that better than me."

"All I could promise him was that we'd take care of Zephyr," Mr. Van Schuyten said. "That was the only comfort I could offer my son as he faced death. I left the office immediately. I headed down to the Village. Erik lived off Grove Street. I got to his building. I took the stairs two at a time. When I got to his floor I could hear Zephyr howling inside the apartment. It was the most pitiful sound I think I've ever heard. I'll never forget it until the day I die. It was almost like listening to Erik himself. He jumped, you know."

There was a long silence in the room.

"So you will do your very best," Mr. Van Schuyten said, tears streaming down his face, "with our precious little Zephyr. You have to, Eli. It's a sacred trust. We're putting all our faith in you."

"So shall we go over the contract terms?" Mr. Van Schuyten's attorney asked.

"I don't think that will be necessary," Mrs. Van Schuyten said. "Will it, Edward?"

461

MAY, 2002

Even a meathead like Yoel couldn't spend all day every day at the gym. And sitting around waiting for his pilot's license and flight instructor's credential to come through was driving him out of his mind. So Cooper and Griffin's Labradors got lots of extra walks. They loved the cityscape and loved showing it off to him. Today's playground was the Marina Green. Strictly speaking, he wasn't supposed to let them off leash. But they loved a good romp, they were invariably friendly with people and other dogs—many of whom were off leash, too—and they never went near the street. What could it hurt? The dogs always returned when he called them, often bringing things they had found. That morning what they brought back was a tall, distinguished looking Englishman roughly the age of Yoel's father.

"Good morning, Yoel."

"Mr. Westerleigh."

"What a stroke of luck, running into you."

But Yoel knew there was nothing random in Ned's sudden materialization. Yoel's handlers had been in touch. Their instructions couldn't have been clearer.

"It was such a pleasure meeting you at brunch last week," Ned said.

Yoel had spotted him then. So this handoff wasn't a complete surprise. Only the identity of his new keeper and the schedule and manner of their contact had been left undetermined when Yoel got on his flight in Tel Aviv.

"You have a beautiful apartment, Mr. Westerleigh."

"You know, Yoel, I believe you'd better call me Ned. It was a pleasure to have you in my home."

■ ■ ■

Yoel had no idea, really, whether Ned had been chosen as his new keeper because Cousin Cooper had agreed to be his immigration sponsor or Cooper had been chosen as his immigration sponsor so Ned could be his new keeper. Cousin Josh could have been called on to sponsor him, which presumably would have meant a keeper in Manhattan. Or perhaps because of Ned New York had never been an option. Yoel hadn't given it much thought. As always, Blumenfeld's people did his thinking for him. So he didn't know the back story and didn't care. Nor did he care about the outcome. He wasn't expected to care. In fact, it was much better if he didn't. He understood this, and kept his attitude properly adjusted. He simply did what he was told and went where he was sent. As always. And anyway, he wasn't going to require much maintenance. Not now that he was inactive.

"No, no," Blumenfeld said that chilly afternoon on the waterfront in Haifa. "You did nothing wrong. It's not your fault that certain parties refused to act on the information you provided. It's their mistake, absolutely. Theirs and theirs alone. We don't even know for certain that your cover was blown. But we can't take the risk. There are too many players involved. Al Quaeda. The Americans. The British. Several governments in our region and elsewhere. Not to mention free lancers of all descriptions. The situation is simply too complex. There's too much to lose, at least potentially. I'm afraid you're going to have to accept that for the foreseeable future our service can't use you. And that's a great loss, truly. Now listen to me. Before you go getting any ideas. . ."

"What ideas?"

"I know you, Yoel," Blumenfeld said. "Probably better than your own mother does. Definitely better than your own mother, come to think of it."

Yoel's mother was a poet. Not just any poet, but one of the most prominent Israeli poets of her generation. Yoel's Grandmother Schlesinger never tired of telling people this, but it was true nevertheless.

"All right."

"Please understand. No shopping yourself to other services. No Americans. No Russians. No Brits. Absolutely none of the regional competition."

"I wouldn't," Yoel insisted.

"Calm down. I know that. But some people think you might. Some people still don't believe that men such as ourselves—you know what I'm talking about—can truly be reliable. Understood?"

"Yes," Yoel said. The people Blumenfeld was referring to had been happy enough to use his sexual orientation as a tool of espionage when it suited them, but it was too much to ask that they'd ever consider him respectable.

"They'll eliminate you at the slightest hint and blame it on terrorists," Blumenfeld said. "They have no compunction whatever. So this is as much a life and death situation as you've ever been in. You must think of yourself as still operational. Even though you won't be, the level of risk you're facing will not change."

"I get it," Yoel said.

"In fact," Blumenfeld continued, "it's been decided that you're too hot even to stay in Israel."

"You're joking."

But it was no joke. There was a brief visit to Tel Aviv to pack his things and make his few goodbyes. His family was let in on his "rehabilitation". It was the only way he could face them. He was no longer that notorious homosexual whose military career had been destroyed by scandalous behavior. He had never been a male prostitute. Except in the line of duty, which didn't count and was classified information anyway. He was a national hero, albeit only a secret one. Still, it was enough to satisfy his father. Yoel couldn't put a price on that. And henceforth, if his loved ones saw him at all, they'd see him in, ironically, the nation where he'd done his most crucial spying. The nation which, in a double irony, now made it impossible for him to live in his homeland. The United States was his destination. San Francisco specifically, where Cooper lived.

■ ■ ■

"You'll be exactly who you are," Ned Westerleigh said. "That's the best kind of legend, really."

Yoel had releashed the dogs. They were napping on the carpetlike grass. The fog was burning off by the minute. If he let himself, he could fall in love with this city. What was holding him back? The possibility of something else, he supposed. Or maybe his recently ended career had left him incapable of believing in the possibility of permanence.

"And who is that?" Yoel growled.

"You know, my boy," Ned said, "your resemblance to your cousin is uncanny. And I'm not just speaking about the physical likeness."

"Everyone says that."

"Who it is, as you say, is Yoel Luxemberg, Israeli Air Force veteran and flight instructor. I have with me your new credentials. Not forgeries like those you were using in San Diego. I'm sure they were excellent. I know your employers' work. Nothing but the best. Foolproof, no question. But good only temporarily, so they won't do in this case. These are bona fide, FAA issued, periodically renewable, backed by documentation, and on file in D.C. Next Tuesday you'll report here." He handed Yoel a business card. "That man will interview you and you'll be hired on the spot. Immediately thereafter, based on your new employment, Cooper and I will help you lease an apartment. All documented and verifiable. It's the start of your new life."

Yoel knew better than to ask a question like "*what if it's not the new life I want?*"

■ ■ ■

"That's terrific," Griffin said. "In fact it's more than terrific. It's perfect."

It was Griffin's last day of school before summer vacation. He'd gotten home early. He was puttering in the kitchen when Yoel came in with the dogs.

"You think so?"

"Why wouldn't it be?" Griffin asked. "I thought that a job like that was the plan all along."

"Of course," Yoel said.

466

II

Most of Cooper's close friends were gym rats, though not all their boyfriends were. Griffin, for instance, fit as he obviously was, rarely set foot in the place. The whole crew met every Sunday for brunch, each week at a different couple's home. Yoel hadn't known it at the time, but that brunch with Ned Westerleigh was a special occasion his handlers had requested as a prelude to handing him off. Today was the real thing. Cooper's friends being who they were, the weekly menus featured lots of things Yoel could actually eat. He wasn't used to guilt-or-frustration-free socializing. For that matter, he wasn't used to socializing at all. He was starting to like San Francisco.

■ ■ ■

"Two time Mr. Israel, isn't that what I heard?" Nick Romanovsky nodded. "You really ought to think about entering the California championships."

"Cooper says I'm at least a year out from it," Yoel said.

"And he should know," Nick's husband Tristan said. He, too, was a gym rat. According to Griffin he'd accumulated almost as much silver statuary—at least the plated stuff they made trophies from—as Cooper himself.

"But don't let that discourage you," Nick said.

"Discourage?" Yoel laughed. "Me? My last name is Luxemberg."

■ ■ ■

Yoel had already met many of Cooper's friends at the gym. Seeing them all here in Scott and Jared's sleek, International Style home, dressed in street clothes rather than workout gear and in their respective pairs, he realized he was being sent a message. This was what his new life was supposed to look and sound like. This was how gay men of his age and social class interacted. This was the kind of identity he was meant to create and inhabit. But this identity, unlike all the ones in his past, was one he shouldn't expect to emerge from three or six months from now. Or even a year or two. This, unlike those previous incarnations, was meant not merely to be impregnable—because they'd all been designed with that in mind—but permanent. The question was no longer how to present an impression of authenticity. The question now was as to the nature of authenticity itself.

■ ■ ■

Though they were first cousins, Cooper and Yoel were a generation apart in age. Which meant, reasonably enough, that many of Cooper's friends were men in or approaching middle age. The kind of men, in other words, whom Yoel's handlers had deployed him against on numerous occasions. Honey traps were far from extinct in that shadowy world. They continued to be a tried and true tactic. You would have expected people to know better by now, but they didn't. Freud had been right about the influence of the sex drive on human behavior. Yoel had an aunt on his mother's side who was an authority on Freud. In honor of this, his Grandmother Schlesinger constantly spoke of Freud to anyone who would listen. Sometimes her explanations of Freudian principles were even accurate. Perhaps that exposure was responsible for Yoel's orientation, though he doubted it. In any case, the experiences with those men had left Yoel with what he thought of as an aversion to the whole generation. But Cooper's friends were different. They were as accustomed to being the prey as the predator in sexual matters. And they were at home with their sexuality, whereas Yoel's exploits had generally been predicated on the fact of his targets' being anything but and thus easily exploited or set up for blackmail. The more time he spent in the company of men like the ones at Cooper's gym and at this morning's brunch, the more it looked as if this dynamic wasn't going to be a problem in his new existence. And since the gang's overall *raison d'etre* was the celebration of the life of the gym rat, age was flexible, both conceptually and existentially. Then too, Cooper's gang included a kind of "junior brigade" consisting of men Yoel's age who weren't merely adjuncts of members but members themselves in full standing. These, it was clear, were meant to become his friends.

■ ■ ■

After brunch, Cooper left to conduct an open house in Pacific Heights. He could easily have detoured to drop them back home, but Griffin suggested they walk. And Yoel, never comfortable with inactivity, welcomed the chance to see more of his new environment on foot. He was starting to understand that he and Cooper were too much alike ever to be truly close, emotionally speaking. Griffin was a far different matter, and much of the time better company somehow.

■ ■ ■

"Tell me about this Westerleigh character," Yoel said as they toiled up a particularly steep block.

"Ned?" Griffin laughed. "What about him?"

"How long have you known him?"

"Over twenty years," Griffin said. "I actually met him before I met Cooper."

"Who is he?"

"Cooper's business partner, of course."

"Right," Yoel said. He already knew that, though it made no sense. "But what else is he?"

"Well, in addition to being a real estate tycoon and the younger son of a British aristocrat, he's an all-around philanthropist and good guy."

"That's all?"

"I don't know what else you might be interested in knowing about him," Griffin said. "I mean, there's his family connection to the Romanovs, of course. But that's generations back. Who's even heard of the Romanovs these days? Outside Russia, that is."

Now they were getting somewhere.

"Is that true? Or just some story?" Yoel asked. Exactly as he had observed back in Israel, American gays were addicted to rumor and gossip.

"And I suppose you'd have to say," Griffin continued, "it's fairly common knowledge that Ned spied against the Nazis during World War II and for a while against the Soviets after that."

Bingo. Obviously, Ned had cultivated the strategy of hiding in plain sight.

■ ■ ■

This explained why he'd been handed off to Ned, Yoel supposed. There was no question as to Ned's professionalism. His tradecraft, at least what little Yoel had observed of it, was flawless, if a little old school. Everything about him inspired confidence in that regard. Yoel considered himself a good enough judge of the type. But it didn't answer the nagging question about Ned's association with Cousin Cooper. Everyone seemed to take it for granted, but what did they really know? Lacking the necessary perspective, nothing sufficient to satisfy Yoel's curiosity.

III

Tuesday morning Yoel borrowed Cooper's ancient Jaguar and drove out to the east bay. He'd studied the online maps the night before and didn't make a single wrong turn. He told himself to think of it as being on an operation. The facility looked like every other flight school he'd ever seen, both back home and in the States. The owner, Jordan Samuels, skimmed his credentials with barely half an eye. Yoel assumed it meant he had no real shot at the job.

"Ned Westerleigh said you'd be coming in today," Samuels said. "When can you start?"

"When can I start?"

"Ned promised me you spoke perfect English," Samuels said. "Something you didn't understand in that question?"

"No," Yoel said. "I can start any time."

"Let's make it next Monday, then," Samuels said. "Lessons start at seven-thirty, so be here at six-thirty, ready to fly. I'll have you some students rustled up. You should come out a couple of times this week to check things out. Take a couple of the trainers up, let me go over the traffic patterns with you. Stuff like that."

"Sure," Yoel said.

"That is," Samuels grinned, "if you're sure we meet with your approval. A friend of Ned Westerleigh's might be too classy for us."

■ ■ ■

"You're welcome here as long as you want to stay," Griffin said.

"But we'd probably just cramp your style," Cooper growled.

There they went again with their good cop/bad cop routine. Yoel wasn't sure how seriously he was supposed to take them.

"He doesn't mean that," Griffin said. "You can come and go as you please. You can even have friends over."

"What friends?"

"My husband is afraid of the word 'tricks'," Cooper said. "The idea that someone else might have an active sex life like he does makes him nervous."

"It does not," Griffin protested.

"All right, queasy."

"What tricks?"Yoel asked.

"Seriously," Cooper said, "I know Ned's been at work on a list of apartments to show you. Drop by tomorrow morning and he'll take you around."

"If you feel like it," Griffin said. "There's no hurry."

"Take Griffin with you," Cooper said. "He's got a good eye for properties. And he knows the neighborhoods."

"He doesn't want to waste his summer vacation on me,"Yoel said.

"Don't worry about that," Griffin said.

■ ■ ■

"A Harley, huh?" Boone said, setting up to do squats. "Well, you came to the right guy."

Boone was yet another of Cousin Cooper's gym buddies, a sandy haired firefighter in his twenties who outweighed Yoel by perhaps ten kilos of rock hard muscle. His pectoral development was stupefying. So far, Yoel hadn't been able to decide whether he'd rather push Boone or his boyfriend Owen under a bus. Perhaps he didn't need to. Perhaps they'd consider a package arrangement.

"Oh?"

"Did a restoration a few months back on a really choice example. Civilian model with police mechanical specs, perfect vintage details, whole nine yards," Boone said. "Gorgeous bike, really."

"Thought you were a Beemer guy," Yoel said.

"I am," Boone nodded. "I have three of them. I refuse to ride anything else. But those old Harleys are beautiful to work on. Real machines, you know? Honest as the day is long. Had a blast getting it back in shape. Then the owner tried to stiff me on the job. Nick Romanovsky helped me put a lien on the bike. Guy ended up walking away rather than pay his debts. And there I was with that gorgeous piece I couldn't do a thing with taking up space in my garage. A friend of Cooper's took it off my hands at a price that paid for the parts, materials, and all my time. Name of Westerleigh. He and Cooper are business partners, actually. Have no idea what he wanted with that bike. Don't think he's ever been on it. Sits in his garage. He'd probably do you a deal."

■ ■ ■

"Very nice flying," Samuels grunted. "You'll do."

Yoel taxied the Cessna toward the apron.

"No surprise, really," Samuels said. "Flew with the Israelis myself back in 'fifty-six. Suez thing."

"Heard my father talk about it," Yoel nodded.

"He a flier?"

"Tanks," Yoel said. "Retired now."

"They were crazy about us over there. American Jews with combat experience from Korea. You'd have thought my buddies and I shit gold bricks, way we were treated. Some of those Israeli women."

"I bet," Yoel laughed.

"Went over again in 'sixty-seven. Non-combatant that time. State Department was all over us former volunteers. Practically threatened us with the death penalty if we got involved. Lucky I got there at all. Probably a good thing they had me flying cargo. Gotten myself killed otherwise. Really was past it by then, though I'd have probably been happier dying than admitting it. Still, Israelis really know about flying in combat. With your pedigree, I'd hire you even without Ned Westerleigh's blessing. Tell you what, let's take the Pilatus up next. Sweet machine, that one. Can't wait to see what you do with her."

■ ■ ■

"What are you doing?" Yoel asked.

"Paying for our purchase," Griffin said, handing the clerk his credit card.

"No, you're not," Yoel said.

"Sure I am," Griffin said. "You didn't think Cooper and I were going to let you buy all the stuff for your new apartment yourself."

"Yes, I did," Yoel said. "Take your card back. I have money."

"I'll tell you what I told your cousin once upon a time," Griffin laughed. "You may be twice my size, but you don't want to wrestle with me over this."

"What if I do?" Yoel growled.

"If you'll just sign here, sir," the clerk said, handing Griffin the charge slip and a pen.

■ ■ ■

From what Yoel had observed around the gym, Cooper and Nick were the undisputed alpha dogs of the pack. Yoel couldn't ask Cooper, obviously. But Nick must know.

"My cousin," he said when he finally got Nick alone at the gym.

"What about him?"

"Business partners with that Ned Westerleigh guy."

"Yeah?"

"How long's that been going on?"

"Twenty-five years," Nick said, "give or take."

"So tell me," Yoel said, "how does that arrangement make sense?"

"I'm not sure I understand the question," Nick said.

"Cooper must have been what when they first teamed up? Twenty-two? Twenty-three?"

"About that," Nick said.

"And even then Westerleigh was a big gun in the business locally, right?"

"You could say that," Nick nodded.

"So why does a man in his position join forces with a young guy like Cooper?"

"Other than the obvious, you mean," Nick laughed.

"Westerleigh's not the type for that, is he?"

"A man can change in a quarter century," Nick said.

"Not that breed," Yoel said. "They're born middle aged and careful and they never get old or stupid."

"You're a keen judge of character, my friend," Nick said, "and you're going to hear the story somewhere. Better if you get it from me."

"So there's a story, is there?"

■ ■ ■

But Nick's story about Cooper acting in straight porn videos to raise money to open his agency didn't really answer Yoel's question. Even after he tracked the videos down and watched them out of morbid curiosity. At least not directly. But then again, maybe it did. A nine month absence from San Francisco, Nick had said. That was plenty of time to shoot those videos as a cover story and do a little something else on the side. Even with training, which for a mid-level operation shouldn't have taken more than, say, eight weeks. And the business partnership with Westerleigh could have been some kind of reward for the risks Cooper had agreed to take. One op, and he was set for life. Or maybe the op had been blown. Maybe somebody's big plans for Cooper hadn't panned out.

It seemed to Yoel he needed to start looking at his cousin differently.

■ ■ ■

"What do you think?" Boone asked.

"It's as nice as you said," Yoel smiled. He had fallen in love with motorcycle culture while on that operation in San Diego. If ever there was a place with the climate and geography for riding motorcycles that was it. Suddenly something he'd never paid attention to before seemed essential, like flying or bodybuilding. And from the first moment he heard one light up, Harleys had been his bikes. BMWs were magnificent in their own way, but the Nazis had killed his grandparents. Japanese bikes were suspect, too. But a Harley was above any historico-political censure. And here was what Blumenfeld would describe as the platonic ideal of a Harley. Yoel's imagination might have dreamed it up. It was that perfect a match for his yearnings.

"You can have it," Ned Westerleigh said, "for what I have in it."

"How much is that?" Yoel asked. When you had a chance to buy the Mona Lisa, you didn't worry about driving a hard bargain.

"I paid off the previous owner's tab with Boone here," Ned said, "for twelve thousand. Isn't that right?"

"Yes," Boone nodded. "We rounded up a little, but that covered everything."

"It's a rare model," Yoel said. "And in this condition, it has to be worth two and a half times that."

"Give or take a thousand," Boone nodded.

"Twelve thousand," Ned said. "Take it or leave it."

■ ■ ■

If Yoel's suspicions of his cousin were correct, what was he to make of Griffin? Had Cooper truly kept a secret like that for over two decades? Griffin seemed too smart, not to mention perceptive, for it to be possible. But also too innocent to have dealt, day in and day out, with such a reality in the event he was in on the secret. Still, there was no question as to the closeness of their marriage, so either Yoel's hunch was wrong, which he could hardly believe, or

Griffin possessed hidden depths. Yoel could just about accept that possibility. That marriage was far closer than the marriage of Yoel's parents. He wasn't sure why those two stayed together at all. What Griffin and Cooper's arrangement resembled, really, was the relationship between the two men who had actually raised Yoel, Cooper's brother, Yakov, and his partner, Naftali Goldman. On the face of it, Yakov and Naftali were as mismatched as Cooper and Griffin, yet they'd been together for nearly three decades. Something held the two couples together. That something, whatever it was, was as unmistakable as a sunset and as inexorable as the tide.

The implication of this was clear. So clear, actually, that Yoel sensed it as an imperative. But where did you find a man who could comprehend your story when the story was as unusual as Yoel's? And not merely comprehend, for that matter. The requirement was more challenging than just becoming conversant with the facts or being able to recount the narrative. Yoel couldn't imagine where to begin. And he was in no mood to ask for advice. But perhaps it could be apprehended through observation. Yoel was good at that. As good, in fact, as he was at flying or making love.

■ ■ ■

Yoel arrived just before six-thirty on Monday morning. Samuels hadn't scheduled him any lessons until nine. The weather was unusually clear that morning, and Yoel didn't want to waste it on the ground.

"O.K. if I take the Pilatus up?" he asked.

"Sure," Samuels grinned, flashing a b-movie thumbs-up. "That machine loves feeling you at the controls."

■ ■ ■

Like a great sea bird the Pilatus soared over the bay, giving an impression of inevitability as it rose. A student of aeronautics since boyhood, Yoel understood the science and technology involved as well as any engineer. Lift increased with speed. And when lift reached a certain point, an object left the ground.

Yet their ascent seemed more like the result of a conspiracy or a joint act of faith—his and the craft's. It was nearly impossible to believe that the machine was just a machine, embodying as it did one of mankind's oldest aspirations. With its slender fuselage and delicate wings, it was a toy. Or perhaps not even a toy. Perhaps it was merely a dream. The canopy shielding Yoel's head and upper body from the elements seemed about as substantial as a bubble.

It was a perfect morning, sunny and clear. The water of the bay was molten silver. The air, often choppy this close to the ground, was as smooth as a caress. Yoel had arrived in this new place, accepted the aid and companionship of new people, found a new place to live and a new job. Still, until that moment, he hadn't felt like the new person all this new context required. But the sun on the water and the gleaming city unfurling before and below him—now was the moment if moment there was to be.

As for the city itself, his new home, you could explore it on foot, by car and bicycle, on public transport. But he was a pilot. And those explorations provided only glimpses. They lacked the coherence only one thing could give to the scene. Now, winging toward that skyline he saw it as his heart needed to see it.

JUNE, 2002

"You have offers from who?" Eli asked, obviously impressed.

Renzo went through the list again.

"Your father would be proud," Eli nodded. "But it won't be a cakewalk. Those top tier firms are ruthless. You'll be working eighty and ninety hours a week. God knows how Horst will stand it."

"How did you stand it?" Renzo asked. "With Dad hardly ever around? Between his career and his family, he hardly had time for you."

"I had no choice," Eli said, frowning.

"Of course you had a choice," Renzo said. "Everybody has choices."

"I was in love," Eli shrugged. "There wasn't anything I wouldn't have done for Eamonn. Ergo, I had no choice."

"Right," Renzo said. "Of course I'm not Dad. And Horst isn't you."

"That's not what I meant," Eli insisted.

"Sure," Renzo nodded. Eli was adorable when he got flustered. The older Renzo got and the more time he spent around Eli, the easier it was for him to understand what Dad had seen in him. It wasn't that Renzo and his brothers had ever been skeptics. They had always been Eli's biggest fans. But as kids they had taken Eli presence for granted. Apparently when you fell in love yourself it made you curious about other people's experiences in romance.

"Relationships are hard work," Eli said. "That's all."

"I'm not even sure I'm going to take one of those offers," Renzo said. "I may set myself up in a storefront practice instead. It's just nice to be able to tell people who I'm being recruited by."

"What you need is an offer from a nice mid-range firm," Eli said. "They won't work you to death."

"Maybe I'll go with the public defender's office," Renzo said.

"Don't you dare," Eli said. "Your uncles in the NYPD will strangle you."

"Hey, put that down," Renzo yelled. Beowulf snapped to attention, but Zephyr went right on chewing whatever it was he'd found in the bushes. Renzo bent over, grabbed his muzzle, and pried his jaws open.

"What is it?" Eli asked.

"Damn," Renzo laughed. "Even in a place like this. I wish people wouldn't dispose of their half-eaten slices of pizza that way. There's a trash can not thirty feet from here."

"Zeph is fascinated with pizza," Eli chuckled. "He seems to think it's the food of the gods."

"It is."

■ ■ ■

"So how did it go with Horst's parents?" David asked, peeling off his wifebeater.

"They were very nice," Renzo said. "It helped that I speak German."

"I'm sure," David said. By now he was down to his jockstrap. For a man in his late thirties, he was astonishing. Actually, for a man of any age. Renzo could only hope to match his physique in time. "But I'm sure they'd have been crazy about you anyway."

"Germans are a tough breed to win over," Renzo said.

"Tell any Frenchman that," David laughed. "Or any Pole."

Renzo followed him down the corridor toward the showers. David's tutoring had revolutionized Renzo's workouts. He'd never really thought about hiring a personal trainer. It turned out that having a guy like this as a workout partner was even better.

"We didn't really discuss geopolitics much," Renzo said, "except when Horst's grandfather took us out sailing. Now there's a tough old bastard. Talk about opinions."

"Survived the war and then survived the Soviet prison camps? Isn't that the story?"

"Mostly he survived Horst's *Grossmutti*," Renzo said. "At least so far."

"Yet you and Horst can't wait to get me married off."

"Please, dear cousin," Renzo laughed. "You want it as much as we want it for you."

■ ■ ■

"God," David said as they emerged from the gym onto Eighth Avenue. "Will you look at that? I wonder where he gets his hair cut."

David's type was ubiquitous in Manhattan, if somewhat unexpected. He liked men a decade or so older than he was. Fiftyish, in other words. Silver haired, well groomed, expensively dressed. He fantasized about busting down the doors of their offices and having his way with them on their desktops. Or so Renzo imagined. Their discussions hadn't actually gotten to that level of detail yet. Still, the type was unmistakable. And absolutely consistent. When David said "get a load of that one" he had either caught sight of a man fitting that description or some variety of terrier. Terriers were his secondary fetish, apparently. They made him melt. Horst had called all this to Renzo's attention first. That's where Renzo got the idea. The look in Horst's eyes as he said it had reminded Renzo uncannily of Dad. Cramming for finals and the bar exam and then taking an extended European vacation had delayed matters, but Renzo was now on the case.

II

Even Renzo's older brothers could hardly remember a time before Eli. They'd known him forever. He was Dad's best friend. Always on hand for their baseball and soccer games, birthday parties, holiday dinners, excursions to museums, movies and the zoo. Usually Dad was with them on these trips, but occasionally Eli flew solo as their escort, such as when they went to the symphony or even once or twice to the opera. It was Liam who first figured the situation out. That stood to reason: he was the oldest. He would also have said he was the smartest, though Renzo had his own opinion about that. There was no overt sign of anything unusual. Dad and Eli were way too careful for that. And Mom kept her cards close to her chest, as well. Adults knew how to keep secrets from kids. But even those three couldn't expect to keep a secret forever. It was the oddness of the pair that caught Liam's attention initially, Dad being a swashbuckler of the old school and Eli such a quiet type. If Eli had been Mom's best friend it almost would have made sense. Once Liam called this to his brothers' attention, it seemed obvious. Tory claimed to have noticed it himself and kept it under his hat, but he was probably just asserting his long running rivalry, as second oldest, with Liam. Renzo was very young at the time the subject first came up. Nothing was obvious to him on its own. His brothers said Dad and Eli didn't really have anything in common. But anyone could see they loved spending time together. They were best friends for no apparent reason. It made perfect sense to a four year old, but as Renzo got older he saw what Liam meant. He no longer had to take his brothers' skepticism on faith. Something was wrong with the picture. Yet it was the picture they were all used to looking at.

The second thing Liam noticed was what clinched it: Eli was always around except for when mom or one of their "real" uncles was. Or their grandparents. Or one of the aunts. Eli was there for special occasions, of course. Weddings, christenings. Things like that. He always had his friend, Jill, with him then and mostly stayed in the background. But otherwise, when Mom or any of their other relatives was present, Eli wasn't. And vice versa. It wasn't that Eli's existence was a secret from the rest of the Lannaghans. But something about his friendship with Dad was. Something was going on that the grownups didn't talk about. It wasn't even clear that all of the grownups knew about it.

■ ■ ■

Renzo had never heard of such a thing as Liam was describing when the time finally came for the brothers to talk it out. But he got the concept immediately. Now he had a name for what he was and felt. Now he never had to be scared of it again. He was like Dad and Eli. Someday there would be a guy who was his friend the way Dad and Eli were friends.

■ ■ ■

Even after they figured the whole thing out, Renzo and his brothers didn't stop calling Eli "Uncle Eli". That would have been to tip off the grownups. Tory said that was unforgivable. Grownups kept secrets from kids all the time. Kids had no choice but to protect their knowledge the same way. Particularly when it was knowledge about grownup things.

■ ■ ■

What really mattered was that when Dad and Mom finally sat them down for what from then on was referred to as "the talk", the Lannaghan boys weren't surprised, much less frightened. Their parents must have been curious about their reaction—or lack of one.

■ ■ ■

The main thing was nothing changed.

III

Until it did. It didn't change, however, in the way any of them might have expected, given the circumstances. Liam got accepted to Princeton. That's when they all found out about the money. Liam got accepted to Princeton and all Mom could do was cry about it. A nurse and a firefighter living in Manhattan with three younger sons couldn't possibly afford to send the oldest one to a school like that. Even with a passel of scholarships, Princeton cost too much. City College was more their league. Which would have been good enough. Mom had graduated there herself. So had a bunch of her cousins. Still, Liam had his heart set on Princeton. Everyone understood it would be a disappointment when he didn't actually get to go there. But it wasn't the end of the world. Lots of people had worse things to deal with. Anyway, just being accepted was a big deal. Wasn't that enough?

But before Liam actually had to answer that question, Eli rode to the rescue. Princeton for Liam? But of course. Here's a check for his tuition. Here's another one for housing, meals, clothing, books. And one for his junior year in Europe. Mom was horrified. "How can he afford it?" Dad just shook his head. He knew Eli well enough not to try and talk him out of it. "What about his brothers?" Mom wanted to know. "It wouldn't be fair for Eli to pay out all that money for Liam's Ivy League university if it meant his brothers would have to do without similar opportunities." It turned out Eli had opened savings accounts for all of them when they were little. He deposited more money in them each month. And he was some kind of wizard at investing.

Liam went to Princeton and on to medical school from there. Was there another second year medical resident in America who was debt free? Maybe so, but not from a middle class family like theirs unless he'd married an heiress. And when Tory and Nancy married, Eli bought them an apartment. Nothing fancy, but nice enough. Nicer than the one Eli lived in himself. Two bedrooms and two baths in a prewar building in Chelsea. The same apartment, in fact, that those two were fighting over now that they were getting a divorce. Renzo's B.A., M.A., and finally law degree—all free and clear. Only Mick hadn't cashed in, and that was only because he hadn't gotten around to providing an occasion for it. As a result, there was now a substantial trust fund for each of the twins.

Eli could have lived like a king, or at least a knight of the realm, on what he spent on Eamonn's sons. Instead he lived in a walkup in Greenwich Village. It was no slum, obviously, but he could have done better. He didn't own a car. He said he didn't want one, but they all knew that every cent he would have spent on payments, insurance, maintenance, gas, and parking fees finally ended up augmenting their nest eggs. He could have gone to Europe more often if he hadn't insisted on bringing them along. Or sending them there with Mom and Dad, as had happened more than once. Whenever they tried to thank him for his generosity, he looked embarrassed. Like he was afraid someone might think he was trying to buy affection when all he really wanted was to express it.

It was one thing to see the "friendship" between Dad and Eli through the eyes of boys or even adolescents. But having your future paid for that way was amazing. What kind of man does a thing like Eli had done? A man who thought of his lover's sons as his own sons, obviously. That was what they all had to get their heads around. They'd had three parents all those years. Lots of kids grew up in blended families. They all had friends with stepfathers, stepmothers, all kinds of connections. But nobody they knew had somebody like Eli. It was unheard of.

Some people might have said "it's only money," or "he's good for it," or even "he's a gay man—what else does he have to spend it on?" But to the Lannaghan brothers it was all the proof they'd ever need of the depth and essential worthiness of the love between Dad and Eli. Over time, they grew extremely vigilant in its defense.

■ ■ ■

It wasn't the kind of thing you could talk about repaying. Whenever the subject loomed, Eli threatened to leave the room. All he would say was that someday they'd have an opportunity to help other people out. And since they had been helped themselves, that opportunity would also be a responsibility.

■ ■ ■

Now Eli needed them. He needed to be reassured that he was still and would always be family. But he needed more than that. And Renzo knew what had to be done. The one thing Eli either wouldn't or couldn't do for himself. And just about that time, Cousin David attached himself to Renzo and Horst like a barnacle. He did so in the nicest possible way, but hanging out with a couple wasn't really what would make him happy. Obviously, he needed taking care of as well.

485

IV

"First of all," Renzo said, "put away that tape recorder. And your note pads. This is just lunch."

"I thought we agreed to discuss a feature article about your father," Caputo said.

"The possibility of a feature article about Dad, yes," Renzo said. "Nothing goes on the record until some things are cleared up."

Caputo and Flash looked at each other for a long three count. Caputo nodded. The equipment disappeared into their backpacks.

"Thanks," Renzo said. "And just so there's no misunderstanding, Horst and I are on a separate check for the meal."

"We're expensed on this," Caputo protested. She was apparently the brains of the operation, as stereotypical a softball lesbian as Renzo had ever encountered. Flash was one of those twenty-something gay boys whose self-presentation screamed "look at me" and "don't you dare judge me by my appearance" simultaneously. This kind of paradox was so unremarkable in what Dad had always referred to as Modern Gay Life that it was practically subliminal. At the same time, the attitude seemed almost obligatory. Everything about Flash's appearance was obviously calculated to elicit outrage. Tattoos, piercings, the configuration of his facial hair, and the color and styling of his coiffure were meticulously calibrated to give optimum offense. His birth certificate probably read Terry or Jim, but a name like that wasn't radical enough to adequately label his alienation from and disdain for everything mainstream. So it stood to reason that he'd chosen a name only a go-go boy could love. Either he was unaware of this or assumed everyone understood the irony. Renzo didn't really care which it was. This was the kind of guy who perennially derided him for being "white bread" or a "narcissistic pretty boy" or a "muscle fascist." He had no use for the type, but he was damned if he'd say as much. He preferred to let others throw the first punch, whether literal or figurative.

"If I don't let you pay for our lunch," Renzo explained, "nobody can imply that I owe you anything."

"Or that he sold out," Horst suggested.

"That's not what buying your lunch is about," Flash protested. It came out in a kind of aggressive whine that matched his exterior.

"No?" Renzo asked. "Good."

"By which he means 'we'll see'," Horst smiled.

They had agreed before arriving that Renzo would do most of the talking. Horst was there to play "good cop". Renzo wasn't quite sure, however, that "good cop" translated into the German psyche, or how.

"So apparently somebody at your paper wants to do a feature on Dad," Renzo said. "That's nice, I guess. Though it seems a little behind schedule."

"I suppose you could say that," Caputo admitted.

"I'm not complaining," Renzo assured her. "I'm just not sure what the point would be after all this time."

"Oh, I don't know," Horst said. "There's still lots of interest in 9-11."

"You do agree, I hope," Flash said, sounding quite superior, "that the part queers played on that day has largely been ignored by the mainstream media. They'd prefer it if our role remained invisible forever. And I'm sure you realize that queers need heroes, too."

"All right," Renzo said, "but this is my father we're talking about, and he found the use of the Q word highly offensive."

"But. . ."

"Scratch that," Renzo said. "I'm not going to sugar coat it. He hated that word. Hearing it made smoke come out his ears. As applied to people like us, that is. If you were just using it to mean strange and unusual—fine."

"See the thing is. . ."

"You don't need to explain to me how we're reclaiming it from the homophobes and in the process destroying its power as a tool of oppression," Renzo said. "I get the theory. Dad understood it, too. He just didn't accept it in practice. He believed it was too subtle for the general public to grasp. As far as he was concerned, when we use words like that we're giving the bad guys permission to keep on using them against us like they always have. If he were here, he'd tell you to walk down the hallway in any American high school and listen closely. You can argue the point all you want, but in the end you can't change the mind of a dead man. So as for being a queer hero, you'd better put that kind of language out of your mind. I won't authorize its use in any article you want me to cooperate with you on. And I wouldn't suggest trying to go around me. I'm a published author myself, and an attorney. I can't shut you down, but I can make your editors and your publisher sorry they didn't make you play nice about it."

"Talbot wouldn't like it, either," Horst suggested. "He hates that word at least as much as your father did."

"That's Talbot Kleinbaum," Renzo said. "He was one of Dad's closest friends, but you probably already know that."

"Actually," Caputo said, squirming a little, "we didn't."

"I'm sure your editor did," Renzo said.

Talbot Kleinbaum, politically incorrect as he might be, had far too much clout in the gay community and wrote far too many checks—with too many zeros in them—to community organizations and causes for anyone to want to cross him. For all Renzo knew, he could buy their newspaper and keep it as a pet. And, for that matter, Talbot had far too many fantastic looking friends and proteges for anyone to willingly give up the opportunity of someday being on his guest list.

"All right," Flash relented. "We won't use the Q word. Any objection to referring to your father as bisexual?"

"He would never have applied the term to himself, so once again I'd rather you didn't do it for him," Renzo said.

"What was he then?" Flash asked, obviously frustrated, "a closet case?"

"Flash, stop," Caputo commanded. "Whatever you think of him, Firefighter Lannaghan was a hero of 9-11. That can't be disputed. And in some way, at least, he was one of us. The community needs to hear his story. And to be helped to celebrate it."

"He was anything but a closet case," Renzo said. "He was out to his family and in the fire department before you were born."

"But out as what?" Flash asked. "That's the question, isn't it?"

"As a gay man," Renzo said.

"A gay man," Flash nodded. "With a wife and four sons. Sneaking around like some pre-Stonewall. . ."

"Get your colleague under control," Renzo told Caputo, "or this meeting is over."

"And our drink orders haven't even been taken yet," Horst said.

■ ■ ■

"I still don't understand what's so wrong about saying he was bisexual," Flash said, spreading aioli on the bun of his veggie burger.

"He would never have described himself that way," Renzo said. "That's what's wrong with it. He was a gay man who happened to marry and father children. Simple as that."

"He never divorced his wife," Flash said. "He stayed with her for thirty years."

"And for a good portion of that time, he was totally honest with her about himself," Renzo said. "The bottom line is he didn't believe bisexuality even existed in males. Every guy he ever knew who called himself a bisexual was either a liar or simply hadn't found his way completely out of the closet yet. He had female friends who labeled themselves that way and were able to convince him that it was real for them. So that's where he came down on it. Female bisexuality was real, but male bisexuality wasn't. I won't agree to have him portrayed as bisexual when he always said he wasn't. He was openly and proudly gay within his own circle, and anything written about him has to acknowledge that. In those words."

"Well, certainly you can't object to our noting that his stance on the issue is problematic," Caputo said. "You might even call it self-contradictory."

"Can object and do," Renzo said. "You and your editors don't get to define him. Or second guess him. Nor do a bunch of activists or queer theorists somewhere. You'd cry bloody murder if he tried to define you. He deserves the same consideration you'd expect for yourselves."

"I still don't see why it's such a big deal," Flash said. "Everybody gets bisexuality these days."

"Wrong," Renzo said. "What everybody gets is what it's politically correct to say on the topic. It's not the same thing."

"This is getting us nowhere," Caputo said. "What I'm hearing you say is we tell the story your way. . ."

"Dad's way," Renzo said.

"All right," Caputo nodded, "his way. Or there's no story."

"That's about the size of it," Renzo nodded.

"You know what I think," Flash said. "I don't think we need to deal with you at all. There was a boyfriend. We can get the story from him."

"If you're referring to Eli Danziger," Renzo said, "the term you need to use is husband. That's what Dad called Eli, and that's what you will, too, in whatever story is eventually published. As his legal representative in this matter, I have to tell you that he doesn't want to be contacted directly. I'll handle arrangements for you to meet him. And by the way, Eli is Talbot Kleinbaum's first cousin. You won't want to go rattling either of their cages."

V

"It's exactly the way he'd want to be remembered by 'our people'," Eli said.

"You think so?"

"I'm certain of it," Eli said. "And I'm so very proud of you. Eamonn would be, too."

"That means everything," Renzo said. Seeing Eli so happy—that always made Dad happy. This almost felt like being able to hug Dad again.

"Incidentally," Eli continued, "the photos you chose to run with the article were perfect. Especially the one of the two of us together."

"Mom picked that one," Renzo said. "She'll be glad to hear you're pleased."

"So is that what we're celebrating tonight?" Eli asked. "The publication of the famous article at long last?"

"Something like that," Renzo grinned.

"Awfully fancy restaurant," Eli said.

"Just your friendly neighborhood hash house," Renzo shrugged.

"On oh, so trendy Bleeker Street," Eli said. "I can't imagine the negotiations it took to make it happen."

"You just call for a reservation," Renzo said.

"Not dinner, you big goof," Eli said. "The article."

"I threatened them with a visit from Talbot Kleinbaum."

"So that's how you managed it," Eli laughed. "I'm sorry you had to do that. But I'm glad it got the job done."

"Name dropping as an act of aggression," Renzo nodded. "I've got to remember the tactic now that I've learned it."

"You know," Eli said, "Your father was as committed to equal rights as anybody. But he always said that 'activist' was the saddest word in all of gay."

"I remember," Renzo nodded. "He thought that whenever real progress was made, it was made by everyday gays and lesbians living their lives. Everything else was just policital theatre. That's what I was thinking about that day those journalists took Horst and me to lunch."

"Don't look now," Eli said, "but your husband is being chatted up by a devastatingly handsome muscledude. Seriously, he's even bigger than you."

"Not more handsome, I hope," Renzo laughed.

"I don't know," Eli said. "He's at least in the ballpark."

"That'll be Cousin David," Renzo said. "Good. They're here."

"Cousin David?" Eli looked blank.

"David Santamaria," Renzo said. "You may not remember him. He hasn't been around much until lately. Dad's first cousin Mary Margaret Farrell married a Puerto Rican guy. David's their oldest son. I'm not sure exactly what kind of cousins that makes us. His brothers are straight and fat and bald. David got all the good genes."

"Good genes is an understatement," Eli nodded. He was a little glassy eyed. That was a good sign.

"He finished his twenty years in the Marine Corps a few months ago. Now he's a physical training instructor at the police academy."

"David." Eli said slowly. It was as if he was pronouncing a new word in a language he was just starting to learn.

"He's been hanging out with us lots the last few weeks," Renzo said.

"You didn't mention it."

"You know me," Renzo said. "Mr. Absentminded Meathead."

It couldn't have been going better.

"Please explain to me," Eli said, "why a man like that is single. He is single, isn't he? Something about him looks single."

"He hasn't met the right guy yet," Renzo said.

"You're joking," Eli said.

Renzo shook his head.

"I'd think he'd have hundreds of applicants for the position."

"He does," Renzo nodded.

"And?"

"He has very specific requirements."

"He'd have to," Eli said. "Otherwise. . ."

"For instance. . ."

"I don't think I want to hear about them," Eli said.

"No?" Renzo asked. "Well, I think maybe you need to. See, what he's crazy about are silver haired guys who wear suits to work. He scopes them out when they stop to get their shoes shined. He fantasizes about what they're carrying in their briefcases."

There it was. That flicker in Eli's eyes. There was no mistaking it. Renzo knew Eli hadn't let himself hope for any kind of future but one spent alone. They stared at each other for a long five count.

"Is this some kind of bad joke?"

"Not that I know of," Renzo said. "Seriously. That's the type that really gets David's blood pumping. Unfortunately, most of the examples he encounters are already taken. Not surprising, really. Guys fitting that description hook up and stay hooked up. They're invested, right?"

"You're not kidding," Eli said, shaking his head slowly.

"No," Renzo said. "I'm not."

"This is an extremely bad idea, Lorenzo," Eli said.

"Dad only called me that when he was annoyed," Renzo grinned.

"Annoyed doesn't even begin. . ."

"But in this case I think it's more a case of cold feet," Renzo said. "And speaking of Dad. . ."

"I'd rather not."

"I know," Renzo said, "but it's time we did. The real live man, not the hero, not the so-called icon. The last thing he would want is for you to live the rest of your life by yourself. If you don't know that, you didn't really know him."

Eli looked down at his drink.

"You know that's true. He wanted you to be taken care of. And happy. Just as much as he wanted Mom to be happy. And his sons. Seeing all of us happy was what made him happy."

"I'm not ready," Eli protested.

"Ready or not ready has nothing to do with it," Renzo said. "Nobody's ever ready. Not really. So you can't think of it that way. What it is is more a question of opportunity."

"No," Eli said. "It isn't."

"Yes it is," Renzo insisted. "David knows who you are already. The whole family's filled him in on whatever he's missed the last twenty years while he was in the Corps. And then when he saw you at the christening something clicked. Unfortunately he was too shy to introduce himself. Shyness is just about his worst fault."

And Eli had been too mopey to notice him there—but Renzo couldn't say that.

"Renzo, please don't do this."

"Eli, tell me who it was that nagged Renzo until he called Horst for a second date."

"That was different," Eli said.

"Every day for two weeks," Renzo said. "You were implacable. It was one of the qualities Dad loved most about you."

"It doesn't matter what I was," Eli said. "This is different."

"If you can explain to me how this is different, I'll leave you alone about it," Renzo said. "Otherwise, we're going over there so I can introduce you to him. And by the way: he's a dog lover. He's very fond of terriers."

"I can't even think about this right now."

"That's all right," Renzo said. "Horst and I already did the thinking for you. Now relax. This won't hurt a bit."

JULY, 2002

Ned Westerleigh had been quite specific. He sent one of those "Burn Before Reading" emails that took Rupert back to the bad old days of Moscow Rules. Marina Green. Nine-o-five a.m. Which actually meant, Rupert knew, twenty–three minutes later than that because today was the twenty-third of the month. These days, Ned Westerleigh's voice was the voice of God. Rupert's continuing presence on the shores of the Pacific depended on Ned's protection, so he wouldn't dream of being late even by a second. Or being off target by so much as a yard. His wardrobe was correct to the tiniest detail. There was a parking space on the west side of the street. If it was indeed west. He didn't really have San Francisco topography mastered yet. In any case, it was on the opposite side of the street from the greensward itself, whatever compass heading that represented. He hadn't expected to find a space so quickly or so close to his rendezvous, so he'd given himself extra time after scouting alternate arrangements the afternoon previous. He steered the Porsche into the space and checked his Breitling. It was the one Cavendish had bought him to celebrate their success in the Seoul Olympics. After sitting in its box for over a decade, it still kept perfect time. And these days it comforted Rupert to wear it.

■ ■ ■

What did Ned have to say to him that couldn't be said in Rupert's newly purchased and occupied Nob Hill condominium? Or in Ned's office, for that matter? Rupert couldn't help wondering. When he desired it, Ned could be as inscrutable and as apparently capricious as an Olympian deity. Whatever it was, Rupert hoped it wasn't bad news. He'd had enough of that. Over the past months, he had thought of Cavendish and Peregrine's deaths as the final straw. But he'd been mistaken. That morning he was freshly back from the U.K. and still a little jet lagged despite his armamentarium of tried and true remedies. Mum, incapable of coming to terms with the loss of Peregrine, had attempted suicide a week or so previous and was currently in a nursing facility. She wasn't crazy exactly. But she surely wasn't sane. And the drinking didn't help. It wasn't the sort of place one checked into specifically for the purpose of drying out, but the staff there were aware that she needed to and would keep her on a short leash in terms of beverages on offer. Once Mum sobered up there would be therapy sessions to help her get back in touch with reality, if such were possible. Rupert had never known her to have more than a nodding acquaintance with the concept and wasn't optimistic.

Usually agnostic on the subject of mental disorders, Dad was being un-characteristically solicitous. Rupert didn't know what to make of it. The whole visit had been depressing, and, worse than that, inconclusive.

■ ■ ■

Whilst back home, Rupert saw Pippa. To her credit, she'd allowed him to see the boys, who were flourishing. That in itself was good to witness, albeit in a manner that still managed to be heartbreaking. Pippa was anything but thriving herself, and the meeting was a difficult one. To Rupert's astonishment, she had truly loved her ex-husband. Indeed, she seemed to have formed the opinion that their divorce had been a terrible mistake on her part. This was probably accurate, but as far as Rupert was concerned that didn't make it any less inevitable. He had always assumed that narcissistic as she was, she viewed Cavendish as nothing more than the ultimate fashion accessory. But she seemed genuinely devastated by his death, as though their divorce had been nothing more than a minor bump in the road, something to be smoothed over in time and never spoken of afterward. Moreover, she absolutely blamed Rupert for his death. Cavendish wouldn't have been on that plane except for him. And an ex-husband was better, she seemed to have decided, than a dead

496

one. The scene was harrowing. Not least because Pippa wasn't the only one who blamed Rupert. Nothing she might say on the subject could possibly hurt more than what he told himself.

■ ■ ■

Nearly as harrowing was Rupert's return to the States. Standing in that line at the immigration checkpoint he was certain that husky young men in dark suits were about to materialize and invite him into a side room for questioning. He'd broken into a cold sweat standing there, which just went to show how out of shape he was professionally speaking. The fact that everyone's nerves were shot these days was no excuse.

■ ■ ■

The extra five minutes passed at a snail's pace. The Breitling's second hand seemed to have slowed to a crawl. At last Rupert unfastened his seat belt and clambered out of the car. He was really too tall and too broad of shoulder for a car like that but wouldn't dream of letting it go. And though he could well afford one, he'd never be able to drive an Aston again. They reminded him too much of Cavendish. But he could just about stick a Porsche. So comfortingly un-British. That's what Cavendish had been—the quintessential Brit. It was as if when Cavendish died, so did that ideal Rupert had worshipped since a small boy. High tea, cricket, and belting out JERUSALEM at the top of his lungs along with the spectators in the stadium during Rugby League matches on the telly. Lost. All of it. As Rupert strode across the street he wondered when he would ever stop expecting an unfamiliar car to speed unexpectedly out of a side street and aim itself at him. That had happened to him once in Moscow. It was a foggy night and an aging Chaika, and he'd never been able to banish the memory of that near miss. The scene around him grew less sinister by the second as joggers trotted past, Chinese nurses pushed affluent toddlers along in strollers that cost as much as a good used Honda Civic, and that trio of Labradors frolicked off leash on the grass.

■ ■ ■

Ned was nowhere to be seen. Rupert checked the Breitling. No getting around it. Ned was late, which was unprecedented. Not critically late. Less than two minutes at this point. But even that slight delay seemed earth shattering. Could the unthinkable happen here? On a peaceful summer morning, surrounded by civilians going about the most mundane and peaceable of activities? Of course it could. It had done, just months ago in New York. Anything was possible.

Ned. Please, God, no. Not here. Not Ned.

One of the Labradors trotted up to him, a neon yellow tennis ball in his mouth. He dropped it in front of Rupert's left shoe and stared up, tail wagging, grinning his Labrador grin, a picture of jovial expectancy. Surely Rupert must know how the game went.

"Loki," a man shouted. "Get back here."

The dog turned, looked over its shoulder toward the voice, and then focused back on Rupert, blinking serenely.

"Loki, I said get back here."

The man had an accent. European? Yes, European, but what kind? Maybe a visual would clarify it. Rupert scanned, located. There, at a range of about thirty yards. A tad over medium height. Extremely broad shoulders. Dark hair in a military cut, gleaming with some sort of grooming agent. Tight white t-shirt and baggy pants. Cargo style, Rupert believed they were called here in the states. Aviator style sunglasses. Rupert ticked off the points of description. Not much detail discernable at that range other than what looked to be a rather impressive physique. The voice was deep. Gruff. Not German, exactly. But not the accent of the speaker of one of the romance languages, Rupert didn't think. Slavic? He needed to hear more. But really what was the point? It was just a man in charge of three dogs. Rupert was meant to be looking for Ned.

"Better go, boy," Rupert said, stooping to pick up the ball. He gave it a toss in the general direction of the man. The dog shot away after it with that astonishing velocity Labradors were capable of when suitably motivated.

Meanwhile, Ned was still nowhere to be seen, and Rupert was becoming more alarmed by the second. In his pants pocket, his cellphone vibrated.

He groped for it. The Labrador intercepted the ball Rupert had tossed and skidded to a halt. He stood for a moment looking in the direction of his master, then turned and trotted back toward Rupert, tail wagging lazily. Typical Labrador. Disobedient in such an amiable manner. Who wouldn't be captivated? Disobedience with impunity. Just like Cavendish.

"God dammit, Loki," the man shouted.

"Ned," Rupert said, gripping the cell phone with fingers that seemed hopelessly clumsy, "where the hell are you?"

"At my office of course," Ned said. "Where else should I be at this time of morning? Just calling to see if you've reached the rendezvous point."

"I'm here on the dot as directed," Rupert said, "and not a sign of you. What the bloody buggery is going on?"

"From your location, you should be able to see a man accompanied by three Labrador retrievers," Ned said. "Black ones."

"Actually," Rupert said, Loki having returned to his position and deposited the ball at his feet again, "I'm apparently in the process of making friends as we speak."

"With the man?"

"With a dog called Loki," Rupert said.

"I see," Ned said. "Take a closer look at the man, if you would."

"What about him?" Rupert asked. "What is it I'm supposed to be looking for?"

The man was quickly closing the distance between them, the other two Labradors at his heels. Rupert looked.

"His name is Yoel Luxemberg," Ned said. "You may believe you know him by some other name, but you don't. You've never seen him before, actually. Not in this world."

Rupert couldn't begin to understand, but Ned was speaking in *that voice*. So Rupert kept looking. Just then, the man removed his sunglasses. Rupert saw. Silly of him to have been put off by such a minimal disguise. He really had lost his touch.

"The rest is up to you, my boy," Ned said.

The End

Also by Jackson Peoples-Rosenblatt:

The Navigators
Lodestar
The Current